A FLAW IN
THE DESIGN

"This American debut explores family and class tensions in a fight over who controls the narrative. . . . Great characterization and plenty of genuine suspense in a psychological thriller par excellence." —*The Guardian*

"A compulsive, richly imagined literary thriller." —*The Irish Times*

"I read [*A Flaw in the Design*] at speed in a state of high stress and anxiety, as the tension built inexorably and I began to feel just as haunted (hunted?) as the author's protagonist. . . . It's all horribly claustrophobic, in the best possible way." —*The Observer*

"A highly literary yet suspenseful debut from Oates, who weaves a stunning tale of obsession, with a surprising ending that begs for a sequel. Perfect for fans of Mary Kubica and Shari Lapena." —*Booklist*

"[A] gripping psychological thriller . . . This immersive page-turner cleverly juxtaposes the writing of short fiction with the production of stories in people's minds. Oates is definitely a writer to watch." —*Publishers Weekly*

"A slow-burn of a thriller." —SARAH LYALL, *The New York Times Book Review*

"Terrifying and amusing . . . keeps you guessing till the very end." —*The Times*

"A tense, taut, gripping thriller with an ending that left my imagination reeling." —*Saga Magazine*

"When fast-paced thriller meets crafted literary fiction in this way, genre preference is irrelevant. There is no question about who will find this enthralling—the answer is everyone. . . . It is a real pleasure to read prose so imaginative and gripping, which is simultaneously naturally tethered to real-world issues such as the complexity of class, family, and of the messiness in between." —*Buzz Magazine*

"*A Flaw in the Design* is not only a deep dive into the things that can rock the cradle of a family but also an absolute page-turner. I read it in a single sitting."

—MIRANDA COWLEY HELLER,
bestselling author of *The Paper Palace*

"A literary thriller of the highest order. Oates manages, with wisdom and insight, to explore the vulnerability of parenthood, the economic injustice of New York City, middle-age compromise, and the fallibility of storytelling, all while telling a heart-pounding tale that commanded my attention from the first sentence to the last."

—JULIA MAY JONAS, author of *Vladimir*

"Brilliantly constructed and psychologically astute, this novel had me turning pages late into the night and left me reeling in the aftermath of its stunning conclusion. Bravo!"

—ANTOINE WILSON, author of *Mouth to Mouth*

"Get ready for a wild ride. Brutal and compelling, *A Flaw in the Design* is the story of a family driven toward destruction as a father takes custody of the nephew he fears will wreck his life. This novel swerves and shocks before smashing into you, a T-bone collision you can hold in your hands."

—JULIA PHILLIPS, author of *Disappearing Earth*

"Menace and mendacity vie with the mundane in this skillfully told tale about ambition and grief and envy. A wealthy, smarmy nephew; an aging midlist writer charged with his care; two daughters; the long Vermont winter—what could go wrong? *A Flaw in the Design* is an impressive debut. Cue the sequel."

—ALICE MCDERMOTT, author of *The Ninth Hour*

"What happens when a (possibly murderous) sociopath takes a writing workshop? This is the premise of Nathan Oates's delicious, inexorable, fast-paced tale of obsession—a thriller that will keep you reading till the end."

—KARAN MAHAJAN, author of
The Association of Small Bombs

"A gripping, twisty psychological thriller about the destructiveness of toxic masculinity hell-bent on protecting its own . . . I couldn't put it down."

—MIRANDA BEVERLY-WHITTEMORE, *New York Times* bestselling author of *Bittersweet* and *Fierce Little Thing*

"This suspenseful debut novel keeps the reader on tenterhooks in a fearful family drama. Oh, this demands a sequel!"

—CHRISTINE SCHUTT, author of *Pure Hollywood*

BY NATHAN OATES

A Flaw in the Design

The Empty House

A
FLAW
IN
THE
DESIGN

A FLAW IN THE DESIGN

A NOVEL

NATHAN OATES

 RANDOM HOUSE | NEW YORK

2023 Random House Trade Paperback Edition

Published in the United States by Random House, an imprint and division of Penguin Random House LLC, New York.

RANDOM HOUSE and the HOUSE colophon are registered trademarks of Penguin Random House LLC.

Originally published in hardcover in the United States by Random House, an imprint and division of Penguin Random House LLC, in 2023.

LIBRARY OF CONGRESS CATALOGING-IN-PUBLICATION DATA
Names: Oates, Nathan, author.
Title: A flaw in the design: a novel / by Nathan Oates.
Description: First Edition. | New York: Random House, [2023]
Identifiers: LCCN 2022017457 (print) | LCCN 2022017458 (ebook) |
ISBN 9780593446720 (paperback) | ISBN 9780593446713 (ebook)
Subjects: LCGFT: Mystery fiction. | Novels.
Classification: LCC PS3615.A355 F53 2023 (print) | LCC PS3615.A355 (ebook) |
DDC 813/.6—dc23
LC record available at https://lccn.loc.gov/2022017457
LC ebook record available at https://lccn.loc.gov/2022017458

Printed in the United States of America on acid-free paper

randomhousebooks.com

9 8 7 6 5 4 3 2 1

Book design by Jo Anne Metsch

For Amy, Sylvie, and Baxter

Everything is a cipher and of everything he is the theme.

—Vladimir Nabokov, "Signs and Symbols"

A
FLAW
IN
THE
DESIGN

1

THERE WAS STILL TIME TO TURN AND WALK OUT, PRETEND HE'D never come. The screen, perched on a pillar near baggage claim, listed the New York flight as arrived. Gate 3. Any minute, passengers would come down the escalator in front of him. But right now, he could leave. Escape before his nephew spotted him. Concoct some excuse to tell Molly: The flight was canceled; no, he wasn't answering his phone. Weird, right? Well, maybe tomorrow. Except no, not really. After all, he was the boy's guardian, and they'd track him down. Or the boy would find his own way to their house and that'd be worse, because then he'd know how much Gil feared him. Hated him. Which was the wrong way to think. He should stop. He couldn't stop.

A loosely strung crowd came down the escalator, hurrying through the nearly empty terminal to claim spots at the baggage carousel. Already it was too late. There he was: Matthew, in a short black down coat that was too light for the Vermont winter, a bright white shirt beneath; hair styled in a swoosh; on his face a smirk,

4 | NATHAN OATES

the slightest turn of his lips, familiar enough to bring loathing into Gil's throat.

He'd known that the boy would look different after all this time, but he wasn't prepared for this. Once a lanky kid, he was now over six feet, a couple of inches taller than Gil. Matthew stepped around an old man who fumbled with a coat and a rolling bag, bored annoyance moving over his face, as if this was routine, as if he was a young businessman sent from the city to check on some far-flung investment.

Gil waved, and in the acknowledging tilt of Matthew's head he caught a glimpse of his sister. Sharon. Who was dead. Who'd left him this. Her son.

"Well, hello, welcome," Gil said, opening his arms, but the boy stepped back, as if he didn't recognize this gesture, or the man behind it. "How was the flight?"

"The flight?" Matthew said, frowning at the darkened check-in kiosks, the empty car rental desks, the snow blowing in streaks across the asphalt outside, his dopey uncle in his black parka and clumpy winter boots. "I guess it was like most flights. Fine, in that I don't remember anything about it."

"That's great," Gil said. "Do you have any bags?" He pointed at the crowd staring forlornly at the unmoving gray belt.

"Nope. All set," Matthew said, tugging at his shoulder strap.

Should Gil offer to carry it? But the bag was small and easily managed, as if the boy was only here for a weekend. Matthew gave him an indifferent squint, knowing he must wait to be led, though the dynamics that subordinated him to this person were clearly a miscarriage of justice, given their true stations in life. Or Gil was just being a dickhead. Maybe Matthew was standoffish because he felt awkward: coming to live with his uncle he hadn't seen in years. That might explain the constricted approximation of a smile. He expected Gil, the adult, to take the lead.

"I'm parked just there in short term," Gil said, turning toward glass doors that held their reflections—blurred and broken by the mounded snow at the curb, the flash of passing headlights—which might've been a tableau from New York. A homeless man (Gil), begging from an annoyed young banker (Matthew).

"You might want to zip up. It's pretty cold," Gil said.

"I'll probably survive," Matthew said, as the glass panes slid apart and freezing air gusted into the terminal.

Waiting for a cab to roll through the crosswalk, Gil caught another glimpse of his sister. The boy had Sharon's profile, the high arch of her cheeks, flushed now with the cold, her gray-blue eyes. Like it or not, Matthew was family, his only nephew, so he should try to see as the boy must: a salt-streaked SUV parked at the curb, the pickup area otherwise empty, a single cop car parked across the way leaking a wisp of exhaust, the lights sharpened in the gusting cold that cut through his coat. A provincial airport in the frozen, depopulated north, where he'd been sent to live among strangers.

Okay, Gil had fucked up the greeting. But he could do better. All of them, Molly, the girls, they could all make this kid feel welcome after what he'd suffered. Except Gil couldn't help noting, as he pointed the way to the Subaru, that Matthew didn't seem in the least upset. Annoyed. Put out. But not sad. Not destroyed, as any kid should be after losing both parents less than a month ago.

An accident on Sixth Avenue. Their sports car smashed nearly flat by a stolen delivery truck. The driver had fled the scene, escaping down into the subway. In that moment, Matthew had been orphaned, though only just. He was seventeen. By all appearances an adult. Except not in the eyes of the law, which was why he was here in Vermont, at least until he turned eighteen over the summer and, a few weeks later, went off to college.

Gil and Molly and their girls had flown to New York for the joint funeral and to make the arrangements for Matthew to come under their care. They'd stayed at Sharon's apartment on the Upper East Side—December in New York, a huge Christmas tree in the apartment's living room, decorated in a way that seemed clearly done by some professional, silver snowflakes and delicate glass balls, white lights—but to their surprise Matthew hadn't been there, not when they'd arrived or at any point after. The family lawyer explained that Matthew would be staying with friends, as that was most comfortable for him in this difficult time. This same lawyer had called after Sharon's accident to inform them that, per the will, they were now Matthew's guardians. Before Gil and Molly had had kids, back when they'd lived in Brooklyn, Sharon had asked if they'd be the boy's godparents. They'd attended the baptism at the Trinity Church near Wall Street, had held the squalling baby, but after the near-total break between the families, Gil had assumed his sister would appoint someone else, a friend from her world, or maybe Niles's parents, who'd retired to Edinburgh, Scotland. Apparently not. Whether this was an oversight, something his sister had stopped thinking about once Matthew was no longer little, or a gesture of familial connection, Gil had no idea. Molly was sure the latter was more likely. People like Niles and Sharon, with real money and assets, didn't pop off a will and leave it untended. If she was right—and of course she was—even after all the acrimony and bitterness of the past six years, Sharon had entrusted them with her only child.

They'd assumed Matthew would attend the funeral, which had been crowded with people from the boy's private school and Niles's investment bank. The men—tall with carefully short hair to obscure their balding, or with expensively maintained styles that looked improbable at their age—shook hands stiffly, heads drawn back, as if remembering an untoward detail Niles had told them about his brother-in-law. A writer, wasn't he? A professor? Didn't they live out in the woods? Maine?

Vermont, he'd corrected, and they nodded to indicate there was no difference. Not New York. Not business. So, not real. Their wives were sculpted and frighteningly thin, with faces that had been tightened and injected so many times they would never again truly smile.

Gil had long scorned his sister's world, but he knew this was partly jealousy. Sure, they were soulless devils, but they had millions of dollars, massive uptown apartments, and lavish vacation homes. The men were math wizards who'd turned to currency trading and market manipulations instead of, say, astronomy or medicine. The women held MBAs, JDs, MDs, and PhDs, but few of them worked. They'd given up their careers for the luxury more easily accessed through a powerful husband. Gil told himself he didn't want any of that. This had, of course, not been on offer: High finance didn't seek out mathematically illiterate fiction writers. So he was safe.

With the service about to start he'd asked a woman whose son was in Matthew's class if she knew where he was.

"Oh, I don't think Matthew's going to make it today," the woman with knife blade cheekbones said. *Today.* As if this was another bit of the routine, soccer practice, or the school play.

"We haven't seen him yet. Is he doing okay? I thought he'd come," Gil said, knowing he sounded pathetic.

"Don't you have his number?" the woman asked, incredulous, apparently not having realized how low on the evolutionary ladder this "person" actually was.

"I've left messages, of course," Gil said. But she'd already turned away, arms out to hug a woman who might've been cast from the same golden mold.

These women were protecting Matthew, shielding him from Gil and Molly. And why shouldn't they? Surely they knew more about the boy than he did. In fact he knew almost nothing, other than what could be gleaned from his sister's annual holiday letters. Even when things were at their worst between them he'd read those. They'd been his last link to her wit, and he'd always found in them glimpses of the young, sarcastic Sharon flickering through. The Sharon of his childhood was otherwise erased, absorbed into this new life as a rich wife.

He backed out of the parking spot and paid for his hour at the booth, feeling sure Matthew noticed the dollar Gil passed across to the bundled and hooded attendant. Not twelve, or eighteen, or whatever it would've been in New York. Here in Hicksville. Among the barbarians who weren't sure how this whole money thing worked.

"Are you hungry?" Gil said. "Molly's making lasagna."

"Sure," Matthew said with a shake of his head, as if this was the stupidest question he'd ever heard. "Everyone likes lasagna, don't they?"

Gil didn't know how to respond, so he snorted stupidly, as if it'd been a joke, a witty bit of repartee.

Usually he took the back roads out of Burlington, but I-89 was faster. Then, as he steered down the ramp onto the highway, he thought the interstate, with its trucks and traffic, might remind Matthew of his parents' death, but the boy went on sneering—no, that could just be his normal expression—at the strip malls and suburban apartment buildings, all crusted with ice and snow.

"It's great that you'll be able to finish high school from up here," Gil said.

"I guess," Matthew said, his face still turned to the window. He reached out two fingers and touched the glass so halos of fog spread around them.

The headmaster of Herbert, the boy's Manhattan private school, had explained in a call last week that Matthew would complete his remaining schoolwork through email correspondence with his teachers. Matthew was, the headmaster had said in a posh English accent, *significantly* advanced in all subjects, so it would be no problem, under these tragic circumstances. There was also the possibility Matthew might take a class or two at Essex College, where Gil taught. The headmaster was looking into it.

Matthew spoke without prompting. "Senior year's a bit of a joke at Herbert. I was going to be breaking my back in Ethics and Yoga, so I won't be missing much."

"Well, that's good," Gil said.

"I took a class at Columbia in the fall, actually. I'm pretty much graduated as it is."

"We'll take you back down for graduation," Gil said quickly.

Matthew recoiled, as if walking through a piss-soaked hallway. "Oh, no thanks. That won't be necessary."

"I thought you might—"

"Yes, I know. I know, and thanks. But I'm fine. It's nice to get away, actually. That school's kind of a suffocating snake pit."

Gil glanced quickly over from the snow-streaked highway, but Matthew looked by all evidence sincere. Maybe it was true. Maybe he hated New York. Maybe he was an unhappy young man and not the spoiled jerk Gil had assumed.

"And all this is pretty nice," Matthew said, gesturing at the landscape, the mountains dark blue in the day's last light. "No suffocating up here, right?"

"You'd be surprised," Gil said. "Wait till it snows. And then snows again."

"Yeah, well, I mean, I can definitely see why you left New York," Matthew said, though now the road dipped and there was nothing but the sludge-darkened snow beside the highway, and beyond, bare trees and lumpy frozen fields.

"If you can hold out until May, all this is worth it," Gil said with a flicker of guilt. Matthew had never once been up here to visit them. They'd never extended an invitation. Though Matthew had surely spent plenty of time at luxury resorts and sprawling estates, second or third homes of rich New Yorkers in Stowe or Killington.

"I bet," Matthew eventually said, after a pause so long Gil almost forgot what it referred to. *The summer. Vermont being pretty. Of course.*

Soon they'd be home. Soon Molly would be there to take over. There wouldn't always be this awkward tension with the boy. He'd just arrived. Everything was bound, with time, to get easier. And better. Everything would get better soon.

2

GIL LOVED HIS HOUSE UNRESERVEDLY, HAD SINCE FIRST SEEING it when he'd come up from New York twelve years ago. With its steep black roof and the low extension off the original farmhouse opening onto a patio at the edge of a field, it was the kind of place he'd fantasized about when he'd persuaded Molly to leave the city. They'd used the inheritance he received after his mother's death to pay off what turned out to be a disconcerting heap of grad school debt, with enough left over for a down payment. Vermont was expensive, but nothing compared to New York, right? Despite drifting almost immediately back into debt—the roof needed repairing, the town tax assessments went up—they'd managed to settle in. He'd gotten a few adjunct sections at Essex and had turned that, after a few years and the publication of his second novel, into a lecturer line, and finally into a permanent position, eventually with tenure. Like most people, they scraped by, but this was their land, and this was their beautiful home.

Of course, there were times he complained—driving through blizzards at night, or when the driveway turned to a sheet of ice, or when hunters strayed down the hillside—but that was healthy. You shouldn't love everything about the place you live. Most people, he knew, loved almost nothing about where they lived, other than its familiarity.

The frozen gravel of the drive crackled under the tires as he turned in through the gap in the stone wall. Matthew stared blankly at the trees—Gil's trees, now—as he had since they'd turned off the highway. Nerves, surely. That accounted for the boy's affectless expression. Not because he was unimpressed.

The front door opened, a spill of warm yellow light onto the icy drive, and Molly, in black jeans and a long denim shirt, hurried down the blue stone steps and up to the car to hug Matthew. She'd been as worried about Matthew's arrival as Gil, but she hid it well now, wrapping the boy in an embrace. As if she loved him. As if she wanted nothing more than to take care of him. The girls, Ingrid and Chloe, lingered back on the steps, nodding tentative hellos.

What did the boy see in this house that Gil and Molly loved so much, this place where he woke feeling lucky: to have such a home, such a wife, two bright, determined daughters? Gil knew his vision of the world was distorted by his love for it. Maybe the boy saw it as familiar bourgeois banality. Predictable and sad, made sadder by Gil's outsized exultation. But Matthew was seventeen. Wasn't everything to be scorned at seventeen? Hadn't Gil done the same? And how could the boy possibly see the house as a home, a place of warmth and tenderness, when he'd been shipped up here like luggage?

Molly, smiling and lovely, short brown hair blown about her face by the wind, rubbed Matthew's arm and said, "Let's get inside. It's freezing."

Elroy was waiting by the door and he leapt up at Matthew with his dopey golden retriever grin. Gil expected the boy to recoil—Sharon had never had a dog—but instead he knelt quickly beside the delighted animal and rubbed his flanks and tousled his head until Elroy collapsed in a heap and rolled over to show everyone his bright white belly.

Gil squeezed past, trying not to feel what he knew was a ridiculous stab of jealousy. His dog! A traitor at the first opportunity.

"Are you hungry? Dinner's almost ready," Molly said, stepping out of her boots.

"Yeah, it smells good," Matthew said.

"But first let me show you your room," Molly said, putting her hand back on Matthew's arm. As if he needed careful tending. As if he was an orphan.

While the rest of them, including Elroy, went up to Matthew's room—formerly Gil's office—Ingrid followed her father to the kitchen. She leaned against the island, glasses sliding down her narrow nose, hair bunching on the hood of her sweatshirt.

"Well, he's here," Gil said, opening the fridge and considering whether it was okay to pull out a Heady Topper. Would that look like he needed a beer? The truth was he did. He really needed one. But Ingrid was watching.

She frowned down at her bulky wool socks, into which she'd tucked her jeans. He shouldn't have said that, as if it was a problem, some long-dreaded event. Even if it was. But his eleven-year-old daughter knew this was wrong. She had, as the cliché went, an old soul. Though it didn't strike him as *old,* exactly, just *better.* More finely attuned to others. She made friends easily, she was appropriately, but not excessively, wounded by the preteen betrayals in her set of girls. Like friendships, school was easy for her, and though she never complained, he worried that the local public schools might be insufficiently challenging. He didn't think she was a genius, exactly, but she did have something of the word's original meaning: an attendant spirit present from birth.

"Yeah, he's here," Ingrid said, with a tone Gil couldn't quite read, if there was in fact anything to read into it.

They'd talked with Ingrid about Matthew coming to live with them, though Gil had preferred the phrase "to stay with us." A temporary situation. Not permanent. Not even close. But they'd wanted to know how she felt about the possibility. Ingrid had said, of course, *It's fine. He's our cousin. He's family.* She was a good girl, generous, maybe to a fault. Could it be that she was actually terrified to have him here? How could she not be? But she was braver than Gil. And there was also the possibility she'd reframed the events at the pool in Montauk in such a way as to make them more palatable. In order to move on with her life. He and Molly had talked to her about it, probably too much at first, and eventually she'd begged them to stop. And possibly, afterward, she'd bottled her feelings up, stuffed them away in the dark.

"So, he's not going to school, right?" Ingrid said, putting her fingers on the cutlery drawer and easing it out and back so it snicked shut, a habit she'd had since she was a toddler, despite numerous pinched pinkies.

"I think the plan is for him to do it online. Or at Essex. I'm not sure."

"That's good, I guess."

"It's only for a few months," he said, which ended up sounding mean, he was sure. As if having Matthew there was a chore. Unpleasant. Which it was. Both, actually.

"Does he seem sad?" she said. "About his parents?"

"Of course," he said. "I'm sure he's sad."

Elroy's nails clicked wildly as he raced down the stairs, followed by Molly, Matthew, and Chloe.

"Laundry's in the basement," Molly said. "But you can leave it in the bathroom hamper. That's what the girls do."

"Oh, no," Matthew said, as they came into the kitchen, "I can do it. Mom always sent it out. Now I can learn a useful life skill."

Elroy half-jumped up to nuzzle his hand, then leaned against Matthew's legs, apparently in love.

"Well," Molly said, "I can show you the machines later, if you want."

"Perfect," Matthew said.

A moment of silence followed. Elroy let out a contented groan.

"Anyone hungry?" Gil said.

"Sure," Matthew said. "I forgot to get lunch." He'd taken off his black coat but still looked formally dressed in his crisp white shirt and gray wool pants. Even his socks, dark blue with white shapes, maybe stars, were elegant. In comparison, Gil was a schlub in his baggy khaki pants and heavy sweater pushed up from his wrists.

"Lasagna," Molly said as she went to the stove, picking her oven mitts up off the counter. "I hope that's okay. You're not a vegetarian, are you?"

"Vegan, actually," Matthew said. Molly looked back in surprise and the young man shook his head. "No, sorry, kidding. I wouldn't do that to you."

"A couple of my friends are vegans," Chloe said. Gil's older daughter was mostly hidden in the doorway. She was fifteen, just a couple of years younger than Matthew, but she seemed like a different generation, innocent and unknowing. Her hair, thick and wavy like her sister's, brown and touched with hints of red, was pulled up in a high ponytail. She wore a bright green sweater, leggings, and the same bunchy wool socks as her sister. "But I think they mostly do it to be skinny."

"Well, that's the only reason that makes sense," Matthew said.

Chloe blushed and clung to the doorframe, as if otherwise she might collapse. She was nervous too, but unlike Ingrid she had a tendency to try to rush into the face of whatever worried her, to try to transform it with her goodwill and energy. That, hopefully, was what accounted for the flirtatious smile on her face now. Gil should say something. Release the strain. He had no idea how to do that.

"Why don't you guys go to the table?" Molly said, lifting the lasagna out of the oven. "I'm going to let this settle and we'll start with some salad."

The table was set as if for a dinner party, with placemats and cloth napkins. A bottle of wine was open beside Gil's plate. Should he offer Matthew some? He was seventeen, but it was hard to believe the boy didn't drink. Still, this was Gil's house. And it might be weird for Ingrid and Chloe.

Molly brought the salad to the table and there were a few strained seconds, the scraping of the wooden tongs against the bowl, the clink of forks on plates, the whisper of ice against glass as Ingrid sipped her water.

"So," Gil said. "Where'd you end up applying to college?"

As soon as the words came out they sounded wrong. He might as well have asked, *When are you going to leave and let us get back to our lives?*

Matthew squinted at his salad, as if taking a moment to process this rudeness. "Well. I applied to Yale. My parents basically forced me. And I was supposed to apply to a bunch of other places, Brown and Princeton, and this whole list they came up with at Herbert. But I missed some of those deadlines. For obvious reasons."

The way he said it, glibly, as if it was a faux pas—*Can you believe my parents did that?*—clouded Gil's head.

"I was actually thinking maybe I'd stay on at Essex," Matthew added, as if this was an obvious choice, barely worth mentioning.

When Matthew focused on his plate, Molly flicked Gil a look of surprise and accusation. As if he'd known and had been hiding it. But why *shouldn't* the boy want to stay up here? Except for all the obvious differences between Yale and Essex. What were those differences? Maybe your classmates weren't as rich at Essex. Fewer had attended fancy boarding schools. Fewer were destined for vice presidencies in their parents' companies after graduation. But Matthew could probably learn as much at Essex as he could at the "best" universities. Isn't that what Gil believed? Elite universities were research facilities for corporations and prestige factories. Matthew already had ample connections and enough money to last several opulent lifetimes. Maybe he wanted to get away from all that, toward something he saw as more, well, authentic.

"Well, at least you'll get to try it out first," Gil said. "Your headmaster mentioned you might take some classes this semester."

"What classes?" Chloe said. It was the first thing either of the girls had said since coming to the table and there was an awkward pause, as if a child had interrupted the adults.

"Oh, I don't know, I think I have to get permission," Matthew said.

Gil should've followed this up, carried the conversation, but he let a puddle of quiet spread over the table.

"Chloe," Molly said, saving them, "tell Dad about debate."

And for a moment normalcy returned. His daughter told him about her victory, about the strategies they'd learned, her voice rising with excitement. Across the table, Matthew slumped in his seat, relieved to have the focus off him. While Chloe went point by point through her arguments in favor of school busing, Matthew leaned over his plate and ran a hand along his jaw. With a shake of his head, he picked up his fork and scooped a bite of salad. No matter how much he tried, Gil couldn't see anything of the boy he remembered. Nothing of the child he'd feared and dreaded spending time with. The child who'd nearly ruined his life, had definitely ruined his relationship with Sharon, had broken for good Gil's first family.

After dinner, Matthew said he was worn out and went up to the guest room. Probably, naturally, he wanted some time to himself, to text with friends, post on Instagram, or Snapchat, or whatever. That's what kids did and Matthew was a kid. A sophisticated, urbane kid. But just a child.

Molly helped Gil with the dishes and, recognizing his distraction, filled him in on Chloe's ongoing tiff with her best friend, Lily. Lily had been acting out ever since her father had moved out, which was understandable, though her coping mechanism seemed to be acting cruel toward her friends. Gil let Molly take the lead in advice for the girls, since his general approach involved little more than saying fuck it and cutting the person loose. Not great advice unless you were a misanthrope, which, thankfully, wasn't a trait he'd passed on.

When they went up to bed, the light in the boy's room appeared to be off. He could've been awake in there, on his phone, but Gil knew he couldn't stay silent all night, needed to vent. Molly settled down next to him in bed, glasses on. She leaned over to kiss his forehead and whispered, "Well, he's here."

"He sure is," Gil said. She knew what he needed.

"And how many days is eight months?" she said, pulling off her glasses and rubbing her eyes. Exhausted from pretending to be happy Matthew was here.

After the funeral, the lawyer had called—how could that have been only a few weeks ago?—to inform them that as the boy's guardians they should begin to plan for Matthew to come and live with them in Vermont. Before Gil could say anything, the lawyer had added that as guardians, they would receive a monthly allowance to offset any expenses associated with the boy's care. Sharon and Niles had stipulated that the amount be generous enough to maintain the lifestyle to which Matthew was accustomed. As such, they would receive ten thousand dollars a month for as long as the boy was in their home, and when Matthew went to college, the amount would be one thousand a month until the boy reached the age of twenty-one. This allowance, the lawyer had explained, was unusually generous, and should be taken as a sign of Sharon and Niles's gratitude.

Ten thousand dollars a month. Every month. For eight months. For food, and clothes, but what else? They'd always managed to pay their bills each month, though just barely, and it had seemed likely they might be in debt until they died, especially once the girls went to college. But now they could be free of all that. A fresh slate. They could even, maybe, contribute to the girls' college funds, in which the initial deposits of five hundred dollars each still wallowed. If they took Matthew in, they'd be free, in a way.

But of course there were concerns beyond money. What if the

boy was a lunatic? Based on what they knew of him, that was a real possibility. And how would the girls feel about it? Would they feel safe in their own home? Would they resent their parents, who, in a way, had chosen money over their comfort and happiness?

After a week of talking it over with Molly, he'd called the lawyer with questions. As soon as Gil had stammered out his concerns, the lawyer had set about shaming him. Of course, they weren't *compelled* to take Matthew. That said, Sharon and Niles had clearly hoped they would. After all, he was Sharon's brother. Her only remaining family. He was, in addition, the boy's godfather, was he not? And hadn't he agreed to be the boy's guardian? Yes, all that was true, but they'd agreed back when the boy was an infant, seventeen years ago. His sister had appointed a backup, right? After a pause redolent with disappointment, the lawyer said, yes, there was a contingency: Niles's parents. But they lived in Scotland and were in their late seventies. Matthew's grandfather was in poor health, and it was likely he'd soon need heart surgery. Gil must've noticed they hadn't attended the funeral? But if indeed Gil was unwilling to honor his sister's wishes, the lawyer supposed he could, in a pinch, see what else might be done.

After another night of fretting, he and Molly agreed: They'd take him. What if something had happened to them instead of Sharon? Wouldn't they have hoped that she, the only family they had left close to their own ages, would have cared for the girls? And so wouldn't they be hypocrites to turn him away? Gil called the lawyer back the next day. Fine, okay. Send him up. The lawyer said he was pleased to hear they would fulfill their commitments and his secretary would be sending along the boy's flight information, as well as bank forms for the allowance.

"At least he seems completely different," Molly said, flipping her pillow and settling her head down. "I mean, compared to when we saw him in Montauk."

"He does, yeah," he said. She was right: Matthew was quiet, polite, even if his privilege simmered just beneath the surface. But the old Matthew, the one they'd known, was lurking in there somewhere. Right?

"And he's handling it pretty well," Molly said.

"I mean, I guess. I guess I just thought he'd be more, I don't know. Sad? Grieving? Or maybe a little, I don't know, scared, disoriented? I mean, his parents. But he—"

"He's a teenager," she said. "His parents died. As far as we know, he's a troubled kid. I'm sure he's upset, but honestly, Gil, my main concern is that we just get through this. You and me and the girls. Make it to July. That's the goal. Right?"

"You're right. We can do it. We'll be fine."

She leaned across again and kissed his cheek, then rolled away to read. He stared at the pages of the novel he was teaching next week but couldn't bring the words into focus. His attention kept sliding back to the boy just down the hall. Gil strained to hear something, even just a cough or the click of the door closing, but other than the rustle as Molly turned a page, the house was silent.

3

HIS FIRST IMPULSE WHEN HE WOKE AT DAWN WAS TO CHECK ON
the girls: a panic familiar from when they were babies, afraid they
might've died in the night while he'd selfishly slept. But of course,
as then, they were fine. Ingrid was twisted in her sheets, and he
opened Chloe's door a crack to peek in at her, face visible above
the comforter, crumpled in concentrated sleep. Matthew's door at
the end of the hallway was open. The boy's bag was tucked beneath the bed, the sheets were straightened, a glass of water on the
nightstand. In a half-sleeping daze Gil felt a brief, ridiculous swell
of hope that the boy was, somehow, inexplicably, simply gone, and
so they were already, unexpectedly, free.

Matthew wasn't in the kitchen, or the living room. It was just
after seven thirty, only a faint dusting of light above the crooked
line of black trees. Gil pushed Start on the coffeemaker. Well,
they'd survived the night. Except where was Elroy? He usually
slept on his dog bed in Gil and Molly's room, and he was always up
with the earliest riser.

"Elroy," Gil whispered, whistling low, but this didn't bring the clicking of nails on the stairs, the thud of his tail against the door as he careened around the corner.

The boy's shoes and coat were gone from where he'd put them last night, and when Gil checked the hooks in the mudroom, the leash was gone too. So Matthew had taken Elroy on a walk. After dinner, Gil had told the boy that they owned ten acres, most of it woods that stretched up a low hill. He said he'd take him out tomorrow, if Matthew wanted. There was a trail that Gil had cut up the slope and down past a pond.

He stuffed his feet into his boots and went out onto the back patio. An arctic blast had arrived overnight and tendrils of freezing air crept through his loose laces. Matthew was out at the edge of the yard, near the trees, Elroy sniffing at the end of the leash. The boy hunched his shoulders against the cold—he wasn't wearing a hat—and he turned toward the house. He was on the phone. The boy gestured angrily with one hand, then curled it against his chest. Gil whistled for Elroy and the dog's ears perked up. Matthew looked at the house.

"You can let him go," Gil called, not thinking he shouldn't until it was too late. He'd probably just woken Molly.

"Elroy, come," Gil called, patting his thighs, and Matthew finally understood. Elroy posed, then raced across the snow, hair rippling, black nose lifted into the wind. The dog slowed when he reached the frozen patio and wiggled around Gil's legs.

Matthew turned his back, so Gil took the dog in to towel him off, then sat at the kitchen counter with his notebook, the one in which he jotted thoughts, ideas, observations. Flotsam was an essential part of the writing life he told his students, and though it was true, now it comprised the entirety of his literary activity. But it was better than nothing. He opened to a fresh page after skimming—not a bad simile on one of the pages, but another entry made no sense at all, as if he'd left out half the essential words—and he forced himself to write before doubt could stifle him entirely. He wrote, without meaning to, about Matthew, about seeing him in the airport, glancing between the page and the boy's shape, pacing the dark wall of trees. As the coffee sputtered to its climax, he heard Molly's footsteps overhead.

"Good morning, loud husband," she said, rubbing her eyes as she came into the kitchen. She wore pajama bottoms and a T-shirt. In the cold, her nipples pressed tight against the yellow cotton, so worn it was nearly translucent.

"Sorry, I was—Elroy—" he said, gesturing at the dog who leaned against her legs. He closed his notebook and got her a cup of coffee.

"Thanks," she said, with a shiver, cupping the mug with both hands.

"Let me get you a sweatshirt," Gil said, checking on Matthew's shape in the yard. Blue and yellow stains stretched above the trees, and the yard went suddenly white.

"You could make a fire," she said, crossing her arms over her chest. Was she thinking the same thing, that she should put something on because if Matthew came in and saw her breasts. . . . But this was her house. And Matthew was family. Ostensibly a kid. But also a stranger. And by all appearances a man.

"Good idea," he said, but first he went to the hangers near the front door and got them both sweatshirts.

He scraped out the ashes of last night's fire, stacked fresh logs, and set the kindling alight. When they'd moved here, there had been lots he'd anticipated needing to learn, but this was the most satisfying: how to make a fire that burned hot and settled into a bed of coals. More than tending the yard, more than the repairs to the house, the plumbing, more than cutting a path through the forest, this had made him feel he'd earned his place in Vermont.

Matthew came in as the larger logs were catching and accepted the coffee Molly offered, took it to sit in front of the fire.

Gil busied himself with pancakes, though he wanted to ask who Matthew had been talking to. Not that it was any of his business. But why stand out there in the cold? Why not make the call from inside? Unless he was trying to hide something. Shit-talking his ridiculous bumpkin cousins? But what teenager was up at seven in the morning during winter break?

The girls came down together as breakfast was nearly ready. Chloe sat on the couch across from Matthew while Ingrid perched behind them on a stool at the counter. Chloe turned on the news. Molly and Gil had always watched the news with the girls, despite its frequent and possibly escalating horrors. Chloe had taken this tradition on, watching the weekend morning shows and often asking if they could keep *PBS NewsHour* on during dinner. She was informed and passionate about politics. After the presidential election she and Molly had traveled down to D.C. for the Women's March in their pink pussy hats, and then she'd run for student government and had started volunteering for Elizabeth Warren's campaign. She'd embraced her parents' interest and made it her own. Of course, soon she'd realize that her purportedly politically impassioned father was in fact full of hot air, never engaged seriously with the issues, wasn't out protesting, hadn't joined anything beyond Facebook groups, had merely spouted off from the safety of his living room.

Onto the screen came a particularly loathsome senator, jowly with the buggy, frantic eyes of one possessed, and Chloe said, "Oh my god, not this guy."

Matthew said something that made Chloe sit up straighter. Gil strained to hear her response, measuring cup poised above the hot pan, a single dollop falling into the butter with an annoyingly loud hiss.

"You're joking, right?" Chloe said.

But then Molly started washing the dishes and the words from the couch were blotted out, though he could tell they were arguing, or debating, or joking around. Thankfully, they were still going when he called them to the table. His daughter muted the television but left it on, so the talking heads smacked their wet mouths in the background.

"I'm sorry," Chloe said, "but it's not a joke. Those laws have a real effect on people's lives. It's not just some idea."

"But it is," Matthew said, pulling out the chair beside Chloe. He looked completely comfortable, as if it was normal for him to be sitting down at this table, with these people. Instead of it being a nightmare. A disaster. Which it was. But there was no evidence the boy felt that way. "I mean, to those guys," Matthew said, gesturing at the TV. "Maybe not in the way the law is applied, sure, but to *those* people, it's *nothing* but an idea. And it's not even *their* idea. Those politicians, all those guys you hate so much, they're ciphers. Those ideas just flow through them and I don't even think they really register them *as* ideas. More like nodes of financial transfer. That's what it's all about, in the end. Money flowing from one place to another."

"Spoken like a real New Yorker," Chloe said, draping a rope of maple syrup over her pancakes. "Those ideas are real. They have real applications. Gay people, women, black communities, all these groups are directly impacted by all this. It's not some postmodern swirl, no matter what privileged white men might want to think."

From beneath his anxiety, Gil felt a flush of pride: His daughter was more articulate than he was now, and so many miles beyond where he'd been at that age. There was nothing she couldn't do. That must be proof they'd done a good job as parents, even if that mostly involved not messing up her natural abilities, which came from her mother.

"Isn't it weird that rich white men are the ones most willing to embrace the truth that it's all just a transaction," Matthew said, raising his eyebrows. "It's almost like they don't stand to lose anything to that truth." Perhaps he meant to be self-deprecating, to poke fun at himself, but this was smothered by fact that *he* was the rich white man here.

"Maybe they should have to live as a woman, or go hungry for a year. Then we'll see how important they find those transactional *nodes*," Chloe said, slicing her pancakes.

When Gil mentioned he was going on campus that afternoon, Matthew asked if he could come along. Surely because he wanted some time out of the house.

Chloe, who'd been fiddling on her phone, looked up and said, "Can I come too?"

"To town?" Gil said, as if this was a ridiculous request.

He glanced at Molly, trying to get a read, but she was at the sink doing dishes. Now he felt sure, from her nonresponse, that he'd fucked up by letting this happen. But how could he say no without it looking as if he didn't want her around Matthew? Which he didn't. Alone, in town, on the boy's first day here. Not that anything was going to happen. Probably. And yet he felt a swirl of anxiety in his gut, a tension that made him wish he'd just slipped away unnoticed off to campus. Before he could answer Matthew said, "Yeah, that'd be good. Then I won't get lost in the big city."

Ingrid watched all this carefully, as she had throughout breakfast, saying hardly a word. At least there was a good excuse not to ask her to join them: She had a riding lesson at the barn. Even in the winter, when the ring was absolutely freezing, she went once a week to ride. This wasn't the sport Gil would've chosen for her. It was expensive, and dangerous. He never felt at ease around those animals. They were far too aware of their physical superiority. Ingrid had explained that this was the problem: The horses could tell he didn't trust them, and that made them nervous. He'd joked and said, *Well, this is the human world now, so they should be the ones to adapt.* Except when you stepped into the pen with a horse you were instantly *not* in the human world, but in the world of a massive, impossibly shaped creature that could kill you quickly. Of course, horses didn't kill people. Or not many people. But everyone, including the horses, knew they could.

After breakfast, they bundled into jackets and boots—Matthew insisted he was fine in his sweater and thin coat, though Gil would never have let the girls out of the house so inappropriately dressed—and into the frigid Subaru.

"So, Chloe, where should I drop you guys?" Gil said, glancing in the rearview as he let the engine idle.

"Church Street?" she said.

"You're the expert," Matthew said, turning to Chloe, who, Gil could see in the rearview, blushed and turned her face to the window.

"Maybe you should look for a parka while you're in town," Gil said.

"Oh my god, Dad, are you kidding? His coat is, like, super nice," Chloe said, leaning up between the seats.

"I know, I'm sure it's nice, I'm just saying, you don't want to be cold."

"Dad," Chloe said, her voice rising. "It's a Moncler."

"Fine," Gil said, having no idea what that brand meant. "Your choice, Matthew."

"Noted," the boy said with a curt nod, chin dipping beneath the collar of his coat.

Gil tuned the radio to NPR, which was broadcasting an interview with a writer. He'd met this writer, had actually shared a panel with her at a conference a few years ago. Well, like, twelve. If it'd been just Chloe in the car he'd have pointed this out, but now, with Matthew there, he kept quiet. To the boy, it might sound like bragging. Trying to prove he was a big shot, though they lived out here in the middle of nowhere. And he was manifestly *not* a big shot.

No one spoke during the drive to Burlington. How did the silence seem to Matthew? As if they had nothing to say, or that he was in the way, obstructing their normal, easy life? Collins Road, which took them out to Dorset, wound past endless snow-humped fields seen through gray trees, an occasional house with a wriggle of smoke, and otherwise wilderness.

The first evidence of town was a relief, and he pointed out

UVM's campus, the lake a gray flatness below town. Matthew leaned forward, as if he didn't want to miss anything. Gil pulled over at the top of Church Street. Two men in filthy parkas and disintegrating boots—homeless, presumably, though the line was often fuzzy in downtown Burlington—argued on a nearby bench, waving their hands, scraps of mist leaking from mouths hidden by wild beards. But Matthew didn't seem to notice them. He was used to it, obviously. From New York.

"I'll text when I'm ready, or you can text me," Gil said, as Chloe climbed across to get out on Matthew's side.

"Sure, Dad," she said, slamming the door so the car shuddered.

Half-sticking out of a parking spot, Gil watched them walk down into the red brick pedestrian mall, past mounds of cleared snow. They could've been brother and sister. Though actually, the way Chloe walked close to Matthew, they might've been a couple.

He had to stop this. Trying to squeeze Matthew into the role of the villain. Chloe would be fine. They were in public, on the pedestrian mall. Nothing was going to happen. Matthew wasn't here to hurt them, he was here because his parents were dead. And so far the boy had been unfailingly polite and good-natured.

If Gil's house matched his Vermont fantasy, Essex College fell well short of the ideal New England college. At the heart of the campus were three rambling old red brick mansions overlooking the lake, but the rest, built in the 1960s and '70s, was a clumsy conglomeration of faux colonial and feeble imitations of the brutalist style—squat, square buildings, rusted and dulled by Vermont winters. Gil's office was in one of the less wretched buildings, the Old Barn, called that either because it was actually a renovated barn or because it stood on the site where a barn had been. The faculty parking lot was empty, and so were the pale yellow hallways, which were cold. The heat had obviously been turned down. To save money. The perpetual budget crisis the university had been facing since its inception.

The first person he saw in the building was the student who'd emailed about an appointment. Susie had been in three of his classes already and would presumably be in many more, as he was the only fiction faculty. She'd been the best writer in his class last semester, one of the best in years. She'd asked to meet about a revision she'd done last semester, and he wouldn't normally have said yes, but Susie was a favorite. She was reading a book and he bent his neck to check the cover: Alice Munro's *Open Secrets*.

When Susie closed her book and looked up, a dark swell of feeling moved through him. This was wrong, a mistake, a grave and foreseeable error. What was he doing here? Keys in his hand. Bag on his shoulder. Ready to chat about whatever. Fiction. Recommendation letters. He was supposed to submit himself to jibber-jabber of no importance, in a world in which his sister had died. Her body had been crushed in a car; her body had been cut free from the wreck; she had been taken in an ambulance to the hospital and declared dead; her body had been burned into rough, heavy ash. Making it all more terrible was the fact that he'd barely spoken to his sister for years. A few texts about the girls' birthdays, the holiday letters she sent each December, but essentially he'd abandoned her. They hadn't seen each other, hadn't hugged, hadn't shown love of any kind in years, and he'd let this all happen, had let her slip away, and now she was dead. Not dead because he'd let her slip away, but somehow those facts were connected. If he'd been different, a better brother, more forgiving, more open, something might've been different. Maybe, somehow, she wouldn't be dead. Ridiculous, he knew.

He wanted to slump into the wall and weep, then find a dark hole to crawl into and bury his face down away from the light. But no. There was only this path on which he went to work in a world without his sister. A world in which he would pretend he gave two shits about this story, or that, or which grad programs his students applied to. But he had no choice. He couldn't walk out on his life.

"Susie," he said, fumbling with the key—his hand trembled, so the metal nicked into the wood—"how was your break?"

4

ROUTINE DID, THANKFULLY, REASSERT ITSELF AFTER THOSE FIRST
few disorienting days. The girls had school on Monday, so Gil woke
early and made breakfast. He drove them and they chatted about
upcoming tests and after-school schedules—debate, horses, Chloe's
plans to try out for the spring musical. Surely this was at least in part
a release: In the car they were safely away from Matthew, could be
their old selves, could remember who they were, out of the shadow
of the tragedy. On the second morning, after Matthew's fourth
night there, Gil asked how they thought it was going.

"It seems like he's doing okay. You know, considering," Ingrid
said from the back.

"Yeah," Chloe said. "I mean, he's a lot different than I expected.
I guess I expected him to be, I don't know, like a jerk, I guess. But
mostly he's quiet."

"He is," Gil said. "I've noticed that too."

"I mean, he's probably quiet because he's sad," Chloe said.

"Of course he's sad," Ingrid said, her voice hitching. "His parents
died."

As they slowed for the junction of Cheese Factory Road, he glanced in the rearview: Tears trembled in her eyes. That boy had tried to hurt this beautiful, gentle girl, and here she was brimming over with feeling for him.

"Yes, it's terrible," he said. "But he's doing okay. Maybe you girls can talk to him about it. I doubt he'll want to with me."

"Why?" Chloe said, frowning over the backpack on her lap. "I mean, you're kind of his dad now, right?"

"That's true," he said. He'd resisted thinking of it this way. Unlike Ingrid, it didn't fill him with sympathy, but rather with a tingling fear. To be responsible for a person he knew basically nothing about. To be required to love a stranger he'd spent so many years loathing. It must end in failure. "But he's a lot closer to your age. I'm just saying, if it comes up."

"It's pretty weird, though, you know? We haven't seen him in so long," Chloe said.

Gil glanced at Ingrid: She squinted out the window. Was she thinking about it: the incident at the pool, what Matthew had done to her?

"You talked to him, when you were in town," Gil said, glancing at Chloe. "What'd you guys do?"

"Not much, just mostly walked around," Chloe said, flipping down the visor and sliding open the mirror, before applying some lip gloss with what seemed to him excessive care. "He had some errands or whatever."

"Errands?" Gil said.

"We went to the Verizon store. He got a phone. So that took a while. And we went to the bank. The ATM, I mean."

"A phone? Doesn't he already have one?" But he knew the answer: He definitely did. Gil had noticed him typing into it the night he'd arrived, had seen him talking on it across his yard.

"Yeah, so I guess it was, like, a second phone? I don't know, he didn't tell me why, Dad," she said, puckering out her lips.

Now he tried to focus on the road, on not going overboard,

but a second phone? What was the boy doing? What possible reason could there be to do that?

"Right," he said. "Okay. Anything else?"

"Well, he did look at coats," she said in a teasing tone. Because the boy owned a Moncler. Gil had googled the brand while in his office that day he'd dropped them in town and discovered that the boy's jacket, short and insubstantial as it looked, cost at least two thousand dollars.

"Well, great, so, I'm just saying," he said, trying to cover his prying, "if he wants to talk to you, you know, you can. Or whatever you feel comfortable with, you don't have to."

Chloe, still looking into the mirror, said, "Of course, Dad. But it's fine. We'll survive."

"Okay," Gil said. "And you're good kids, you know that, right?"

"Not just good. The best," Chloe said.

"In the whole wide world," Ingrid added, imitating how he used to croon when they were younger.

Matthew required almost nothing from them, or at least from him, beyond food. The boy spent a lot of time in his room, presumably on his phone—or on one of his phones—though he did go each day to the basement, where Gil had a mildly rusty, chronically underused set of weights. One afternoon Gil went to swap the laundry and heard a metallic clank, a grunt, and there around the corner was Matthew, benching. The boy was wearing a tank top: Lean, roped muscles pulled tight across his shoulders, triceps stood in sharp geometric relief as he lifted the bar back up and let it down with a bang.

"I can spot, if you ever need it," Gil said, as Matthew sat up, slicked with sweat, panting and staring at him with eyes half-lidded from exertion.

"Thanks," the boy said, swiping at his face with a hand towel, then he lay back and fitted his hands around the bar.

Later that afternoon Gil went down to check. The boy had been benching two twenty. More than Gil could manage. A lot more. Which shouldn't bother him. But it did. Felt almost like a threat. But no, the boy was just exercising. Burning off some energy. Still, there'd been anger in the boy's face as he'd sat panting on the bench. Maybe it'd been surging testosterone. And yet Gil was convinced he'd seen hate in that look, a glimpse of the boy's true feelings.

Molly seemed to have accepted Matthew, at least better than Gil, which wasn't saying much. When he joked, "Survived another day," she squinted over the frames of her reading glasses and said, "I think we're going to be fine, Gil."

"Of course we are," he said, his voice inadvertently rising. He took a deep breath, closed his eyes, focused on keeping his tone down. "But I'm saying, who is he? Don't you wonder? It's almost like I picked up the wrong person at the airport. I just don't see anything of the kid he was in the person he is now."

"Isn't that good?" She was peering at him over her frames. Why didn't she take them off if the lecture was going to be so extended? Except it wasn't a lecture. He'd brought it up.

"I know, I'm just saying, I'm a little surprised. Not in a bad way. I expected more, more, I don't know." He picked up his book as if they might drop the conversation. But she sat there, watching and waiting. "I guess I expected him to be more work. More difficult."

"Me too," Molly said. "And let's hope it stays like this. For the girls' sake."

"Yeah, the girls." He blew her a kiss and opened his book. A moment of agreement to smooth over his ugly need to villainize his nephew.

He spent the next day refining his syllabi, sending a flurry of emails, uploading readings onto the course website, and in the afternoon, so as not to go crazy, he decided he'd take Elroy on a walk in the woods. The sky was clear and for the first time in weeks the air was filled with light, a glare reflecting off the snow. Expecting a no, he asked if Matthew wanted to come.

"Sure," the boy said, lowering the phone into which he'd been furiously typing. "Sounds good. I've been wondering what's out there."

"Mostly trees. And snow," Gil said.

Elroy, ever a fanatic for a walk, kicked his excitement up another notch when he realized his new best friend was coming. Dancing around the living room in anticipation, he lunged through the door as Gil opened it and bounded down the steps, skidding and slipping so his back legs went out from under him for a second, before shooting across the snow toward the trail.

From the patio Gil saw a faint line of smoke rising from the garage's chimney. They'd converted the space into Molly's studio years ago. She must be in there working on the new series: intricate, precise drawings of wooded landscapes. He couldn't see her, the window was too high on the wall, but it comforted him to know she was working. Somehow it relieved the tension he felt over neglecting his writing, as if she absolved him with her diligence.

The crunching of the crust covered the need to talk, but once they were under the quiet of the trees, he slowed to let the boy catch up.

Matthew was wearing an old pair of Gil's boots, and one of Gil's old jackets. Both coat and boots were too big, making him look like a kid playing at adulthood. Matthew was actually taller than Gil, or at least the same height—Gil hadn't any desire to find out for sure—but he was thin, without any of the accumulated bulk of fatherhood and age. Not that Gil was fat. Of course, he wasn't skinny. The boy was just young. Don't begrudge him that. Soon enough, age would catch him. But by then Gil would be a gnarled old Vermonter.

Shortly after entering the woods the trail bent up the hill and he had to focus on not slipping, forcing his boots down into the ruts of the snow and pushing down from the knee. Elroy skittered up and down the trail, leaving an occasional sprinkle, racing back to check on Matthew, then past Gil and on out of sight. After the hill, the trail followed the edge of a plateau before sloping down toward a pond.

Elroy waited for them at the curve in the path. Gil loved the way the slope here met the pond and the boundary between land and water was only the slightest bump in the snow, then the severe evenness of the ice. Deer gathered there, and hawks often sat in the trees.

Matthew came up beside him, hands stuffed into his pockets, breathing plumes, squinting into the glare.

"Not too shabby," the boy said.

As they watched the white world together, Gil felt an unexpected closeness to Matthew. Almost affection. Maybe all this time he'd been wrong. Once, the boy had been a beast, but he had changed into a better person, capable of finding beauty in Vermont's winter fields.

"Do you ever skate?" the boy asked, pointing at the lake. "It must freeze solid."

"It's not our land," Gil said. "The edge of the trail is our property line. That's our neighbor's. His place is through those trees."

"Too bad," Matthew said.

Where did he skate in New York? Central Park? What else didn't Gil know about him? The answer was everything.

"There's a rink in town. And a few ponds nearby," Gil said.

"Whatever," Matthew said. "This weather. No joke, huh?" He hadn't worn a hat and the tips of his ears were a violent red.

Gil wanted to tell him to put his hood up but kept it to himself.

"Don't worry, it'll only last another three months," he said, tugging his hat down, before they followed the path as it looped back around toward home.

5

HE HADN'T NOTICED MATTHEW'S NAME ON THE ROSTER, HAD only glanced at the list that morning after grabbing it from his departmental mailbox, so seeing him there, back near the windows, made Gil stop in the doorway to double-check the room number, though of course it was 105. For a few dizzy seconds he was sure the boy was there to hurt him. All the good behavior and kindness had been cover for this moment. Why else would he smile like that, an edge of teeth showing between curled tight lips? The boy couldn't be there to take Introduction to Fiction Writing, as, of course, turned out to be the case when Gil dug the already crumpled roster from his bag and called roll.

None of the other students noticed anything out of the ordinary. Matthew was just another student, albeit more handsome and better dressed in a crisp dark blue gingham shirt. But there *was* a difference, Gil thought as he read out the course description, which sounded more wooden than ever. Unlike the other students, who stared with intent start-of-the-semester nervousness at their syllabi, Matthew fixed his gaze on Gil, as if he'd long hunted him and wasn't going to let him out of his sight.

Why hadn't Matthew told him he was taking his class? How had he gotten in? The class had been full since the second week of registration and he'd fended off a half dozen requests to add in. Yesterday Gil had driven the boy to campus for a meeting with the dean of students to discuss which classes he might take. And now here he was, listening as the other students introduced themselves. When it was his turn he leaned forward and put his elbows on the table.

"I'm Matthew Westfallen. I'm taking this course as an elective. I'm from New York City. Um, favorite book? I've been reading a lot of Nabokov recently. Favorites I guess are *Despair* and *Pale Fire*." He sat back in his chair, then jerked forward quickly and added, "Oh, and Gil up there, he's my uncle."

A murmur of laughter ran around the table.

"Susie?" Gil said, gesturing to the young woman beside Matthew, as if they could move past this blip.

"Sorry, what?" she said, flustered, glancing at Matthew, who looked delighted at the stir he'd caused.

"Susie, can you introduce yourself, please?" Gil said. Probably he should make some kind of joke, some comment about how, yes, unfortunately for Matthew, they were related. But any mention of that might lead to the fact that the boy was living with them, which would lead, inevitably, to questions that could be answered only by the truth of his sister's death. Thinking about it there made him sick, and he squeezed his pen in a weak, trembling fist.

"Oh, sure, sorry," Susie said, smiling at Matthew.

When he dismissed them—forty-five minutes early, though he warned them that that wouldn't be a regular occurrence—he wanted to ask Matthew to stay behind but couldn't think of how to phrase the first sentence, how to make it seem reasonable, not like he was singling the boy out, and then it was too late.

Instead Gil went to the English department. The only way Matthew could've added in at the last minute was through the chair, Simon, who'd directed the department for four years following the turbulent reign of a crotchety Victorianist who'd clung to power like a mad dictator all the way to his belated retirement. Unlike some of the other faculty, Simon seemed to see little difference between a fiction writer and a scholar, and he'd sided with Gil's preference when they'd hired a poet last year. Simon's field was Elizabethan theater, and he had a bit of the whimsy of those plays in his behavior, along with a quirky formality of speech.

A line of students snaked out of the chair's office and down the hall. Gil stepped past their scowls. Simon, white frock of frizzy hair standing off his head, squinted into his laptop. A petulant young woman sat across the desk from him, chomping away at her pen cap.

"Simon, could I have a minute?" Gil said.

Squinting, baffled, into his computer, Simon said, "Sure, Gil. Stop by in March?" Then his face brightened and he said, "Here, I found it! It's an issue with your AP credits. You're going to have to go down to the registrar, sorry." And with that he ushered the young woman out, her face now flushed with rage.

"How about lunch?" Simon said, putting a hand on Gil's arm as he warily checked the line of malcontents. "Half an hour?"

"Sure," Gil said.

Simon shouted "Next!" and a young man in sweatpants and a sweatshirt forced himself into the doorway so Gil had to squeeze aside.

After Gil had worked through emails from frantic students who wanted to add his classes there was no sign of Simon, so he went through his class paperwork, something it usually took him weeks to get to. In addition to going over the syllabus and introducing themselves, the students had signed up for workshop. Matthew's name was in the first slot and beneath it was Susie's. Usually no one signed up for those early spots and he had to cajole experi-

enced students, or pile up workshops toward the end of the semester. *The first slot.* The boy was showing off. Not only could he get
into a full class, one that freshmen never got into, but he could
hand his work in before anyone else. This school, this class, these
assignments, they were kind of a joke. After all, he was, essentially,
Yale bound.

Done with busywork, Gil took out his notebook and opened
to a blank page. He wrote about a professor who walked into his
first class to discover his nephew there, a nephew he hated, and
feared. It was awful how good it felt to write the truth, or some
version of it.

Simon knocked on Gil's door, pulling on his parka. A white
fringe of hair stuck out from beneath a tight wool cap.

"Ready? If we don't go now I might never escape."

Hurrying out the back door of the department and down the
stairwell, Simon talked nonstop about the chaos of the new semester, asked what creative writing classes they should offer next year,
mentioned the lecture next week by a literary scholar that Gil
should encourage his students to attend. Outside, freezing gusts
cut their conversation short. The faculty dining hall was on the top
floor of the University Center, hidden away with the offices of
poorly attended student clubs. They paid five dollars to Sandy at
the desk, gathered some desultory food—fried chicken chunks
from steaming metal bins, salad consisting almost entirely of ice-
berg lettuce cores—and managed to get a table to themselves. As
they arranged thin paper napkins on their laps, Gil said, "This
morning, in my fiction class, I was surprised to find my nephew is
enrolled."

Simon poked at his salad with a fork, clearly unsure how to take
this. Was Gil simply making an observation? A complaint?

When Gil said nothing, Simon nodded and said, "Oh, yes, yes,
I meant to tell you that. Sorry. He came by my office yesterday,
asked if I would give him an override." He adjusted his small, round
glasses. "And you know how ardently I loathe overrides, but, well,

he's your nephew, so I assumed he'd cleared it with you in advance. I take it I have erred?"

"He hadn't mentioned it. Maybe he just assumed it was fine."

"Well, is it?" Simon said, slipping half a cherry tomato into his mouth.

"Of course. Sure. I . . ." but Gil wasn't sure what to say. Now that he was discussing it with Simon, whatever problem he'd felt must be there had faded.

"In my defense," Simon said, raising both hands as if surrendering, "he had a letter from a dean asking chairs to allow him into classes. I realize it's unusual. If you'd prefer, I can talk to him, get him to take Intro to Poetry with Nicole."

"No, I'm sure it'll be fine," Gil said. He was an idiot. He'd felt so strongly that something was off but hadn't articulated to himself what that might be. Just looking at the fried chicken made his face greasy, but he forced a butter knife into its rigid hide.

"How *is* your nephew doing?" Simon said, his face crumpling with real concern. "Both his parents, the poor boy."

"He seems okay. Considering." A corner of chicken broke away, fibrous and nearly as dry as the crust, but he forked it up.

"And your sister, I'm so sorry. I wish I could've made it to the funeral," Simon said.

As he swallowed a semi-masticated lump, Gil remembered the call he'd gotten yesterday. He hadn't exactly forgotten about it, but had put it aside in the frantic rush of the start of the semester. A detective from New York had left a voicemail saying "I wanted to go over a few things from the investigation, if you can give us a call back." And she'd left a number.

"I actually thought it might be good for him," Simon said. Gil had missed the sentence or two before that. *Good for whom? What might?* "Make him feel more comfortable. More at home, if that's not too much of a cliché."

Oh, Matthew. Of course.

"I'm sure it'll be fine. How were the MLA interviews?"

Delighted to change the subject, Simon rolled his eyes and related the travails of setting up campus interviews for the Nineteenth Century American Literature position.

Gil half-listened, trying to articulate to himself what the problem was. Why had he wanted to talk to Simon? What had he been afraid of? Because, if he was going to be honest with himself, he *was* afraid. Had been. No, actually, you know what, still was.

Maybe Matthew didn't remember the incident. But no, of course he must: He'd been eleven. Not a baby. Which was what made it all the worse. Which was what made it, at least in Gil's mind, an act of evil.

6

"THAT'S IT, NO, YEAH, THAT'S DEFINITELY IT," MOLLY SAID,
pointing to a roof visible above the dunes. Gil had thought they
were lost. The town of Montauk had dwindled behind them, and
now they were driving through what looked like a nature preserve.
Only glimpses of mansions flashing between the brush and trees
suggested otherwise. Private estates, he supposed you should call
them, as he turned in to the narrow lane that wasn't on the GPS,
but there was a wooden sign nailed to a spindly pine: The Westfallens.

He'd never been able to get used to his brother-in-law's sur-
name. Now his sister's name. So archly WASPy. Niles probably
traced his lineage back to 1066, or beyond. To the Romans, maybe.
And if anyone had the resources to do—or fudge—the research, it
was Niles. Because look at this fucking house that emerged from
the landscape, as if rising from the sand for King Niles's delight.

The house was modern, sharply angled, made almost entirely
of glass. The sloping roof was lined with solar panels, and there in

the driveway, parked beneath the wraparound deck, was a shining red Ferrari. Gil parked the rental—a Mercedes, gone shabby in comparison—far away.

They hadn't seen Sharon and her family for two years, not since she'd called and said she was bringing nine-year-old Matthew to Vermont, wasn't that fun? They were heading to Stowe with friends. Maybe they could meet up on the mountain?

The day passes cost almost as much as a season's pass at their usual slopes, but with both his parents gone, Gil felt the thinness of his family, the near erasure of his past, and he knew the girls longed for some connection, to cousins, a larger family.

This was all hard to keep in mind once they were actually on the mountain. At check-in, his sister barely acknowledged them, spent all her time whispering like a sorority girl with her friend, a beautiful, haughty woman in form-fitting black ski pants who eyed them with weary contempt and didn't direct a single word to them all day. Gil spent most of the afternoon on the easier slopes with Ingrid, so reports of Matthew's behavior came through Molly. Apparently, the boy had attacked his nanny, a young French woman, with his poles while they were putting on their boots, screaming that he hated her, calling her a bitch, saying he wanted to kill her. Later, on a run, the boy had cut in front of the nanny and intentionally tripped her. She'd fallen, losing her skis. Thankfully, she hadn't been injured, but she'd been crying as she scrambled back upright, clipped on the skis Molly had fetched, and started down after Matthew's dwindling shape. Molly and Chloe had seen the nanny and Matthew at the café atop the mountain, where the boy was drinking a huge mug of hot chocolate while the young woman stared despondently out the window, as if considering hurling herself down the nearest triple black diamond.

Gil didn't interact with his nephew until the end of the day while they were taking off their boots. Ingrid was tired and quiet and Chloe sipped hot chocolate beside her mother, watching her cousin warily.

"Did you have fun?" Gil asked Matthew as he tugged at his daughter's boot.

"Did you have fun?" the boy said in a high, whiney imitation. His cheeks were flushed with the cold, his blond hair damp at the temples, lips twisted in a snarl.

"Excuse me?" Gil said, flustered.

"Oh, what's wrong, Uncle Gil?" the boy said, light blue eyes glittering with malice. Gil had always assumed that that didn't actually happen, had told students to never include glittering eyes in their stories. But his nephew's glittered with hate, as if they might shake free from his face. "You hard of hearing? Or just stupid?"

"What?" He held Ingrid's boot in one hand, his daughter tense, staring at the boy.

"Deaf?" the boy shouted, leaning close so spit jumped from his lips onto Gil's cheek and eyelids. "Are you deaf, Uncle Gil?"

Gil blinked back the urge to grab the little fucker's spindly throat.

"Well, I guess so. And also stupid," Matthew said, jumping up and walking away.

Seething, Gil finished getting the girls' boots off, took the girls to the bathroom, then looked around for Sharon. He texted her but got no response. Then tried calling, but went directly to voicemail. While Molly and the girls sipped hot chocolate, he tromped out into the parking lot, looked stupidly up and down the row of cars, then at the hotel. His sister had a room, but he had no idea what number. They eventually found her at the bar, seated around the far side, as if hiding with her friend, drinking a glass of white wine. Sharon half-heartedly invited them up to their place, ignoring her son, who knelt on the carpet emptying sugar packets into a heap. Gil said they needed to get home, the kids were tired, school tomorrow. Sharon was obviously relieved, though she did at least deign to climb down from her chair and give them all quick, tepid hugs. Matthew didn't look up when his mother told him to say goodbye to his cousins.

It was physically painful not to say anything until the girls fell asleep, but as soon as they did, he and Molly whispered their disgust all the way home. You know what? They were done with them. Hadn't Matthew always been awful? From birth? Gil's mother had told him how when he was a baby Matthew had bitten her when she'd picked him up out of the crib. Kids sometimes bite, but this had been different: Matthew had laughed. His mother had rarely discussed his sister's family with him, but during that conversation she'd cradled her bandaged hand to her chest and said the boy had looked evil. He'd enjoyed it. But then, perhaps realizing she'd been too forthcoming, she said it was surely just a stage. All kids went through bad patches. Some patches were just a little deeper than others.

There was some truth to this. Their neighbor's daughter had turned overnight from a charming young woman into a brooding, angry hooligan who no longer returned their greetings. And in a few more years she might morph into someone else. As soon as he'd had kids, Gil had started writing about children, fascinated by their fungible natures, which confirmed what he'd come to believe, that one's "identity," or "self," or whatever you wanted to call it, was nothing but the thinnest mask. A scrap of paper fluttering in the hand. All it took was a surprise, a change of weather, and it went skittering across the sidewalk, catching and melting to mush in the gutter.

After the ski trip, he and Molly often talked about—shit-talked, really—Matthew and, for that matter, Sharon and Niles. Could you even call what they did parenting: constantly shifting their son into the hands of nannies who seemed chosen more for their looks and European accents than their ability to take care of a kid, especially a difficult (evil—let's just be honest) kid? Through this routine of complaint and judgment he'd felt himself growing to dislike his sister, to scorn the woman she was now, someone he didn't know at all. Which might, in the end, be the real problem: He'd lost touch with her, and the pain this brought was intense. He was losing contact with the one person left in the world who'd known him as he'd been long ago, the boy who'd slept with his stuffed seal throughout high school, a secret she'd never once told anyone. That boy he'd been was nearly gone, except in the mind of his sister. Sure, her son was a pain in the ass. And sure, she wasn't at all the person he used to know. He was pretty sure she'd botoxed her face. It could've been the cold, but her cheeks and eyes had been eerily stiff. Who was she? And beyond that, a deeper question: Had he ever really known her?

That he should follow in his parents' path toward an academic and intellectual—however modest—life had always been a given. It was a good life in most ways. Meaningful, or at least potentially meaningful, and there was the social status of being a professor, summers off, a steady, if small, paycheck. He'd assumed Sharon had felt the same, but when she'd dropped out of graduate school, married Niles, and transformed into this new person, he'd looked back and seen signs of her discontent everywhere: her childhood obsession with horses and her constant annoyance at her parents' insistence that they couldn't afford riding lessons; befriending, in high school, the richest set of girls at the private school her parents took a second mortgage out to afford, then bitterly complaining when they wouldn't send her on a New Year's ski trip to Deer Valley or a spring break jaunt to the Bahamas. Sharon, he realized later than he should've, had resented their middle-class life. She'd resented their small house in Alexandria with its one full bathroom—a second toilet and sink in the basement—a setup that had required scheduling morning showers. She'd resented, more vocally, their ten-year-old Volvo, which she'd driven only when there was no other choice. She and her friends had nicknamed it the Purty Turd, which came to be the only way she ever referred to the car, even in front of her parents. So, Gil could see at last, she'd always longed for a different life, one built on the comfort of wealth. And yes, she'd given academia a meager go: majoring in philosophy at Yale, starting an MA at Columbia. But at the first real opportunity she'd dropped it all, moved out of her studio in Morningside Heights and into Niles's Tribeca apartment, then together into a massive uptown classic six. Gone were her black jeans and boots, replaced by a new, billowy wardrobe of discreetly expensive styles. Her hair was cut and dyed, her face tightened and sculpted. She stopped calling and Gil almost never saw her, and each time he did there was that small shock at realizing that the woman, clipping along in her heels, a leather handbag in the crook of one arm, was his sister. Who was she, he'd wonder as she waved with the tips of her fingers and then leaned in to peck his cheek?

But there was only one way to find out who she was as they crept into middle age and their lives drifted further apart. He wasn't going to get to know his sister by avoiding her, by bitching about her family. Instead, he should make an effort. Spend some time with her. Despite her terrible son.

And so this trip to the Hamptons. It was a chance to reclaim something. Not just his relationship with his sister, but his past, the kid he'd been. If his sister had turned into a vacuous shell as he feared, if her son was an unrepentant monster, if her husband was a greedy, condescending snob, well, at that point maybe he'd let the relationship wither. But something in him needed to give it one more shot.

Molly and the kids scrambled out of the car, babbling amazement at the house, and, well, it *was* amazing. And beautiful. Terrible, unjust, ridiculous, and utterly gorgeous. His sister had bought this house last fall, after renting in East Hampton for decades, but, as she'd put it when she'd called to insist they use her private jet service, she had to get away from that scene. He couldn't imagine Montauk was much different. A bit farther down at the tip of Long Island. Still the land of millionaires who built impossible mansions perched on the dunes. These houses would be swept away by the rising sea levels, but that was part of the point. They were emblems of excess, symbols of outrageous consumption, the very thing that had led to the rising sea levels, those collapsing glaciers in Greenland. This house was an act of defiance—fifteen or twenty million dollars poured into a place that could, next year, or in any year to come, be wiped out by a hurricane—and an embrace of that very precarity. *Here we are. Do your worst.* When the worst came, Sharon and her family would no doubt be safely installed at their mountain house in Vail, guarded by a well-paid cadre of soldiers, while the world below crumbled to ash.

If he'd dared say any of this to anyone, even Molly, they'd think he was ridiculous. And jealous. Because he was ridiculous. And jealous.

"You're here!" his sister cried, a glass pane sliding away to let her onto the deck above. She wore a tennis outfit, white skirt, white shirt, her dark hair clipped back from her face. "Come in, come in, the door's open." As they started in she added, "And please leave your shoes down there!"

Sharon met them at the top of the stairs, kissed and hugged them. Unlike Gil, who was balder than when they'd last met up, not to mention five years ago when he'd first felt the cold of Chloe's zipper against his head while carrying her on his shoulders and realized what the dwindling future of his hair would be, Sharon still looked young: no bags under her eyes, no crow's-feet, her jawline sharp and clean.

The house was no less dazzling on the inside. It seemed to be a single enormous space and yet was broken into discrete parts, rooms, or some more contemporary approximation: walls that eased apart when his sister touched a panel to reveal themselves as doors. The front of the house facing the ocean was entirely glass, a smooth unbroken line of white, breaking waves.

Out one of the windows Gil caught a glimpse of a pool, a bright blue oval, darkening deeper at one end. His sister hadn't included it in the tour, as if it didn't bear mentioning.

"Niles and Matthew are out on the boat," Sharon said, pointing to the ocean, as if they might glide by. Gil had seen pictures of the boat on Facebook and was pretty sure it should be called a yacht. "But you guys should totally get into your suits while the sun's out."

The girls raced through the house to the guest room. Guest rooms. Guest wing.

"I'm so glad you're here," Sharon said, squeezing his arm and steering him into the glittering kitchen. Black marble counter—or who knows, likely some rarer stone—futuristically smooth chrome appliances, a sink in which you could've bathed a large child. As they came into the room a woman slipped around the corner so Gil caught only a glimpse of her hair, tied up in a bun, and her white shirt. Sharon made no move to introduce them, so he assumed she must be a maid, or a nanny.

"Thanks for having us," he said. "This place is amazing."

"Well, we like it," she said, flipping a hand at the windows, bright across the expanse of the living room, as if it was no big deal. And as difficult as it was to process, twenty million on a house was, for Niles, like buying a used Subaru might be for Gil. Notable, requiring research and paperwork, but definitely manageable.

"The girls are really excited to be at the beach," he said. Realizing that might sound as if they didn't care about seeing Sharon, or her family, he added, "And you guys. I mean, they haven't seen Matthew in a while."

"Matthew, yes, well, Matthew," Sharon said softly. She shook her head and said, "You better get going. Cocktails at five. We're very strict about that here."

They wound along a path through the dunes to the beach. Following the girls, each lugging a boogie board and various flotation devices, he decided coming here had been the right call. He'd missed his sister. She was all that remained since his parents had died. Without Sharon, he'd have only Molly and the girls, and of course that was enough, but soon they'd get older and then go off to college, exactly as they should, and it would be just the two of them in the house in Vermont. He'd tend the garden, chop the wood, take walks in the woods, which would be indistinguishable from the woods behind his house now except that through them would walk not a middle-aged man but an old man, his fully bald head covered with a black cap. And when he returned the house would be quiet, the whisper of the radio in the kitchen where Molly might be cooking, or the snick of a lamp as she sat down to read. With Sharon, his world was a little bigger. And no matter how bad her son was—what a relief it was to arrive and have him out of the house—they could bear it.

When they were kids, their parents had taken them to the beach, though nowhere like this. Usually they'd camped, driving down the spine of the Outer Banks to Ocracoke. They'd set up their tents in a cove behind the dunes—one for their parents, with an anteroom where they hid in the afternoons from mosquitoes, and a two-person tent for the kids—and spend three or four nights, sleeping bags slowly filling with sand so they'd wake each morning feeling scoured. Their dad would take them early in the mornings while their mom dozed in the sun-splashed tent. They'd often go out into the ocean on their own, Sharon holding his hand as they dived under and went far enough out that they could bob around while their dad sipped coffee. Gil remembered so clearly his father sitting cross-legged on the sand, a sweat-stained Orioles cap pulled low to cut out the early sun so nothing of his face could be seen between beard and brim.

Out in the water they'd play imaginary games, all the way through their last such trip when Sharon was twelve. *Star Wars,* usually, or they were orphans, or there were battles with mosquitoes who'd followed them from the dunes.

In the afternoons they'd drive around the island, or go to the one store for supplies to get out of the sun, then their father would make dinner. He was a terrible cook but was the only one who knew how to keep the gas stove lit—a finicky German model he'd bought mail order years before Sharon had been born. Their mother sat in a folding chair, reading, or watching her husband squat above the blue flames over which he cooked potatoes in foil that were always hard in the center, then steak, which he left too bloody, and finally scorched mushrooms or green beans. They ate with special camping utensils: wide-handled metal sporks that didn't fit right in their mouths, and knives from their father's collection, so sharp they had to be careful not to cut through the paper plates on their laps as they ate in the dark. Their father's dinner would go cold while he attended to the stove, detaching the small propane tank, setting the burner aside to cool, then pouring himself wine in a blue speckled tin coffee mug and draining it in several mouthfuls while he watched the rest of them eat, before finally settling himself, disappointed to be done with his chores, in his seat.

Back at home, Sharon had already begun to turn into an adolescent—she spent hours on the phone, hogging it, though Gil had no one to call—but at the beach she'd let herself be a kid. Each time she'd said "Come on, let's go play" and they'd run off into the dunes, or to their tent, he'd felt a swell of joy, as if he'd known that that closeness couldn't possibly last.

And now they were here, in the Hamptons, in a neoliberal fantasy of beach life. A mansion instead of a tent, marble-lined bathrooms instead of Porta Potties, private chefs instead of freeze-dried lasagna. To see Sharon's house as a betrayal of how they'd been raised by their academic mother and journalist father was maybe too simplistic, but he was sure their dad would've agreed. Still, Sharon had invited Gil and his family. She wanted them here with her, in this bought paradise, and it was hard, once faced with the softly crumbling waves and the pale yellow sand of the beach, to feel bitter.

The girls shrieked in and out of the water, which, since it was June, was cold. By the time he and Molly had the towels and umbrella and bags set up, the girls were begging him to take them out over their heads so they could get wet. Flinching at the first touch of the waves, he clung to Ingrid's hand—she was only six, too little to swim in the ocean on her own—but Chloe, an independent nine-year-old, refused to take his other hand. They waded out, turning their backs on the breaking waves, then, on the count of three, ducked down into the water, came up sputtering, and raced back to the warm sand.

Ingrid wanted to swim in the pool, which they passed on the way back, but they needed to shower before dinner. It was, according to his phone, which got only a single bar of service out here, nearly six. There'd be plenty of time for the pool. They'd be here all week.

After washing off the sand in the downstairs shower—which instead of a poured concrete floor was lined with what he thought was slate, smooth but somehow not slippery—the girls ran upstairs wrapped in towels.

The house seemed at first to be empty, but through the glass doors he spotted his sister's head in one of the deck chairs.

"Throw your towels in the bathroom hamper," she said. "And FYI, you're late." She held up a mojito. "I'll give you a pass this time, brother. Now go get yourself a drink so I don't have to wallow alone in my debauchery."

In the kitchen, Gil was greeted by a handsome young man with a European accent who asked what he could get him. Molly soon joined them on the deck, while the girls stayed back in the room to watch shows on the wall-sized television.

Sharon asked Molly what art she should be paying attention to and Molly admitted she hadn't been down to the New York galleries in years. It was so easy to drift out of touch and the art world was constantly changing and . . . She sounded embarrassed, which Gil would've felt if Sharon had asked who she should be reading. Did this house, the grounds, all the opulence, amplify those feelings of having slipped out of sight? Even if you regarded the world of finance as a scam—which Gil definitely did—Niles had un-questionably conquered it, while Molly and Gil had, by the same measurements, failed. They weren't famous, weren't well known. Yes, they'd made work, had sold some work, but where were the monuments they'd raised to themselves?

"We haven't been as much as we should either. The last great thing we got to see, really, was Abramović at MoMA," Sharon said.

"Oh my god, that sounded amazing," Molly said, sitting up. "I so wish we'd gone."

She'd been, he remembered, somewhat obsessed with that per-formance: had watched the live stream on the museum's website for hours. He'd found her teary, watching a woman sit across from strangers for hour after hour. He hadn't grasped what she found so profound, had always been—regressively, pathetically—resistant in some dumb way to performance art.

"Yes, it really was amazing. We got to go to the opening, actu-ally," Sharon said. "And we got to sit with her."

"You did?" Molly said, pulling off her sunglasses, as if she could barely stand this excitement. "How?"

"Well, you know, Niles is on the board. So when they offered us the chance we of course said yes. It was early on, and of course part of the performance is about endurance, all those faces, day after day, but even so, it was intense. And terrible. I only sat across from her for seven minutes. She really *looked* at you. Relentlessly. But also, somehow, gently, which almost made it more awful. We're just not used to it, I think."

"The recognition," Molly said.

"Yes, exactly. The sense that you are so fully seen. With our family and friends, we don't look at each other in that way. Which makes it sound like our everyday lives are missing something. And maybe they are. I don't know. But it's what we think of as our lives, these glimpses of each other. And sitting there across from Marina was too much. Too human, someone said. But it went beyond the human. A religious moment, I heard other people call it, with all the fear and mystery of religion."

Gil felt he was hearing, for the first time in years, a faint flicker of the old Sharon, the person she might've been if she hadn't met Niles just after starting her MA program.

She laughed and shook her head. "So, of course, then Niles gets up there and sits for over an hour. Longer than anyone had done to that point, and then we went to dinner, as if nothing had happened." She said this as if it was both funny and, at the same time, proof of what they all knew: Niles was superior. Or maybe Gil wasn't reading her right. Maybe she was teasing Niles, lightly mocking him. Gil could happily take the teasing several steps further: Sharon's husband was a dead-inside narcissist who tried his best to turn an art piece about human connection into an exhibit of his will to dominate.

This was the Sharon he didn't want to know. The housewife, the wealthy woman, the person who fawned over her arrogant husband. His mother had insisted, the one time he'd brought this complaint up to her after Sharon's wedding and the purchase of their Upper East Side apartment, that Sharon was the same person Gil had always known: She was still intelligent, still interesting, but this now expressed itself in new ways. Was it, she'd asked him in her most professorial tone, so unbelievable that someone would give up on academia, with its low pay and constant competition and underlying sexism? Was it so shocking that Sharon would want comfort and pleasure and travel and the freedom to do anything, go anywhere? Hadn't she always loved travel? Hadn't she thought of transferring to Oxford after her junior year abroad there? And with Niles she could have at least a version of the life a part of her had always wanted, which was what everyone was trying to do in their lives, wasn't it? Sure, he'd conceded, yeah, he understood that. But *this* was what she wanted? A life among unctuous braggarts? Maybe, his mother had gently suggested, he was simply jealous of Sharon's wealth and comfort. *Bullshit,* he'd said angrily, but it was hard not to sound defensive: At the time he'd been scraping by on adjunct pay. His father, a journalist hardened by the brutalities of reporting on the world week after week, had listened to all this with a frown, then said that Gil should be happy for his sister even if he couldn't understand her choices. Sharon was happy, as far as anyone could see. And they were her family. No one was asking Gil to approve of Sharon, only to accept her, be happy for her. It would, his father had said, make Gil happier too, to put his grudges aside. There had, as far as Gil could tell, never been proof of this final claim, or more likely he'd failed to heed his parents' advice.

A young man—Giovanni, from Rome, Sharon explained—brought them fresh drinks, and as they collected them from the tray, Niles and Matthew returned.

First came the shouting.

"No, Dad, fuck *you!*" Gil heard from below, where presumably a car had pulled in, though one so finely made it was undetectable to the human ear, and he started up in his chair against which a negroni and the rumble of the waves had pinned him.

"Matthew!" Niles roared as a door slammed downstairs.

"Well, they're back," Sharon said, lifting her sunglasses to peer at a bird perched on a flagpole at the end of the deck.

"Leave me the fuck alone!" Matthew screamed, inside now, closer. Did he not see them out here? Had he not noticed their car?

Gil resisted the urge to turn around. The boy was probably visible now through the glass. And Sharon might find it rude. Gawping at her terrible son.

The door to the deck opened and the boy was there, panting, his handsome face twisted with rage. Beyond the rage the boy was unnerving in other ways: eleven years old but not a doughy preteen. Instead, he looked like a small, finely chiseled version of an adult.

"Mom!" he shrieked, as if she wasn't four feet away. "Mom!"

"Yes, Matthew," Sharon said, turning her head but not getting up.

"Mom, can you come tell Dad to stop being such a fucking dickhead?" All of this was shouted as the boy leaned out, arms flung across the doorway so his arm muscles flexed.

"Honey, maybe you need to take some time out and calm down," Sharon said.

"No!" the boy screamed, clenching his eyes shut and throwing his head back, then snapping his head toward Gil, baring his teeth like a crazed dog.

"Say hello to your uncle, please," Sharon said, as if pleasantries were possible.

"No, Mom, get your ass in here. I need you to tell Dad to stop being such a dick sucker." His tone had shifted into a whine and he bobbed in the doorway as if about to pee his pants.

Sharon let out an elaborate sigh and sat up, lowering her sunglasses to squint at the waves. "Hold my spot," she said. In that moment, Gil could feel a shift in the atmosphere, and he knew the rest of the week wouldn't resemble those first few relaxing hours.

Sharon squeezed past the boy, who stayed in the doorway, glaring at Gil as if considering spitting in his uncle's face. With a toss of his head he swiveled to follow his mother, the whining rising quickly into shrieks.

"I'd better go check on the girls," Gil said, hoisting himself up, a wave of dizziness—the drinks, but also the brackish backwash of adrenaline—making him clutch the side of the lounge chair for balance.

"You can't leave me out here alone," Molly whispered, leaning out of her chair to grab his hand. "What if he comes back?"

"Then you'd better come hide," he whispered, as if anyone could hear him over the swell of screams.

They skirted the side of the living room farthest from the kitchen, where Matthew was shouting, "This is such bullshit. You fucking liars! How fucking dare you lie to me like that?"

Gil closed the door to the guest suite, blunting the boy's voice. There was a lock on the door. He should flip it. After all, his nephew was apparently insane. Once his parents were dead the boy would make his way back here with the blood-soaked knife.

The girls were watching *The Parent Trap* with worried frowns that made it obvious they'd heard.

They should leave. Call a cab and take a train to New York. Clearly Matthew was disturbed. Their presence would only make things worse.

If only he'd listened to that intuition, everything might've been different.

All the next day Gil struggled to stay awake. He hadn't fallen asleep on a beach since he'd been twenty-four years old and had passed out on a strip of black sand in Guatemala, where he'd been traveling, purportedly trying to write, though in fact he'd spent most of his time drunk and stoned in gringo bars. He'd woken from that Guatemalan nap to find his friends gone, mosquitoes swarming over him. But now he had people to take care of. He had to make sure the girls didn't go out into the waves.

He forced himself to sit up beside Molly who lay in the umbrella's shade, book open across her chest. His head throbbed, a dull, dry pulse out of sync with the crush of the surf.

Each time Niles had opened a new bottle Gil had said *Sure, thanks,* long after he knew he should stop. When else would he get to drink such wine? Niles was a braggart, but he had impeccable taste. Or a sommelier who stocked his cellar had impeccable taste, which Niles took credit for. What did it matter when there were bottles of 2000 Valentini Montepulciano, and a Latour, also from 2000, and a La Tache that Niles declared "something really special"?

Sharon had set the girls and Matthew up in the theater's plush leather seats before a huge screen to watch *Up*. She'd let Ingrid pick the movie, and after half an hour, while they were still on salad, Matthew had stomped past, saying he wasn't watching some dumb baby movie, he wasn't a baby, he hated that movie. From far off, a door slammed. As dinner wound down, Gil went to check on the girls, who were huddled together with a huge container of popcorn. The nanny—an older Asian woman—smiled at him from the back row, nodding to indicate everything was fine. Matthew was, thank god, nowhere to be seen. For a minute or so he watched the screen: An ornate house floated through the sky, carried along by balloons. They'd seen this movie in the theater, but as he stepped forward to say something about that to the girls, he felt his drunkenness keenly, the wine on his breath, the pleasant dizziness, so he put a hand on a seat for balance. He probably looked drunk, at least to the nanny, so he turned back into the bright house to rejoin the adults.

By the time they switched to bourbon Gil could barely taste anything, yet he'd held the glass beneath his nose, swirled it, listened to the story of how rare this or that vintage was, how Niles had bought this bottle from a quirky Japanese collector who let a pack of wolves run loose on his estate, and on and on. Gil found himself saying how interesting it all was, and he stayed at the table when Molly went to put the girls to bed, and Sharon excused herself soon after.

It *was* interesting, even if made ridiculous by the nauseating sums of money paid for a few sips. But Niles wasn't a normal person, as his brutally crisp persona let you know the second you met him. He was preternaturally fit and wore elegant jeans, a white shirt, and leather shoes that looked so soft Gil had to resist the urge to reach down and touch them. Niles's face was Hollywoodesque—Christian Bale, or Viggo Mortensen, somewhere in that line—though he would only ever be cast as the malevolent male beauty: the abusive husband, the charming serial killer, the community-devouring banker. At least one of those, and hopefully not more, was a role Niles did in fact inhabit, hence this house, those wines.

As the night went on and drunkenness soaked through him, Gil realized this was the longest conversation the two of them had ever had. Maybe if he kept listening to Niles he'd come to understand his sister, who she'd become over the past fifteen years. Niles told a long story about a feud between Russian mobsters who owned neighboring Greek islands that ended with someone getting run over by a power boat. Niles might've been present at the accident, but this was during the bourbon portion of the night, so it was foggy. All Gil knew for sure was that Niles expected Gil to be impressed, and maybe a little scared. Intimidation leached at the edges of the man's charisma. Subtle, soft, but definitely there. Not quite observable. Only felt. Because, actually, Niles had only ever been polite and kind, if cool and removed, with Gil and his family.

At his wedding to Sharon—most of which Niles had insisted on paying for, to the consternation and relief of Gil's parents—he'd been gracious, had teared up during his toast. And Sharon loved him. Purportedly. No. She did. Hopefully. Maybe Gil was just bigoted toward the rich. He assumed the worst, without evidence. Though the horror show that was Matthew must have its genesis somewhere. The sins of the father, visited tenfold upon the son? Wasn't that in the Bible? Or it could just be his histrionic drunken stupidity. Here he was, in the man's house, drinking hundreds— maybe thousands?—of dollars of his alcohol and he was critiquing him?

Eventually, Gil begged off more drinks and staggered to bed, where Molly was still up reading. "Ho, boy," she said, as he collapsed onto the mattress beside her. "You're going to have a fun day tomorrow, sweetie."

She'd let him sleep in, but when he woke at ten his head felt battered and his mouth was eternally parched and a desperate need to sleep draped over him like a leaden shroud. Any attempts to free himself, such as chugging four and a half cups of coffee, only cinched it tighter about his shoulders.

He thought maybe the waves would knock the hangover out of him, so he walked down to where the girls were digging for sand crabs and asked if they wanted to go in. They squealed yes and ran back up to get their floaties. Frigid water tugged at his ankles and the sand slid out from beneath him, slick and traitorous. As soon as the first big wave slammed into him, he felt like he was going to barf. The grip of the water around his legs as he tried to stand, the thud of the next wave as they tried to move past the break to where they wouldn't get pummeled, it was all too much. Unnatural. When a wave shoved him back he nearly lost his grip on Ingrid, who shrieked "Daddy!" and panic grabbed his throat: He had to get the fuck out of that water.

Though her eyes were wide and frantic, hair plastered over her face, Ingrid begged him to stay in, tried to pull away as he lunged toward the receding shore. Gasping, he screamed for Chloe to come back, get out of the water now, right now, out.

He staggered up and collapsed on his towel, heart heaving, head spinning. He thought he might fall asleep but then began to worry about burning—the back of his neck was hot, as was his bald spot, as was the side of his face turned up to the sky—so he flopped into one of the folding chairs beneath the umbrella. The seat was low, so he tried to let his head fall onto his chest.

"You okay there, champ?" Molly said, poking his arm.

She was unaffected by last night's wine, sunglasses pushed up into her hair so locks of it fell down around her face. The sight of her gorgeous breasts in her black suit sent a wave of lust through him, followed, weirdly, by a swell of despair that made his eyes water.

"Don't go in that ocean," he said, pointing at the waves as if they'd tricked him. A heavy crash nearly drowned his words.

"Daddy!" Ingrid shouted from where she was pouting at the tide line. "When can we go back in?"

"Never," he said. "Just never. Unless your mother wants to."

"Your mother most certainly does *not* want to. That's Daddy's job. Right, girls?"

"That's right, Mom," Chloe said, glaring with arms crossed over her chest. "And Daddy's not doing a very good job."

"That's a bad ocean," Gil said, too tired to lift his arm to point. "Never going back."

"Daddy!" Ingrid shouted, slapping her towel. "Please, Daddy!"

"We'll swim in the pool at the house," he said. When he was a kid he'd spent hours alone in the surf. When he was her age, he was pretty sure. Or more like Chloe's age. Nine? That sounded right. But now he wasn't sure he'd let Chloe go in unattended either. As if the ocean had grown more dangerous in thirty years. Or maybe his parents had just been negligent. Or his generation was a bunch of spazzes.

"Promise," Ingrid said, throwing a fistful of sand at the waves.

"I promise," he said. "When we go back. After lunch."

"We all heard him," Molly said. "A deal has been struck."

They lapsed into quiet, everyone reading or watching the ocean for fifteen minutes, then Chloe and Ingrid asked if they could take a walk and Molly said she'd go with them—they wanted to see how far down it was to the next house, its white turret rising above the dunes. Left alone, he tried to nap, but again failed. This place, this beach, the house, the privacy—there was another family, so far down the sand they were specks—was excessive. And yet there he was. And, god, it was beautiful. What was the alternative? Refuse to come? Not see his sister? Lecture her about the evils of her husband's work in finance, with a digression into the fact that her son needed intensive therapy? Shock therapy. Possibly a lobotomy.

The girls returned from their walk and took the chairs down to the surf, let the waves wash around their legs, squealing when the swells lifted them. Gil expected his sister to come down, but by lunch she hadn't, so they went back up to the house for a break from the sun.

The house was empty. The cook, already in the kitchen, said he'd bring them lunch, so they went out onto the deck and played Uno beneath a table umbrella. Sandwiches arrived with a bowl of chips and another of fresh vegetables and a pitcher of lemonade with chilled glasses. They played until Ingrid lost too many hands in a row and quit, which Molly said was the international sign for siesta.

"Daddy, the pool," Ingrid said, tugging on his arm, still angry about the cards.

"Siesta," he moaned.

"You promised, Daddy," Ingrid whined.

"You sure did," Molly said, standing and stretching. "Have fun at the pool, you two."

Well, he could nap later. Presumably. And the lemonade had burned away the worst jabs of his hangover.

The pool was now half in shade, but it was warm, and they played basketball on the hoop in the shallow end. Ingrid flailed wildly any time she went too deep, immediately giving in to panic so he had to scoop her up and calm her down. He wasn't sure why she had so much trouble learning to swim. Chloe, by the time she was six, had been doing laps. Or maybe she'd been more like eight. He knew bringing it up would sound like criticism, so he withheld the lecture about how she needed to relax, float, don't fight.

They played for an hour, and when he begged for a break she surprisingly relented. He pulled a lounge chair into the shade and told Ingrid to stay away from the pool. She sat at a nearby glass table, coloring in the books they'd brought, his good girl.

And then he must've fallen asleep. He hadn't meant to. A mistake. To fall asleep with his kid beside the pool. Why hadn't he sent her inside? Or gone to nap in the air-conditioning?

The splash might've woken him, though he didn't remember hearing it. He sat up sharply, blinking, his heart pounding. Matthew, in a gray T-shirt and black shorts, stood at the edge of the pool looking down into the water, and for a moment Gil watched the boy, uncertain if he was in a dream.

"Matthew?" Gil said. The boy didn't turn, and then Gil thought to look for Ingrid. She wasn't there. She could be playing somewhere he couldn't see, behind his lounger, or in the cover of those bushes at the edge of the yard, but when he stood he saw the shaking of the water, settling down after some agitation, and then, beneath the surface, Ingrid.

Not swimming. Down at the bottom of the pool. He screamed her name and stepped past Matthew, who flinched away from him as if his uncle was being a brute—Gil caught only a tiny glimpse of the boy's face, his sneer, or, he'd think later, his smirk—and flung himself into the deep end.

Water sloshed and frothed and for a few seconds he thought he might be drowning, but he thought: *Ingrid*. Tipping himself down he dived to the bottom of the pool where she was suspended, eyes open, watching him approach. He got his arms around her chest and pushed off the bottom with both feet and surged to the surface. Flailing and sputtering, he pulled her to the edge, telling her to hold on, grab the edge, Jesus, honey, grab the edge, and though her face was bluish, she put a limp hand on the side and he heaved her from the water, then pulled himself out and rolled her onto her side and put his arms around her stomach and tugged so she vomited onto the soaked gray stones.

"Ingrid, are you okay? Honey, answer me," he yelled, right in her face, turning her around. She blubbered, her brow crumpling, and began to cry.

Molly found them like that, Ingrid sobbing against his chest. When she shouted, "What's wrong? What happened? Is she hurt? Gil, Jesus, what happened?" he could only stare in stupid incomprehension and say she was fine, she was fine, he had her. She was okay. Just scared. But Molly, he would later think, already understood better than he did, probably understood as soon as she'd heard him scream Ingrid's name, certainly did when she saw them beside the pool, understood that with a small twist their lives could've been shattered. Molly dropped to her knees and pulled Ingrid from his arms and carried her away to one of the lounge chairs, away from the water that quivered and shook, as if reaching for them, for the one it had meant to claim.

Ingrid was incoherent, unable to begin to explain. She didn't seem injured, but maybe she'd been submerged long enough to damage her brain. Gil's frantic internet searches while Molly soothed the hiccupping girl on their bed were no help, since he'd no idea how long she'd been underwater.

"I don't, I don't, I don't," Ingrid kept saying, each time Gil pressed her, and eventually Molly threw up her hand to silence him and gave the girl an iPad and put on an episode of *Phineas and Ferb*. Ingrid settled into the pillows, damp hair clumped around her shoulders, eyes puffy from crying, lips a bit blue. Or that could be the reflected glow of the screen. Chloe cuddled next to her sister, close enough that Ingrid put her hand on her sister's leg, as she used to when a baby.

Molly led him across the room and said, "Gil, what happened?"

"I fell asleep," he said, knowing there was no point in hiding it, and, as he'd feared, loathing flashed across his wife's face. She hated him in that moment. And he deserved it.

"I fell asleep and she was playing, but not by the water. I told her to stay away from the water. But I woke up and she was in the pool and I jumped in and I pulled her out and I think she's okay, right? Isn't she okay?"

"How can she be okay? She almost drowned!" Molly cried. Chloe scooted closer and put her arm around Ingrid, who let her head fall onto her sister's shoulder.

"Matthew was there," he said. "By the pool. When I woke up."

"What?" Molly said.

"When I woke up. He was just standing by the pool, I mean, he was looking down at Ingrid. Just standing there."

"So, what are you saying, Gil? Are you saying Matthew, that he had something . . ." She gestured at the door.

"I don't know, Molly. I didn't ask him, and by the time I got Ingrid out of the water he was gone." But Molly was right, and the thought had flickered through his panicked brain as well: Matthew standing by the pool, Ingrid in the pool. He'd done something. Somehow, surely, Matthew was to blame.

Molly squinted at him, then opened the door and asked Chloe to pause the show.

Ingrid said, "No! What are you doing? It's not over."

"Honey, I know, but first can you tell us what happened?" Molly said, sitting down beside the girl on the bed. Gil stood behind, banished by guilt.

"I want a *show*," Ingrid whined, slapping the pillow.

"Just tell us what happened, honey. How did you fall in?"

"I didn't fall," Ingrid said, as if they were being intentionally dumb.

"What do you mean, honey? What happened?"

Ingrid let out a sigh, rolled her eyes, and said, "I was playing and Matthew came outside while Daddy was sleeping and he pushed me in the pool."

She said it as if it was nothing, as if they should've known. Stupids!

What Gil felt was something he'd never have told anyone: a thrill. He'd been right. Matthew was to blame. Not Gil. Well, he'd still fallen asleep. But his daughter hadn't nearly drowned because he was negligent, she'd nearly drowned because of her evil fucking cousin. As the relief spilled into anger he didn't hear Molly's next question—his heart roaring in his ears—but forced himself to listen to Ingrid's answer.

"I was playing and then he asked if he could play and then he threw my rock"—her face flashed with indignation and frustration, but thankfully she kept going—"in the water and then we looked for it and he pushed me in."

She studied their faces and added, "So, can I watch another show?"

"Wait, honey, no. Tell me what happened. Was it a mistake? Do you think maybe you tripped into the pool?" Molly said, her voice wavering.

Gil swallowed back the urge to tell her of course Ingrid wasn't wrong. The boy had pushed her in. Probably knowing she couldn't swim. And even if he hadn't known he'd watched her sink, left her there at the bottom so he could watch her drown.

That vile weasel. That little fucking murderer.

Of course she was sure, Ingrid said. Matthew had grabbed her under her arms and thrown her into the pool.

So not pushed? Molly's voice quavered. With anger. Not pushed, but threw? He *threw* her into the pool?

Chloe had her arm around Ingrid and she'd stayed quiet through all this, but now she said, "Mom, she's telling the truth."

Ingrid's eyes welled and Molly said, "Oh, I know. I believe you, honey. I'm sorry, finish your show, okay?"

Gil followed Molly to the bathroom, where she shut the door and turned to him. "We have to leave. Right now." He was frightened of her in that moment, the anger that tightened the skin of her face, that reddened the rim of her eyes. She looked wild. Feral.

"Okay," he said. "I can pack."

"No. You have to go tell your sister."

She could see his resistance, though he barely paused. His cowardice. "You have to tell her, Gil. Her son threw Ingrid into the pool. She can't swim. That . . ." Molly stopped, pushed both hands to her eyes, and let out a shuddering breath.

"I will," he said. "I'll tell her."

"Good," she said, blinking away tears and reaching around him to open the door. He squeezed against the linen closet to let her pass.

The mirror across the bathroom cast back his ludicrous reflection: thin hair flattened to his head, wet beard sagging, bare chest smeared with coarse dark hair, crotch chilled in his bathing suit, pale, scrawny legs poking down to large, awkward feet. He should change before going to Sharon. To end his relationship with her. Because that's what this meant. He couldn't imagine their connection, strained and brittle as it had become over the past decade, surviving a blow as severe as this. Not if he told the truth. Not unless he lied to his sister and betrayed Molly, and Ingrid. Not unless his cowardice was more important than his family's safety. His hands shook as he pulled off the adhering suit and stepped into boxers and jeans. He misbuttoned his shirt. Did it wrong a second time. Molly watched all this, rage pulsing off her.

Sharon was on the couch reading a magazine, and he stammered out a version of what had happened, what he'd woken to, what Ingrid had said. Sharon's face slowly fixed itself into a mask of disgust.

When he finished, she said, "No, Gil, I'm sorry, but that's ridiculous. That sounds very scary for Ingrid, but she's a kid and kids get confused. I promise you, Matthew did *not* do that."

Sharon called her son into the living room, and Niles must've heard something in her tone, because he came as well, arms folded so his biceps bulged beneath his T-shirt.

"What?" Matthew said, an iPhone held in front of his face.

"Honey, were you out by the pool?" Sharon said, haughty. Right here, Gil's stupid delusions would be put to rest.

"Yeah," Matthew said, not glancing up.

Gil saw his sister flinch, her narrative faltering at the first step.

"What were you doing?" Sharon said. Now she was afraid. Because she knew what this little fucker was capable of. In denial about it, blocking the truth with nannies, private schools, tutors, summer camps, but, fundamentally, she knew.

"I was talking to Ingrid. That girl," he said, flicking a hand at Gil.

"And what happened?" Sharon said.

Niles took a step forward, as if to intervene. Matthew noticed his father's movement and glared at him as he answered.

"I don't know. She was playing some stupid game."

"And what happened?" Sharon said.

"What?" Matthew said, slapping his phone against his thigh.

"Sharon, please," Niles said.

The intervention of his father spurred Matthew and he glared across the room and said, gloating, "Yeah, she was like, she had this, I don't know what, like a rock or something? And she dropped it in the pool and then she tripped, I guess. She must've like tripped, and she fell into the pool."

"She fell?" Sharon said, her voice lifting, as if this was better news than she could've hoped for.

"Yeah, I mean, I guess. Like, she tripped. Or, whatever."

"Or whatever?" Gil said, louder than he meant to.

Matthew turned to his uncle. "Yeah, that's right, Uncle Gil. She tripped. Or *whatever*."

"You didn't push her?" Gil said, stepping toward the boy. Out of the corner of his eye he saw Niles straighten.

"Push her?" Matthew said.

"Gil," Sharon said, holding up her hand. "Please, Gil, just let me—"

"Sharon," Gil said, closing his eyes to try to keep himself calm. It didn't work. "Ingrid told us what happened. She said he pushed her into the pool."

"Well," Niles said, strolling across the room as if this was all no big deal, just a normal afternoon at the Westfallens'. "This sounds like it's just a misunderstanding. Ingrid's fine now, right?"

Gil couldn't look at his brother-in-law, could imagine the condescending smile on the man's face: Gil, a purported adult, getting upset over adolescent hijinks. Ingrid's fine now. Why are we even talking about this?

"Why would Ingrid lie?" Gil said. "What possible reason could she have to say that Matthew pushed her into the pool? Because she was pretty clear about that."

Before Sharon could answer, Matthew let out a bark of a laugh. "Jesus Christ! Give me a break. You think I pushed her into the pool? That's what you think?" He leered at Gil, his face wolfish and sharp.

"I'm—I was just telling you what—" Gil stammered, but the boy cut him off.

"You know what, fine. I pushed her." He folded his arms over his chest and leaned back, as if he'd just won a decisive point. "I did it. She wanted to get her stupid rock or whatever, so I pushed her in."

"Matthew, come on," Niles said. "Cut this crap and tell us what actually happened."

"No, *Dad,* that is what happened. I pushed her," the boy said, rage in his voice.

Sharon put a hand on Matthew's arm, but he whipped away, yelling, "Don't touch me!"

"Matthew, you need to stop," Niles said, his face hardening, authority radiating off him. But the boy ignored it, as if his father meant nothing to him.

"Hey, you wanted the truth. Uncle Gil wants the truth. So here you go: I threw that girl in the pool and she sank to the bottom. The. Fucking. End."

Niles grabbed Matthew's arm and dragged him out of the living room, the boy squealing for him to let go, goddamn fucking asshole.

"Gil, oh my god, that, I don't. Matthew didn't mean that. You have to understand," Sharon said, her hands trembling and fumbling together in front of her. "He's had trouble at school, and this last year was so stressful, and, well, I hope you understand that he didn't mean it. He didn't mean any of that."

"What didn't he mean?" Gil said, trying to keep his voice even, almost managing.

"Any of it," Sharon said, throwing up a hand, as if it was all so ridiculous. "He's just angry. When he loses his temper, well, things like this happen. He doesn't like being accused."

"Sharon, he just confessed," Gil said. "You heard him."

"Please, Gil, you don't really think he pushed Ingrid into the pool, do you? You don't really think he tried to, to, you know, to *kill* her?" Sharon said this as if he was just being silly. Couldn't they be serious for a moment, please?

"So I'm supposed to pretend I didn't hear him, just now, standing right there?"

"No, of course, no, and I'm sure there's an explanation. You know how these things are, you know how children are."

"Sharon, Ingrid's a kid, but she's not a liar. Can you think of any possible reason *Matthew* might lie?"

Sharon flinched, her mouth moving, but no words escaped. When Gil turned away she stammered, tried to explain: Matthew had been having a hard time at school. He was, well, and his therapist, and she was sure it was all a mistake, and she, and he, and they. Gil didn't respond. He couldn't look at her. She said she was so sorry. This was such a mess. They were leaving, weren't they? Oh, god, of course they were. Fine, yes, that was fine, she understood. Did they want her to set up the plane to take them back? He said, no, they were fine, they'd drive.

As he went past her in the hall with the suitcases she grabbed his arm, and in that moment he could feel it all falling away. The anger was missing, though it'd return soon. In the car, as the girls slept, he felt it roar through him, and he and Molly let out their hatred of Matthew, of Sharon, of Niles, makers of that monster. Impossible not to heap blame on the two of them. They hadn't thrown Ingrid into the water, but they'd made it possible. For months afterward he'd felt the aftershocks, the dreams that woke him shouting in the night, and through it all his sister slipped away. He wouldn't see her for years and would never again feel what they'd had, the love and companionship. All that was dead.

And now she was too. And he was left alone with her son, the monster who'd tried to kill their girl, living with them in their house.

7

THE PLAN HAD BEEN TO MEET IN THE ENGLISH DEPARTMENT AT the end of the first day, but Matthew didn't show up and Gil's texts went unanswered. After an hour, while he fumed over paperwork, checking his phone every few minutes, a reply finally came.

Getting myself back. Head on without me.

No explanation. No apology, either.

You sure? It's a long way.

No response.

They'd given the boy too much freedom. After all, here he was, in a university, being treated as if he was a freshman, when in fact he was a high schooler. Of course, the difference between him and these students was minimal. Nonexistent, even. Most came from small New England towns, and so in many ways Matthew was more sophisticated, more capable of handling himself. Still. He was orphaned. He'd only been in Vermont a week. He shouldn't just be cut loose on the first day.

Stalling, Gil replied to a couple of emails, then rearranged books in his bag. All that took about seven minutes. He checked his phone and headed out, letting the office door fall shut with a thud. Walking across campus through a slow-drifting snow, he knew this was a mistake. Leaving him behind. But what choice was there? What could he do if the boy didn't want to be found?

He took the circuitous route home past Church Street: He'd spot Matthew, pretend it was a coincidence, offer him a ride, but that was unlikely. It was too cold for anyone to linger outside.

Molly was with Ingrid at the barn and Chloe had tryouts for the musical, so he arrived to an empty house and was grateful for the reprieve from the inevitable inquisition. He'd left Matthew in Burlington? Who was he with? When would he be back?

Elroy trotted out into the yard, picking daintily over the ice-crusted snow, stopping to sniff a bush. As he watched, Gil's phone rang. That same 212 number. The detective from New York. He pried off his glove and tapped the screen.

"Hello?"

"Hello, yes, is this Gilbert Duggan?"

He recognized the voice. The woman detective.

"Yes, hello."

"Mr. Duggan, this is Detective Simpson. Is this a good time? I've been trying to reach you."

"Yes, of course." Elroy had moved to the tree line and leaned into the path that wound through the forest, nose lifted to catch a scent.

"I'm calling to check up on Matthew Westfallen. You're his guardian?"

"I am. And my wife."

"And he's there with you, in Vermont?"

"He is."

"Okay," the woman said, and there was a pause. She wanted more.

"Is there a reason you're calling?" Gil said, worried that sounded aggressive.

"We wanted to be sure Matthew is with you. As our investigation continues."

"Of course. Yes, he's here. He's staying with us until he goes to college. In the fall."

"And if we want to talk with Matthew, is this the number we should call, or is his New York number better?"

Talk to Matthew? About what? The investigation? What about the investigation? Did they want to question him? Interrogate him? Wasn't he a minor? Wouldn't he need a lawyer? Distracted, it took Gil a second to say, "Yes, this number's good."

"And you don't have any plans to travel. Internationally. In the coming weeks?"

"No, the semester just started here, I'm a professor, and—" He stopped. Travel internationally? They didn't want Matthew leaving the country?

"If you do plan something, can you let me know? You can call at this number or," and she gave him another number, but he didn't write it down.

"Have you found him?" Gil asked, realizing what this might be about. "The driver?"

"I'm sorry, sir, I'm not permitted to disclose information about an ongoing investigation. We'll be sure to let you know if any charges are pressed."

"Oh, okay," Gil said. "It's—well—fine."

"You know how to get in touch with us?" the detective said.

"Of course. Yes, I've got it," he said. Then added, "Thanks."

"Goodbye, Mr. Duggan. And thank you for your time."

He returned from a walk to find the house empty. It was five thirty. He hadn't seen Matthew since class, so around two thirty. The boy could be gone. He could've sent that last text—hours ago, now—from the road, phone held up in front of the steering wheel as he headed north.

Fleeing the country. Canada was just forty-five minutes north, or somewhere more remote. He felt this possibility expanding, the bulge of an alternate reality. This was how he felt when a new short story came to him, arriving, as they did every few years, whole and urgent and waiting to be poured onto the page. He could see Matthew behind the wheel of a car, the windshield flecked with the spray of melted snow. Every minute or so he clicked the wipers so they rushed across and back. Gil could smell the car, the faint hint of someone having smoked in it, that slow metallic tang that builds to a burn in your nostrils. Not the boy's car. Someone else's. The radio was off. Because the boy was focused. Focused on getting north, getting away, to safety.

Impossible. Matthew was a teenager. Where would he get a car? At his age he couldn't even rent one. Gil was replacing the real boy with a construct. Superimposing fiction on the observable world.

Molly returned with Ingrid and Chloe and the anticipated interrogation commenced. He answered Molly calmly, said it was no big deal. Matthew was fine. Nothing to worry about. They had dinner, and he did his best to pretend not to be worried. Twice, before and after eating, he sent the boy a text, but neither was responded to. Maybe this was how he'd been allowed to behave back in New York. Take off without a word. Ignore the adults. Niles had worked endless hours at his investment bank, and Sharon's social calendar had been more crowded than a high government official's. Matthew had probably been on his own most of the time. Gil and Molly would have to set some ground rules. For example: You couldn't just stay out on a Tuesday without explanation. When Molly asked about his classes, he mentioned that Matthew was enrolled in Intro to Fiction.

"Oh, well, that's good," Molly said, cutting up a filet of breaded chicken.

"Good?" He was confused. How could it be good?

"I think it's nice that he wants to be in your class," she explained. Simple. Human.

"Right. That's what Simon said. Anyway, I guess we'll see," Gil said.

Molly frowned at this, baffled by his hesitation. The call from New York, the boy's continued absence, all this let back in the fear Gil had struggled to suppress. He should tell her about the call from the detective, but Chloe was in the living room, texting and probably half-eavesdropping. There was no rush.

He'd just finished washing the dishes when headlights filled the drive. Through the window over the sink he watched a salt-stained Honda Civic pull up behind his Subaru. The interior of the car was dark for a moment, then the door opened, the dome light came on, and Gil could see Susie behind the wheel. Matthew was in the passenger seat, one leg already swung out, laughing. Made sense, they were in the same class. But he felt a sinking in his gut, a twinge he'd never describe to anyone else as jealousy but was just that. He wanted to go out and warn her away from his nephew.

Eventually Matthew slammed the door and turned toward the house, a backpack on his shoulder, several shopping bags in his hands.

Gil pretended not to be watching and only called "Hello" when the front door slammed shut.

"Hey," Matthew said, coming into the kitchen, boots on, carrying a puff of cold air and bits of melting snow onto the stone floor. "Sorry about that. Missing dinner, I mean." He pulled off his scarf and tossed back his head, ran a hand through his hair. He was wearing a parka with a fringe of fur around the hood. Woolrich. Gil had admired that parka in a window in Burlington. Until he'd seen that it cost twelve hundred dollars. But maybe the boy saw that as a bargain, considering what he usually wore.

"No problem. There's leftovers in the fridge, if you're hungry."

"No, I'm good. We got something in town," Matthew said, bending down to unlace his boots. Also new. So he'd been shopping. After all, the boy was a millionaire. Or would be soon. And he had his own account. The lawyer they'd met with, when signing the custody documents, had outlined all the various trusts and accounts, including Matthew's personal checking account, into which a monthly allowance flowed.

"How were classes?" Gil said, as the boy pried his feet free.

"Fine. Except I had this one weirdo professor. Teaches creative writing?" Matthew straightened up, smiling, a boot in each hand.

"Oh, yeah, I've heard that guy's a nut," Gil said.

"Seemed okay," Matthew said, twirling a finger beside his head. "Just a little."

Gil didn't pursue the joke any further, wary of where it might lead.

Molly came downstairs and asked Matthew to sit with her in the living room and tell her about his classes. To Gil's surprise the boy did, apparently willingly.

When Gil brought in two glasses of wine, Molly was saying, "Yeah, I think that'd be fine."

"What's that?" Gil said, handing her a glass and sitting beside her on the couch, Matthew having taken the leather chair.

"Matthew was saying it might be easier if he had a car. He started looking this afternoon. But he needs one of us to sign for him."

"Right," Gil said, wanting to object. Did he have a driver's license? How had he learned to drive in the city? Was it valid up here?

"I'll pay for it, of course," Matthew said. "And I'll keep my New York license."

Totally reasonable. Nothing to get upset about. The desire to say *No, sorry, that isn't a good idea* was wrong. Despite his beautifully tousled hair, his crisp shirt, his probably Japanese denim jeans, despite all that, the boy wasn't trying to show off. This was simply who he was. And he wanted a car. And he had the money. A seventeen-year-old who could pop out on a whim and buy a car. Would it be easier if he had a car? Yes, it would.

Ingrid came into the room, her hair damp from a shower, wear-

ing a T-shirt from Shelburne Farms and pajama pants with snow-
men on them. His baby. And here they sat, chatting away about
buying a car for her attempted murderer.

"Mom, can you help me with math?" She leaned in the doorway as if she might be intruding, or feeling self-conscious in front
of Matthew.

"Sure, honey," Molly said.

Apparently the conversation was over. Matthew would get a
car. Without Gil ever saying okay. Not that there was any reason
to deny him. And yet it felt good to leave the request unaddressed,
to put it aside. A moment of uncertainty for Matthew. The possibility he wouldn't get what he wanted. Petty. But a real pleasure.

Gil's head was woozy with exhaustion as he lay down in bed. He'd
stayed up waiting for the kids to go to sleep, but Matthew was
down in the living room, poking away at his cellphone. Research-
ing dealerships. Or texting friends in New York.

That was something the boy had hardly talked about at all: his
life back in New York. Surely he missed his friends, his school, the
city. But if so, he kept it entirely from Gil. Presumably he kept
nearly everything from Gil.

"Classes were good?" Molly asked, sliding her phone onto the
bedside table and picking up her book as he struggled to keep his
eyes open.

"Syllabus day," he said. "Pinnacle of excitement."

"Good," Molly said. "My class starts next week."

That's right. He'd forgotten. She was teaching a drawing class
at UVM this semester. Now he felt sure she knew he'd forgotten.

Molly had already opened her book, reading glasses perched on
her nose.

As he clicked off his light and rolled away from the glow of her
lamp he realized he hadn't mentioned the call. Tomorrow.

8

THE PURCHASE OF MATTHEW'S CAR—OR, TECHNICALLY, GIL'S
car, since as a minor Matthew couldn't be listed as the primary on
the title—was disconcerting. Gil had called the estate lawyer to be
sure the purchase was permitted. The lawyer said that was accept-
able and the money would be transferred to Gil's account along
with the first installment of the caretaking allowance, and two days
later it was in their account. Fifty-two thousand dollars. An email
from the lawyer confirmed the amounts: forty-two thousand al-
located for the car, ten thousand for the allowance. Any money left
from the car purchase could be used for additional expenses associated with the boy's care, such as initial insurance and registration
fees. Never in all his life had Gil had that much money in his
checking account at one time. Soon, of course, chunks would slide
out, but there'd be extra to send to credit cards. Gil had long assumed he'd die in debt, and yet apparently they'd be set free by
Matthew's leftovers.

Matthew wanted an Audi, so Gil took him to the dealership in
South Burlington and a couple of hours later left with a car that

was more expensive than anything Gil had ever owned, except his house. Gil had tried not to flinch as the boy chose the most expensive of the available cars, as he agreed to this add-on, to that one, to all of them. It was the boy's money, after all. Not just the car money, but all of it. And yet there it sat in Gil's account and he could see how easily he might begin to feel it was his money, no sharing. Maybe this was another terrible truth Matthew brought to light: Gil had never cared about money only because he'd never had any. One month of a flush account and out came his greed and meanness.

Now, with his own car, Matthew spent most days out of the house. Gil had no idea where he went, though of course he asked. The boy was always vague. *Around,* he usually said. Around where? Burlington. Doing what? Nothing much. He spotted him out only twice: once walking near the Church Street mall with several other students, laughing, as if he'd known them for years, and another time through the windows of the gym on campus. Matthew had been on a treadmill, running, his legs pumping so his shorts rose up around the sharply articulated muscles, arms moving quickly, face soaked in sweat, a look of grim determination on his face. Not merely determination, but something darker. His mouth was twisted into a snarl, his fists were clenched, as if he was ready to strike out. He'd set the speed so high the machine trembled, rocking slightly from side to side, as if it might shake apart. That glimpse had felt like a peek into the boy's true self, the one he kept carefully hidden away.

Admittedly, he didn't press the boy about what he'd been doing, tried to see it the way Molly encouraged: The boy's freedom meant Gil's freedom. And his family's freedom. From the boy's dampening presence. From Gil acting like a nutjob when the boy was around. They could carry on with their lives. Could spend afternoons with the girls, guiding them through homework, shuttling them to various extracurriculars. And there were times Matthew seemed a part of the family, as if he'd been there years instead of weeks. One evening Gil had come back with Chloe from debate practice and found the boy chopping onions, blinking back tears with a laugh while Molly directed him from the stove.

"No, that's good, those are fine," Molly said. "Bring the board over here and scrape them in."

Gil watched from the foyer as Matthew lifted the board with one hand, knife in the other, and stepped across to the stove. Onions cascaded into the sizzling oil.

"You can stir them with the spoon there," Molly said.

It should be—would be, to other eyes—a touching domestic tableau. A mother and her son, cooking dinner. Neither of the girls was interested in helping in the kitchen, other than Chloe's occasional half-hearted attempts at cookies.

A few days later Gil arrived home to the lights on but no one around, as far as he could see. But when Elroy finally calmed down and stopped prancing, Gil heard voices through the wall, coming from Molly's studio. First the rumble of Matthew's voice, then his wife's laugh. How long since he'd heard that: her high, fluting laugh? Weeks? Months? Longer? Gil walked quickly back into the mudroom and knocked on the door, then pushed it open an inch.

"Hello? Molly?" Elroy squeezed around his legs and bundled open the door.

Molly's studio had formerly been a garage, and converting it was the only change they'd made after moving into the house. They hadn't really been able to afford the renovation, but Gil had insisted. It'd been important: an expression of his gratitude for all she'd given up when they'd left the city. In New York, she'd never have had a space like this, with its huge windows flooding the room with light, a view of the yard and trees beyond now dazzled by the low sun on the snow. The furniture was simple: pale wooden tables, tall narrow stools, mason jars filled with pens, pencils, brushes, arranged in rows.

Matthew and Molly stood before her slanted studio desk, on which lay a large white piece of paper. Gil could only make out dark lines, a woven cluster that seemed to spread out from the center. Elroy already leaned against Matthew's legs, grinning joyously, fluffy tail flopping side to side.

"Oh, Gil," Molly said, smiling: not at him, but at whatever Matthew had been saying.

"I heard you guys," Gil said. "Are the girls home?" He knew they weren't, but felt he needed an excuse for interrupting.

"They're out," Molly said. "Matthew asked to see some of my work." She looked happy. Happy that someone was interested. Not that Gil wasn't interested, but he also knew she needed space to work privately for long stretches without anyone prying into her process. Or maybe all this time he'd been wrong. Maybe that wasn't what she'd needed. Maybe *this* was what she'd wanted: someone to show interest, to ask to be shown her work.

"I did, and it's beautiful," Matthew said, gesturing at the long table against the windows that was laid out with drawings already fixed in matting. The last Gil had heard, she was nearly done, would soon be sending them to her gallery in New York.

Gil stepped closer to look at the pictures—he'd seen them before, but never all together. For the past couple years Molly had been working with blue and black ballpoint pens, the cheap kind that came in packs. With these she drew intricate, hyperrealistic forest scenes: heavy underbrush, a tumble of broken branches braced against the trunks of trees, the land and layers of leaves rendered with naturalistic precision, but then the density, the forest's complex depths of shadow and patterns of light, also shone with the inks' metallic hue. They were beautiful, with a claustrophobic intensity, as if all light was crushed out and you were lost in a forest.

"Gil, this is crazy, listen to this: Matthew knows Caroline," Molly said, and again it took Gil a second to make the connection. Caroline. Molly's gallerist.

"Well, my mom knew her," the boy said. "But we met a couple times. And I remember my mom saying Caroline has great taste, which"—Matthew gestured at the drawings before Gil—"obviously she does."

"Hopefully she'll like them," Molly said.

"Oh, she will," Matthew said quickly, and Gil felt as if he'd been usurped by the boy, as if Gil should've been the one to say it, to praise his wife. The boy was smiling at Molly, kindly, but also maybe a little flirtatiously. And in the pause that followed, as he failed to think of something to say, Gil realized that they were waiting for him to leave.

"Okay, well," Gil said, "I've got some emails. Sorry for interrupting."

As he let Elroy into the yard he heard Molly laugh again, and again Gil felt another pathetic stab of jealousy.

She brought up the Caroline connection again as they were getting ready for bed. Wasn't it kind of incredible? Of all the galleries in the city. Matthew said Sharon had been collecting art for years. Had Gil known? Didn't it seem like something Sharon would've mentioned?

"We didn't talk much," Gil said, as if this needed pointing out.

"I know," Molly said. She was sitting up with her reading pillow, tracing her finger slowly over the letters in the title of the new Rachel Cusk novel. "I just, I guess I think it's sad. All that time, all those years, there was this connection, you know? Between us and Sharon. And Matthew. And we didn't know."

"Sharon might've known," Gil said. "She might've seen your work on Caroline's website, right?"

"Maybe," Molly said. "But not unless she was really looking for it."

"So, you're probably right. Just a coincidence," Gil said, trying to feel the same tug of sadness his wife obviously did. Sharon, in a gallery whose storage room held Molly's drawings, a connection that was almost there. But even if Sharon had known, would it have mattered? Because if she'd known, she still hadn't reached out, not even in an email, to mention the connection. She'd stayed silent, because of Matthew. Because Gil had accused her boy of trying to kill Ingrid. Because her boy *had* tried to kill Ingrid. And now the boy was here, living in their house, admiring art, chatting up his aunt about New York gallerists.

Though actually Matthew wasn't in any visible way a *boy*. By all evidence, he was an adult. They could leave him at home while they took the girls with them to Harriet and Frank's for dinner. They invited him—Molly, not Gil—but the boy said he actually had a lot of reading, if that was okay. Of course, Gil said, trying not to sound too eager.

Molly had met Harriet when they first moved here, at a group art show in Burlington, and it turned out their kids were the same ages. Chloe had quickly become friends with Harriet's daughter, cementing the connection. All this had conscripted Gil into a tepid, obligatory friendship with Harriet's husband, Frank, a contractor who'd grown up in Vermont and so was, like most of the locals, pathologically in love with everything about the state. Gil had worked to kindle a genuine friendship, but nothing had taken. Frank wasn't offensive, just boring, and unfortunately the dinner parties quickly split conversations along gender lines. Did any man actually prefer the talk of other men? Maybe the women just wanted to be free from the monstrous male egos for a while so they could enjoy their wine. Gil was left to sip his Heady Topper while Frank told him about a neighbor who'd cut down three trees between their houses. Now the branch cover was thin enough to see through, at least in winter.

"I guess I shouldn't complain though, you know, considering what you guys are going through," Frank said, raising his thick eyebrows.

"Right," Gil said, sure he'd missed something.

"So, how's he doing?"

"He?" Gil said.

"Your nephew," Frank said. "He's living with you guys, right?"

"Oh, yeah. He's fine. I mean, he seems fine. It's hard to tell," Gil said.

"And this is the same kid. I mean, the one with the whole pool thing. And Ingrid?"

"It is, yeah," Gil said. They'd told the story of Montauk to all their friends over the years. It was how he explained why none of them had met his sister, why they were estranged.

"Man, that must be tough," Frank said. "I mean, for the kid. Awful. And you guys."

"Right," Gil said. "Terrible."

"And how're the girls?" Frank said, taking a pull from his beer, a dribble of foam running down into his heavy beard, eyes wide with the effort. Gil hemmed and hawed and tried to say basically nothing. It was fine, of course it was fine. The girls were great, they were doing great, Matthew was fine.

"Just awful," Frank said and gave the table a slap, and went to get himself another beer. Driven to drink by Gil's meager conversation.

Probably having picked it up from them, Molly was now telling Harriet about Matthew, how surprisingly easy it had been, but how tragic and sad the accident had been. Harriet's delicate face, framed with wild, curly hair, crumpled in sympathy. You could see how hard Matthew was trying, Molly said. He was almost too polite, but he just seemed to want to fit in. It was sad. She almost wished he would break down, show how he must really feel, but he kept it all stuffed away. *Oh, that poor boy,* Harriet said.

So, Gil was the only one who felt it: the burden. The boy was a weight, a stress. And though everything Molly said was true, Gil had felt that burden growing heavier. He should be adjusting, adapting, making the best of it, like his wife, like his daughters, who were still children. But he couldn't. He floundered, felt himself somehow to be a victim. Victimized by the presence of his orphaned nephew. This was an ugly, possibly evil, attitude. He knew that. He wouldn't say it to anyone, ever.

The Audi-bought freedom meant Matthew started sleeping in, so Gil went to campus on his own. On days he taught he didn't see Matthew until class, where the boy was already seated, chatting away with Susie.

In Intro to Fiction, Gil used "classic" stories—Joyce, Mansfield, Porter, O'Connor—which were usually new to his students who came from Vermont towns, but apparently not to Matthew, who must've encountered some at Herbert. Or they *were* new and he was just able to absorb them with astonishing depth and precision. Beyond the assigned story, he'd often read the entire book in which it appeared. Matthew talked about "Flowering Judas" in terms of Katherine Anne Porter's other early Mexican stories, "Araby" in relation to *Dubliners*. He talked about the different uses of free and indirect discourse in Katherine Mansfield's "Bliss" in comparison to "At the Bay." Matthew's comments were far above the heads of the other students, and Gil had to resist the urge to engage with the boy at this unusual—at least at Essex—level. But that'd leave everyone else out, build animosity—toward the boy, but also toward Gil—so he nodded and said "Good point" and asked for other thoughts.

He wasn't alone in his estimation of the boy's intelligence. Alice, who taught American Literature I, in which Matthew was also enrolled, stopped Gil in the hallway one afternoon on the way to class. They chatted about the semester, about break, and she said how sorry she was to hear about his sister.

"And I've been meaning to tell you, your nephew Matthew's in my class." Gil braced for bad news. The boy had disrespected someone. Instead, she said, "He's really kind of wonderful, isn't he?"

"Oh, that's good to hear," he managed.

"You know what it is? He *reads*," Alice said, putting her free hand—the other curled about an anthology and a stack of print-outs—on his arm. "It's so exciting. To have a student who reads so deeply, who really *thinks* about the books."

"I know what you mean," Gil said. "He's in my fiction class. Maybe I should send the girls to that school he was at in Manhattan." A joke, but it sounded bitter. Was bitter.

"Good luck affording that," Alice said, shaking her head. Then she added, "Do we get to keep him?"

"What?"

"Next fall. We should keep him. What a prize that'd be."

"Right," he said. She looked curiously at him, at his lack of enthusiasm. Luckily, they were on a schedule: Class was about to begin, Matthew awaited him at the far end of the seminar table.

As the stragglers came in, Gil reminded them that next week would be their first workshop. Matthew and Susie would bring copies of their work to class, and they'd begin by reading the stories aloud. Reading the stories aloud was mostly a teaching short-cut, but he justified it by imagining it helped the students regard their stories as works in progress, malleable, far from finished. Anyway, all the students really wanted from class was to be seen. This gave them the chance to perform, to claim ownership of their work, and it saved him hours of class prep. Win-win.

They started off with a discussion of a Denis Johnson story. Most of the class had found it confusing. "I mean, when does that ending even happen, like, in relation to the rest of the story?" one of the women said. What was her name? He scanned the roster but couldn't find a match. Eventually, thank god, Susie stood up for Johnson's approach, and Matthew raised his hand to say that he just wanted to admire the writing, especially the line about entering traffic like running aground. "That's perfect," he said.

Gil gave them the rest of class for a writing exercise and tried to concentrate on his own writing—using his black notebook, the kind he encouraged them to buy and use, though most were typing into their computers now—but couldn't help watching Matthew. The boy typed steadily, pausing now and then to squint into the screen. Each such squint was followed by an explosive burst of writing. Gil had covered only three lines of his notebook. He read them over: total crap. Part of the process, he might tell the class. Write through the shit. Which was, in practice, as much fun as it sounded.

"Don't forget," Gil said, as the class began frantically packing up their bags seven minutes before the half hour, "be ready for workshop."

Susie left with Matthew, shoulders brushing. He walked behind them on the path—not following, but they were headed the same way—and watched as their hands slowly entwined and Matthew pulled her against him. He supposed he should be happy for the boy. Susie was better than Matthew deserved. When they turned off the path—toward the parking garage—Gil watched them for a moment. Susie laughed, tossing her head back theatrically, rising up on her toes to kiss Matthew's cheek. He could only see a bit of the boy's face, but knew he was beaming. That's what bothered him, he decided, turning back to Dahly Hall. The boy's contentment. His happiness. As if everything was fine. As if his parents weren't, at the moment, and for all moments to come, dead and gone. And now the boy was carrying on as if he didn't care, as if nothing had happened. That's what Gil was jealous of, he decided. Not Susie, not having a lovely young woman on your arm, but to somehow, incomprehensibly, be free of grief, to stroll along as if nothing was wrong, as if nothing in the world could ever touch you.

9

NO MATTER HOW CLOSELY GIL WATCHED HIM, MATTHEW NEVER acted like a grieving orphan. He puttered about the house, drove his car too fast down the driveway—given that Elroy was often out roaming the yard—and stared into his phone.

Gil could only assume social media was what kept the boy riveted, along with texting, given the manic fits of typing. Maybe he missed his friends. But when Gil mentioned to Matthew that they could take a trip down to Manhattan if he ever wanted to go—there was no mortgage on Sharon and Niles's apartment and the building fees were paid by a special trust, so they could stay there—the boy had said no, that was okay. He was fine.

Once or twice he'd caught what he thought were glimpses of the truth in the boy's face, a carefully hidden wickedness, a just-suppressed smirk that crept out when he thought no one was watching—at dinner, while Ingrid told a "funny story" that meandered on and lost its way, or while the girls laughed at one of those awful sitcoms they watched with Molly. But no one else seemed to catch these flickers, making Gil wonder if he was making it all up, if he was so desperate to have outward signs, however subtle, confirm his feelings he would twist reality out of shape. A mean, stupid way to think.

Gil had long since stopped being nervous when he taught, but the day of Matthew's workshop felt as if he'd drifted back two decades, as if he was a young man in front of students for the first time, fumbling uncertainly along. Before workshop they were supposed to talk about the assigned reading, a story by Donald Barthelme. He'd braced himself for the students' scorn, despite the fact that it was manifestly a masterpiece. Today he was lucky—they'd enjoyed it.

As usual, it was Susie who swept in early and set the tone.

"By the time he gets to the puppy you can sense where the story is going, and you think you're ready for it, but then he has the Korean orphan thing, and then all those parents and grandparents dying. I mean, that line about grappling with a masked intruder. I couldn't stop laughing after that, so it carried me along right into the philosophical debate they have at the end, and I don't even care at that point that it doesn't make sense in a kind of realistic way." She said this all quickly, leaning forward in her seat, brushing dark hair behind her ears.

"But," said one of the other students, a young man who'd announced on the first day that he didn't like reading, preferred video games, "I mean, like, kids don't talk like that. I mean, 'fundamental datum,' and . . ." Here he paused to search for a phrase. A few others looked down at their anthologies, while most watched the windows, past which slow snow drifted. Eventually, the student found it and said, "Oh yeah, and like, 'the means by which the taken-for-granted mundanity of the everyday must be transcended in the direction of—' I mean, kids don't talk like that. It, like, it pushed me out of the story."

"But it's *supposed* to push you out," Matthew said, speaking for the first time. Gil had assumed his unusual silence—typically he spoke more than any of the others, except Susie—was a result of nerves. But Matthew didn't sound nervous in the slightest. He radiated his usual imperturbably arrogant calm. "I mean, obviously kids don't talk like that, but isn't that the point? I mean, it's funny. That sentence you read, they're about to give an answer, some, you know, real wisdom, but the teacher interrupts before they can and says, 'Yes, maybe.' That's just perfect."

Susie's head bobbed. She clearly adored him. Who wouldn't? Smart, handsome, confident, and attuned to the pleasures of Donald Barthelme.

There was a lull, and Gil tried to determine whether it was one into which he should insert himself or if it was better to wait, let another few comments percolate up. Over a decade of teaching, and this part—enduring the silence that was either the prelude to thought or the echo of indifference—still flustered him. But he waited. Patience. Which was greeted only by more silence, so he tried to make it sound as if he was taking all the points of view evenly, though hopefully also making it clear that in the end he agreed with Susie and Matthew. But no need to worry about favoritism, as most of the students were now mesmerized by the snow outside, and it was time for a break, after which, he reminded them, they'd start workshop.

Coming back in after a few minutes of poking at their phones in the hallway—a habit only slightly less destructive to their health than smoking, as he'd done in college—they reassembled around the seminar table.

Susie's fiction wasn't up to the standard of her other qualities as a student. But Gil had taught long enough to know that the smallest flicker of talent could rear up into something surprising and lasting, and that the most talented writers could flame out, or quit writing despite early success. The writing life was mostly about endurance, about feeling the vocation strongly enough to carry you through those first years of occasional ups and abundant downs until it became your life. Often Gil had wished his life had taken some other turn, one with greater financial reward, for example, or one in which he wasn't judged over and over and usually found wanting. But this was his life now. He'd published two novels and a dozen short stories. Not much in the past eight years, but he'd made a life of it. Susie might get there. Or she might stop writing after college, or after an MFA, and cut some other path for herself. There was no way to know. Which was why he favored gentleness in workshop, why he thought it best to guide toward craft but away from judgment. They would, if they kept writing, get plenty of rejection without his having to feel like a jerk every week.

Susie read in a "poet voice," each word freighted with questionable emotional emphasis, but he knew critiquing their performance would do nothing to help students. Her story was set on her grandparents' farm in the Northeast Kingdom, where she'd grown up with hippie parents who often left her for months at a time. These stories were vivid, full of the bright, sharp-edged summer months, the fall slaughter of the chickens, the frozen stillness of winter in the remote north. But this wasn't one of her better submissions. She was going back to the chickens, but not with the same urgency and fluency she had last year, in a story that had ended up in the campus literary magazine. But this was a good sign: Instead of rushing away after some new, likely half-baked idea, she was returning to the source of her best writing, to try to dig deeper, unearth more.

Gil tried to help them see what was working—the descriptions—and what might need to be improved—what was at stake here for the character, other than the fearful descriptions of headless animals spouting blood as they blundered into tree stumps? Susie furiously scribbled notes, nodding constantly. A few weeks from now he'd get a copy of her revision in his mailbox.

Matthew was mostly quiet through the discussion, pointing out a couple of sentences he liked, and during the critique portion he watched with a thoughtful frown.

Susie got to ask questions—she didn't have any—so Gil said, "Matthew, you're up." He could feel his heart speed up, prickling in the tips of his fingers, a rush of lightness to the head as the boy rose to hand around copies of his story. Gil blinked a few times and, through his anxiety, took a few seconds to make out the title: "Ways in Which She Might Have Died and How She Did."

Matthew read well. No poet voice, at least. But Gil had trouble focusing, kept trying to scan ahead while following along. The story was about a three-year-old girl in New York City, heading to the park with her father. The father tells her to hurry as the Walk signal begins to flash red and they step into the street. It's been raining all morning, and the girl drags on her father's hand, slowing to watch drops speckle a puddle. She wants to "stomp in the dark skin of water, thinly ribboned with oil, a mashed newspaper dissolving into sludge in one corner." Gil wrote *Good* next to this line, though it needed work, he knew, still: not awful. He crossed out "thinly," not sure if that actually improved the sentence. Whenever the students read their work he jotted notes throughout. He told them this was the main lesson of workshop, learning how to edit sentences quickly to find the natural rhythms within their work.

After this came a paragraph about all the things the girl doesn't know about her father: his work at the investment bank; the affair he'd had three years ago when she was a baby; how, on a trip to Bermuda for work, he'd considered driving the rented scooter through the low shrubs and out over the edge of the cliff. The sentences twined further back into the father's life: his years in business school, where he met the girl's mother; back to college, where one night at a frat party he slept with a girl, how afterward she'd accused him of rape, how he remembered it differently, how scared he'd been she would report him; back to high school, where he'd played soccer until he tore his MCL and LCL, the sound of the tendons snapping, the face of the boy who'd tackled him blocking out the sky, the sneer on the kid's mouth before the ref pushed him aside; the time he'd found the neighborhood boys pouring motor oil over a bird they'd trapped in a bucket. He can still remember the bird, opening its beak, the soft pink interior, bright against the slick blackness of the oil on its feathers, no sound coming out as the beak snapped open and shut, gasping for air.

The point of view shifted to a deliveryman on a motorized bicycle, racing back toward a restaurant. His phone says there are three orders waiting. He has twenty-seven minutes to pick them up and get them delivered or his rating will drop, which he can't afford. If he loses even one shift he won't be able to cover his share of the electric bike and then he'll have to use that beat-up old ten-speed, which means he'll get in a deeper hole, and he'll have to borrow money to cover rent and then, fuck, he'll probably have to go back to Stan for another loan, but Stan will say no this time, and he'll start pressuring him about the loan he's already got and hasn't paid back any of yet. This is what the driver's thinking as he rips through a red light and leans forward to make the next, the intersection where the father and daughter are crossing, though, with the water smearing across the cheap laboratory goggles he wears when it rains, the deliveryman doesn't see them.

New York. An accident. A driver running a red light. The piece wasn't about Sharon and Niles, but it was close enough to cloud Gil's head with the stirrings of panic.

But the girl and her father aren't struck down by the driver. He roars past, splashing through the puddle, lifting a "tattered lace of filthy water that sloshes over the father's legs and shoes so he turns to scream, but the man is already gone."

After a space break was a shorter section, a single long paragraph. This one was about a girl, eight years old, at a riding lesson. She's too small for the horse and sits up in the saddle, "red curls escaping out beneath her helmet, hands clutching the reins up beneath her chin, legs jutting like a stiff-legged doll, flapping like stunted wings as she prods the animal forward." Gil wrote *Mixed metaphor here?* but the description wasn't terrible. In fact, it reminded him of Ingrid from a few years back, when she'd just started to ride. Matthew wouldn't have known all those details unless he'd seen it, been at a barn. Maybe Sharon had ridden. Maybe they'd had a horse out in the Hamptons, finally fulfilling that childhood dream.

The paragraph wound through a contorted description—Gil wrote *Awkward* in the margin—of the horse cantering around the ring. As the horse circles around, another rider comes into the ring, tacking toward them at a trot, then the horse shakes its head and speeds up, as if to charge the little girl's horse, Smudge, who shies and rears up with a whinny. The girl throws out her hands, letting go of the reins, and topples back off the horse's rump and falls onto the packed dirt of the ring.

Smudge. That was the name of the horse Ingrid rode. Matthew must've heard her mention it, which meant the little girl was supposed to be Ingrid, though she had red hair, so maybe some kind of blend of Chloe and Ingrid. Which meant the girl in the first story was the same kid—that red hair. Matthew had written a story about the ways Gil's daughters might die. A murder fantasy. And he'd turned it in to class. So they could fucking discuss it.

There were several more sentences, about the jostling of the horses, the noise, the blowing and the shouting and the girl on her back, staring blankly up at the distant white of the dome's ceiling, unmoving. Her teacher sinks to the dirt beside her, touches her shoulder lightly and asks, "Are you okay, honey? Can you get up?" The girl thinks, for a second, that she can't move, can't even move her head to nod, but then the numbness passes. Her fingers wriggle. She twitches a knee, then pushes her hands into the dirt and sits up.

Gil glared across the room at Matthew, that piece of shit. Using the girls in his little death fantasy, that worthless little shithead. This wasn't okay. The boy didn't look up, turned the page and kept reading.

In the final section, a young woman—Gil wrote *Why no name?* in the margin—is skating on a pond. The oval of ice is surrounded by rolling fields and snowy pines. From the description, it sounds like the pond beyond Gil's woods. And, as the scene develops, the girl sounds more and more like a version of Chloe: Her hair is curly and tinged with red. And her hat is Chloe's exactly. "A bright pink hat with a white Adidas symbol, pulled down to her thick eyebrows."

She wears earphones, and so she doesn't hear the long, low groan, like an old man waking up in pain, then a sharper pop, and then a resounding crack. The sun is out, the girl can feel it on her face, the warmth of it, heating up her hat so she thinks about plucking it off, but with nowhere to put it, she leaves it on. Beneath her, as she skates and turns, listening to Imagine Dragons, the ice softens, the cracks widen. Then she glides into the seam of a split, and her weight, compressed into the narrow metal surface of her blade, breaks the ice.

There's a crack so sharp she hears it over the music, then the world seems to pause, as if stilled in anticipation. The weightless glide turns into a lurch, a stagger, and then a fall and as the ice opens and the water, so safely sealed away a moment before, is a yawning blackness reaching up and taking her in, pink hat going askew with her thrashing. Her arms break the ice around her, the jagged black water slaps at her face, and she begins to sink, pulled down by her skates, filling, despite the tightness of the laces, with water. And then, already, so fast, she's gone. There's her pink hat, floating now in the gap in the ice rim, before it too slips beneath the surface and there is only the white and the black and the quiet and the calm.

Matthew looked up as if expecting applause. Anger thickened Gil's tongue. A drowning story. About a girl who was, obviously, Chloe. The pink hat. The way he kept returning to it.

The silence expanded with terrible slowness. He could only blink down at the page that drifted out of focus with each pulse of rage.

"Well, I'll start," Susie said. "I think the writing's really good."

"Yeah," the video-game-loving-Barthelme-hating young man beside her said. "I mean, it's like pretty disturbing and everything, but you definitely made me want to keep reading. I actually even kind of wish it was longer, you know. I know there's a page limit and everything, so it's cool like this."

As the students cycled through their compliments, Gil's anxiety deepened. All he wanted to ask was: *How fucking dare you?* Except, even in his rage, he knew the boy had cover. This wasn't exactly like Ingrid and the pool. And anyway, the class didn't know about that incident, would probably defend Matthew. That fucking weasel who sat nodding as Alice said she loved the horseback-riding part, because he so totally got the details right.

"I don't know if it's okay to move to suggestions now?" Susie said.

She waited, but Gil didn't respond, afraid that if he tried to speak, he'd end up screaming at Matthew across the table. Which was probably what the boy wanted. Why he'd enrolled in this class in the first place: to provoke, to taunt, to make trouble. The only way to deny him was silence. Susie said something about how the three pieces could be more fully woven together: The looseness was interesting, but also maybe too thin?

Smudge. That pink hat. And the father in the first part was him, maybe. He scanned the first page, but couldn't find evidence it was set in Brooklyn. In fact, now could find no proof it was even New York. The story was a series of gaps, holes into which Gil could pour his fears. How could Matthew have known he'd do that?

He managed to look out at the class. They were waiting. Or not. At least half stared vacantly at the snow drifting by the windows. "So, Matthew," he said, pausing to clear his throat. "I have to ask, are you serious with this?" His voice cracked, but at least he'd managed the sentence.

Matthew snorted a laugh and cocked his head, as if he was confused. As if he didn't know exactly what Gil could be referring to.

"Come on, Matthew, Jesus. Smudge? The pink hat? Do you want to say something?"

"About what?" Matthew said. "Do you mean about the details?"

"About using them, Matthew. About using the girls in your story. I don't think that's— I think you're fully aware of how— You can't—" Flushed and dizzy with anger, he looked up at the class, but they were frowning, baffled. He wasn't making sense.

"Using them?" Matthew said, leaning forward and narrowing his eyes. "Is that what I'm doing?" He threw up his hands and sank back, as if he was the victim of some meanness himself. "Well, sorry. I thought I was just following one of the rules. Write what you know. Isn't that like a mantra? *Write what you know.*" His voice shifted, at the end, into a deeper register, as if he was imitating Gil. Who never said that, who didn't believe that cliché, but, no, that wasn't the point.

Gil took a shuddering breath and looked down at the table. "Is this all just a game to you?"

Matthew laughed, loud and sharp. "A game? Yeah, actually, I guess it is. I mean, it's *fiction.*"

"Um, so, like, I have an idea on a different point?" Alice said, with a happy tone, as if she hadn't heard anything they'd just said, as if she was utterly oblivious. "I think the character should have a name. The girl, I mean."

Flustered, Gil could only glare at Alice until her acne-splattered cheeks flared scarlet. But now he'd lost it, the point, Matthew's transgression. If he went back to it now, the students would think he was a nut, if they didn't already. The boy had slipped by. But he hadn't escaped. He didn't need to let this go. Except, well, right now he did, class was over.

"Okay," Gil said. "See you next week."

The students whispered and hurried out of the room. He couldn't help now but notice Matthew: The boy was out of his seat, pulling on his gray wool coat. Susie had a hand on his arm and was laughing. At the boy's triumph.

On his way out of the room, Matthew stopped beside Gil's desk. "Sorry, uh, Professor, can I—" he said, tapping the barely marked manuscript.

"What?" Gil said. "Oh, I—" He wanted to stop him, to keep the pages, as proof, for Molly, but the boy jerked them out from beneath Gil's fingers, tucked the pages between his books, and was gone.

10

THE AUDI WASN'T IN THE DRIVEWAY WHEN GIL GOT HOME. HE'D
texted Molly but got no response. Throughout the drive home it
had been hard not to let what he knew were paranoid fantasies
overwhelm him. There was nothing to worry about. Or, well,
okay, not nothing. But nothing obvious. Nothing major. Probably.
In all likelihood, Matthew wasn't a danger to them. It was possible
the boy didn't know what he'd done. But no, that was stupid. He'd
written about a traffic accident, and, more importantly, a drowning. The boy wasn't stupid. All this time he'd been living in their
house, eating their food, sitting at the table and pretending everything was fine, when in fact nothing was fine because Matthew
was not a normal person, he was a deranged maniac who wanted
to drown them in a pond. Finish what he'd started six years ago.

When Gil got into the house Ingrid was at the kitchen counter,
homework spread around her, iPad tinkling teen pop.

"Where's Mom?" he said, after stopping for a second to listen
to a creak from overhead. Maybe Matthew *was* here, somehow.

"I don't know," Ingrid said.

"She's home though, right?" She had to be. Her car was in the drive.

"Yep," Ingrid said, trying to block him out.

And fine. Of course. She was doing homework. As far as she knew, there was nothing to worry about.

She erased something on her paper and said, "Actually, she took Elroy on a walk. Like, out on the trails."

He went to the bay window that faced the yard, framed by the line of dark trees. He watched the path, as if Molly might appear and wave. What if Matthew had gone with her? What if he somehow got her out onto the pond he'd been so interested in? What if they were out there now and the boy found a way to crack the ice, have her fall through, water riding up into her mouth as she cried out, flailing, hat pushed down over one eye, the other wide and frantic as her boots filled with water and her shoulders slipped beneath the black surface?

Spots flared across his vision and his chest went tight. He took a breath, got no air. Panic. A panic attack. The kind he used to have in Brooklyn, the tightness in his chest spreading over his ribs and into his hips, shooting quickly up his back to settle over his shoulders and tighten its grip around his neck. Those feelings had been banished, he'd thought, when he'd come to Vermont. That was the old Gil, the New York Gil, gone, buried, now crawling up out of his distant grave, a revenant.

"I'm going out," he said, not saying more because he knew his voice would break.

"Okay," Ingrid said, clicking the volume on her iPad up a couple of notches.

"Honey, I'll have my phone if you need me," he said, but Ingrid ignored him. Annoying, nutty Dad.

He jogged around the side of the house, zipping his coat as he slowed to cross the yard in case Ingrid saw him out the window. No reason to scare her. Except it meant she didn't know to be on guard. At the table, framed in the window, she was tiny and vulnerable, bobbing her head to the music, then bending to jot an answer.

Grass poking up through the snow dragged at his boots as he turned toward the woods. He suppressed the urge to call out. At least the path was a loop. There was a chance they'd pass each other going in and coming out.

The dark was already thick under the trees. He should've brought a flashlight. Presumably Molly had one.

As the path climbed the hill the pines mixed with a few oaks and maples. This was where he built forts for the kids years ago. Through the branches, he could see the boards nailed between two trees, only their unnaturally straight lines distinguishing them in the dark.

Beyond there the path split. He stopped to listen for footfalls, or the scampering of Elroy, Molly whistling for the dog, but there was only the soft clicking of trees, the whispery rush of a bird's wings as it lifted from a high branch that wagged like a scolding finger against the pale sky.

"Molly?" he said. "Molly, you there?"

Anxiety had its grip about his throat and he blundered ahead, feet slipping on the pockets of ice bedded among the slick coat of needles.

Nearly running in the dark was how he didn't notice it. A shape moving at the edge of his vision, then pulling upright. He stepped toward it, opening his mouth, but then heard its snuffled breath, saw its body shift, the shoulders roll, the huge shape beneath the narrow head with small, faintly lit eyes.

There'd been a bear here over the summer, come for the blackberries, but bears should all be asleep now. Except here was one, sniffing furiously. Gil stepped back, lifting his arms slowly, jerking up his hood to make himself bigger. He couldn't glance back to see if he was about to step into the thorns. The bear watched him, not moving, then it dropped onto all fours. Gil wanted to shout, to warn it off, but his throat closed, and it was too late. The dark shape moved across the path and ran down the steep hill toward the creek.

Immediately Gil turned and walked back down the path, forcing himself to check behind, but the bear was gone. Before he reached the end of the loop he had to turn on the flashlight on his phone, and when he did there was a text from Molly.

Elroy's with me, picking up Chloe at play practice. Ingrid said you were on a walk.

Holding his phone out to light the path, Gil ran the rest of the way to the yard, forcing himself to breathe, calm down, just calm the fuck down.

In the window, he saw Matthew sitting across from Ingrid: She laughed, pulled her brown hair back behind an ear. Matthew leaned back in his chair so that only two legs were on the floor. Gil watched while he gestured vaguely with his hands, rocking the chair back and forth.

Matthew tipped his chair forward and stood. Gil's breath caught as he watched, waited for the boy to move toward Ingrid, to loom, to strike, but he only turned and walked past her into the kitchen, opened a cabinet for a glass, filled it at the tap, drank it down with his head back as if he was just a thirsty teen, an orphaned kid, and not at all what even now Gil saw in him: a terrible, violent monster, waiting patiently for the moment to strike.

11

BY THE TIME HE GOT INSIDE, INGRID HAD MOVED TO A CHAIR beneath the lamp to read, and Matthew was heading upstairs. The boy glanced through the railing, then jogged up out of sight.

Gil's hands shook as he diced the garlic. He wanted a whiskey worse than he had in months. After checking on Ingrid in the living room, he found a bottle and poured some into a coffee mug, drained it with a wince. Eyes watering, he hid the bottle back up behind the vinegar and rinsed out the cup. That was better. Though not much. Molly and Chloe returned with hellos and kisses and bags slung against walls, and soon everyone settled in for dinner. Ingrid told a story about the new trainer at the barn, how awful he was: Apparently his parents were wranglers out west, where they ran a slaughterhouse.

"How can you take care of horses all week and then spend the weekends chopping up cows? It's so weird," Ingrid said.

"Maybe they're poor," Matthew said, sprinkling cheese over his pasta. "I mean, that might be why they have a slaughterhouse." He said it with a shrug, like he was just guessing.

Ingrid opened her mouth, then realized, surely, even at her age, that the boy was right. They were poor. They didn't want to kill animals. And she shouldn't shame them. Ingrid blushed, blinked down at her plate.

In the awkward lull Gil said, "I went on a walk this evening. Down the path. And guess what I ran into." No one was willing to hazard a guess—it was as though they hadn't heard—so he went on. "A bear."

"What?" Molly said, lowering her glass of wine. "Are you serious?"

"I was up by the blackberry bushes." He could see they didn't believe him. "We looked at each other for a few seconds, then it ran down the hill."

"It's February, Dad," Chloe said. "Aren't bears all hibernating?" She said this as if he'd revealed himself to be a total idiot.

"Yeah, they *should* be," he said, and wanted to add that it'd been warm at the beginning of January, climate change, the unmooring of the seasons. Such a digression might save him from the doubt. But actually, it hadn't been warm in January. That had been last year.

"Are you sure it was a bear?" Molly said. "Could it've been something else?"

"Like what?" he said, heat rising painfully into his face. What possible reason did they have to not believe him? Why didn't they just say: *Really, Dad? That's so crazy!*

"I don't know. A hunter? Or a badger."

"Well, unless this badger was five feet tall, or I ran into the hairiest fucking hunter in all of Vermont, who only communicates through grunts and snorts, then I'm going to have to say no, it couldn't have been either of those."

"Well, honey," Molly said, her face tightening with annoyance. "I'd have to say that a hairy hunter is as likely as a bear with the weather we've been having."

"Right, so we'll leave it up there. Hairy hunter"—he flung up one hand—"or bear." He lifted the other hand. "Guess we'll never know."

He'd shouted this last bit, not realizing he was doing so until it was too late and the words had surged from his mouth. After a few seconds of silence in which Chloe vigorously rolled her eyes, amazed at her father's madness, and Ingrid visibly fought back her too-ready tears, and Molly squinted in disappointment at him across the table, Matthew spoke up.

"We didn't have a lot of bears on the Upper East Side. I doubt I'd be as calm as Uncle Gil. I'd probably still be out there, crying up in a tree."

"Oh, no, don't ever climb a tree," Chloe said. "They can climb. But they're only really around in the spring and summer. And it's mostly just this one. Ingrid calls him Teddy. Or, I mean, she used to. He eats blackberries down the path."

"Okay. So, no going outside come spring," Matthew said, but beneath the surface jokiness there was a taunt in the boy's voice. Pleasure in Gil's disgrace.

Molly changed the subject to the plans for the rest of the week. Did Matthew have more classes?

"One, tomorrow afternoon," he said. "But I have to do some things my high school wants. Reports and stuff. For graduation. I was planning to do it in the morning."

"Must be nice," Chloe said. "To basically be in college early."

"Well," Matthew said, "I have to admit it's way, *way* better than high school."

"Oh, I believe it," Chloe said, blushing down at her plate, as if she might burn in the glare of her cousin's radiant charm.

"Well, two more years, sweetheart. And then you can escape. And your father and I can weep and weep and weep," Molly said.

Normal family life had resumed, despite madman Dad.

After dinner Molly started on the dishes, and he suggested the kids watch something—they settled down on the couch, Matthew in the middle, and he pulled up some YouTube video on his phone he said was hilarious. Wait till they saw this idiot. That wasn't what Gil had meant, but they were way too old to watch what he'd had in mind—cartoons, or whatever—and Gil went to help load the dishwasher.

"I can do it," Molly said. "You made dinner."

"It's okay," he said. Penance.

"So, how were classes?" she said, running water into the sink so a mound of bubbles bloomed over the dishes.

"Matthew's workshop was today," he said, whispering. This was what he needed. To talk to her about it. She'd know what to think. Take some of the burden off him.

"How was it?" She scrubbed plates and forks and set them aside for him to load.

"It was actually—it was pretty— Hold on," he said, and leaned into the doorway. The three had broken away from each other, each on their own device—Chloe and Matthew with phones, Ingrid, who didn't have one yet, on her mother's iPad. All three had headphones on, zoned out.

"It was fucked, Molly. Really fucked."

Molly squinted at him. "What's it about?"

"It's this triptych thing, three stories, and they were all about this girl, and—" He stopped and pulled off his glasses to rub his eyes. It shouldn't be this difficult to describe it. "Trust me. It was fucked up. One of the parts was about a little girl with her dad, they almost get run down. And then there's a girl, she's horseback riding, at a lesson. And her horse is named Smudge. She falls off, almost gets trampled. And the story ends with a drowning. This girl, she's skating on a pond. Like the one in the woods, Jim's pond. She's skating and the ice breaks."

Molly shook her hands into the sink, the droplets fizzing down into the heap of bubbles. "Smudge?" She frowned at him, but she looked confused rather than scared.

"And the girl, the one who drowns, she was wearing a pink Adidas hat. You know, like Chloe's."

"What?" Molly said, turning to face him. Finally there was something like fear in her expression. "Do you have it? Can I read it?"

"He took it back. After class. But he has a copy, obviously you could," and then he noticed Molly looking past him and he turned to find Matthew leaning in the doorway, as if he'd been there for some time. More than a few seconds, anyway.

"Is it okay if I take Elroy out?" the boy said.

"It's cold for a walk. And don't forget about the bear," Molly said, smiling at Gil. Teasing. Fine. As long as it distracted from the fact that they'd been whispering like conspirators about Matthew's story. "But I'm sure Elroy would love that. There are flashlights by the front door."

In silence, they watched him grab his jacket and a leash from the hooks, then whistle for Elroy, who wiggled and pranced with excitement. Gil should pretend they'd been having a normal conversation. But he couldn't think of anything through all the time it took Matthew to push his feet into his boots, lace them up, find his scarf, his hat, the flashlight, open the door—a blast of cold—and he was out.

"So, how did the class go? What did you say?" Molly asked.

"I mean, what could I say? I couldn't lay into him right there."

"Well, you should talk to him," Molly said, turning to the sink and scrubbing at a pot with a sponge. "I don't know, because I haven't seen the story, but couldn't it be a misunderstanding? Like, he used details, which I know you're always talking about in your class, right? And he just picked details from life, so, maybe . . ." She shook her head, scrubbing, trying to rationalize. To justify Matthew. Even now.

"Maybe, Molly, I don't know. It's kind of hard to see how it could just be a misunderstanding," he said. "But I'll talk to him."

Maybe he should ask the boy to come to office hours? Give him the benefit of the doubt, as Molly was obviously willing, or maybe even eager, to do. Because he was their nephew. Because he was living in their house. Because he was brown-nosing her about art, flaunting his connections: He knew Caroline, could put in a word, or the opposite, maybe. Which was probably ridiculous. Anyway, he already knew there was no point in confronting the boy. No matter what Gil said, Matthew would play innocent, cast Gil as the oppressive, censoring professor.

"Good," she said, hunching her shoulders into the scrubbing.

He went up to their bedroom, and as he reached for the switch he saw, out the window, down in the yard, the white bobbing of Matthew's flashlight. Leaving the room dark, Gil went to the window, off to the side in case the boy could see him with the hall light on behind. Elroy loped into the white circle of light, then off into darkness. As if he was going to walk in the woods in the dark, but he stopped and the flashlight clicked off. A second later there was a new, softer light illuminating the boy's face. He was making a call. The blue light died and the boy vanished into the black tree line.

Gil sat at his desk, but couldn't concentrate on the paper proposals he needed to grade. Was Matthew on his new phone, the one he'd gotten in Burlington? He'd tried to take note whenever he saw the boy on his device—which was often—but it was always the same shining black iPhone, with no case, because what did it matter if it broke? The boy stayed out in the yard, talking in the dark. Because he didn't want them to overhear. His friends wouldn't believe these people, how they lived. If you could call huddling in the woods living.

But Matthew knew nothing about them, not really. He regarded them with his cool New York irony, but what did he know about them? His regard of them, or rather his disregard, ran beneath the words of his story, through every line. And when he talked to his friends—or texted them, probably—he must've told them all about his bumpkin cousins, their dinky house with its sad kitchen. The mother, with her little art studio, making drawings that barely sold. The father, his uncle, a failed writer who also happened to be a terrible professor. The girls, well, they were okay, at least the older one wasn't a freak. No wonder, he surely told them in his weary, droll voice, they'd fled the city. Couldn't hack it. No wonder they'd fled and had let themselves be swallowed by the winter dark. They were pathetic. Because, let's face it, they were losers.

But Gil loved this life. Without this place, without Vermont, without the girls, without Molly, he'd have been lost long ago.

12

HE HAD NO MEMORY OF *NOT* WANTING TO WRITE, NO MEMORY OF wanting to be, or to do, anything else. And from the time he was in high school he understood New York meant writers. Publishing, agents, readings, bookstores. After graduation from the University of Virginia, most of his friends moved to Washington, D.C., and the lure of those filthy Adams-Morgan apartments was strong. They could basically carry on as they had in Charlottesville: drinking cheap beer, blasting Archers of Loaf, dancing on chairs until three in the morning. An extended, ironic, possibly pathetic adolescence. But he knew that Washington, D.C., and those friends, and most of all those cheap beers and late nights, were the obstacles between him and the life he wanted, the only life he could imagine he'd happily endure. The life of a writer. Whatever that might be.

The final push came from his favorite professor, a woman who'd written one novel, then nothing. They'd been conferencing after his workshop—not his best, he knew, but he was distracted—and she told him, "If you want to be a writer, go to New York. Then you'll find out if you really do."

The only person he'd known in the city was a woman from the upper-level workshops who'd moved to the city the year before and worked as a literary agent. Or an assistant to a literary agent? An assistant agent? Anyway, she lived near Gramercy Park in an apartment with five other women, all of whom worked in publishing. He called her and said he was moving up and wondered if they could meet for coffee, and if she knew of anyone who needed a roommate. She said of course, and actually she knew someone who had an empty room. It wasn't a great apartment, but it was cheap. She gave him the guy's phone number. Jake. The man who answered the phone sounded drunk and said sure, fine, whatever, he was a friend of Jessica? Any friend of Jessica was good enough for him. Four hundred a month. His own room. Plus, you know, whatever they had to pay for electricity and shit. No, he could pay when he got there. He gave Gil the address and hung up without saying goodbye. So that was it. He was moving to New York.

Feeling foolishly and delightfully like a character in a Paul Simon song, he took the Greyhound from D.C.—bye, drunken past—up the monstrous Turnpike and through the hellscape of the Lincoln Tunnel to the deeper hellscape of the Port Authority. He couldn't remember much of his first few hours in New York beyond his confusion in the subway, despite a childhood of taking the Metro in D.C. But this was apparently an altogether different world, one built on chaos and fear. He got on a train going the wrong way, switched to the other line, made it across the city to a nondescript red brick building. He shouted his name into the intercom while Jake screamed "Who?" half a dozen times before buzzing him in. The building hallways were grouted with dirt, and down one wall were dried brown streaks that might've been blood. The apartment was on the top floor, five flights up. The wooden railing was worn shiny. Noises came from inside the apartments as he climbed—a roaring television commercial, a man shouting "No, you shut up, you fucking cow!"—and then there was the apartment itself: dingy, awkward walls put up to carve a small box into tinier sections with a kitchen between them. The place was Jake's uncle's, a rent-controlled lease he'd had since the eighties. Jake's room faced the street and was full, at that time of the day, with light. Gil's was on the shaft, perpetually dark, with frantic pigeons occasionally clattering past the window. The one light in the room was on the admittedly high ceiling, a low-watt bulb that filled the room with shadows. There was, however, a mattress.

"The last dude left that and I told him there was no fucking way I was hauling that shit down to the street, so you can have it. No bugs," Jake said. He always spoke this way, it turned out. Nothing bore mention unless adorned with a shit or a fuck. Jake was a lawyer. Or was going to be a lawyer. Right now he was a paralegal. But after he went to law school he was going to be a lawyer. At least that was the fucking plan.

"Have at this shit, or whatever," Jake said, flicking a hand at the room, and went back to his room, pleasantries completed.

Gil dropped his backpack on the bed, unslung his shoulder bag, and noted all the things he'd need to buy: sheets, a pillow, a lamp. A table for the lamp? Though, it turned out, he'd go without this last one, putting the lamp on the floor—after all, the bed was on the floor—and piling books around in mounds.

Jessica met him for coffee a few days after he arrived. She was transformed, so much more beautiful and adult than he would ever have imagined back at college when she'd been, at least to his superficial and self-absorbed eye, unremarkable. He asked her to let him know if she heard of any jobs in publishing and she said of course, but nothing ever came of that, and instead it was Jake who helped him get his first job, temping at his firm. The work consisted of making copies of files. That was it. Eight hours a day, walking between the offices and the copier. Standing over the copier until his thighs were hot from the machine's exertions and the smell of ink painted over the inside of his nose. The job lasted only three weeks but he made enough to cover rent, though he could barely afford food to get through the days.

A good percentage of his meals came from a bagel shop on First Avenue where the men behind the counter bantered with the regulars, though they refused to recognize him, no matter how many times he went in. Mostly they noticed the women. One man in particular, Ati—that was the name written on his white hat—seemed to be in love with some of the customers, most of all a young woman named Emmy. She was probably about Gil's age, tall, blond, strikingly beautiful in the way of so many women in New York, but also shy and gentle, blushing when Ati handed her a white paper bag on which he'd drawn a huge heart, calling out, "I love you, Emmy! Emmy, I love you!" Gil could commiserate. He too was in love with Emmy, though he never did more than make eye contact with her once or twice, trying whenever he saw her to not stare as she ate or walked or stood in line, her hip cocked, her tight skirt slit gorgeously up the side of her thigh, the glimpse of her perfect stomach when she reached up to take her tray from Ati. Back in his cave, he masturbated to fantasies of her— she'd rescue him, carry him away to her own apartment, brighter, cleaner, bigger, where she'd support him with her business job, make love to him every day, make him happy in a way he'd never been before and couldn't imagine.

He only ever saw her at the bagel shop, except once on a bench in Stuyvesant Square. He'd assumed she worked in midtown or downtown, but there she was, and not dressed for work on a Tuesday in early October at noon. She wore jeans that showed her ankles, and slim shoes like ballet slippers. She didn't notice him— wouldn't, couldn't, since she had no idea who he was—but he felt he should go over. Sit beside her. Profess his love. Or ask her name, though he already knew it, had whispered it to himself in a way he was sure was creepy but that he intended with the deepest possible adulation. Her hair wasn't tied back in her usual ponytail, fell blond and bright in the sun to her shoulders. Instead of stopping he walked past slowly, hating his cowardice, sure that despite the fact that this woman was far too beautiful to have anything to do with him, he was leaving behind a chance at happiness. But this would be good for him. To suffer. To feel real loss. Even if they'd never met or spoken. Even if now, he felt sure, as he passed her bench and she didn't look up from her book, they never would. And he was almost right. A few months later she stopped showing up at the bagel shop. Maybe she'd moved to another neighborhood. She was lost to him now, swallowed by the city.

He wanted to love New York—everyone else professed to—but wasn't sure he did. The noise was too much, though his otherwise awful room helped with that. Maybe he should leave the city. Go home to D.C., which he found himself doing more often than he could afford. He split his time there between friends' apartments in the city and his parents' house, which felt like home in a way it hadn't since high school. A refuge. A place he was safe. Which was kind of sad, he knew. He was supposed to be an adult. Striking out on his own. When home he went on evening walks with his dad and his parents' dog, a black shepherd mutt named Heaney after his dad's favorite poet.

Over Thanksgiving of Gil's first year in New York his dad had asked to read some of his work and Gil had anxiously given him a new story he'd just finished. The story was of a canoe trip in Alaska that goes terribly wrong, and Gil felt sure it was his best work. As they walked through the suburban streets, past the warmly lighted houses, some of which had wisps of smoke curling from their chimneys, despite the weather that was barely cold enough for a jacket, his father said, "I read your story. It's excellent, Gil, really good."

A surge of pride making his neck tingle, Gil said thanks, he wasn't sure it was done.

"That ending, that's just perfect. And the raft, those Danes. That was all just so well done," his dad said, squinting ahead at a car turning toward them off the main road, shortening Heaney's leash. "It reminded me, that end, of Hawthorne. Or Flannery O'Connor," his dad added, reaching out and putting his hand on Gil's arm and giving it a small squeeze.

In fact, Gil had stolen the ending from Chekhov, but he didn't say anything, knowing that by naming those authors, his father was giving him the highest possible compliment. His father, the son of Irish immigrants who'd worked sixty hours a week to put himself through college and then worked his way through the brutal career of a journalist, was not one to heap false praise on anyone's writing.

"Thanks, Dad," Gil had said. Heaney tugged along at the leash, tongue lolling, delighted, which was just about how Gil felt in the moment. Maybe he could do this writing thing. Maybe his dad was right. After all, his father was a writer. So, in her academic way, was his mother. Maybe it was in Gil's blood. Maybe it's what he was meant to do.

Back in New York he spent his time between temp jobs browsing at bookstores or sitting in coffee shops trying to write. In the evenings, he went to literary readings, and though he'd been told he should wait, give it a few years, live in the "real world" for a while, he applied to MFA programs that winter. He missed university life, saw nothing of value in the world of business, at least beyond, you know, money, and though he'd been counseled, by that same professor who'd advised him to go to New York, to get an MFA in the Midwest or the South, somewhere with a low cost of living, he applied mostly to New York schools, with applications tossed in at Iowa and Brown and Johns Hopkins, because what the hell. A stream of rejections rolled in. He knew it was impossible to get in anywhere and blah blah, but he was different? Right? In the end only one school accepted him, the New School, but at least with a partial fellowship. He told himself it was fine as he submitted his FAFSA for loans he would then take out every semester for the next three years. An investment, sort of. At least he wouldn't need to leave New York, could have it both ways: the experience of the city, the literary culture, and the MFA.

At orientation, with all those other nervous young writers, he'd felt he was back in a world he understood—his mother was a professor of religious studies at George Mason—and in which he belonged. In workshop, sitting around a seminar table like those he'd sat around in Charlottesville, he was sure he'd made the right decision.

Of course, like the rest of his peers except the trust fund babies, he had to work, but now it was in decent jobs. He sent the story his father had liked out to literary magazines and after a dozen rejections he received a call from a number he didn't recognize and answered to find the editor of *The Antioch Review* on the line. They would like to accept the piece for their winter issue. When the issue came out his parents bought a dozen copies, which they had stacked on their coffee table when Gil came down for Christmas.

In his second semester, he was given a stipend to help with the reading series, and through that he got a part-time job at Coliseum Books after being introduced to the store managers by his workshop professor at an event.

Then Sharon moved to the city to start a master's program in philosophy at Columbia, and that helped: It was nice to have family nearby, even if they saw each other only occasionally, busy with schoolwork and different social circles. Then, a year into her program, she'd started dating Niles. He seemed to Gil an obvious mistake, at least for Sharon. Niles was a native New Yorker from a wealthy Brooklyn family. They met at a symposium at Columbia on ethics and artificial intelligence: Sharon had published a paper that year on something about artificial consciousness, drawing on Thomas Nagel's bat simile. Gil had read it but hadn't understood much. Niles was there presenting on AI innovations made by investment banks.

Over drinks with Gil the next week, Sharon had gushed about him: Niles had an MBA from Wharton and a master's in computer science from MIT, where he'd been lured out of the PhD program to Wall Street. Banks were where, she'd insisted, so much of the cutting-edge work was happening now. Gil doubted this, guessed that the real work was being done at places like, well, MIT, but one didn't make millions in academia. Maybe he just resented Niles for pulling Sharon away from him, just when he'd felt they might be reconnecting. She was his only sibling, they should be close, and for a brief window there'd been a possibility they might remake their relationship. But as soon as Niles had sunk in his wealthy claws, he quickly dragged Sharon away from Gil, away from academia, toward, even Gil had to admit, the life she'd always wanted.

Despite this frustration, for a little while Gil felt he'd achieved a decent life: thirty or so hours a week shelving books and helping customers, evenings in class, followed by nights at bars downtown arguing about that recent essay in *Harper's* and whether minimalism was a thing, if it was over, and what came next.

Later he'd see that the anxiety that had been building in him, even during this good year, was beyond the normal range. He thought it was weakness, indecisiveness. That same weakness that squirmed in his writing. All writers thought this way at some point. He'd read the self-doubt in Virginia Woolf's diary, the fear of failure and irrelevance in Cheever's journals, the elation chased away by despair in the letters of F. Scott Fitzgerald. Normal. But still, it was debilitating. Or nearly. He wrote for hours every day. He filled a manila envelope with rejection letters, taped the occasionally encouraging ones to the wall until he'd drained them of meaning and they began to seem cruel, or pathetic. When he'd rip them down the wall glittered with bits of tape, like taunts.

When Sharon told him she was engaged to Niles and, not long after, that she was dropping out of her master's program, it had seemed like another sign that New York wasn't for him, wasn't a place for a writer or an artist, or actually for anyone without a trust fund or a rich spouse. He'd tried to be happy for Sharon, tried not to feel resentful at the lavish wedding at a loft and rooftop in

Tribeca. Among her new friends Gil had never met, Sharon seemed happy, and after the wedding she retreated into her new world of the wealthy wives of financiers.

He might've floundered, washed out, given up writing altogether, if not for Molly. He met her at a reading downtown. He remembered seeing her for the first time, the keen, focused expression on her face as she read from a book while the crowd hobnobbed around her, hair loose, clothes all black, a leather jacket with a complex system of zippers, black jeans, bulky military-style boots. The reading was a combo art opening and literary event, with poems and short prose pieces that might've been related to the art on the walls. The gallery was set back from the street, through heavy plastic flaps, past a room cluttered with broken shipping pallets and wooden boxes with stenciled Chinese characters, to an open space with a poured concrete floor that might once have been, you felt, a slaughterhouse.

He didn't talk to her until the after party, shouting over the blasting music. She was too cool, too pretty, but she edged closer and closer, then kissed him when he got back from the bathroom. They went to her apartment in Brooklyn and fucked, eagerly, first on the kitchen floor, again in her bed. Not a romantic courtship you could tell your kids about. Fucking on the first date. *Don't do that, honey.* But at the time it'd been wonderful. Confidence poured off her and he was happy to shelter behind her directness and calm. She called him the next afternoon after he got home. He'd been in bed, staring at his faintly fluttering overhead light. Jake came to his room with the cordless and said "Phone call," with a baffled tone that made Gil realize this was one of the first calls, other than from his parents, he'd gotten since moving in.

"What are you doing right now?" Molly said.

"Sitting on my bed."

"Naked?"

"Not quite," he said.

"Well, why don't you come over here? And we can be naked over here. Together."

"That's a long subway ride," he said.

"How about this? Shut the hell up and get over here."

After that, even his job at the bookstore became a burden, as it took him away from her, all the way across New York. Four months after they met she suggested he move in. "You're here all the time. And we could split the rent. And I bet Jake would survive the disappointment."

The following spring, as he was graduating from his MFA program and she was in the process of stalling the end of hers so as to be able to take out another semester of student loans, they moved into a one-bedroom a few streets over. That was when he felt he became a writer. Those early years with Molly. Fortified by her, he could do it. When he expressed his hesitation about asking a friend to refer him to his agent, Molly said, "Don't be an idiot, Gil. That's how it works."

That agent, after getting a few of his short stories placed in magazines, sold his novel to a small publisher in San Francisco. This, in turn, made it possible to get a few adjunct sections around the city. It wasn't much money, but it gave a brief flicker of relief to the endless pressure, which they tried to relieve by moving to Fort Greene, an eventually desirable block featured in films and Volkswagen commercials on which, back then, crack vials crunched underfoot.

Molly loved the neighborhood, loved the city, loved their life, so he'd tried to hide his unhappiness. But he knew his true feelings leaked out despite his best pretense. The city was too expensive. Their neighborhood was too dangerous—muggings in the park half a block from their apartment were so frequent he rarely went in—and his adjunct pay was pitiful and they would, at this rate, fall deeper and deeper into debt. They were mortgaging their future, and for what? To jostle his way into a vomit-splattered Q train at rush hour and ride swaying out over the bridge? To live in their roach-infested apartment with the dryer that had a faint gas leak? And they were among the lucky ones. That location! A dryer! Amazing, apparently.

But he couldn't admit he hated the city, not after 9/11. He'd been at home, at the desk they called an office, when the first plane hit. Their internet was dial-up, which he tried not to log on to when he was writing, and he'd left his phone in the other room so had missed Molly's calls. There were sirens, but they were near the hospital, so that was normal. Then he heard people shouting in nearby apartments, and out the windows he saw people on the roofs of the brownstones across the street, pointing toward Manhattan. They held hands to their mouths, pointed, squatted, sobbed.

He tried calling Molly, but the network was down. He went into the pantry and pulled down the ladder. With a ripping sound the hatch lost its grip and he climbed onto the warm, tar-spotted roof. He couldn't see the towers, or much of Manhattan, with the bulk of the high school and the hill of the park in the way, but he could see the helicopters, the black smoke, and he was up there when the first tower fell, heard the roar of it, saw the pale yellow cloud rise up over the tops of the buildings, surging toward Brooklyn.

Molly walked home from Manhattan, where she'd been adjuncting. By the time she arrived he'd seen the first of those returning from downtown, painted white with dust. He'd watched a man knock on the door of a brownstone across the street, watched the door open, a woman with a stricken face reach out, but the man brushed her away and limped inside. The woman stepped out onto the stoop and looked up and down the street, as if expecting more, or someone else.

Though he knew it wasn't about him, he felt as if he'd missed the event, was left out of the trauma that bound the city together. But he hadn't. He'd been there on the roof as the first building fell.

So where was his grief? Of course he'd cried, sick at the thought of the people in those buildings, sick with a petty fear for himself, but the deeper panic and love of the city that he saw all around him was missing. Because he didn't love New York. He was a traitor. Or a coward. Molly slept terribly, drank too much wine, didn't ride the subway unless she had to, afraid it might happen again. Not only to her, but to her city. Her home. His home too, though in some important way he knew now it wasn't, would never be.

Not until his father died a year later did he let his hatred of the city take hold.

Gil was only thirty-one, too young to lose his father, who was only fifty-seven. But his parents took a trip to Prague, and his father got sick. A terrible, virulent flu that had first manifested on the flight home. The phone calls went from "Your father isn't doing well" to "His doctor's worried" to "We had to admit him to the hospital" with shocking speed. When his father had the strength to talk on the phone he sounded nothing like himself. None of the old humor or wit. His voice was raspy, a dwindled whisper, as if hiding a shameful secret.

Gil got to the hospital just in time. His father's blood pressure was crashing, only a cocktail of drugs—lethal if administered for more than a week—keeping him alive, and then only nominally so. As soon as he walked into the room and saw his father's face, sallow and white and spotted here and there with blue, thin tubes in his nose, a thicker one down his throat, needles in his hands and arms, Gil knew he was dying. His father's fingers seemed to have gotten longer, each one sharp and cold and dry. The only warmth was at the very center of his palm. Gil pressed the tips of his own fingers there, trying to feel the feeble beat of his father's heart.

Sharon arrived a few hours later, tears pouring down into the tracks of all those that had preceded them, and Gil collapsed into sobbing, as if none of it had been real until he'd seen it there on his sister's face. She climbed onto the bed beside their father and wrapped herself around him, curled her face to his neck, spoke to him. But their father didn't respond, except that his breath, a death rattle, the noisy gurgle of his drowning lungs, quickened. Gil stepped to the bed, took his father's hand and lifted it to his lips, kissed the cold fingers.

His father never regained consciousness, never knew his children hadn't left him to die alone. Except he hadn't been alone. Gil's mother, the person who'd taken care of him for his entire adult life, had been there all along. At the end, before they turned off the machines—his blood pressure had sunk to 40/62, numbers that Gil didn't understand but evoked sluggish drowning—his mother asked for time to say goodbye. Gil stood in the hallway, watching her through the gap in the curtains as she crumpled over his father, head on his chest. He heard her begging him not to leave. But she came out into the hallway wiping her eyes and said, "I'm ready."

Molly had taken the train to D.C. that night. As soon as she arrived she took Gil's hand and led him to the guest room and lay with him on the futon until he let himself go again. They stayed with his mother for two weeks, but eventually she said they should go home. They were in her way. In the way of her grief.

Six months later, Sharon convinced their mother to move to New York. Both her kids were there, she'd loved the city, and Sharon would buy her an apartment. Their mother could sell the house in Alexandria and put that money in savings or investments. Niles already had an agent scouting one-bedrooms in doorman elevator buildings on the Upper East Side. She'd been teaching for over thirty years. Wasn't that enough? Why not enjoy herself? Be near her grandchild, Matthew, who'd just turned one?

Gil had been astonished at his sister's generosity, though in his more jealous moments he told himself it wasn't much of a sacrifice, considering how monstrously rich they were. Molly told him that was ridiculous, that it was incredibly kind, that he should be happy to have his mother closer. And he was. But tangled up with the kindness was the fact that this act was a justification of Sharon's new life: Yes, she'd given up any hope of a career, had dropped out of her master's program soon after meeting Niles, but wasn't it, in the long run, the right choice? You couldn't do *this* on an academic salary, and beneath that was the implicit suggestion: An academic life, the life their parents had lived, the life Gil was muddling through, the life Sharon had seemed headed for, that life could never adequately provide for your family, and Sharon was smart enough to see that this compromise had been the right choice. She could care for their mother in ways Gil never could.

The following summer Gil and Molly went to Vermont for the first time, renting a cottage on Lake Champlain with money Molly had made from selling three paintings. Standing on the porch above the water, Gil had started to cry with relief, though he hadn't told Molly, or anyone else, how he felt. Driving back to the city at the end of the week he was surly and snappish. Meanness took hold of him. When his mother moved up to the city he could barely bring himself to attend the dinner party Sharon threw in celebration. After a lifetime of work, after losing her husband, his mother got to live in a city she loved, in comfort. Which was great. But meanwhile Gil was scraping by, the money from his book was gone, and the piddling amounts he made adjuncting at universities where at first he'd been so delighted to be offered a class only deepened his anger.

All he could talk about was leaving. This might've killed his relationship with Molly, who was worried and wary during his rants, but then she got pregnant. They hadn't meant to. They couldn't afford it. Their apartment was too small, and how could they possibly afford childcare? But now it was there, and it was the only thing Gil wanted. Sharon was delighted, gave them all her old baby stuff, including a stroller that was worth a month's rent. Molly tried to protest: What if they wanted another kid? Oh, no, Sharon had said. One had been the plan all along. They'd just spoil their one rotten. Gil had wanted to sell the stroller, but Molly told him not to be a dipshit.

Matthew was largely sequestered behind a squad of nannies, already a danger to himself and others. When they'd brought baby Chloe over the first time, toddler Matthew had stood over her blanket on the floor where she lay sucking her fist and said, "Babies can't do anything, right? If you hurt them?" Gil had wanted to snatch Chloe up. Sharon had knelt beside him and said, "You wouldn't want to hurt a baby, would you, Matty?" He hadn't answered, studied the helplessness of the child before him, clearly imagining hurting her. Sharon had kept a hand on his back, Gil had noticed, ready to pull him away. When Matthew turned three Sharon got a puppy, a gorgeous Bernese Mountain Dog, but a few weeks later the dog was gone. "Matthew was jealous," Sharon said. "I should've thought of it." Gil asked if the dog had snapped? Growled? But his sister was so unforthcoming that he suspected it was worse: The boy had tortured the dog. Slammed its tail in a door—the boy loved to slam doors—or some other violence. Molly agreed the boy had probably done something, but it wasn't their problem. They rarely saw Matthew, far less than he'd have thought, considering they lived in the same city with kids only a couple of years apart.

For a while Gil had thought Chloe would save the city for him. She learned to walk in Fort Greene Park, clambered over the equipment in the camel playground, went in her stroller to the farmers market most Saturdays. They took her up to visit her grandmother on the Upper East Side, where his mother, delighted to have at least one grandchild who didn't bite and punch, lavished her with attention.

That same year Gil got a one-year visiting assistant professor position in the city. Molly taught classes at Pratt, only adjunct, but it was better than nothing. That was a lesson of parenting: Everything was better than nothing, because now you could see what nothing meant, how much further there was to fall than previously imagined. Ignorance happily lost, fear happily gained. They went back to the same cabin in Vermont that summer, and seeing Chloe there, playing on the grass, shrieking atop her floaty penguin in the lake, made him dream again of leaving the city, though it didn't feel as urgent as before Chloe had arrived.

But when Chloe was two, his mother got sick. Had already been sick, though no one had known. Cancer. Which spread before it was caught, despite the fact that Sharon had been sending her to the "best doctors." But money couldn't stop this and his mother shrank, went bald, faded gray.

Though he knew it wasn't true, he felt as if his mother had stopped talking months before her death. What had she told him? What had she said during those afternoons he'd sat beside her bed? Change the channel. Please turn that TV off. Call the nurse, she needed more pain meds. Please, hurry, call her! Where was she? Where was the fucking nurse, oh god, oh shit, please.

There must've been more, some wisdom. After all, his mother was wise. But if so, he'd missed it. The TV had been too loud. He'd been asleep. Simply not paying attention. And then she was dead. The dark hole he'd fallen into after his father's death now revealed itself to be not a hole, but an abyss.

It was at that point that he knew for certain they had to leave the city. Each ride on the subway blackened his soul. He'd never believed in the idea of a soul. Watching both his parents die, being there in the room with them, there'd been no evidence of anything departing. Just beeping machines, labored breathing, slower breathing, beeping, then only the beeping, then silent machines. But when a young man in a business suit pushed him aside to exit the train at Canal Street, Gil felt a surge of hate, as if that fuckhead had ripped off a piece of him and carried it away.

The night it happened, what Molly and his therapist called his "suicide attempt," had been unremarkable. Nothing particularly bad had happened. He hadn't meant to do it. That's what he told them. That's what he told himself. His therapist tried to convince him that wasn't the case, tried to convince him he'd been planning it. When Molly and Chloe went to bed, he'd stayed up watching that alien invasion movie with Tom Cruise for maybe the twentieth time. He drank a couple of beers. Six beers. Nine. Shaking with drunkenness he took a couple of sleeping pills, planned to sleep on the couch, not wanting to get into bed, where they co-slept with Chloe, worried he might drunkenly smother her. But he hadn't fallen asleep. So, two more pills. Did he forget he'd taken the first two when he took two more? After that, he doesn't remember anything. Certainly not taking the rest of the bottle. How many had been in there? He didn't know. Not full. Half full? What would that be? Fifteen pills? Apparently not enough to kill you, but enough so that when your wife wakes up at three in the morning to check on why the TV is so loud she finds you there, froth in your mouth. Ambulance, stomach pumping, IV, Molly at the foot of his hospital bed with Chloe in her arms, fear and betrayal in her face, a look he never wanted to see, one he couldn't bear, one he promised he'd never bring on her again. Hence the therapy, which he hated. Why wouldn't he just say what he wanted?

Fine. To get out. Out of the city. Okay, yes, he understood the city hadn't tried to kill him. He'd tried to kill himself. But the city wasn't helping. He couldn't live there. He knew that now. Now he could admit it. They had to leave.

Molly still loved the city, always had, even as it'd eaten away at him. She'd never wanted to live anywhere else. She hated driving, had a large network of friends—from grad school, from the art scene, from the playground—and her work was here, her gallery, which she'd finally broken into earlier that year. How could she maintain her life, as it was, outside the city? Sure, people did, but could she? She wasn't sure.

But she loved him and was, he knew, even in the depths of his desperation, loyal. She wouldn't leave him like this, when he needed her. And so she agreed they could try it, they could leave the city.

But how they could afford to get out he had no idea until Sharon called him and told him their mother's will had, after some delay, been fully executed. His mother had left each of them half her money: their father's insurance money, her own retirement fund, and the proceeds from the sale of the house in Alexandria. With the inheritance, Gil and Molly could buy a house in Vermont and spend a couple of years putting together new lives. Molly, he was sure, didn't want to leave the city. But they did, together. For him. She'd done it for him. Given up her life. A year after they moved to their new house, Molly was pregnant again. They'd be happy. He was sure of it. They'd found their proper place. Where they belonged. A place where that old misery and uncertainty couldn't touch him.

13

WITH MATTHEW'S WORKSHOP BEHIND THEM AND THE SEMESTER grinding up through the gears, he might've been able to put aside his fears. The boy had taunted Gil with that first story, but that was all it had been. A taunt. He'd promised Molly he'd talk to Matthew, but the moment never seemed to arise, at least not at all naturally, and each time he decided he should force it, anxiety overcame him. The boy would act baffled, would pretend he had no idea he'd done anything wrong. That was the boy's nature, after all. He was a natural liar. He'd plead innocence, claim he'd misunderstood, claim the story had come out of that exercise Gil had assigned in class: Collect fifty details from paying attention to the world around you and then use at least thirty of them in a piece of fiction. Had Matthew done it wrong?

And what would be gained through confrontation? The boy wouldn't change his nature. Probably he couldn't change if he wanted to. Maybe Gil should ignore it, as one would any bully. Soon the boy would be gone and they'd be free. Seven months.

Well, no. Seven and a half. That's what he'd done. Taken the cowardly route. No surprise there.

Molly, on the other hand, had no such hang-ups: They took Matthew and the girls snowshoeing over the weekend, and while the three of them raced ahead out of view into the woods, she explained to Gil that she'd asked Matthew about workshop.

"And he knows it didn't go well," she said, with a tone that suggested this should settle the issue. Remorseful, mistaken Matthew.

"Wow, perceptive," Gil said.

"I asked him about using the details, like Smudge, and he said it was just a mistake. He'd meant to change the name before submitting, but turned in the wrong version."

Gil scoffed, but they were mounting a small hill and he focused on his foot placement, then stopped at the top to take a few breaths. Through the trees he could hear the high laughter of the girls.

"You believe him?" he said.

"Shouldn't I?" She lifted her sunglasses up into her hair. She looked so lovely, flushed cheeks in the cold, in her black down coat and snow pants, her hair curly with the moisture of snow and sweat.

"Because, Molly," he said, but the rest of the answer, the why, was inarticulable. Because of what the boy had done in Montauk. Because of the person Gil was sure he still was. Because of those small moments, carefully hidden for the most part, when Matthew's true self peeked out.

"Because you say so?" she teased. "Well, I think we should give him the benefit of the doubt." Lowering her sunglasses, she adjusted her grip on the poles and pushed off down the trail. Gil had to hurry to catch up, unable to say what he wanted, which was that this was exactly what he could not do: Give the boy the benefit of the doubt. And yet she was right, of course she was right: There was no reason to assume the worst of Matthew. To do so was, for now, irrational.

But then the detective called him that afternoon in the middle of his literature course. Already, only a few weeks into the semester, and the students were dragging. This was partly his fault. Failure to sufficiently entertain. This was, he knew, just part of teaching, which was often less about expertise than performance. Ideally, he supposed, it was both: the performance of expertise. And, like any performer, he had off days. Earlier in his career he'd been better at managing these lulls: He'd push harder and carry the students—well, some of them, anyway—across on the tide of his enthusiasm. But with time and repetition, that ability had faded. The lessons and readings had become rote and stale. So often now the work that excited them read to him as naïve and simplistic, while the work he preferred had been deemed by the students to be dense and boring and—a bad thing now—weird. He finished his lecture and the students were unwilling to help fill the gaps, so he started to wing it. He should be able to do this. After all, he got paid for exactly this.

Unable to remember how his tangent about an essay by Walter Benjamin the students hadn't read related to the Nadine Gordimer novel they'd (theoretically) read, he ended class early. The students scampered out of the room. Rats from a ship.

The call had come in during class, while his phone was silenced in his bag.

"Hello, Mr. Duggan, this is Detective Simpson from the NYPD. Can you please give me a call back when you have a moment?"

He'd heard something in the detective's voice: a tick of excitement. A break in the case, surely.

He half-jogged across campus toward his office, jacket flapping open, the loose buckle on his shoulder bag clinking maddeningly, faster when he sped up, slower when he skirted around a patch of ice in the freshly shoveled walkway.

In Dahly Hall he kept his eyes down, studying his phone. *Busy, busy, can't talk, sorry.* He got the office door open, wrestled himself out of his coat, which seemed to be adhering wetly to his sweater, sat down, pulled a piece of paper from the printer, and grabbed a pen from the Essex University Research Center mug.

He mistyped his security code three times, took a breath, and told himself to calm down. It wouldn't do to call a detective with a shaky voice. Gil hadn't done anything.

"Hello, this is Detective Simpson."

"Oh, hi," Gil said.

"Mr. Duggan," the woman said, not pausing, as if she'd seen his name when he called, as if he'd entered his name into her contacts. Not an idea he liked. But maybe it was just caller ID. She was police, after all.

"Yes, hi, sorry. I'm calling you back."

"Yes, thank you. I wanted to let you know that an arrest has been made in the death of your sister and brother-in-law, Sharon and Niles Westfallen."

"Oh," he said, his heart pounding so he was momentarily blinded by bursts of white across his vision.

"We have a suspect in custody and we will be pressing charges tomorrow. I was thinking of waiting until the formal arraignment to call, but I thought you'd want to know as soon as possible."

"Well, thanks," he said, then his mind clicked back into place. "What are the charges? I mean, what will you charge him with?"

"It *is* a man," Detective Simpson said, "and I'm not sure what the final charge will be. Leaving the scene of an accident, certainly, and likely manslaughter. This is a pretty clear-cut case of hit and run. I can't say much more now. I wanted you to hear from us before it shows up in the papers."

"Well, thank you," Gil said.

"No problem. And as we discussed, please let us know if you have any plans to travel with the son of the deceased, Matthew Westfallen. As the next of kin and a minor it's important that we keep track of his whereabouts, especially if this goes to court."

"Do you think it will?" Gil said. "Go to court."

"I really couldn't say," the detective said. "That's up to the DA.

I'm sure you'll hear more soon. As I said, we're early in the process."

"Yes, I understand," Gil said. "Thank you. Thanks for calling."

"You can reach me here if you have any questions," she said, and after he said that sounded great—as if they'd set up a meeting—only then did he think of it.

"Wait, I'm sorry, but who is it? The driver. The person you arrested."

As if she'd been waiting for this most obvious of questions she answered immediately. "His name is Thomas Gashi. He's an Albanian national, here on an expired tourist visa."

"Thomas," Gil said. Albanian. The driver was from Albania. Gil could feel it: gears catching, facts, data, falling into place. Albania. Matthew had been to Europe last summer. Eastern Europe, so maybe Albania, though Gil had thought it was Croatia? He'd been traveling for a service project Herbert had been involved with for several decades. Sharon had written about it in her last holiday letter. Not a coincidence. No way. Not an accident. Maybe.

"A lot will depend on what his lawyer wants to do, and how the DA wants to handle it. I imagine they'll be in touch with you soon."

"Okay, thank you," Gil said.

As soon as the call ended he felt a surge of panic. What the hell was he doing not asking more questions? But what were the questions he should've asked? What questions would've led to the truth, the one he knew now must be: Matthew was somehow involved. He set the phone on his desk, stared at the light reflected off the now dark glass. In his other hand he clutched a pen he'd held throughout the call. His office was lit only by the desk lamp and it was nearly dark out. Snow had started again.

14

HE DROVE HOME QUICKLY OVER THE NEWLY FALLEN CRUST OF
sleet. How easy it would be for Matthew, unused to these condi-
tions, to lose control, overcorrect, turn against the skid. How
easily his car might strike the side of the bridge, break through
the metal barrier, land upside down amid the rocks of the frozen
stream, curls of blood sliding beneath the skin of ice. And then
the money with which the boy was buying luxury automobiles
would come to Gil. Every concern they'd ever had would be
wiped away. The girls could attend any college they wanted.
Ingrid could have a horse. Several horses. They could build a
barn on their land. They could buy a pied-à-terre in the city for
Molly.

As he approached the bridge he leaned forward, as if it might
already be there, the wreck, wheels still spinning. Of course there
was nothing: the intact guardrail, the river rimmed with white
ice that thinned into the clear running water that made his neck
cold.

The driveway was empty. Molly was with Ingrid at the barn, and Chloe was at debate practice. Elroy hopped off the couch and wiggled across the house as Gil tugged off his boots. While the house was empty, he needed to search the boy's room. Elroy, grinning and wiggling, if less eagerly now that he'd gotten only a few quick pats, followed him upstairs.

The door to Matthew's room was closed, and Gil knocked. No response, so he turned the knob and peeked in. Empty. There wasn't much indication anyone lived there at all, other than three books on the nightstand. One was a Nabokov novel, *King, Queen, Knave;* the other two had their spines turned to the wall. A pair of shoes was tucked under the bed, which was pushed up close against a set of bookshelves, obscuring the bottom two rows. Atop the bed was the old, tattered comforter, which Matthew must scorn: Poor fuckers were so broke they couldn't afford a proper duvet. Beside the bed was the desk where Gil used to write.

On the desk were stacks of papers. One was next week's workshop stories, already marked up with notes—*Good line; Not sure I can see this clearly; maybe continue this dialogue a few beats longer*—and Matthew had written long endnotes to the authors.

Beside the stories were papers from his American literature class, printouts of essays from the JSTOR database about Edgar Allan Poe's "The Fall of the House of Usher." Gil was fairly sure Alice didn't require them to use scholarly sources in that class, but Matthew was of course going above and beyond. The diligent little psychopathic parricide.

On the corner of the desk was a third pile: a syllabus for a history course the boy wasn't taking, and beneath it three stapled pages. He read the first paragraph hurriedly.

I'm fairly certain that with a little effort I could've fucked my father's secretary. She's an adult, I'm a child, at least nominally, if in no other way that any reasonable person could claim—

I look and act more adult than most Americans ever manage— and yet legally I'm still bound to that ridiculous space of purported innocence.

Gil scanned the rest quickly, trying to find a connection to the accident, but he couldn't focus. He took out his phone, thinking he could photograph the pages and read them that way, but out the window that faced the road he saw headlights turn in to the drive. Molly and the girls. He took a photo, but it came out a blurry mess. The car had come to a stop in the driveway. The only thing to do was to take the pages. But Matthew would notice their absence. And yet if Gil put them back he might lose his chance.

Holding the pages lightly in one hand he looked quickly at the bed, at the dent in the pillow. Beneath the Nabokov were the two books: a Norton edition of Poe's selected writings, and Gil's first novel. There'd probably been a copy here in the guest room when Matthew had arrived. Gil wanted to see if there was any indication the boy had actually read it. Gil could hardly remember having written that book. He'd been closer—much closer, sickeningly so—to the boy's age than to his own.

The front door slammed and Molly called hello. He closed the door to the guest room and went into his own bedroom and slid the pages into his bedside table drawer. Matthew might guess what had happened to them, but he'd have no proof.

While Gil put the broiled chicken beside the bowl of green beans shining with olive oil, Chloe told them all about her upcoming debate tournament, down at Putney Academy. He'd forgotten about that. That'd put him on barn duty with Ingrid, which Molly usually handled, as he could barely stand the horse world: mothers in their riding boots, miming claps when their daughters bounced past; just girls and their mothers, except for him, and maybe a stray brother playing on an iPad. The world of the dilettante rich. He never said a word about these feelings to Ingrid, or Molly, who didn't share his antagonism. Ingrid was passionate about horses, and that was enough for Molly. Probably it should've been enough for him, but the whole thing stank of excess, stank of the world his sister had lived in, if in a minor key.

"Lots of subjects," Chloe answered to a question Matthew had asked. "Should the federal income tax be abolished? Can the use of nuclear weapons be justified? Should transgendered people get to use the bathrooms of their choice? Stuff like that."

Whenever she started talking about debate, Chloe slipped into a news anchor tone. Gil found it nerdily cute, but worried now that it would be an affectation Matthew couldn't help but mock. He'd not really been able to look at Matthew since the boy had gotten home, just before dinner. Now he noticed what he might've earlier: The boy's expression wasn't its usual placid, amenable smile. There was a tightness around the boy's eyes, an edge in his look like anger.

"So, which side are you on?" Matthew said, poking at his salad.

"On which issue?" Chloe straightened her back, more fully inhabiting her debating persona.

"I don't know. How about income tax?" There was a light mocking tone in his voice.

"Well, actually, the point is you're not really on a *side*. You have to be able to argue any position, but to do it in a way that you get more points than the other teams."

"Right. I know how debate works. So, you don't actually be-lieve any of the stuff you're arguing," Matthew said, putting his elbows up on the table, the fork dangling from one hand. Now Molly must've finally heard the edge of aggression, because she looked warily at the boy.

"No, I definitely have my opinions. Like, the transgendered thing. I think they should get to choose their identity and their bathrooms. But I could argue the other side if I had to," Chloe said, apparently oblivious to the boy's aggression.

"I have to say, I'm not sure that's a great idea," Matthew said, setting his fork down, as if now this had gotten serious and needed his full attention.

"What isn't?" Molly said, glancing protectively at Chloe, whose cheeks were already blotting as she blinked wildly at her plate.

"To argue for an idea you don't believe in. I mean, I know it's the Sophist tradition or whatever, but there were a lot of people back in ancient Greece who hated the Sophists. People said they were a corrupting influence, that they shouldn't be allowed to teach. And I kind of see that point. Doesn't it seem like a bad idea to teach people that how you say something is more important than saying what you believe?" Matthew said this all in an earnest tone, as if it was a real problem.

"But isn't that true?" Gil said. "Look at the president. Or anyone in politics. The way to get power is to master rhetoric. Once you're in power, then you can change things. But good intentions don't change anything on their own. Rhetoric, persuasion. That's how you change things, in a democracy anyway."

"Really?" Matthew said, squinting at him. "It seems to me the way you change things is with money. And teaching kids that persuasion is an effective tool, that they can actually change the world with words, well, that's basically a lie."

"Give me a break," Gil said, his voice rising. Molly flashed him a warning look—*Don't engage*—but he couldn't let this go. "Sure, money is a form of power. But you can't just say it's the only way to make change. Not unless you just cherry-pick history."

Matthew was grinning now, delighted. Chloe looked like she might cry. *This little bastard.* At Gil's own fucking table, eating Gil and Molly's food.

"So, what's an example, Uncle Gil? In history?"

"Okay," Gil said, his mind flailing and then, thank god, landing on one. "Hamilton."

"Oh my god," Matthew said with a laugh. "The world turned upside down, right?" His scorn was palpable, though he'd surely heard the girls listening to that album.

"Or," Molly said, leaning forward, "how about some people enjoy debate and some people don't? Why does it have to be some moral endgame?"

Gil nodded as she spoke, knowing she wanted him to stop, to drop it, but that would mean the last word was the boy's mockery and cruelty.

"What I'm saying," Gil said, "is that he was poor, not rich, and he managed, I mean, we all know the story, so I'm saying—" Except he didn't actually have an argument. Just as the boy's scornful smile suggested, he was reverting to pop culture for evidence, the way any ignorant kid might.

"Well, maybe the real lesson of Hamilton is: Marry rich. Am I right? Because he was rich, eventually. And if he hadn't been, I don't see how he could've possibly made any difference," Matthew said.

"What about Lincoln?" Gil said. "And Obama?" His voice was shaking. He should've followed Molly's lead, turned the conversation back toward his daughter, her feelings. The boy didn't want to have a real conversation. He wanted to taunt them.

Matthew nodded, but in a way that clearly radiated his disgust. This man was a professor? This ignorant, naïve man-child? "Well, history aside, it seems to me a bunch of college kids are pretty convinced being on the right side is more important than how well you can argue a point." He smiled, to show it was a joke—those silly idealists! But it was also a criticism of Gil. From a seventeen-year-old kid. Gil was out of touch. He didn't understand his own students. Which might explain why he was such a shitty professor. Oh, but Matthew wasn't done yet. "I mean, if anyone is to blame here, it's not the students. What choice do we have? Right, Chloe? If they tell us to do debate, we do debate. If it helps us get into college, we do it. It's the people who are telling us to do this stuff, but not telling us what the right way to think might be, how we should be, they're the ones at fault. I mean, isn't that what we really want to know? Isn't that the whole point? How are you going to live your life? Aristotle and all that ethics stuff?"

Chloe smiled weakly, surely wounded by this snark: Matthew had suggested that instead of evidencing intelligence, wit, charisma, dexterity, all the qualities she prided herself on, that in fact debating was a form of mindless obedience in pursuit of paltry rewards that a young man like him could simply pluck without any effort. Aristotle? What kid his age knew jack shit about Aristotelian ethics?

"Well, the young are sometimes overly idealistic," Gil said, forcing his voice to stay level, calm. The reasonable adult. Or at least the performance of reasonableness. "And debate gives them real life skills. And teaches reasoning, logic," he said, fumbling and trailing off, apparently his words so banal there was no way to follow them up, as a curdled silence settled over the table. Molly opened her mouth, but the damage was already done. Best to try to defuse the situation.

"And," Chloe said, her face flushed, her tone sharpening around a point, "debate's really about learning the tools that can help you make *actual* change in the world. If you're a privileged white man, I can see why you'd get upset about other people gaining access to the tools of a culture you've dominated for, you know, forever. That's a direct threat to your hegemony, so of course some people will try to deride and belittle it. But too bad. We're not going away, and you'll just have to deal with it."

"Ouch," Matthew said, but his look had softened a little, a smile of grudging respect. "The hegemon surrenders." But then he narrowed his eyes at Gil, a fresh target.

"What about you, Uncle Gil? Don't you think education is about teaching people how to be good? That's kind of the impression I get, you know, from class."

The problem was that the answer was yes. That is what he

thought, basically. But if he said that he'd be taking the boy's side against his daughter and somehow, also, against himself: After all, here was one of his students at the table, not being good.

"I think," he said, winging it, "that education should help people make up their own mind about how to be, by giving them the tools to make smart, rational decisions. And that's exactly what debate does." Here he looked at Chloe, but she was watching Matthew, a challenging, but also flirty, look on her face.

Now that he'd said it he supposed he believed it, in contradiction with other beliefs. But wasn't that supposed to be an example of a refined mind or whatever, two ideas held in opposition? That's not how it felt. At that moment, it felt like confusion. Stupidity, actually, as Matthew's smug smirk suggested.

"The tools of the patriarchy, though, right?" Matthew said this to Chloe, who gave a little laugh.

"So we can burn the patriarch's house down," Chloe said.

"Uh-oh, Uncle Gil," Matthew said, still smiling at Chloe. "Better watch out."

"Oh, don't worry," Chloe said, leaning toward Matthew, distinctly flirting now, "this is a matriarchy here. I would've thought you'd noticed."

"Okay," Molly said, "well, the matriarch says it's time for a new topic. Matthew, you should be hearing from colleges soon, right?"

Gil nodded along as the boy mumbled about deadlines sometime in March. Molly always knew how to manage things: The boy was a jerk, so she looked ahead to the time they'd all be free of him.

15

MOLLY WAS DOWNSTAIRS ON THE PHONE WITH HER MOTHER, AND
Gil was in the bedroom, about to start on the stolen pages, when
he saw, out the window, Matthew's dark shape moving across the
yard. The shape stopped, his face illuminated by his phone, then
he was gone. This was it. A chance. An opening. Gil could just stay
up here, pretend he hadn't seen, or he could act. For Sharon. For
his family.

Putting the stapled pages under his pillow, Gil hurried downstairs. Molly was there, in the kitchen, but she was listening to her
mother, adding an occasional "Okay" and "Uh-huh." He hadn't
gotten a chance to tell her about the detective yet. Chloe had
needed help with her math homework, which Molly had done
while starting on the dishes. Chloe was there, glowering into her
hated textbook, twisting a strand of hair tight around her index
finger. He jammed his feet into his unlaced boots, grabbed a jacket,
and slowly opened the door. The cold was urgent and his hands
were numb by the time he got his jacket zipped, moving around
the side of the house, away from the motion sensor lights in the

driveway. At the corner of the house he stopped, listened, and caught snippets of Matthew's voice. Keeping away from the squares of yellow falling from the windows, he moved toward the trees and stopped as the branches brushed his jacket.

"I told you. No, I told you. What the fuck are you talking about?"

The boy was nearly shouting and Gil took the chance to move closer, wincing at the squeaks of his boots in the snow.

"That's my fault? I'm supposed to be in charge of that moron? What does that have to do with me? Did I tell him to do that? Did I? It's a simple fucking question, so why don't you just answer it? Did I go down there and tell him to shoot his stupid fucking mouth off? Did I? Right. That's right. So don't threaten me."

In the bay window across the yard Molly came into view, talking into her headphones, and the boy turned to watch. She laughed, then leaned toward the window, as if she'd spotted something. Matthew. Or—god, shit, no—maybe Gil.

"Look, I'm done with this, you hear me? I did what we agreed. My end is over. The rest of this shit, it's your problem." After a pause he added, "Man, fuck him, okay? That dumb bitch can rot for all I care." Another pause and then he said, softer, "Dude, fuck this, I have to go," and in the phone's sudden light Gil could see Matthew clearly for a second: his deep scowl, eyes tightened, scanning the dark. He turned the phone toward Gil, the blue glow catching the shapes between them—fallen branches sticking up through the snow, the sagging pine branches. If he turned on the flashlight he'd see his uncle, creeping about in the dark. Spying on him. But Matthew slipped the phone into his pocket and crunched out across the yard.

After the boy went around the side of the house, Gil started back, keeping close to the trees. Molly was in the window. Watching her husband skulking around the yard like a lunatic. Matthew had been talking to someone connected to Thomas. About how

Thomas had gotten arrested. It was all right there, he could see its shape, but he couldn't reach it. Patience. That's what he needed; though, as he skirted the tree line, he wasn't sure how long he could wait.

Teeth brushed, face washed, he took the pages from the bedside table and got into bed. He read quickly, half his mind perked for the sound of feet on the stairs.

I'm fairly certain that with a little effort I could've fucked my father's secretary. She's an adult, I'm a child, at least nominally, if in no other way that any reasonable person could claim— I look and act more adult than most Americans ever manage— and yet legally I'm still bound to that ridiculous space of purported innocence. But if I'm right, and you'll have to trust that I am, this very fact of my youth and its attendant indiscretion makes Rebecca hot. Or I could say horny, except that it is in itself a stupid word, and one I won't use in reference to so gorgeous a person as Rebecca, who was sitting when I entered the anteroom to my father's office that afternoon behind a little glass desk that allowed everyone to see her shapely legs, her small sharp heels, her flat stomach gliding up to C-cup breasts, the tops of which were always, at least in my admittedly small sample of experience, exposed by a V-cut at the neck of her dress. Today the dress was blue.

She's beautiful, as are most of the women who work for my father. Presumably because he chose them for that quality. Who wouldn't want to surround themselves with beauty, if they could? And not only could he, but he was arrogant enough to make decisions like that nakedly, as if there was nothing wrong with choosing female employees based on their looks alone. Though, actually, not alone. Most had attended colleges like Yale and Harvard, and were working for my father because the firm at which he was a partner was a path to greater wealth, and if they had to use their beauty to accomplish those ends, so be it. Who am I, the son of this monstrously rich man, with every possible privilege, to judge those women who would have to work harder than me, and do things I'd never consider, to get ahead? Except they probably won't. Get ahead. Of me, I mean. There was in fact almost nothing they, or even I, could do to change that.

I was there because Rebecca kept meticulous track of my father's whereabouts, his many appointments, his liaisons, his whatever-the-fuck-he-did-all-day. Despite growing up in that world, surrounded by fathers who spent all day making piles of money swell into larger piles, I had no sense of his "job." For most of human civilization his "work" had been regarded as a sin. Usury. In an earlier age, it would've cost him his soul. His social standing. He'd have been killed in a pogrom, or burned at the stake, or cast out of the court, or whatever. No longer. Now he and his buddies were the court. That was at least part of his job. Holding court. With investors, with eager young men from Stanford and MIT with start-ups they hoped my father's firm would devour and digest and so defecate out those techies as millionaires.

All my father's presiding required a lot of riding around in cars. One office to another. Downtown to midtown. He took helicopters, though only in extreme instances. He'd volubly scorned those showboats who flew out to the Hamptons on July weekends, landing their water planes in the ocean before taxiing up to their docks and jumping out as the family skittered down from their mansion to greet them. We, as a mark of our class, slogged it out in the traffic on the LIE with the sweaty schlubs, though we did so from the back of our armored Chevy Tahoe with Andrei or Vlad or some such Russian special-forces turned bodyguard/driver behind the wheel.

I feel I'm getting off the point too often. Too easily. Almost as if I'm avoiding the ending, or just the story itself, since as of the writing of this story it has not yet in fact ended, is still unfolding, as it were, like these crisp, well-ordered letters slipping across the screen with just the lightest pressure of my fingers on the softly clicking keys. So, I'll try to stay on course. Though I do, as they say, beg your indulgence, dear reader.

Gil had just finished when Molly started up the stairs. She stopped at Ingrid's room to say good night, giving him time to slip the pages back into the drawer.

Molly only glanced at him as she entered, but he knew she saw something amiss. His face was probably red. Certainly his heart was skittering. If he had a heart attack, no one would know the truth. Matthew would keep living in his house with his wife and girls. Until he killed them. Or maybe they weren't worth the effort. Who were they anyway, the Duggans? Redneck cousins. Soon he'd be free, a multimillionaire devil, able to wreak havoc wherever he wanted.

"You okay?" Molly said as she closed their bedroom door and opened her dresser drawer for pajamas. The curtains weren't pulled fully shut, so if Matthew was out in the yard, making another call, he'd see his aunt as she pulled her shirt over her head and unclipped her bra, running her fingers beneath the curve of her breasts before pulling on a T-shirt from a 10K she'd done in New York over a decade ago. Holes dotted the seams of the shirt, but Molly had said she'd wear it until it disintegrated. The same was true of her scrub bottoms, which a doctor friend had given her, and though she could've bought replacements on Amazon, she still had them, twenty years later. How did Matthew see her? As the beautiful woman she was, or as a fading middle-aged woman who'd drifted beyond youth's orbit?

"Fine," Gil said. "Lots to do."

"I'm going to sleep. Exhausted," Molly said.

"Right," Gil said. "So, I got another call today. From the detective. In New York."

Molly, who'd been bent over her dresser, straightened up. "About what?"

"They made an arrest. The driver. Of the truck."

"Oh my god," Molly said. "Really? When?"

"She didn't say. I mean, all I really know is that they have someone."

"Did she say who it was?"

Gil stepped around the bed so he could speak more softly. "The guy's name is Thomas Gashi. He's from Albania, here on a tourist visa."

"Thomas?" she said, twisting the hem of her T-shirt in one hand, clearly struggling to process this news.

"From Albania," he said. Still, she squinted at him, confused. "Remember? Matthew went there, right? Wasn't it Albania? I told you when we got Sharon's letter. Last summer. That school trip?"

Molly let go of her shirt, brushed at the crumpled cotton, frowning, but he could tell she still wasn't making the connection. Possibly because there wasn't one. Or not as much of one as Gil had hoped. But there could be. Of that he was sure. It couldn't just be dismissed.

She sat on the edge of the bed. "So, wait, Gil, you're saying, what? That Matthew knew this guy?"

"Maybe?" Gil said. Hearing it through Molly's skepticism made him feel sick. Because now it did sound unlikely. A leap. Possibly a crazy one. "Otherwise, it's a pretty big coincidence? And the accident. Remember? The police told us the truck didn't slow down. And the driver ran. Maybe that's because he planned it. Because someone paid him to do it."

"And that person is Matthew?" Molly sat with a stiff back. Tense. Afraid. Or angry at him. For acting like a psycho, perhaps. But all he could do was forge ahead.

"I'm saying, it's possible. Isn't it?"

"I guess, but, Jesus, Gil. If you think that, why aren't you on the phone with the police right now?"

"I wanted to talk to you," he said. "I don't *know* that's what happened, Molly. But it's possible, isn't it?"

"I don't know, Gil, is it? He's a kid. How could Matthew hire someone, if that's what you're saying? And the money, how could—"

"He could do it, Molly," he said. "You know he could. He's got endless cash. I mean, that fucking car out there? And you know what he's like. I'll admit he's been on mostly good behavior, but that could be cover, right? If he did this, if he was involved, wouldn't he be going out of his way to appear innocent? Maybe that's why he seems nothing like the person we remember, because it's all an act."

"So," she said, standing up and crossing her arms over her chest, "are you going to call the detective?"

"Do you think we should?" He knew he sounded pathetic. Like a whining child.

"Gil, if you actually think Matthew had something to do with the accident, then yes, we should. But that's a big accusation without any real proof. Isn't it?"

"I know. You're right. I need proof. That's why I didn't call yet."

"Jesus Christ. What a nightmare, Gil," she said, covering her face with both hands, then running them through her hair.

"And that's not all, Molly. I heard him on the phone. This evening. He was talking to someone."

"You heard him? Where? When?"

"Yeah, he was angry, he was talking about someone and it sounded like it was about Thomas."

"Oh my god, are you serious, Gil? If he's on the phone, talking to someone in our house about Thomas, about a man who's just been arrested, if —"

"No, honey, I don't know for sure it was about Thomas. I just heard him talking, and he was angry, and, well, I'm saying it could be connected." As he said this he saw something move over his wife's face, flicker through the fear that twisted her mouth into a grimace. Doubt.

"Could be connected? What exactly did he say? On the phone. Did he say Thomas's name?"

"No, but, shit, Molly, I can't remember exactly what he said. That the guy could rot. He said that. So, maybe he meant in jail?"

The skepticism in Molly's face spread and she shook her head.

"I know it doesn't all add up, but, Molly, come on." He forced himself to keep his voice low. The boy could've heard them. Even just from Gil's tone, that weasel would know. "How can all these little pieces not fit together? How can it all just be a coincidence? And, I mean, we *know* him, Molly. We know what kind of person he is. He could've killed Sharon. He could've done it, you know it's true." He stopped to breathe—his head had gotten light and loose—and noticed her look: worried. That he was losing it. Had come unhinged, as she'd so long feared he would again.

"Why don't we just watch him?" she said softly. "And if he does something, then we get in touch with the detective. At this point, it could all be a coincidence, right? The Albanian thing, I mean, Europe is big." She gave him a placid smile. To calm him down. The raving lunatic in her bedroom.

"Fine. Okay. If that's what you think," he said, sounding petulant, he knew. But he couldn't help it. He felt fucking petulant.

"If the cops thought there was a link they'd have said so on the phone," Molly said. "They have the guy in custody, after all. Surely he'd tell them Matthew was involved, if that's true. So we should just wait. And, you know what, you should call the lawyer. From the estate, ask him if there's someone Matthew was talking to in New York, like a therapist. We don't need to do this all on our own, Gil. So let's try to keep calm and see what happens."

"Right, I know, you're right, Molly," he said, but knew it was unconvincing. Even he could hear the small edge of panic in his tone, the frantic energy scrambling to get out, like a trapped animal.

"Gil," she said, as if about to scold him, but then she closed her eyes, overcome, it seemed, with exhaustion. He should go to her, hug her, but before he could move she turned and went into the bathroom. He heard the faucet go on, the clink of her toothbrush as she lifted it from the metal cup.

Now he looked like a fool. Like a lunatic, desperate to frame the boy. Now Matthew would use this, Gil's fumble, to further insulate himself. There had to be a way in, a way past the boy's defenses. Matthew was a child, surely he'd made mistakes. Gil just had to stay calm and find them.

16

THE NEXT MORNING AN OPENING APPEARED. MOLLY HAD DRIVEN the girls to school before going to teach her Intro to Drawing course. Buttering a piece of toast, Matthew said, "Hey, actually, I was wondering if it might be okay if I go down to New York this weekend."

"New York?" Gil said. The phone call last night in the yard. The anger in the boy's voice, though now he was utterly calm.

"It's my friend Eric's birthday and he called last night to see if I could make it. It'd only be like one or two nights."

"How would you get there?" Gil said, anxiety rippling through him: the call in the yard. It might've been Eric, and no more than teenage bluster.

"Drive?" the boy said, squinting as if not able to believe Gil's hesitation was real.

"Can you do that, on your permit?"

"It's a New York license," Matthew said, his tone sharpening.

"I'm not sure you're allowed to drive on the interstate with a permit," Gil said.

A flash of anger moved across Matthew's face and it was clear he was checking himself from lashing out and telling this wizened piece of country trash to fuck the hell off. The boy focused on spreading his butter and adding honey.

"I could take the train," he suggested.

"Or I could drive you," Gil said. "There are a few people in the city I've been meaning to meet with."

"Sure, okay," Matthew said, clearly trying not to frown. This wasn't what he wanted. But guess what? Tough shit. Because he was a child and Gil was the goddamn boss.

"I don't teach Friday. We could leave early and get there in plenty of time."

"Whatever," Matthew said, as if none of it was his idea. "The party's Saturday."

"Midmorning, then? That way we'll get to the city before rush hour."

"Whatever, fine, sure," Matthew said, taking his toast to the table.

Probably Gil should've run this by Molly. What was the schedule for this weekend? There was always some tangle of events and hobbies.

Teaching had rarely been more difficult than it was that afternoon, distracted as he was by his plans for New York. Or rather, his lack of plans. He wanted to see what Matthew was up to, but how was he going to do that? Follow him? The boy would notice, and he could easily lose Gil on the subways, or the streets.

But at the very least they'd be staying at Sharon and Niles's apartment and there might be evidence there. Which, Gil felt as he released his class a few minutes early, there *had* to be. In Vermont, Matthew had been careful to erase any evidence; this was hostile territory. But New York was home, and if Gil went with him, the boy wouldn't have time to scrub it free of traces. Maybe that had been part of the reason he'd wanted to go down in the first place. To cover his tracks now that Thomas had been arrested.

The horse barn, where he took Ingrid after school, seemed to thrum with the same anxiety that rippled out of him. The smell of the animals, their shit, the rich, tingling scent of hay, so out of place in frozen February, made the twisted wire in his stomach thicken until he was nearly choking with the pressure. Ingrid rode a brown horse with a white streak down its chest around the ring. Her helmet and knee-high riding boots were clearly no protection from the whims of that animal, skittish, bouncing hard in its stride. Horses always looked this way to him: barely contained, on the verge of lashing out. What chance did his hundred-pound girl in her tan riding pants and green UVM sweatshirt have against that beast with muscles twitching up and down its legs? And then there was a moment at the end when the trainer was holding the bridle and talking to Ingrid, who leaned forward to listen, and the horse jerked back, stamping its hooves, tugging itself free from the trainer's grip. Gil half-rose from the wooden bench, his heart pounding and his mind leaping immediately to Matthew's story, as if by writing about it the boy had made this happen, as if this had somehow been his plan all along, to cause this accident, to finish what he'd started. But Ingrid tightened the reins, straightened up, and brought the horse under control. The trainer laughed as she came over and they did a last loop of the pen before Ingrid swung her leg over and hopped down. The horse let itself be led away.

"Well, that was scary," Gil said as they walked out to the car afterward, Ingrid's unzipped jacket blowing open around her.

"What was?" she said, head bent down so the words muffled into her scarf.

"The horse, at the end. When it bucked."

"He didn't buck. Smudge never bucks."

"Okay," Gil said, pushing the Unlock button so the car chirruped and flashed its lights. "Didn't buck. But he got nervous."

"He was just antsy," Ingrid said. As if this was no big deal.

"You weren't scared?" he said.

She didn't answer until they were both inside the car and Gil had turned the key and a feeble breath of warm air was leaking out of the vents.

"I don't know. The horses don't scare me. I mean, I don't feel *scared*. Sometimes they can be a little goofy," she said with a laugh. "But they're not scary. Just bossy."

"Well, for the record, *I* think they're scary," he said.

"That's because you don't ride them. I mean, what's scary if they're going to let us ride them? Because they let us. And if they do, then I don't see any reason to be afraid." She zipped her jacket all the way to her neck and hid half her face beneath the collar.

"But they're giants," he said, backing up slowly, avoiding a patch of ice he'd noted on the way in.

"Big things don't always hurt you. A poisonous spider is as dangerous as an elephant."

"I'd choose neither, if I could," he said.

"Fine. But I choose horses," she said, defiant. She'd told him many times she was going to have three horses of her own when she grew up. He'd said good, because it meant she might stay in Vermont. Her attitude struck him not as admirable, as she surely intended, but as preteen presumption, a false wisdom for her not-thought-through theories about horses and consent and power, her fantasies of owning a bunch of horses on a stretch of land in Vermont with no thought to how she could possibly afford such a life. He remembered this stage with Chloe, confident she'd mastered already the logic of adulthood but not yet stitching it together, especially the dark reality of money. What both girls were missing was an understanding that power was violence, and for that matter, money was only another expression of power. Contained power was contained violence, and it took almost nothing to switch it over to real violence. This was innocence on their part. And there was no reason to rush them out of that. Life would do so eventually, and likely too soon.

By the time they got home, Matthew's Audi was in the drive, and he could see, from the way his wife watched him pull off his boots, that the boy had already brought up the trip to New York.

"So," Molly said, drawing the word out. "I hear you're taking a trip."

"Shit, Molly, sorry. I meant to tell you. Matthew asked if I would take him down to the city. Does that work?" Gil put a hand on the wall and tugged his foot free, putting his sock down in a puddle of melted snow.

"He asked you to take him?" Molly said, raising her eyebrows.

"Well, he wants to go. A friend's birthday. And he can't go by himself," Gil said.

"Of course he can't," she said, and he strained to hear some irony in her voice.

"I said I'd take him. I need to meet with Peter at some point anyway. He's available Friday afternoon." Gil hadn't spoken to, or emailed with, his agent in six or seven months. He was supposed to have sent Peter a new draft of his novel, the one Peter had said he couldn't sell in its current form after Gil had sent a draft last year. Gil hadn't touched that book (any book, actually) in months. He'd often forgotten about it, only to have failure lurch into view whenever someone asked the dreaded question: *What are you working on?* Which probably meant it was well and truly dead.

"Did you finish a new draft?" Her tone had shifted, softened. Because she wanted what was best for him. All this time she'd held out hope for his dead book. She had faith in him, for some reason. She'd always been excessively generous about his work. She'd given up so much of her art, her friends, connections, galleries, to move to Vermont, but she'd never held that against him. She showed in Burlington, Stowe, and Bennington, but he assumed she must often wonder what would have happened if she'd stayed in New York. If she'd refused to leave with her broken husband. Might things have been better?

"Not yet," he said. "But I sent him some pages and he wants to meet, and since Matthew wants to go down anyway . . ." This was, at least in a way, the boy's doing. Driving him to lie to Molly.

"Do you think it's a good idea to let Matthew go at all?" Molly said. "Just yesterday you were convinced—you know, the driver?"

"I know, Molly, I understand, but if I'm going to meet Peter anyway—"

"I don't know that this is a great idea, Gil."

"I know it isn't, but what are we going to do? Tell him no? Now?"

"Why not?" Molly said. "Just tell him something came up. Because, honestly, you're not making a lot of sense. If you really think Matthew had something to do with this Thomas who was arrested, why on earth are you taking him to the city?"

He couldn't answer that, at least not honestly. Because the answer was: to spy. To gather evidence. But if he said that out loud he was afraid it would sound, well, insane. Which it nearly did in his head.

"And did you talk to the detective? Did you call her?" Molly said.

"No, not yet, but I will. I can call her tomorrow. And we can't just let him go on his own. And since I have this thing with Peter, I thought—" He was circling that particular lie, pathetically, probably exposing himself. "We'll be back Sunday."

Molly frowned at him in a way that made him feel sick. She doubted him, and was worried. Maybe even afraid. He'd seen that look before, but not for years. It was a look he'd seen often during their final years in Brooklyn, especially after he came out of the hospital. He would be sitting with Chloe, playing with blocks—mostly she liked him to build, then she demolished with a delighted squeal—and he'd find Molly watching from the far side of the room, eyeing him carefully, fearfully.

"Molly, don't worry, okay?" She snorted, but Gil kept going, otherwise he'd lose the chance the trip offered. "And it'll be good for the girls to have him out of the way." He couldn't tell if she believed him, not really, but some of the tightness went out of her face, so maybe. Hopefully.

"Actually, I think Chloe would probably want to go with you," Molly said.

"To New York?"

"Except she has rehearsal all weekend."

"I mean, I'm just going for a meeting, and—"

"Um, Gil, I don't think she'd want to hang out with you. She'd want to go with Matthew."

"Matthew?" Gil said, as if this was an absurd idea, but of course Molly was right. They were close to the same age, and Matthew was the older, more experienced city boy who could take her to parties. Thank god for the spring musical.

"They've been hanging out. Haven't you noticed? And Chloe told me the other day that he's been helping her with geometry, and apparently he's even been helping Ingrid with her Civil War presentation."

Gil nodded as if of course he knew all this. After all, he lived in this house and he wasn't so self-absorbed, so fixated on, say, well, his nephew to have not noticed Matthew worming his way into his family's affections. That time he'd been out in the woods and had seen Matthew and Ingrid at the table together: Maybe he'd been helping her. Not threatening her. Nothing untoward at all.

"Oh, I forgot, I talked to my mom this morning," Molly said. "She suggested we come down there for spring break."

"To Maryland? With Matthew?" Gil said. His in-laws knew all about Montauk and had quietly loathed Matthew—and Sharon and Niles, whom they'd met only once—ever since.

"Well," she said, turning back to poke at the fish sputtering in the oil on the stove, "we can't all go, because Chloe has that debate thing at Sarah Lawrence that weekend. But I could take Ingrid. We haven't seen my parents since July."

"And I'd stay here," Gil said. "With Matthew."

"I asked him if he wants to come. But he says he has some papers for Herbert to finish," she said. "And you could use the time to work on Peter's edits."

"Sure, right," he said. "That sounds good."

At dinner, the girls chatted with Molly about their day—horses, debate, the usual. Then Molly asked Matthew whose birthday he was going down for.

"Eric's," the boy said after a moment's hesitation, as if he couldn't remember what she was talking about.

"He's a friend from Herbert?"

"Yeah," Matthew said, taking a bite as if that'd excuse him from further inquiry.

"Are you excited to go back? To the city, I mean?" Chloe said. "You must miss your friends." As soon as she said this she blushed, as if she'd just made a ridiculous mistake. Missing people. How banal and childish!

"I stayed with Eric after my parents died," Matthew said. "His family was good to me, so I thought I should try to go down for the party."

"Well, I'm glad we can make it work," Gil said, suppressing a flicker of guilt. No. All of this was a show.

"Yes, it'll be nice, I'm sure," Molly said.

Matthew narrowed his eyes slightly at Gil, then refocused on his chunk of fish. Had Molly seen that, the meanness in the boy's eyes, the flicker of barely contained malice?

17

FUNERAL ASIDE, GIL HAD LAST BEEN TO THE CITY THREE YEARS ago. That was also the last time he'd seen Sharon alive. A friend had invited him to join a panel at the Brooklyn Book Festival, and Gil had immediately said yes, having long feared he'd let himself drift so far from the literary scene it no longer knew who he was. That he was clearly a last-minute sub didn't bother him—as it might have years ago—which said something troubling about his self-regard, or maybe just his realistic appraisal of life. The theme was city versus country, and the impact of place on the writer. He was the only writer on the panel not living in New York, and he'd been introduced by his friend, as they sat on stools on the stage in the middle of the book fair, as "the one who got away." This elicited half-laughs from the large crowd.

They were probably mostly here for the poet beside Gil, a brilliant young Vietnamese American who'd grown up in Queens and presumably stood for everything good about the city. And if you were to compare them—the bearded, balding man with his too-baggy cotton sport coat, shapeless jeans, and boxy shoes versus the sleek, impossibly thin young genius in black, his pointed shoes glittering, his hair precisely mussed—it wasn't hard to see which to prefer. And those superficial surface details were affirmation of the deeper distinction. The poet had a natural ease and eloquence, a wit, a generosity of spirit that was nearly visible in its intensity. In comparison, Gil felt childish, dim, and a little awed.

He took the 4 from Borough Hall to the Upper East Side. Sharon had asked if he could possibly come "in to the city" to meet up. She hadn't been to Brooklyn in years and was sure she'd get lost. Imagining he'd want an escape from the festival, Gil had agreed, though as he rode the clattering, jam-packed subway—it was a fucking Sunday, why was it so crowded?—he bristled. What exactly did Sharon have to do? Here he was doing an event at a major festival, and instead of coming out to see him she'd asked him to come up to her ossified neighborhood where the streets were haunted by wizened vampires intent on sucking the life from the planet to further their rapacious existence.

Some of his bitterness arose from the fact that there'd been no apology, or even any apologetic tone, in Sharon's recent emails. No admission that the reason they hadn't been in touch was that her son had tried to drown Ingrid. Instead it was: *Let me see if I can fit you in.* Between her fitness classes and facial treatments, presumably.

She was his sister, but she'd compartmentalized him as the unfortunate relative that must occasionally be humored. A chore. How had this happened? When they were little, they'd been close, had spent hours playing together, often in an imaginary world of Sharon's making. He had many such memories, but the one he most often returned to was the summer they'd spent in Ireland, just outside Galway, where their mother had been doing research. Gil had been seven, so Sharon must've been eleven. While their parents worked inside, Sharon took him to the playground down the street from their apartment and showed him how to pump his legs hard enough to get the swing to the end of its chain so that for a second he could see out over the gray slate roofs of the houses across the street before falling back with a lurch.

Gil had brought only one toy to Ireland, his stuffed seal, Sookie, and they built an adventure around him: The crows that clustered in the trees were spies and assassins, screaming threats in a twisted tongue. In the gaps between the sharp branches of the hedge they built a hideout: delicate furniture of sticks and bark, and, buried in a shallow hole beneath a bed of moss, the prize the crows were after, a code book of secrets. Sharon had made it: a few pieces of folded paper, stapled, covered with meticulous rows of inscrutable symbols. This, she'd explained to him, holding the book out with both hands, must never fall into the hands of the Lord of Crows.

One morning, halfway through their stay, Sookie was kidnapped, and after a giddy, nearly tearful search, they found him in the crook of a tree. His flipper was broken, and he had a concussion, so Sharon nursed him back to health in the hedge. This was one of his clearest memories of his sister: Sharon lifting a stone—the seal's teacup—to the stitched line of the seal's mouth, cooing encouragement, her face soft with care, patterned with bits of light that found their way down through the branches.

And then, just a couple of years later, all that was over. She became a teenager, too self-conscious to play, too distracted by her burgeoning social life, phone calls with friends, trips to the mall. By the time he began to catch up she was off to college. His parents had taken him along when they'd gone to visit her in Oxford over winter break during her junior year abroad. Throughout their visit she'd been distracted and distant, insisting she had to work, she had papers due to her tutors in January, and so she'd stayed behind when they'd gone down to London. Though he was only sixteen, he'd hoped that maybe she'd take him to a pub, or that at least they'd walk around Oxford together, but she'd barely noticed him, had clearly found their visit a burden. It was her boyfriend, his mother had insisted at dinner in London when his dad had brought up Sharon's rudeness. She was in love. Young love often did this to people, made them selfish, self-absorbed. Which Gil would find to be true, eventually, himself. But still, it was that visit, his sister's aloofness, the quickness with which she'd turned away from them in their hotel lobby after showing them around her college, that had marked for Gil the definite end of their closeness, the beginning of her drift away that would lead to Niles, to Matthew, to what had become her life.

They were meeting at a coffee shop on East Seventy-fifth Street a few blocks from her apartment, where Gil was perhaps no longer welcome. Sharon was seated in the window, wearing a drapey black sweater, black jeans, and high, spiky heels. She glanced up from her phone to wave.

In her email, she'd said she had only an hour, and after he got his cappuccino and sat beside her on the bench he was glad. From the outset, the conversation was strained. She asked cursory questions about Molly and the girls, checking her phone throughout. Were his annoyance and anger as obvious as her indifference?

"How's Matthew doing?" he eventually asked.

"Oh, Matthew," Sharon said, lifting a hand to brush hair behind her ear, the sleeve of her sweater drifting down to reveal a glittering band of diamonds. "You know Matthew."

"I don't, actually," Gil said, glad for the flinch in her face. "I haven't seen him in three years. He must be, what, fifteen?"

"Just," Sharon said. That's right. A July birthday. Gil hadn't called, written.

"How's his school?"

"He's had some trouble, to be honest," Sharon said. "But then I think partly it's all so easy for him. *Too* easy. He gets bored. And then he acts out."

That, or he's evil, Gil wanted to say.

"But he's going to be spending next summer in Europe. Working at an orphanage. It's a service project, through his school. Niles doesn't want him to go, but I think it'll be good. Get him out in the world."

"That sounds like a great experience," Gil said, trying to hold down his bitterness. Because it *would* be a great experience. One that Chloe should get to have. Or Ingrid. She'd love that.

"I'm sure," Sharon said, glancing down at her watch.

"How long will he be there?"

"Oh, three weeks, I think," she said, stirring the ice in her plastic cup with the straw.

"Maybe it'll help him."

She squinted at him, defiant. "With what?"

"His trouble," he said, gesturing at the table, as if the answer was in there, clearly visible before them. "You said he was having trouble."

"Hmm, yes," she said, sitting back. "Matthew's fine. He knows how to take care of himself. He's resilient."

Like a weed, Gil wanted to suggest. *Like a virus.*

"Right, he'll be fine."

"Of course he will." Her tone had hardened. She reached for her plastic cup but then pulled back and glared at him. "It hasn't been easy for him, you know."

"What hasn't?"

"All of this. All the accusations. His own family suggesting he's a murderer or something. *That* hasn't been easy for him."

"Easier than nearly drowning," he said, spots of light flicking across his eyes. He should've let it go, not engaged. That would've been Molly's advice. But now he felt this was why he'd come: to have it out with his sister. To make her face what her son had done.

"Jesus, Gil, do you believe that? That's what I want to know. That's why we're sitting here. Because I need to know if you think my son tried to kill your daughter. Do you think he intended to drown Ingrid? Or do you think maybe it was an accident? Maybe they were playing, or maybe Ingrid fell into the water." Her tone was cool, as if he were a bad student in need of correction.

"You think Ingrid's lying? What possible reason could she—

She was six years old, Sharon. And Matthew *admitted* it. I was standing right there." His voice had risen and the barista glared at him: the violent man. If only she knew!

"I'm saying it's possible she didn't remember correctly. They were kids, Gil. And Matthew has been working on this, you know. With a therapist, ever since. I know he was a difficult child—"

Gil snorted so loud she flinched, but after a pause went on.

"But that doesn't mean he's a murderer. Don't you see the gap between being difficult and killing someone?"

"I don't think the problem here is that I can't see some nuanced gradation in Matthew's personality. I think it's that you don't want to see what's down there. In your son. He tried to kill my daughter. I saw my daughter"—his voice began to hitch, but he forced himself on—"I dove into the water and I pulled her out. And you're going to say she's a liar? To protect your son? Who tried to kill her?"

"He's my son," she said, softly.

Gil's mouth went dry. He went to get a glass of water from the pitcher on the counter, and when he came back to their seats, Sharon had her purse on her lap, clutching it with both hands. "Well, I'm going," she said.

"Okay," he said.

"I'm sorry, Gil," she said, but he knew she wasn't. This was his sister, his only family left, and she wanted nothing to do with him. That completely fucking sucked. And he knew exactly how she felt. Because he felt it too.

From his seat in the window he watched her step to the curb and fling out her arm. A cab immediately slid up, as if it'd been waiting for her. Gil tossed his cup out and walked over to the Met, trying not to fume as he paced the galleries. Seeing Sharon had reminded him intensely of what had been affirmed that morning: This city wasn't his, and his family wasn't here.

18

NEITHER OF THEM SPOKE FOR THE FIRST HALF HOUR AS GIL drove the Audi—a far nicer car than their Subaru, than any car Gil had ever owned. If Molly and the kids had been along he might've taken 22A down along the lake to 149 and through Lake George, but with Matthew faster was better, so he chose the highway.

Thankfully, the boy fell quickly asleep, head on his balled-up jacket pressed to the window. Gil usually listened to the radio while he drove—NPR, with occasional masochistic forays into right-wing talk shows when bored. But if he turned it on it might wake Matthew, and then he'd have to apologize. For listening to the radio.

They were nearly out of Vermont before Matthew woke up, blinking in a way that looked fake.

"Tired?" Gil said.

"I can never stay awake in cars," the boy said, rubbing his eyes and zooming out on the dashboard GPS.

"Good thing you didn't drive yourself, then," Gil said.

"Yeah, thank god."

"Do you want to listen to something?" Gil said.

"I don't care, whatever."

Gil found the NPR station out of Brattleboro. There was a piece on the refugee crisis in Eastern Europe, the miles of fencing put up at the Hungarian border, the flood of people moving through the Balkans, cold and hungry and desperate. At the break for local weather, Gil turned the volume down.

"You were over there, weren't you? In Eastern Europe?" He tried to sound calm, collected, just chatting.

"Yeah," Matthew said, with a not-this-again tone. "Just a couple weeks, though."

"Where was it, again?" He could play the fool, if it might get him the truth.

"Albania," Matthew said. "And we went to Croatia. And Venice, at the end."

"That must've been interesting."

"Yeah, you could say that. I guess you could say it was *interesting*."

Gil gripped the wheel tighter but stayed calm, let the comment pass. The rat wouldn't slip away that easily.

"What were you doing there?"

"Working in an orphanage," Matthew said. "Part of Herbert's community service thing. You know, giving back and all that. Good citizens." He said this as if it was the most risible idea ever concocted.

"And you lived at the orphanage?"

"Yeah, outside Tirana." Matthew's whole body was turned away toward the window so his breath fogged the glass. He didn't want to talk about Europe, or anything, actually. Not with this fossilized hick.

"How'd you get around, while you were there?" This was a risk: too direct, maybe. But Gil was sick of tiptoeing around.

Matthew shifted up in his seat, gave the volume knob a mean-

ingful stare. The program had returned. When the boy didn't answer, Gil pushed harder. "Did you get to travel? Or, you know, go
into the city at all?"

"A little," Matthew said. "The orphanage was pretty far out,
like, in these hills. But if we wanted to go into Tirana they had a
couple of drivers. They had these big black Land Rovers. Former
military, I'm pretty sure. Anyway, they'd drop us off downtown and
we'd go to a café or whatever. And a few times they took us on
weekend trips. Like, we went camping up in the mountains, near
some Greek ruins."

"Well," Gil said, "that sounds like a great experience." *Drivers.
Thomas Gashi.* Gil could almost see him leaning over the wheel of
the truck as the light turned red, as the Ferrari, heading uptown,
swerved around the traffic and into the intersection, into his path.

"I guess," Matthew said, and he turned up the radio. This was
Matthew's car. Gil was the boy's guest. His rude, jabbering, idiot
guest.

They hit traffic in the Bronx and from there crept along until they
passed the accident, visible through a cordon of police and ambu-
lances: a gray car with an obliterated front and a minivan with a
scrape on the side, a bumper hanging loose. He checked the boy's
face—would it bother him to see an accident?—but Matthew
looked no different from any other rubbernecker clogging the
highway.

"How are your classes going?" Gil said. "I hear you're doing
well."

"Do you?" the boy said, smiling, as if he assumed his professors,
especially at a rink-a-dink clown school like Essex, would spend
their free time extolling his virtues.

"Dr. Holden mentioned it," Gil said, as if he couldn't help but
feed the boy's boundless ego.

"Yeah, my classes are fine. I mean they're, whatever."

"And you're up in workshop soon, right?"

"If you say so," Matthew said, as they rose onto the bridge that would take them into Manhattan.

"What's the new one about?" Gil said. This might be too obvious. But Matthew apparently didn't find the question any more annoying than any of the others.

"I'm working on something, but I'm not sure if I'm going to have it done in time."

"I guess I'll have to wait."

"With bated breath, I'm sure," Matthew said, and despite his head being turned, Gil could see the corner of his mouth curl up in a smirk.

In Manhattan, Matthew shut off the GPS and gave directions. Gil's hesitant driving provoked honks from careening cabs and shouts from pedestrians who stood in the road when their light was red and launched into the crosswalk as soon as Gil's light flicked yellow.

Sharon and Niles had owned several spots in a parking garage on Second Avenue. An attendant frowned as they pulled up to the barrier, but as soon as he spotted Matthew he smiled, revealing two dead front teeth. The man leaned down to Gil's window but talked right past him, a reek of stale cigarettes pulsing off his gray jumpsuit.

"Mr. Westfallen. So good to see you, sir. And I'm so sorry to hear about your parents. They were beautiful people. Really beautiful." The man clapped a hand to his chest, close to Gil's ear. "I've been wanting to tell you. Awful. A real tragedy."

"Thanks, Sammy," Matthew said. The man waited a few beats, as if hoping for more, then patted the roof and went to raise the barrier. They parked in the spot where, Gil assumed, the Ferrari had once been.

The man waved as they passed his booth, but Matthew pretended not to notice. The boy led the way, a few steps ahead, to the building, where he was greeted by a phalanx of doormen. They offered to carry Matthew's shoulder bag, asked how he liked the country. They hoped he was doing well, it was so nice to see him. All three men ushered them into the elevator with great solemnity. This was how rich people were treated: Even a routine ride up to their apartment was a grand occasion to be admired by the subalterns.

From the outside, the building was regal, untouched, and within, two classic eights had been combined into a sprawling palace. Gil had recently searched the price: sixteen and a half million dollars.

The foyer opened onto a gleaming kitchen on the left, and straight ahead lay the living room—wide swaths of empty wood floor across which a set of white couches surely too big ever to have passed through the door faced a wall-sized television. Off the living room was a separate dining room, and behind sliding doors was a library with floor-to-ceiling dark wooden shelves. He checked for his own books, and of course they were there. Hardbacks, which he'd signed: the first to Sharon, the second to her and Niles. On the back flap was his face. Or the face he'd once had. He looked pompous, as if certain of his importance in the world of literature. A cocky, deluded fool. Did other people think the same thing when they flipped to the back? Or *had* they, since who knew how long it had been since anyone had picked up one of his books?

"Anything good?" Matthew said.

Gil snapped the book shut.

"So, I'm going to head out," Matthew said.

"Okay. Will you be out late?"

"I might end up staying over somewhere."

"Right," Gil said. Should he give him a curfew? But curfews might not be a thing in his world.

"You have meetings?" Matthew put a hand on the edge of the

door and pulled it out a few inches, shoved it back so it gave a bump.

"Right. My agent."

"Well, see you later," Matthew said.

Gil stayed where he was until he heard the front door click shut. He slid his book back into place, went to the desk in the corner, which he knew his sister had used, and opened the drawers.

He'd searched the library, the living room, the kitchen, Niles's office, Sharon's office, their bedroom, and of course the boy's bedroom. He'd spent so much time hunched over that his lower back ached and his knees had gone stiff.

The bedrooms looked staged, white sheets tucked tight. Sharon's and Niles's closets—two walk-ins—were empty, save for dozens of wooden hangers. Their clothes and shoes had been donated to charity. That had been one of the items ticked over while Gil had sat in that fine leather chair in the lawyer's office. The receipt for the clothes donations had been used for a tax write-off. Some of the jewelry had been sold—the money going to charity—and the rest had been put into a bank lockbox. Gil remembered thinking, bitterly, that if that money had come to them instead of going to a charity they could've afforded college for the girls. But maybe that was grotesque: profiting off his sister's death. And he already was, what with the caretaking stipend. It was terrible how death immediately called up the accountants, the dissolution of boundaries between wealth and self, as if you were nothing but the assets you left behind.

But money might be a link to the truth. If Matthew had hired Thomas, he'd have had to pay Thomas a significant amount. Matthew could have managed that. When they'd gone over the will, the head lawyer of the Westfallen Trust had been explaining the tax ramifications and had slid a piece of paper in front of Gil. The number was over four and a half million dollars. Was that supposed to be the amount of the taxes paid? And at what rate? Which meant there was, at bare minimum, ten times that in the trusts. More. Well over fifty million dollars. The truth was horrible—to have so much wealth hoarded in one family, his own family, and to be unable to touch it, to use it to improve the lives of his own children. All of it, that bottomless reserve, was headed to the least deserving person imaginable.

Best way to deal with this monstrosity was not to think about it. Best to look away, whistle some tatty, distracting tune in your mind. But now it was the only clue he could follow. He'd told Molly he'd call the lawyer about the therapist issue. A way in.

A secretary answered, and asked if he had an appointment.

"No, I'm, well— This is Gilbert Duggan. I'm calling about the Westfallen Trust. I'm Matthew Westfallen's uncle. I just have a couple of questions."

Gil could hear accusation in the pulse of silence that followed. Here he was, right on schedule, the greedy relative trying to disinherit the poor orphaned boy. But that was exactly why the boy's thoughtful parents had hired this august firm: to protect their son. Because the firm well knew, as did this woman on the phone, that people are pigs. Ravenous pigs eager to devour one another to get at a pile of cash a fraction the size of the Westfallen Trust. And, on cue, here he was, scratching around like a pig—no, actually, like a rat, crawling up out of the subway to drag its trail of wet slime across the platform and scramble up into the dark mouth of a trash can—in search of scraps he might carry away for himself.

"I'm afraid Mr. Ripley isn't available at the moment. But I can take a message, if you'd like," the woman said.

"Sure. Matthew and I are in the city for the weekend"—*Who's the rat now? Would a greedy rat bring his nephew down for a weekend in the city to see his friends?*—"and it occurred to me to follow up on a couple of questions. Nothing urgent."

"Is your number—?" and she repeated it back to him.

"Yes, that's right."

"Well, I'll pass along the message."

"Okay," he said, suppressing the urge to apologize. "Thank you."

"Goodbye, sir," she said, nearly spitting the last word. Or maybe, he hoped, that was the sound of the call disconnecting.

19

A FREE NIGHT IN NEW YORK AND HE SPENT IT IN THE APARTMENT doing nothing. He ordered Chinese delivery and flipped around on the television, which was, weirdly, still connected to cable. Presumably because it didn't matter. What was a couple hundred dollars, autopaid out of some trust? Worth maintaining in case Matthew ever came down. At midnight Gil lay down in the guest room, but it was hours before he managed to sleep.

The apartment was spacious and elegant, but also dead. A mausoleum. As soon as he woke the next morning—no sign of Matthew—he knew he had to get out of there. Go somewhere, get breakfast. Was food the only thing he missed from the city, he wondered, as he squeezed onto a downtown 6 train? He'd lived here for more than a decade. There must be other things. Well, bookstores. And museums. He'd never been to the new Whitney. So that was it. Try to act like a normal person. Take a break.

That evening, by the time he got across town from the Meatpacking District to the East Village, Momofuku was jammed, but since he was alone, he got a stray seat at the bar. In the din, after he ordered, he texted Molly, sent her some photos he'd taken at the Whitney, but as soon as he did, it felt wrong. What was he doing in the city, exactly? Sightseeing? Going out to dinner? The text was delivered, but not read.

Dazed by ramen, pork rolls, and IPAs, Gil walked down First Avenue and over to the Bowery, which had, at some point in the past ten years, been converted into a string of high-end boutiques. Wealth leaked out of the storefronts and off the people he passed. The city had become a diamond, buffed and cut, rising each time in value, beyond the reach of all but millionaires. But some things remained as he remembered them. For example: Beside the McNally Jackson bookstore was a bar where he'd gone once with Molly after his first novel had come out and he'd entertained delusions that he was a big shot, or could be a big shot if he just wrote another novel quickly, and, of course, went to the right parties. Whose release had it been? His friend from the New School who'd written that memoir? The crowd inside was as it'd been then: sleek, handsome young people, preening. He slowed, caught in the sharpening moment of nostalgia, and that's when he saw Matthew.

The boy was laughing, his hand on a woman's arm. In Matthew's other hand was a slim glass of beer, nearly empty, the sides streaked with faint lines of foam. When he tipped his head back to take a sip, his eyes moved toward the street, and Gil ducked his head and went next door to the window of the bookstore, pretended to study the display.

He tried to slow his thudding heart, but he couldn't. This was a gift. Not a miracle. And yet it *felt* like a miracle. Wandering around the city, and there was Matthew. Because someone, or something, wanted Matthew punished as much as Gil did. He wasn't alone. Chance was on his side. If he hadn't gone to dinner he wouldn't be here now, at this exact moment, wouldn't have seen him. He knew it was crazy—the beer talking—but it felt like an offering. Now he could see who the boy was when adults weren't watching, while his guard was down.

It was only eight. They wouldn't stay in the bar all night. He probably had time to go into the store. Cover in case the boy spotted him. He browsed quickly, picked up a couple of books, hurried to the register, and was back on the street in a few minutes, but he was sure they were already gone.

More luck. Matthew was still there, half-perched on a stool, talking with a young woman. Gil slowed. It was Susie. From Essex. Here, in the city, with Matthew. The tips of Matthew's fingers touched Susie's hip, and as Gil watched her lean toward him, laughing, holding a glass of wine beneath her mouth, the boy's fingers curled into a belt loop of her black jeans.

Across the street there was another bar, mostly empty except for a few tourists with their shopping bags, slumped over beers. Gil took a stool at the bar with a view of the brightly lit windows across the street. The bartender barked "Yeah?" and poured Gil's beer so it was half foam. No matter. He wasn't here to drink.

"Another?" the bartender asked, as Gil glanced between his phone and the window—no emails, no texts from Molly.

As the new beer was poured he took out his notebook. If he was just sitting here, he might as well make use of the time. But when he opened the notebook the tidy lines were a taunt. When he wrote "The boy" atop the page, his handwriting was the scrawl of a child learning his letters. Or maybe that of a madman.

His phone was silenced beside his glass, but he saw the call come in. Lang, Ripley and Lyons, with (Sharon's Trust) below. They were calling now? Well, one did hear that lawyers worked nonstop, didn't spend a lot of time bumming around bars, stalking their nephews.

"Hello," Gil said.

"Yes, Mr. Duggan? This is Albert Ripley, calling you back. I apologize for the hour, but things were busy here. I'm told you have a few questions about the Westfallen Trust?"

"Yes, hi, thanks. I was calling to ask about one of Matthew's accounts," Gil said, his voice shaking. Nervousness had a hold on him. As if he was doing something wrong. Because he was. Spying on his nephew. Trying to get evidence that probably didn't exist.

"You mean one of the trust's accounts?"

"Right," Gil said. He hated that bullshit idea: that the trust was someone in possession of accounts. An embodied corporation. The corruption of language that has led to— But no. Focus.

"So," Mr. Ripley said into the pause. "Which account is this?"

As with the secretary, there was wariness in the man's voice. He had made it clear to Gil in their various discussions that the trust was an entity distinct from his role as guardian. While it was useful for him to have a sense of the boy's assets and future inheritance, the day-to-day management would be handled by the firm. The message was clear enough: none of his business. And here he was, butting in. Already. The villainous ne'er-do-well uncle of a nineteenth-century novel.

"See, that's the thing, I'm not sure. I don't have the account number. But I know that there was a withdrawal. A large one."

"Can I ask what the money was for?" the lawyer said, and now his voice was full of concern.

"Right, see, Matthew probably made the withdrawal. Is there a way to look that kind of thing up?"

"When was this?" The man's voice hardened each time he spoke, a brick in a rising wall. A wall to keep the barbarians out.

"I'm not sure. I guess, maybe, December?" It would have to be, for Matthew to pay the driver before the accident.

Now the pause was more pregnant, and Gil realized what the lawyer was piecing together. In December. When Sharon and Niles were alive. Which meant it was truly none of Gil's fucking business.

"Matthew asked me to check on this" was what he came up with.

176 | NATHAN OATES

"Interesting. I saw Matthew this morning," the lawyer said. "He didn't mention it."

"Oh, he asked me a while ago, and, well, I forgot about it, unfortunately, and then we were in the city, up at Sharon and Niles's place. . . ." Matthew had seen the lawyer this morning? The boy had preempted him, gone in and come up with some explanation of those funds, had warned them that his uncle was overbearing, didn't understand how this all worked, you see, and so if he called, well, do Matthew a favor and just ease him out. This wasn't his purview. Not his world.

"Yes, Matthew told me," was all the man said. Was that an English accent? How had Gil not noticed it before? Or maybe, like other rich men he'd met, the man's voice lilted into that cadence when he needed to put the plebs in their place.

"Well, if you spoke with Matthew . . ." Gil said.

"Yes, we had lunch today. Niles was a good friend."

"Right, well, I'll make sure Matthew has everything he needs," Gil said. The dutiful uncle. The thwarted thief. "Actually, there is something else."

"Yes?" the man said, annoyed now.

"I was wondering if there was someone Matthew was talking to. Before. In New York."

"Talking to?"

"We were thinking, a therapist?" Gil said. "Sharon mentioned something. A while ago."

"As far as I'm aware," the lawyer said, his voice guarded and formal, "Matthew has not been seeing a therapist, but if you think there's a reason he should, I can certainly get a recommendation. Is he doing okay up there? My impression is that, considering, he's okay. But he can be rather stoic and hard to read."

"Yeah, no, you're right, he seems fine," Gil said.

"Has something happened?" the lawyer said.

"Well, I thought, as you said, he's hard to read, and, well, we were worried," Gil said, flustered, though this was what he'd called about. This man was paid to protect Matthew. If Gil brought up his suspicions, the man wouldn't be sympathetic. He'd probably tell Matthew. Give the boy a reason to take action.

"I can have my assistant put together a list of contacts. But you should discuss this with Matthew. He's old enough to be a part of this decision." The man's voice was scolding: Gil was failing his nephew.

"Of course, yes, I will," Gil said.

"And now that you've brought this up, I meant to ask: Did you hear from the police about the accident? About the arrest?" the lawyer said, his tone sharpening.

"I did, yeah. She called."

"I heard. In the future I would ask that you let me know as soon as you hear anything from the police. After all, we're all in this together."

"Right," Gil said.

"I heard from the detective myself, of course. And I spoke with Matthew, but I do want to be sure there are no loose ends. There is no reason to add to Matthew's stress."

"Of course not," Gil said.

"Please do contact us if you've any questions," the lawyer said, and hung up.

Gil's second beer was nearly gone. Swirling the last of his foam, he gave it a few more minutes, typing up a text to Molly, who hadn't responded to his earlier notes. Because she was busy taking care of both kids while he was museum-hopping and drinking in bars and fucking up conversations with Matthew's lawyer.

But Gil's persistence was rewarded. As he half-rose from his stool to slide his phone into his pocket, the glass doors of the bar across the street opened and Matthew emerged amid a crowd, shouldering into his jacket so it spun out around him, charcoal-gray wool with a flash of blue silk lining. Susie was there too, eyes fixed on the boy, who stood at the center of their group like the king while they huffed clouds of cold air, checked their phones, lit cigarettes, and started, a jocular heap, across the street.

He gathered his coat and watched their heads bob beneath the window, a clatter of hard, mocking laughter. He went to the door, counted to twenty, and stepped outside. He thought he'd lost them, but then he saw Matthew's coat, his profile, his head thrown back to laugh. Gil let them get farther ahead.

At Bowery they turned right, deeper into SoHo. He hadn't been in this part of the city at night, certainly not on a Saturday, for a long time. What had been abandoned warehouses and flop-houses were now boutiques and art galleries. Matthew and his crowd passed all of these, ran across Grand in front of a shrieking cab, and Gil had to wait to follow.

A full block ahead they turned, and Gil jogged to catch up, knowing how the streets tightened here into a tangle, and he nearly ran into Matthew, who was standing just around the corner. The boy looked up from his phone, without surprise.

"Uncle Gil," he said, reaching out a hand and putting it firmly on Gil's shoulder. "What a nice surprise."

"Matthew," Gil said. The boy's friends were a block farther on. Susie trailed behind, glancing back.

"What are you doing here, Uncle Gil? You weren't, wait, no, you weren't *following* me, were you?" Gil tried to shrug off his hand, but Matthew tightened his grip.

"What, no, of course, no. I was book shopping." He held up his bag, which crinkled loudly in assent.

"Down here?"

"I think maybe I got lost," Gil said, tried to step away, but Matthew didn't let go.

"I think," the boy said, his face narrowing into a leer, drawing close so Gil could smell the beer on his breath, "you're following me, Uncle Gil. That's what I think."

"Don't be—" Gil started, but the boy squeezed his shoulder

and Gil gasped, then ducked and freed his arm and stepped away, wanting to run.

"If you're not following me, what are you doing here? I mean, is it just a coincidence? You just happened to be spying on me in that bar? Just happened to follow us down the street? Just happened to be running around the corner here to catch up? What are the odds? Must be some kind of fucking miracle!"

Here he was. The Matthew Gil had known lay behind his polite smile. A cruel, sharp-faced piece of shit, leaning toward him there on Orchard Street at the edge of the deli's blue light.

"Or maybe you're after Susie. Your pretty little student. Is that it? Because I'm afraid that's probably going to end in disappointment, Uncle Gil."

"I have no idea what you're talking about," Gil said. Down the street Susie watched them, though now he was mostly obscured by the deli's awning. At least he hoped so.

"No, I think you do. But I'm afraid that's not going to work, because, well, not to be crass, but I *had* planned to fuck her tonight. Only if you don't mind." The boy held up his hands, as if afraid he'd transgressed some subtle code of propriety.

"Grow up, Matthew," Gil said, feeling, finally, a little resolve in the face of the boy's brutishness. "You're drunk and you should probably—"

"Drunk? I'm not drunk. Maybe you are, Uncle Gil. For your sake, I fucking hope so. Because otherwise, I'm going to have to tell you, it's pretty creepy to follow a bunch of teenagers. That's weird shit. I mean what do you think Susie thinks? Maybe we should ask her. Or you could just come along with us to the bar. We could talk about books. Fiction writing."

The boy stepped closer and Gil flinched, tripping on an uneven piece of sidewalk. He stumbled toward the street but managed to catch himself against a streetlight.

"Hey, watch it, Uncle Gil," Matthew said. "Wouldn't want you to fall out into the street. Wouldn't want you to get hit by a car.

That'd be a real shame. Your poor daughters, up there all alone with no one to take care of them." He grinned: rows of white teeth that glowed in the deli's haze. "But don't you worry, professor. I'll make sure they're okay. And your wife. Kind, gentle Aunt Molly. Molly, Molly, Molly."

A cab swerved off the Bowery and roared toward him, weaving slightly in its lane. He tensed, waiting for the boy to grab his coat and shove him into the street. But the cab passed with a rush of air and he was still there on the dark sidewalk. When he looked back, Matthew was walking away.

All the boy's politeness was a flimsier mask than it appeared. He'd just seen it more clearly than he'd hoped might be possible. He shouldn't be happy about this. But, Christ, he was. Happier— despite the hammering in his chest, despite the feeling that with each step the ground might lurch and dissolve and tip him into the dark—than he could remember feeling in a very long time.

20

GIL FLIPPED THE LOCK ON THE GUEST ROOM DOOR BEFORE GET-
ting into bed. His head ached from the beer, and everything he
probably should've felt there on the street poured over him, rest-
less, irregular waves of confusion and anger.

How dare that fucking punk talk to him like that? He was the
closest thing Matthew had to a father. And sure, yes, Gil had struggled to be anything like fatherly to the boy, but the boy had spoken
no differently to his real parents. That's how you speak to adults,
apparently, if you're a vicious, steaming streak of shit.

They had to drive back to Vermont in the morning. Matthew
could reach over, grab the wheel, and tip them off the road, or into
the path of a semi, or he could hit Gil, knock him out, steer the
car off the highway, down a state road, onto a rutted dirt track
marked with yellow posted signs, and there he could take out a
gun from his shoulder bag, or maybe a knife he chose from the
block in the kitchen, drag his uncle from the car, and slip the blade
into Gil's pulsing throat, pull his head back to open the artery,
careful to not get any of the spouting flow on his nice gray coat.

Somehow he fell asleep. The beer helped. He'd sent Molly a fourth text before bed and there was a reply when he woke, groggy and stiff, but alive:

You're coming home today? ETA?

She hadn't wanted him to come to the city, but she'd been wrong. It hadn't been a waste. The truth was here. Gil had seen it, faced it on that street in the deli's fluorescent glow.

The hallway was empty, but Matthew's door, down at the end, was closed. It'd been open last night. So, he was here. Gil went to the kitchen and fiddled with the excessively complex coffee machine until he figured out how to make a pot, then sat on a stool at the counter and let the headache ebb and swell behind his eyes while the water hissed and gurgled.

"Oh, Professor Duggan," a voice said, and Gil turned quickly on his stool, nearly fell, just catching himself on the slick stone counter.

It was Susie, wearing only a white button-up shirt. Skinny legs poked out the bottom, her bare feet splayed pigeon-toed on the tiles.

"Oh, hi," Gil said, standing up—he was wearing the stretched T-shirt he'd gone to sleep in, but thankfully had pulled on jeans before coming out here. Tugging his shirt away from his gut, he pointed to the counter and said, "Coffee."

"Oh, sure, okay. If there's enough," she said, squirming and looking behind her down the hall.

"Sure, plenty," he said. Then remembered he wasn't supposed to know she was here. After all, it's not as if he'd been spying on them last night.

"What are you doing here? I mean, in the city," he said. *And here. In my dead sister's apartment, with my evil nephew?*

"Matthew, he, well, his friend's birthday was yesterday, and—" She fumbled with each word as if they were gears of an unfamiliar engine she was somehow meant to assemble.

"How was the party?" Gil said.

"Oh, it was fun," she said, smiling. For a moment, he couldn't place what was different about her—other than her relative state of undress—and then he realized she wasn't wearing her glasses. Hopefully she couldn't see him clearly, how shitty he looked. Not that she cared what he looked like. But *he* could care a little, couldn't he? Out of basic self-respect? Not lust for her, as Matthew had suggested. Yes, she was a beautiful young woman, with her dark hair mussed about her head. But he'd been a professor long enough to know that they were, at this age, basically children. They didn't look like children, but their adolescence, that part of themselves they were so eager to shed, clung on into their twenties. He liked Susie, but not because she was pretty. He liked her because she was smart, thoughtful, and hardworking. Though apparently not smart enough to stay away from Matthew.

The coffeemaker beeped and he occupied himself finding mugs, searching for milk—none of that—though there was sugar. He set a cup on the counter for Susie, and she said, "Actually, could I get another one?" She gestured down the hallway, blushing.

"Right up there," he said, pointing.

She came up to the counter beside him so he could smell her hair, a faint scent of vanilla, and she rose on tiptoes, shirt riding up along her legs, revealing, for an instant, the curve of her butt, her lacy black underwear. She filled the cup and went slowly down the hall with a mug in each hand.

Gil took his coffee back to his room, where there was, thank god, a bathroom attached. While showering he forced himself to not think about Susie's legs, her ass, the smell of vanilla. No. He turned the tap to the middle so cold water poured from the rain spigot over him in a scolding deluge.

They'd made no clear plans about what time to head back, but Gil packed—it was already after ten. The door to Matthew's room was half open and he heard Susie's wild giggle. He tried to read in the living room but mostly stared at the townhouses across the street: blank, reflective windows revealing nothing.

A voice startled him from the twitchy half-sleep into which he'd drifted. "Hey, Uncle Gil, how was your night?" Matthew was leaning in the doorway as if he'd been watching him.

"What? Fine. Ready to go soon?"

"Pretty much," Matthew said. "Susie's going to catch a ride. She was going to take the bus, but I told her that was crazy."

Susie was nowhere to be seen, but surely listening, and there was no reason or way to say no. And at least now he wouldn't be alone in the car with Matthew. He'd decided he had to talk to the boy about last night, about the way the little shit had spoken to him. He couldn't let him get away with that, but he could only imagine that conversation as an absolute disaster. And now he had cover for his cowardice.

"Of course, no problem. We should head out in, like, twenty minutes?"

"Whatever," Matthew said, giving the wall a slap and turning back toward his bedroom. For a quickie, Gil guessed, from the enthusiastic slam of the bedroom door.

Matthew sat up front, twisting in his seat to talk to Susie while Gil drove out of the city. Could she believe what a fucking dipshit so-and-so was? And how about so-and-so? Total slut. Absolutely, she was. No, listen, some people were just sluts. That girl, trust him, she was a straight-up whore.

"Whore, Matthew, really?" Susie said, slapping his shoulder. "You're a dumb frat boy now?"

"Frat boy? I'm sorry, but a whore's a whore."

"Spoken like a true frat boy," she said. "But you're young. There might still be hope for you."

Gil glanced at Susie in the rearview, disappointed to find she was smiling. Maybe this was part of their relationship: Matthew acted like a thug and she laughed it off, because of course she thought he was in fact a refined gentleman with impeccable clothes, rich friends, and a Manhattan mansion.

In the rearview Gil could see the corner of the wrapped frame beside Susie. Matthew had brought it with him from the apartment. In the elevator Gil had asked what it was. Something for his room in Vermont? Even as he did he felt like a fraud. Chatting away with the thug who'd threatened him on the street just a few hours earlier.

"Actually, it's for Molly," the boy said, adjusting the frame beneath his arm so the paper crinkled.

"Molly?" Gil said.

"It's by this artist she likes. And my mom had a couple of her works. So, you know, I thought she'd like it." Susie beamed at Matthew as he spoke, her magnanimous, gift-giving boyfriend.

Gil felt a tremor of jealousy and anxiety run through him. An artist Molly knew? Which meant, expensive. Which meant, a gift for Molly the likes of which Gil couldn't possibly match. And, worse still, he hadn't thought to get anything for Molly and the girls. He was obviously an asshole, and Matthew would now look like a good guy.

On the more open stretch of highway, Matthew's interest in the conversation with Susie waned and he turned around and closed his eyes with a loud sigh.

"Oh, Professor Duggan, I meant to tell you," Susie said, leaning forward, her hand curling around Matthew's seat, touching his shoulder, "I read that book you suggested."

He had no idea what she was talking about. He suggested readings for all his students.

"And I did a tour, I mean, while I was in the city. Of her neighborhood. That part of the West Village. Donald Barthelme lived right around there too."

Now he had it. Grace Paley.

"Which book?" he said.

"I already had her *Collected Stories,* but I found a signed first edition of *Enormous Changes at the Last Minute* at a bookstore downtown. And Matthew got it for me."

He glanced in the rearview to see her gazing fondly at the boy, who was, ridiculously, still pretending to be asleep.

"That's a nice gift," he said. Matthew ignored him, kept his head to the window. A sleepy, magnanimous gift giver.

"'Wants' is my favorite," Susie said. "Or maybe 'A Conversation with My Father.'" She described what she loved about the stories, the way the metafiction was there, playful, but not too heavy and overbearing. She compared Paley's work to Barthelme's, and to John Barth's. Yes, okay, she'd made a bad choice in dating Matthew, if that's what they were doing, but she was one of the best students he'd ever had. It was students like Susie, bright lights of enthusiasm cutting through the fog of indifference that hung about most college kids, that made his job meaningful.

She asked what he was reading and he had to struggle through the hangover to remember. That new novel by the Italian writer he'd tried to like but didn't. They talked about translations and new podcasts. He asked if she'd ever heard the audio recording of a particular Barthelme story. She hadn't, so he found it on his phone, and they poured up the highway, laughing, and for a moment, it was almost possible to forget about everything: Matthew's face, twisted into a sneer in the deli's blue haze; the painting, a judgment on Gil in so many ways, jostling along in the back seat beside Susie.

Matthew didn't say a word for the rest of the ride, his face rolled to the window, pretending to sleep. Only when Susie pointed to a tall wooden house north of Church Street did he pretend—surely he was faking—to drift awake.

"This is good, right here," she said, and Gil guided them to the curb.

"Well, it was nice talking to you, Professor Duggan. See you in class," she said as she scooted across the back seat.

Matthew didn't say anything, and Gil wanted to tell him not to be a dick.

"See ya," the boy managed once she'd climbed out. "I'll text you."

"Okay," Susie said, unable to hide a pang of hurt.

She paused, hand on the door, as if hoping Matthew might say more, but he stared blankly ahead, and she shut the door. In the sideview mirror Gil saw her watching them from the sidewalk, backpack dangling from her hands.

Matthew hopped out of the car as soon as they stopped in the drive, took the frame from the back, and was inside the house before Gil got his bag out of the trunk. As Gil pried his feet free of his boots in the mudroom he watched Molly lay the picture, still wrapped, on the coffee table as she said, "Oh, Matthew, you didn't need to do this."

"I just thought, you know, it's sitting down there in an empty apartment, and, well, you'll see," Matthew said, arms crossed, grinning, delighted with himself.

Molly teased loose the tape and folded back the paper. Gil couldn't see the picture, but he could see the look on Molly's face, the shock, a look of—there was no other way to describe it—joy.

"Oh my god," she said, reaching out with one hand as if to touch the picture, then stopping herself and touching her mouth instead.

"My mom loved this one," Matthew said. "And I know you said you like her work." The boy looked pleased, smiling, his hands in his pockets as he rocked up onto the balls of his feet, then back down.

Gil dropped his bag and crossed the kitchen: a drawing, it looked like from his angle. Sharp, jagged lines, coming from the eyes of a woman in the center of the image, as if she was shooting beams from her eyes that bounced around the frame.

"Oh, Matthew, a Kiki Smith! This is too much. I can't possibly—" Molly said, not looking away from the drawing.

"My mom would've liked knowing it belonged to someone who appreciates it."

There'd been something in Matthew's voice Gil hadn't heard before: a wobble. A tenderness. *My mom.*

"Gil," Molly said, looking up at him with her tear-shimmering eyes. "Did you see?"

"I did," he said. "It's beautiful."

"My mom loved her work," Matthew said. "And some of yours reminds me of hers, so I thought it was the right one."

"Matthew, this is beautiful, thank you," Molly said, turning and hugging the boy, who, Gil saw, returned the hug, his eyes closed. Because he was being comforted. Because he was a boy, a child, an orphan, in need of care.

When Molly released him the boy turned to go upstairs with his bag. Gil and Molly watched him ascend. "Jesus, Gil, did you know about this?" she said to him when the boy was out of sight.

"The picture?" he said, stupidly.

"You shouldn't have let him do it. I mean, it's a Kiki Smith. It's too much." Her voice was still trembling with emotion.

Gil looked more closely at the picture. What he'd taken as beams shooting from the woman's eyes could be more like, well, tears. The beams were multicolored, bands of blue and yellow and red glittered with sparkles. Or maybe tears wasn't right, as they went down from her eyes but then came back onto the page around her head. Tears turned into beams of light.

"Well, he didn't ask my permission," Gil said, immediately hearing the bitterness and jealousy in his tone, so he quickly added, "and I guess he just wanted you to have it."

"Where should we put it?" she said. "Down here? Our room?"

"Wherever you think," he said.

She touched the frame with the tips of her fingers. He couldn't tell her about the encounter on the street, about the glimpse he'd gotten of the real Matthew, not now. Who'd believe Gil's version now? Who'd believe the boy he'd faced on the street would give a gift like this? And Molly, in her skepticism, would know he hadn't run into the boy by chance. She'd know Gil had been following Matthew. And what real proof was there of anything in the encounter? The boy had been a drunken prick. Not surprising. Not news. He wouldn't be able to convey the menace, the violence he'd felt pulsing off the boy. That encounter had felt to Gil like proof of the boy's nature, his capacity for violence, his—well, the word was *evil*. But it wasn't proof, was only a feeling. It couldn't be explained, or described. Or at least he couldn't explain it or describe it. And now she'd already walked away, leaving him with nothing to do but carry his bag of dirty clothes down to the laundry.

21

YOU WOULDN'T CALL IT A DREAM. NOT EXACTLY. THERE MUST BE some other name for that process when your mind returns to the quivering space between imagination and memory, worrying over it, twisting and bending it until it takes on a new shape, until some new version blots out the original, so that when you think back on that day what you remember is the construction, the false narrative, the mostly fiction.

Gil saw Matthew throw Ingrid into the pool. In his dream. Daydream. Half-waking state in which he'd been both asleep and watching, paralyzed, unable to move. The sun pinned him to the lounge chair. Ingrid played in the shade, far from the water. His good girl.

Matthew must've been watching them for a while. Making sure Gil was asleep. When the sliding door eased open, the boy's wolf-lean face focused on him, watching for a flicker of disturbance. Gil didn't make a move, because he couldn't. The sun. And he was asleep.

Matthew crossed the sun-blasted concrete on the balls of his bare feet to the shadows where Ingrid squatted, playing with rocks.

"Whatcha doing?" he said, in imitation of a kindly adult.

Ingrid squinted at him, wary. Her parents had warned her that her cousin was mean.

"Playing?" she said, softly, glancing at sleeping Daddy.

"With rocks?" he said. "Are they characters?"

"Kind of," she said, looking down at the handful of pebbles, some clear and bright, others dark. How could she explain? It'd just been pretend. Some voices, but mostly silent.

"Can they swim?" Matthew said, plucking up her favorite, a bright clear pebble, like a magic crystal.

"I don't think so. They're rocks."

"But maybe they can," he said. "Let's see."

He walked over to the pool, bouncing the pebble on his palm. She followed, wanting to see—it would be amazing if it swam!—but also afraid. She didn't want him to throw her rock in the water. It'd sink to the bottom and Daddy wouldn't be able to find it, but she couldn't cry about it because it was just a pebble and it was silly to cry about a pebble, she knew that.

Matthew glanced at Gil, who was watching but couldn't move, as if the boy was immobilizing him with his stare, forcing him down into the hot lounger.

"Here we go," Matthew said, bouncing the rock on his palm high, higher, then with a big bounce he sent it out over the water and down with only the faintest plop. The stone sank, shimmering. She lost track of it before it hit the bottom.

"Do you see it?" Matthew said, bending to whisper in her ear. "Look!" He pointed into the water. All she could see were broken bits of light wriggling through the water. "It's swimming, look. It *can* swim."

He sounded like he believed it and Ingrid leaned out, trying to see it, and for a second she did, the clear rock, struggling up through the layers, rising to the surface. Then his hands were under her arms and he was lifting her up and he was throwing her into the pool and the water closed around her and she sank to the blue bottom.

The splash woke him, pulled him up through the heaviness. The boy stood over the water, watching the girl drift down, her arms waving, her feet kicking. With a flash of disappointment the boy saw her father stagger up, stumble forward, groping at the air with both hands before he launched his pale body into the water with a howl.

22

MARCH 2018

OVER THE NEXT TWO WEEKS GIL FLOUNDERED, THOUGH HOPE-fully to others it just looked like his typically harried midsemester routine. Teaching, grading, working on lectures, reading student work, skimming scholarly texts from which he gleaned—in the most exact definition of that word possible, with special emphasis on "with difficulty"—ideas to use in teaching W. G. Sebald. Though, based on the recent reading quizzes, most of the students hadn't opened the book. Or they'd opened it, seen those blocks of text, struggled for a few minutes with a couple of syntactically complex sentences, and said *Fuck it*.

His fiction workshop had fallen into its usual groove: Students barely read the assigned stories from the anthology, overwhelmed as they were with the onslaught of midterms, but they managed to prepare for workshop, and Susie led the way, guiding them along better than Gil. In this work she had Matthew's help. Her sidekick. Or partner. That's how the other students surely saw it. At this point, Gil felt you could unequivocally say they were dating. He'd seen them at a sandwich shop in Burlington, holding hands across the table; had seen them walking across campus through a heavy snowfall, shoulders bumping; had heard Matthew talking to her on the phone while he sat in the living room, the boy's voice sometimes drifting down into a whisper, a giggle, then a sudden burst of laughter.

There was no escaping the boy. Gil came home one evening to find Ingrid jubilant: She'd gotten an A+ on the presentation Matthew had helped with. Her teacher had said it was the best presentation she'd seen in twenty years of teaching. Wasn't that wonderful, Daddy? Of course he was proud of her, but he was repulsed by the way the girls and Molly acted as if this success was largely due to Matthew's involvement, as if it was Matthew's achievement. And the boy never deflected the praise, never said *Really, Ingrid did all the real work.* And even at Essex, beyond the classroom, the boy was there. A novelist Gil admired came to give a reading and meet with creative writing students. Molly, a fan of his work, joined Gil at the event. They met the writer in an auditorium: a tall, shy man with a deep, resonant voice and a shockingly thick head of hair, tiny metal-framed glasses. He lived in Brooklyn, and Molly excitedly talked with him about the city, about the neighborhoods where they'd lived, about how much she missed it.

Gil hadn't noticed Matthew come in, but as they settled into seats he scanned the room for students and saw him, just two rows back, Susie whispering into his ear, and there was a sly grin on his face, as if what she said was snark, or sex talk.

During the Q&A, Matthew, of course, asked a question. The boy's voice, posh and smug, droned about how the writer would situate himself in relation to the European novel, as opposed to the American tradition, as his work seemed so clearly in conversation with Bernhard and Handke and Nabokov. The question, which was really more of a comment, was just Matthew showing off, but the writer nodded throughout and said, "That's a really excellent question, and yes, those writers are incredibly important to me."

Molly went over to say hi to Matthew after the reading, but Gil stayed chatting with his colleagues until it was time to head to dinner down on Church Street, a dinner that Gil tried to enjoy but that was, like so much, tainted by the fact of Matthew. It was irrational, maybe. Molly would tell him the boy hadn't come to the event to hound Gil, just to see the writer read. *Be reasonable, Gil.* But he couldn't. The boy didn't belong here, it was wrong, and wrong of everyone, including the detectives in New York, to do nothing. He hadn't heard anything since they'd pressed charges, weeks ago. Worst of all, Matthew would never, it seemed clear now, be held to account for what he'd done. And Gil was sure of that: The boy had done something. Murder. He'd murdered Gil's sister, and here Gil sat, eating calamari and carrying on with life as if nothing had changed.

On the way home Molly said, "Well, that was wonderful. And a lot of your students came?" She was driving because Gil had ordered an after-dinner whiskey, and the darkness of the countryside jostled past his window. Far ahead a pair of headlights shuddered through the trees, vanished.

"I think so," he said, sounding petulant. Grumpy. Because he *was* grumpy. "And yeah, a great reading."

Molly flicked him a frown as they slowed for a stop sign at Irish Hill Road, but she let it go. Maybe she'd wanted him to say something about Matthew. What a diligent student he was, what a smart guy, blah, blah. No. Gil wouldn't.

The second caretaking allowance flowed into their back account and felt like another rebuke: How could he complain about the boy when last month they'd paid off six thousand dollars of debt and would be able, this month, to send another chunk? So, deal with it. The rest of them were.

Gil had barely spoken to the boy since New York, couldn't bring himself to return to normal after the encounter on the street, which struck him as more and more threatening the longer he worried over it.

A week after the trip to New York, as he fidgeted with his pillow, cursing softly at the tangled sheets, Molly said, "Is something wrong, Gil? Because you're acting weird."

"Exactly what every man hopes to hear from his wife," he said, trying to joke it off.

"Come on. Talk to me."

"I do want to talk about it," he said. "I—but, Molly, I mean—"

She waited for him to go on, eyebrows slightly raised. "Is it Matthew?"

"It's just, you know. He was a jerk," Gil said. "In New York."

"How?" He could hear the skepticism in her voice. Because of the Kiki Smith. His helpfulness with the girls.

"Well, he brought a girl back to the apartment," he said. He wouldn't mention it'd been Susie. Somehow that might implicate him. Maybe it was the lust he'd felt, seeing her there in her white shirt.

"What girl?" she said.

"Someone from the party, I guess. And he was an asshole, in general. Not a single thank-you."

"That's rude, but what'd you expect? I mean, you wanted to go with him."

"I know, Molly, it's my fault, I'm an idiot," he said, trying to make a joke, but it came out wrong. Snarling and aggressive.

"What about the lawyer? Did you talk to him?" she whispered.

"I did. He said he didn't know anything about a therapist."

"That's weird," Molly said. "Didn't Sharon tell you he was seeing someone?"

He strained to remember, couldn't.

She reached across the bed and rubbed his arm. The warmth of her fingers against his skin for those few seconds reminded him that they hadn't had sex since Matthew had moved in. Explanations abounded. They were in their late forties (the list could, he thought, stop there); it was the start of the semester; they were tired; they were so tired; the kids were usually in the house. Their marriage had gone through dry spells before. It didn't signify, in itself, anything. But it was another mark of the distance that Matthew brought between him and his family. Molly was smiling down at him, thinking she understood, but she didn't. Couldn't possibly. Because he hadn't told her everything.

Two weeks after the trip to the city, Matthew went to pick up Chloe at play rehearsal, and as Gil set the table, he realized they still weren't home.

"Oh, sorry, I forgot," Molly said, looking up from her book. "They texted."

"They?" Gil said, fingers tightening around napkins and knives.

"Chloe and Matthew. There's a get-together at Lily's. I said it's fine."

"A get-together? As in a party?" Gil said. "And Matthew's there?"

"Apparently Lily thinks he's cute," Molly said with a smile, as if this was charming.

"So, when're they going to be back? It's supposed to snow later."

"I told Chloe midnight at the latest," Molly said, already lifting her book again.

Gil ground his teeth and set out the napkins, then went back to the kitchen to check the chicken, which, he could see by the skin, he'd overcooked. All throughout dinner he tried to act normal, be normal, but he couldn't bring himself to chat, instead half-listening as Molly and Ingrid talked about the foibles of her sixth-grade classmates.

They let Ingrid pick the after-dinner movie and she stayed up later than usual. By the time Molly came down from checking on her, it was eleven thirty.

"Well, I'm going to bed," she said.

"Up in a bit," he said, wiping at the table with a dish towel, though it was already clean.

"Gil, Chloe texted at nine. I'm sure they're fine." As if he was being ridiculous. Which he felt sure at this moment he wasn't. *She* was the one being ridiculous. Leaving their daughter out there with that boy.

"You're sure, huh?" he said, unable to keep from snapping. "You're sure everything will be okay? Because Matthew's out there driving our daughter around in the middle of the night, and I just don't get it, I can't understand why you keep giving him a pass." He sounded abrupt, unhinged. Probably because he felt fucking unhinged. His daughter was out there with Matthew, doing who the hell knows what.

"A pass from what?" she said, arms folded defensively over her chest.

"I just don't understand this, this, all this acting like Matthew's some kind of nice guy. Molly, he is *not* a nice guy. If you'd been in New York, if you'd seen the way he talked to me, if you— Look, you have to," Gil said, flustered with rage. "I'm just, I just want—" There had to be some way to make her understand, to see past the boy's deflections and seductions, but before he could finish, lights turned in to the drive, pulled up beside the Subaru, and clicked off.

Molly gave him a chastising look as the door flung open and Chloe staggered in, arm around Matthew's neck. Gil's head went light, his legs wobbled, and he clutched the side of the couch to keep from falling: Here it was, what he'd so long feared, what he'd tried to warn Molly of. Matthew had hurt her, his Chloe, and now he'd dragged her back to show off what he'd done.

"Chloe?" Molly said. The girl looked up at her with heavy-lidded eyes, mouth slack.

"I told her to stop," Matthew said, guiding Chloe into the kitchen where the girl slumped against the counter with a groan. "Jell-O shots," the boy added.

"Oh my god, Chloe, no," Molly said, brushing hair away from her daughter's red, puffy eyes.

"No," the girl moaned, swatting at her mother. "Bed. I just, I just need bed."

"She threw up at Lily's," Matthew said. "But not in the car, so I think she's okay." His voice was calm, parental: *These crazy kids, what can you do?* His hair and shoulders were dusted with snow, and he looked tidy and handsome, while Chloe, slumped on the counter, coat falling open, one pant leg bunched atop her boots, looked a wreck.

"Matthew, how did, you weren't, you, you didn't—" Gil stammered. "Were you drinking?"

The boy squinted at him, held up his keys and shook them. "Of course not. Designated driver. And, actually, Susie's in the car and I need to run her home. So, if you've got—" He gestured at Chloe whose head swung, mouth open like a drooling fool.

Before Gil could stop him, Matthew opened the door and stepped back out into the cold. Gil hurried to the window in time to watch him settle into the driver's side beside Susie, who burst into laughter at something he'd said as the interior went dark and the headlights flooded the house.

"Gil, a little help," Molly said.

They guided Chloe up the stairs, the girl, loose-legged, mumbling about how she was fine, god, stop it, she was fine, she was just so tired, didn't they know she was just so tired?

Molly got Chloe changed, forced her to drink some water, and did some mild scolding. Yes, they understood she was almost sixteen and there was going to be drinking at these parties, but hadn't they talked to her about hard alcohol? Yes, Chloe shouted, suddenly wide awake. She was *sorry*, okay? My god, couldn't they just know she was *sorry*? Tears sprang into her eyes, but Molly asked what would've happened if Matthew hadn't been there. Mom, *stop it,* she *knew,* she was *sorry.* Gil stood in the doorway, adding nothing, the oily residue of the fear he'd felt when they'd come in the door clinging to him. Chloe's slack face, Matthew hauling her in like a sack, then waltzing out again at midnight. Free as a fucking bird.

"Okay, well, for now, go to bed," Molly said, brushing hair from the girl's face.

"I'm sorry!" Chloe shouted, for the last time, hiding her head under the pillow.

In their bedroom, Molly said, "Well, at least she's okay. And thank god Matthew was there."

Gil let out a sharp bark of a laugh from the bathroom where he stood before the mirror: bags beneath his eyes, age spots along his thinning hairline, dark hairs in his nose that hung down and caught the glare of the bulb above.

Molly stood up and came to the door of the bathroom. "I'm serious, Gil. He got her home. He stayed sober. It could've been a lot worse."

"Well, sorry if I'm not thrilled Matthew brought our daughter home drunk," Gil said.

"From *her* party, Gil. They were at Lily's house. It's not Matthew's fault. You understand that, right?"

"Why are you defending him?" Gil said. "Our daughter gets drunk and Matthew's with her at the party and he hauls her in here, then takes off—" But he wasn't sure what came next.

"Chloe's the problem here, not Matthew. She's the one in trouble," Molly said.

"Of course, you're right, I know. I'm just," but there was, still, nowhere to go with this. "You're right. I was just, I don't know. I just don't trust him. I can't."

"That's clear," Molly said. "But when he does something good you can't flip it into something bad. That's just crazy."

"Fine," he said, hating how that word felt coming out of his mouth.

Molly looked like she wanted to say something else, something not about Matthew, but about Gil. How he was acting. He trembled in anticipation, sure that if she started down that road, he'd lose control. But maybe she saw that was true, and instead she said, "It's late. Everyone's tired. Let's just go to bed."

He brushed his teeth, avoiding his reflection, then lay beside her and pretended to read as she drifted off, calm, while down the hall their daughter lay in a drunken stupor. Just a normal night at the Duggan house. He should just adapt, as they all had, apparently, without complaint. He waited to hear the sound of Matthew's tires on the drive, see the wash of headlights against the trees of the yard, but sleep came before they did.

When Gil spoke with Chloe the next day, he couldn't keep his questions from drifting toward Matthew. He knew this was wrong. What Chloe had done was normal, sure, even to be expected—especially since she persisted in hanging out with goddamn Lily—but still, the focus should be on her, on her mistake, on making her understand how dangerous it had been, how careful she should be in the future. But he couldn't help himself. Had Matthew given her the Jell-O shots? he asked, interrupting her rambling account of the night. No, of course not, Dad. Was she sure Matthew hadn't been drinking? Not even one shot? No, no, he'd helped her, Chloe said. He was super nice and they were, like, friends.

Now that Matthew had given them some expensive gifts and then ferried their drunk daughter safely home, Molly had apparently put aside whatever anxieties she might have felt after the arrest of the Albanian driver. Nope, that didn't matter anymore.

She tried to explain her position to Gil one afternoon on a walk with Elroy on the town trails near their house. They'd talked of other things at first: what they might do for spring break, looking ahead to summer when, now that they'd cleared so much debt, they might take a long-hoped-for trip to Maine. But as they stepped out of the snow-draped trees into the wide clearing, Molly turned the subject to Chloe and how lucky they'd been. How lucky they were Matthew had been there.

Elroy sniffed out across the snow, pausing where bent grass formed mounds, then lifted his head, catching a scent. Gil watched Elroy's ears ripple in the wind, trying to bring himself to agree with Molly. Wasn't there a chance, no matter what Chloe said, that the boy had encouraged her to drink? That he'd manipulated her into bad choices? They were supposed to believe Chloe's first serious lapse just happened to coincide with Matthew's being there?

At least they agreed on the punishment: Chloe would be grounded for two weeks, other than play rehearsal, and that would bring her right up to her next debate tournament in March. All settled.

It began to seem that the only way to get through this would be to stay silent about the boy, which is what he tried to do—despite the ludicrous freedom afforded Matthew, who was out doing who knew what most of every day—until one night they sat down to dinner, and only then did Gil realize he hadn't seen Matthew since class. He asked Molly if she knew where he was.

"He texted this afternoon," Molly said, scooping gnocchi onto her plate from the steaming bowl they'd bought eighteen years ago in Italy, their last international trip, funded by a grant he'd gotten before his first book came out. There were several chips along the rim, and a fine, dark crack down its side. Maybe they could go back. Once Matthew was out of the house. For the first time in, well, ever, they might actually be able to afford it if he picked up a summer class. "He's spending the night at a friend's. In Burlington."

"Spending the night?" Gil said, thoughts of Europe shattered. "It's a Thursday."

She raised her eyebrows. "So?"

"I just don't think he should be staying out," he said, hearing how deeply stupid that must sound. But he felt betrayed. She was just going to let him run around Burlington, free to wreak havoc, all night, no supervision? While Chloe was there, grounded. And Matthew had been with her. Was only a couple of years older, was still, in a legal sense, a child. Was this what Sharon had had in mind when she listed them as guardians? "We don't let Chloe stay out on weeknights," he added.

"Actually, yes you do," Chloe said, lifting a piece of gnocchi to her mouth. "I stayed over at Sally's last month. Remember? When we were working on that project?"

"That was different," Gil said, having no memory of that. When had he and Molly agreed on this policy? "And that won't be happening again for a long time."

"I *know,* Dad," Chloe said, glaring at him, then quickly down at her plate.

"How was it different?" Molly said, smiling placidly, then turning away, apparently done with this conversation. She'd decided this was the best course: no need to consult the erratic husband.

"Molly, come on," he said.

"Come on, Gil. I think it's best for everyone if Matthew has a little space."

Reasonable. Even to him, it sounded like maybe this was the right course. But it *felt* wrong. Matthew was free to do whatever he wanted and Sharon was dead. Sharon had been killed by an Albanian driver. What seemed so obvious to him was worryingly opaque to everyone else. Even the police, who he supposed now would never call. So it was left to Gil, and yet here he sat, doing nothing. Fretting. As he'd done far too often for most of his life.

After dinner, while he was loading the dishwasher, she refilled his wineglass. A consolation? Ignoring his madness?

"So," he said, scrubbing at a clotted pot, "do you know who he's staying with?" He tried to sound casual, failed.

"He said it was a friend from Essex. From your class, actually."

"Who? Did he say?" There was only one possibility.

"He didn't, sorry," she said. "Do you know?"

"Nope," he said.

"Do you have a problem with it?" she said. "I thought you'd be relieved. A break."

"I don't have a problem, it's just—" he started, but he couldn't explain.

"Well?" she said.

"Nothing. It's fine, just forget it."

"Gil, just try to enjoy it, okay? A break. It's pretty clear you need one."

"Right, whatever," he said.

Molly's plan, clearly, was to get the boy out of the house, carve out as much space as she could until he left for college. Keep him away from Gil. Erratic Gil. In which case the "break" was for Matthew. Their generous benefactor. Bringer of gifts and art and cash. Fuck. This was a mess. Now he'd have to go this alone. Not that he hadn't been doing exactly that so far. But then it was his problem. His family. His nephew. His responsibility to protect Molly and the girls.

By the time he finished the dishes, the girls were in their rooms and Molly was upstairs. If he went up there, he'd have to either pretend he agreed with her approach, or tell her the truth. About the encounter on the street. And about Susie. Somehow make her see what seemed so clear to him but she couldn't see. Or *wouldn't* see. Because she didn't want to. Willful blindness. Must be nice. But that wasn't available to him anymore. He couldn't close his eyes now, not when he'd seen the truth in Matthew's face in the blue haze of the deli. That snarl, the threat pulsing off him. The truth of his nature. That had been the boy's one slip: showing Gil the truth. He was evil. Gil knew this. In a way, he'd always known it, and nothing the boy had ever done had shaken his certainty: No amount of money, no lavish gifts of art, no helping out with homework, nothing could change the boy's true nature. And now Matthew simply did whatever he wanted, and he got away with everything. Soon he'd grow bored with this freedom, would push out, find new entertainments. Bringing Chloe home like that, drunk and staggering, had been a warning. A caution. And no one could see it for what it was except Gil, because only Gil had seen the boy's face in New York, had seen his mask slip. Matthew would not be content to tease for long. Soon he'd hurt someone. Like he had in Montauk. And that person, Gil realized now, would not be Chloe. No, first Matthew would hurt Susie. She was vulnerable, alone, a young woman from a poor country family. In danger. Right now. And Gil had, in a way, put her at risk. This was his responsibility now.

"You want to go on a ride, Elroy?" he said, turning to the dog, who was flopped on the floor eating with his face tipped lazily into the bowl. His ears perked up, but he continued rooting, as if he didn't believe it. Not until Gil took the leash from a hook near the door did the dog hop up, scrambling across the kitchen, wiggling with surprise. He pulled on his boots, jacket, and scarf, couldn't find his hat, and grabbed his keys.

From the car he texted Molly.

Need some stuff at store. Taking Elroy on errands.

He wasn't sure she'd believe it. Not many stores were open at this time of night, but there was the Walmart in Williston. He hadn't thought this through. Another mistake. But too late. He couldn't turn back now.

He went quickly down the drive, made a right onto the empty, snow-slicked road. Glancing down at his phone he saw a text from Molly.

What?

Flipping his phone over so he couldn't see the screen, he drove on, Elroy panting and prancing across the back, shoving his head up beside Gil's face to stare out at the headlights cutting through the thin snow falling through the trees that bent their dark shapes overhead, making a tunnel of the road.

On North Winooski Avenue he pulled over and picked up his phone. Two texts from Molly:

Where are you going?

If you go to the store, pick up milk.

There was no note he could send to explain, so he wrote only "OK." He put the car in Drive and rolled up the street, turned right, and parked at the corner. He'd passed the house where he'd dropped Susie after that New York trip. He looked up her address through the Essex Portal. Apartment H.

"Want to take a walk, buddy?" So that's why he'd brought the dog. Cover. Pretense. Flimsy as it might be. *Just out for a stroll with my dog in subzero temperatures, seventeen miles from home.*

Pulling his hood up against the freezing air that swept around them, riffling the dog's fur, he went up the sidewalk, letting Elroy sniff at everything, trying to come up with a plan. Sneak around their neighborhood? Why would they be out walking in this cold? But they were young. Young and stupid. A lovers' stroll, heedless of banalities like weather, carried away on their affection. Love. Lust. Susie might imagine she was in love. Not Matthew, though. For Matthew love would only be a pose, a means to manipulation. A way in, so that he could hurt someone.

Susie lived in one of the wooden houses downtown that had swollen with slipshod additions over the years. The house seemed to sag and bloat, as if all the cheap beer spilled over the decades had leached into the frame and foundation. Lights were on in most of the windows and in one a woman sat, blowing smoke out through a screen.

They might not be here, might be in some coffee shop downtown, or at a party. Or at the library. But no, he was just trying to give himself an excuse to be a coward. They were spending the night together. They were here.

Elroy sniffed the sidewalk and looked up at Gil.

"Come on, buddy," he said, and walked up the shoveled path to the front steps. Beside the front door was a line of buzzers, A through F. Which meant H must be around back. In the driveway, Matthew's Audi gleamed amid an array of battered, salt-streaked compacts.

The ground floor at the back was G. Which meant H must be up a rickety set of wooden stairs tacked to the side of the house. Stepping back, he could see the door.

"Shhh," he said to Elroy, who eyed him warily, not sure what he'd done wrong. "Keep quiet, okay, buddy?" Gil said. He'd have to take the dog with him. If he tied him up down here Elroy might bark.

The handrail wobbled when he grabbed it and the steps sagged with rot beneath his boots. Snow and ice clung to a few steps, making them slick and treacherous. Elroy picked his way uncertainly, pressing against Gil's legs. Near the top he stopped, listened, heard nothing, then went up the last four steps. On either side of the smudged door were narrow windows, only partially covered with flimsy white curtains so that, stooping, he could see inside: a pale yellow wall and the edge of cheap fiberboard kitchen cabinets with chipped corners. One cabinet was open, the shelves nearly empty: a jar of peanut butter, a box of pasta with open flaps, a salt shaker. Damp curls of mold-spotted wallpaper peeled off the back.

"Shut up!" a voice shouted from inside. Susie's voice, high and flirtatious and stupid-sounding. "No you didn't!"

He edged over to the other window. From there he could see into the living room. Susie lay atop Matthew on the couch. She wore a tank top and boxer shorts. Matthew was in a T-shirt, and Gil couldn't see his legs, covered as they were by a mix of Susie's own and a blanket. They were talking, but Gil couldn't hear the words, so he pulled down his hood and pressed to the wall.

"Seriously," Susie said. "Don't be a dumbass, Matt."

She sat up and with a quick motion pulled off her tank top and sat above him, breasts small and high, nipples nearly as pale as her skin, her stomach with a firm line of muscle down the center as she pressed her hands into Matthew's hips. The boy admired her for a couple of seconds, then squirmed out of his own shirt: a ribbed row of muscles, hard, flat pecs.

Just as Susie bent to kiss Matthew, pressing her breasts down so they swelled against his skin, Elroy barked. First a single, sharp report, then again, then a flurry.

Down in the parking lot a young woman getting into her car looked up. Gil saw only the movement inside, not its details, but knew what it meant. Grabbing the loose railing, he started down. Elroy lunged ahead, so he dropped the leash. With a final bound the dog skidded on the snow and stood at the bottom, barking at the woman who was now closed up in her car.

Gil didn't know if anyone was following, couldn't check, could only scramble wildly down. But he looked at the girl in the car and so missed a step. As he fell the railing swung away from him, as if it might break, and his elbow extended with a bright flare of pain, and then his back hit the steps, a flashing white heat. Somehow he was immediately back on his feet, blowing pain through his teeth. He whistled for Elroy, but the fucking dog just wagged his tail as Gil lurched past the woman in the car who stared at him, her phone up in front of her face, possibly calling the cops.

Out on the sidewalk he turned and whistled through a dizzying swell of pain. Elroy came bounding down the drive, tail wagging, tongue lolling from a grin.

He couldn't see the back stairs as he hobbled away. They'd been half-naked. It'd take time to disentangle and put clothes on.

Pulling up his hood he limped down Converse toward the dead end—he could cut through a driveway and onto the far sidewalk. Halfway across the yard, he looked back. A woman was there, pointing, shouting, the words indistinct, carried away on the wind.

Tugging Elroy's leash, Gil ran behind the house and thank fucking god his car was there at the corner. He urged the dog through the driver's side door and climbed in after, pain spiking when he sat, and after gasping for a few seconds he started the car. Only as he waited for a light to turn right onto River Road did he take a deep breath, heart pounding, head light. They hadn't seen him. There was no way they'd seen him. And the girl in the car couldn't have seen much. It was dark. The stairs had been dark, without any safety lights. He'd been running.

"Bad dog," he said as they rushed alongside the river, his back, elbow, ass, all throbbing. "No barking, Elroy. No, no. Bad boy."

The dog cocked his head at this incongruous scold, decided to ignore it, and turned his panting face to the glass, fogging it over entirely.

23

BY THE TIME HE WENT UP TO BED THE PAIN HAD DEEPENED TO A
wild heartbeat in his back. His elbow was stiff and at some point
he must've injured his knee: It slipped as he climbed the stairs
and he caught himself on the railing with a groan. When he lay
down he ground his teeth to contain a squeal, and when Molly
leaned over to kiss him he pretended it wasn't excruciating to have
her weight on his shoulder.

"You got milk?" she said, settling back on her pillow.

"Of course," he lied, somehow without moaning.

"Great. Thanks," she said, and lifted her book to let him know
the conversation was over. Thank god.

He tossed the blanket aside in the morning and a whip of fire
went up his back. He froze, awaiting another lash.

Molly was in the shower and he limped into the bathroom. Her
shape moved beyond the fogged glass, her head tipped back, a soft
lilt of some hummed song. He shook out Advil and dry-swallowed
three, gagged, sending a tornado of pain up his back, then shuffled
downstairs, made coffee and toast, which he ate hurriedly standing

at the counter. By the time the ladies emerged from their rooms and showers, the pills had blunted the sharpest edges of pain and he offered them coffee and breakfast as if nothing was wrong. As if he hadn't nearly broken his neck falling down the stairs after watching one of his students strip naked atop his nephew. What the fuck had he planned to do? Knock? Tell Matthew to come home now, young man? Yes, that was pretty much it, no matter how ridiculous.

When Molly refilled her coffee she frowned into the fridge but didn't mention the milk. Which was a bad sign. As if his lying was no surprise.

That morning he felt his debasement powerfully. This must be what the devout felt when faced with their sins. A swollen wave of self-loathing, fear at the coming retribution, a desperate desire to do better, but with no idea where the path to redemption lay. Except, actually, he could see two paths. The first, the one Molly had, by all evidence, chosen, was to ignore the suggestions that the boy had been involved in the death of his parents. Drop it. Forget it. Move on. The other path, the one Gil wanted to follow, was the path to the truth. Unless it wasn't. Unless he was as nuts as his throbbing back suggested.

He went to campus early, afraid of giving away his injuries if he stayed in the house, and convalesced uncomfortably in his office. Four hours after he'd taken the first pills the pain overcame him and he took two more. Possibly he'd broken his tailbone, though the stabbing ache radiated all over his lower back and butt, not in one spot, as a Google search suggested would be the case. Keeping the office door closed, he graded two papers, looked despairingly at the remaining stack. Maybe he was unfit for this job. Too late now, though. He was in his midforties. Okay, late forties. There was no other life but this one. Just this cluttered desk, this dark, cramped office with its cinder block walls and its narrow glimpse of an ever gray winter sky, this low pay. He'd felt this job was a way station, a holding pattern while he got on with his real life. Which

was his writing. Which now had fallen entirely away, lost somewhere back on the path, and the way station had become his home.
He hadn't noticed, hadn't known to object. Lulled by happiness.
The clichéd enemy of the writer. But maybe it was true. Maybe
he'd have been better off miserable. Though as far as that went, he
felt pretty fucking miserable right now, and still no writing.

As if to drive the humiliation deeper, he took out his notebook
and flipped through the pages. Notes on Matthew. That's all he'd
written in the past few months. Scattered paranoid jottings. A record of his shame. But no reason to stop now. He turned to a fresh
page and wrote at the top "Idea for a story," and below that "an
account of last night, an old man huddled at the window, peering
in at the young lovers."

A knock came at the door and he fumbled the notebook under
a pile of quizzes and called, "It's open." Susie came in, shoulders
sagging, as if the burden of her backpack was too much. Her coat
hung limp over one arm, dragging on the floor. "Hi, Professor,
can I talk to you?"

"Susie, of course, come in," he said, standing up quickly, pain
flaring in his back at the ill-advised movement. Gritting his teeth,
he eased himself down into the seat, let the pain ebb, and said, "So,
what's up? Did we have an appointment?"

Fear flared in his gut. She'd seen him. That's what she was here
to tell him. She'd seen him peeping in the window, and she'd already told the dean. An email from the university would be coming, putting him on leave. He was a creep, a criminal.

"No," she said, tugging at the cuffs of her sweatshirt. Dark bags
ringed her eyes, her skin was splotchy, her hair greasy. It was, at
that moment, hard to believe this was the same person he'd seen
through the glass last night. As if Matthew had drained her. A
vampire. Which was how Gil felt, too: wizened, life seeping out,
stolen by the boy. "I just thought I'd drop by."

"Of course, great. How are you doing?" It was hard to look at
her, as if by not doing so he could avoid knowing whether she'd

seen him. Whether he'd been caught. Whether his life, at least as he understood it, was now over. "Is everything okay?"

"What?" She glanced up, cringing, as if he'd said something uncouth.

"I just, I know it's a busy time of the semester," he said. He'd gone too far. Showed he cared. A dangerous no-man's-land for professors now, full of explosive misunderstandings. Especially professors who spied on their fornicating students.

"I don't know," she said, taking a deep breath. "Yeah, busy, I guess."

"I'm sure," he said. She was enrolled in eighteen credits. He'd warned her against it at their last advising meeting, but she'd insisted it wouldn't be a problem. But the problem wasn't her classes. He knew that. It was Matthew.

"I actually wanted to talk to you about changing my major," she said in a rush, as if otherwise she might not get it out.

"Your major?"

"To accounting."

"From creative writing?" he said, trying not to sound hurt.

"Yeah. I mean, at this point I'm going to do the minor, since I have so many credits. But I'm a junior and I thought I better do it quick. I've taken some accounting classes already, in my freshman year. I think I can manage it." All this was said as she stared into her lap, her voice wobbly and uncertain.

"But why?" he said.

She glanced up, as if she'd been waiting for this opening. His whine. His weakness.

"I need to get a *job*," she said. "My parents aren't rich, and this is basically killing them, sending me here. They never wanted me to major in creative writing, but you talked me into it and I've been thinking about it a lot and I need to get a job."

"Maybe I'm biased," he said, forcing himself to stay calm—she was just a student, his favorite student, but merely one of hundreds, of thousands—"but there are plenty of things you can do with a creative writing major." As he said it he could think of only one or two such things. The English department had a flyer, *What You Can Do with an English Major,* for advising sessions, but he'd never read it.

"Yeah, well, I can't afford to do a publishing internship in New York. I don't have the money to stay in the city and not get paid, and otherwise I don't see what I'll do," Susie said, sneering. At his stupidity. Or maybe it was a trick of shadows, the room dark but for the lamp's white puddle on the desk. The sky had gone black in the window. This lighting was all wrong: too intimate, the two of them huddled over the desk. Though actually Susie leaned away from him, as if she didn't want to be there. The overhead fluorescents, with their flattening, industrial glow, should be on, but to do that he'd have to get up and go past her to flip the switch on the wall, and if he stood she might take that chance to leave.

"What about graduate school?" he said, which felt like offering her a rotten banana when she'd complained of starving.

This got no response, so he said, "Are you sure about this?"

Still she didn't answer and he sat forward, spoke quickly so she wouldn't cut him off.

"Is everything okay, Susie? Because you don't seem like yourself. Is everything okay? With Matthew?"

"Matthew?" she said, as if he had no business knowing about that. As if he hadn't seen her standing in his dead sister's kitchen in nothing but the boy's shirt. Seen her peel off her shirt while straddling— No. Focus.

"You guys are dating, I assume, or, well, whatever." He tried to smile, felt it come out awkward, unconvincing, and she leaned back, disgusted. "I just hope you're okay."

"Like what would be wrong?" she said, futzing with the zipper of her sweatshirt, jerking it up and down. "You think he might try to drown me or something?"

He sat back quickly, as if she'd tried to slap him.

"No, I, why would—" But now she did cut him off.

"Matthew's fine. I'm just here about my major." As she said this, staring past him, she jerked the zipper down so her sweatshirt sagged open. Beneath, she wore a loose, wide-necked T-shirt, and along her collarbone spread a red mark. A love bite. Or maybe the start of a bruise. A mark left by Matthew's hand as it closed around her throat and tightened. She must've realized he could see and, with fumbling hands, zipped her sweatshirt shut.

"Are you sure you're okay?" he said.

"Yeah, actually, I am. I already talked to the chair of the accounting department and he's signed all the forms. I don't actually need anything from you. I just kind of wanted to let you know." Her voice had gone cold, angry, almost, he felt sure, accusatory.

"Oh, well, we'll miss having you in workshop," he said, as if she was leaving that minute, never to return. He needed to stop her. To stop Matthew from hurting her more than he already had. But she was standing, pushing the chair in close to the desk.

"Yeah, well, bye," she said.

This was Matthew's doing: ruining Susie's life. His wealth, his privilege, his ability to do whatever he wanted without thinking—this had infected her, turned her mind from art, literature, a life that would bring her happiness. A hard life in some ways, but worthwhile. And now she was gone. He shouldn't care so much. But, that mark. Matthew had done that to her. Not long after Gil had seen them through the window. Matthew's hands closing around her neck, her mouth opening in a scream, the boy clamping his other hand down over it, pressing his face close to her ear, asking, *Does it hurt?* Does *this* hurt, because he could make it hurt so, so much more. Would she like that? Why don't they try it?

The boy could abuse, terrorize, do whatever the hell he wanted, all because he was rich. Anything you want, Mr. Westfallen. We'll mop up the blood, cart away and burn the bodies, all with a smile in the hope that you might favor us with an approving nod. Well, fuck that. Gil didn't need to just sit by.

24

GIL PICKED CHLOE UP FROM PLAY REHEARSAL ON THE WAY HOME from campus. She was sullen, her new mode since the night of the Jell-O shots. Teenagers went through these darker periods—god knows he had—but he couldn't separate her new funk from Matthew. The boy had done this to her, had poured poison in her ear about her stupid parents, their stupid restrictions, what a bunch of crap, she didn't have to listen to them. Why not just be more like Matthew? Look at him: free to do whatever he wanted.

"Your debate tournament's soon, right?" Gil said, trying to be a good father.

"I guess so," Chloe said, turning her face more fully away from him.

"Is this nationals? Or regionals?"

"Regionals," Chloe said. "Or, I mean, whatever."

"Whatever? Cut it out, Chloe."

"What, Dad?" she said, turning to him, her face flushed and angry. "Cut what out?"

"This mopey crap," Gil said. This had gone all wrong.

"This *crap*, Dad? That's nice. That's really nice." Chloe flung him a look of disgust and turned back to the window.

"I had no idea you're so sensitive," Gil said, trying to make a joke out of it, but Chloe curled farther away from him. "After hanging out with Matthew, I'd think you'd be used to that kind of talk."

"Matthew? What does Matthew have to do with it? Matthew's been *nice* to me, Dad. Don't you get it?"

"Get what?"

Chloe turned back to Gil, her face hard and angry in a way he wasn't sure he'd ever seen before. "He's not like you said, not at all. I mean, all those years you acted like he's this monster, or whatever, and it turns out he's *not*. He's nice, Dad. He's actually really nice."

Gil snorted and said, "Right. That sounds like Matthew."

"Jesus, Dad, what's your problem? Why do you hate him so much?"

A flash of anger tore through him and he gripped the steering wheel, focused on the road as it climbed the hill, past the auto body shop, around the next curve. "I'm pretty sure I don't have a problem, Chloe." Then he added, through his teeth, "And I don't hate him."

"Okay," she said, but now her voice had softened, surely knowing she'd gone too far. "I'm just saying, like, you should give him a chance. That's all I'm saying."

"Great, well, thanks for the advice," Gil said, then reached for the radio, turning on NPR to cut this off now, pain shooting up his back with the sudden movement so that he had to clutch the steering wheel and hold his breath so as not to moan.

That evening, Molly asked what was wrong when he sat on a stool with a wince and he used the lie he'd prepared: He'd nearly fallen off the treadmill at the gym. Lucky not to have split his head open.

"Might be time to switch over to the elliptical," she said. "You can join the rest of us middle-aged fogeys. It's not so bad, as long as you put aside your self-respect."

"Well, in that case it'll be a snap," he said. At least now he could grimace openly.

"So are you okay if Ingrid and I go to my parents'? We're supposed to leave on Thursday, but we could go Friday."

"No, that's fine," he said. He'd completely forgotten this plan, which now, after New York, after the fall down the stairs, seemed a huge and obvious mistake. How, with the old man alone, could Matthew not take his chance to rid himself of this bothersome tail? "And Matthew will be here, of course."

"Right," she said. "If you're sure you're okay."

"I'm sure, Molly." He knew it sounded snappish, but the pain flared up his back and he couldn't, in the moment, bring himself to apologize. Catching sight of Molly's worried frown made the anger flare again, so he went to let Elroy out.

In the living room Chloe and Ingrid were doing homework, and Matthew was apparently upstairs, since his car was in the drive. Gil stood outside in the cold while the dog picked across the packed ice—it had melted last week, then refroze into a slick sheet—and tried to push away the anger. Unreasonable. Especially that he was angry with Molly. That was just a proxy, a misdirection. From the real target. And himself.

Molly called him in to dinner and then called up to Matthew. A few minutes later, after they were all already at the table, the boy bounded down, leaping the last few steps, landing with a thud that made the house shudder.

The boy thrust his plate out for Molly to lift chicken onto and pulled it back without a thank-you, then he reached across the table, nearly bumping Chloe's nose, for the salt. Throughout the meal the boy's anger mounted, covering his end of the table with a dark, forbidding cloud. Ingrid leaned away, and when she got up for more water she scooted closer to her mother. The boy wore only a tight white T-shirt, and the wiry muscles of his arms flexed and jumped while he sliced and stabbed up his food. Over the boy's shoulder, at least from Gil's angle, was the Kiki Smith, and though he knew Molly had chosen the spot—not too close to the fireplace, not where it would get direct sun from the bay window—it felt like a rebuke: *Don't criticize the bringer of gifts. Matthew may be a petulant jerk at the moment, but look what he provides.*

They were nearly done before Matthew deigned to speak.

"So, this was pretty crazy," he said, cutting off Ingrid who'd been telling them about the bad kid, Mark, who'd gotten suspended. She flinched and looked down at the table, obviously afraid. Wise girl.

"What's that?" Molly said, a scold in her tone, but the boy ignored it.

"Someone tried to break into my friend's apartment last night."

"What?" Chloe said, perking up for the first time. "Seriously?"

"Seriously," Matthew said. "Some guy. And his dog." As he said this he stared at Gil, a smile leaking through his glower.

"His dog?" Chloe said.

"What time was it?" Molly said. "Were you asleep?"

"Oh, no," Matthew said, his eyes flashing. As if he was high. Maybe on speed, or coke. "It wasn't late. I mean, it was dark, or whatever, but we were sitting in the living room and then we heard this rattling at the doorknob, then a dog barking. But by the time we got out there he was gone."

"That's scary," Molly said, shaking her head. "This was in Burlington?"

" 'Downtown,' " Matthew said, using air quotes, since it was a city only in some farcical way.

"Maybe it was one of those homeless guys who hang out down there," Chloe said.

"Maybe," Matthew said. "Some of those guys have dogs. Anyway, a neighbor got a photo."

"Of the guy?" Molly said.

"It's pretty blurry, but, well, here, you can see it." He tugged his phone from his pocket and unlocked the screen with a flicker of fingers, held it up.

All Gil could see was a man's shape, a black coat with a fringe of fur. His coat. Him. Shoulders hunched, hobbling down the driveway. He took a slow breath in through his mouth, but the air didn't reach his lungs and his heart pounded, head light, as if someone was holding him under water.

Matthew was talking, but a ringing swelled in Gil's ears and he missed it.

Molly said, "Can I see?"

The boy passed the phone to Ingrid, who looked, shook her head, and handed it to her mother. Gil leaned forward, but spots flared in front of his eyes and he sank back, raked in another useless mouthful of air.

"Did you send this to the police?" Molly said. She hadn't recognized him. He could see that much. There was no shock. No horror. "I mean, it's not very clear. But maybe he's been doing this around the neighborhood."

"No," Matthew said. "We didn't want to have to deal with the cops."

"Did you get a picture of the dog?" Ingrid said.

"Nope, unfortunately there're no photos of the puppy," Matthew said, snide and condescending. Ingrid looked down at her plate.

"Here," Molly said, bumping Gil's arm. She was trying to hand him the phone. The screen had already gone half dark and he took it with a shaking hand, but Molly didn't notice.

No one would look at this picture and know it was Gil. That was his coat, but plenty of people had parkas with fur around the hood. The side of his face was blurred. But you could see the beard. More than half the men in Vermont had beards, especially in winter. There was nothing clear here, nothing to implicate.

"What kind of dog was it? Did anyone see?" Chloe asked. *Stop it,* Gil wanted to say. *Stop asking questions, right now.*

That girl in the driveway, holding up her phone, not to call the police but to snap a picture. Thank god he hadn't known. He might've stopped, tried to do something. But what could he have done? Grabbed her phone?

"She said some kind of mutt. Like, I don't know, like Elroy's size." The dog, who'd been sprawled beside Matthew's chair, hopped up, hoping this mention might result in some chicken. When it was clear no treat was coming he flopped his head down with a sigh.

"Let me see, Dad," Chloe said and he slid the phone along the table toward her.

As she studied it, he watched for a flicker of recognition. Would she say it? *That looks like Dad!* Not that she'd think it was him, but, no, she wouldn't compare her father to a vagrant caught breaking and entering.

"Your friend should be careful," Molly said.

"Oh, don't worry. I got her some pepper spray. Told her next time she should open the door and blind the crazy fucker," Matthew said, as if this was normal dinner conversation.

"Well, I hope she calls the police if there's a next time," Molly said, clearly surprised by the news she'd just gotten. She. A girl. Matthew had spent the night at a girl's apartment in Burlington.

"I told her she should get a gun," Matthew went on, caught up in a feverish tone, nearly a rant. "Shoot the crazy fucker."

"Well, that's not very good advice," Molly said. "But I'm just glad you're okay."

"The guy fell down the stairs. That's what the girl who took the photo said. So let me know if you see any hobos with a limp."

No one laughed at this joke, if that's what it was, and an awkward silence fell over the table, all of them trying to piece it all together: spending the night at a girl's apartment. An attempted break-in. A limping hobo.

Gil realized he hadn't spoken during the entire conversation. He'd meant to say what Molly had: scary, be careful, call the police. All that. No wonder she was giving him that frown again.

"They've had some problems on campus, too," Gil said. "Over the past couple months. Guys sleeping on the heating vents near the library. That kind of thing."

Matthew let out a loud laugh, totally out of proportion to the conversation. "How'd they even know?"

"What?" Gil said.

"How'd they know they were homeless? I mean, the way those Essex kids dress, it must've been hard to tell."

"Right," Gil said, as if he agreed. Here he was, the real Matthew. Showing himself at last to Gil's family. Not that they wanted to see it.

25

MOLLY DIDN'T SAY ANYTHING ABOUT THE INCIDENT ONCE THEY were in bed, which was worrying. Normally, they'd have whispered about all the attendant dangers and possibilities and they'd have worked out how to address them. In bed was where they did most of their serious parenting, managed whatever mini-crisis had reared its head. But now there was only a curt "Good night," followed by the click of her lamp. When he said "Love you," she whispered, "You too."

Possibly she was feeling the stress of having Matthew in their lives as much as he was. Without freaking out. That was his specialty. When a hooligan boy in pre-K had punched Chloe in the eye, Gil had stomped around their Brooklyn apartment saying he'd like to get his hands on that brat's father, that smug faded rock star jackass who probably taught his kid to assault nice girls. Molly had stayed calm and guided them through the meetings with the teacher and principal, even the one attended by that leather-jacket-wearing father, with his absurdly dense English accent. Gil had seethed in the man's pompous presence, but Molly directed the conversation so that the blustering fool revealed himself to be just that, and after he'd stormed out the teacher and principal assured her they'd keep Chloe safe. And when Matthew had thrown Ingrid into the pool, Molly had stayed calm while Gil had been consumed by nightmares of what might have been if he hadn't woken up with the splash, if he'd found her floating facedown, hair fanned about her head, drifting between sun and shade.

Or, worst case, she'd recognized him in that picture and now lay tense and afraid beside her maniac husband. Thankfully, Matthew hadn't mentioned, as far as Gil could remember, the time of the attempted break-in. Anyone would assume late, at least midnight, not right after dinner, when he'd been out doing errands with Elroy. Or had Matthew said something? Fuck. Maybe he had. Maybe he'd said seven thirty, eight. His wife might be deciding that he, Gil, was the psycho.

He tried to stay out of the house that weekend, to avoid Matthew, and to avoid, now, his wife. He took Elroy on a walk on the nature trails behind the elementary school a few towns over, and Ingrid joined him. The pain in his back persisted and he went slow, accepted it as a kind of penance. The path went out of the woods into open prairies flattened by snow, sloped down along the banks of the frozen Brown River, then back up the ridge, where they stopped and ate the sandwiches he'd picked up in Essex Junction. Gil eased himself onto a mossy rock, and as the pain subsided to a low growl he asked Ingrid what she was reading. She gave an extended analysis of the connections between *The Lord of the Rings* and *Harry Potter*.

Biting into his Italian sub, pain spasming up his back, he was rocked by a wave of sadness. How many more times would he get to do this? To sit with his daughter in the woods and listen to her excited sentences? Chloe wasn't here, nor was Molly. Just Ingrid, his baby. In seven years she'd be off to college, leaving him behind. Just as she should. He wanted her to go. But her going would be the end of him, or at least this version of him, the father taking his kid on a hike in the woods. Then she'd graduate and move away, just as he'd moved away from his parents, and he'd hear from her as often as his mother had heard from him.

Molly and Ingrid left Thursday morning for Maryland. Gil helped them load the back of the car. Elroy, who followed them in and out to the car, sniffing his bag of food and toys thoroughly as Gil placed it in the trunk, was going with them. Molly's parents had two shepherd dogs Elroy adored. Ingrid explained that a farm down the road from her grandparents had a new horse she might be able to ride.

"Call when you get there," he said, hugging Molly, the pain flaring in his back. "And tell your parents hi."

"Be good," she said, squeezing his arm. "And try to get some writing done. Try not to worry about Matthew, okay?"

"Yes, ma'am," he said. "I'll try."

She kissed him on the mouth and gave him a worried look. He thought she might say they should stay, it was fine, maybe they could all go in the summer. But, resigned, perhaps, she slid behind the wheel.

He watched them pull out, waving until they were out of the drive, then went inside. Chloe was already at the high school, waiting for the bus that would take them down to Sarah Lawrence for the debate tournament. A weekend alone. Molly was right. He should try to write. Maybe, with all this time away from the draft, his novel would look different. Salvageable, even. Over the past two months, with Matthew here, he'd let himself get entirely off track, but he could correct that. Not today, though, since he had class this afternoon. Matthew's workshop, no less. Gil was ready. This was the last story of Matthew's he'd ever have to read. Soon the semester would be over. Summer would arrive. The boy would

226 | NATHAN OATES

go off to college. They'd be free. Until then he just had to stay calm, focused, stop stalking the boy, accept that his nephew was a monster but not entangle himself further.

The classroom was dark when he arrived and the gathered students groaned with disappointment when he flipped the switches and filled the room with a wash of bluish light. Matthew and Susie weren't there. This was the first time he'd arrived before them. The room was hot and dry. The windows creaked, buffeted by gusts of snow and ice. Some of the kids wore T-shirts, others were bundled in their coats, as if the room contained several climates at once.

At two minutes after, Matthew and Susie were still missing. Maybe they wouldn't show. Maybe they were with the dean, informing the administration that a faculty member had watched them do some wholesome, college-appropriate fucking, and in fact that pervert was upstairs right now, about to teach a class. As he took roll, they came in and slouched across the room to their seats.

Again, Matthew's story was up second, so they had to first slog through a discussion of Ned's piece. To call it a story would defame the genre. Per the young man's own admission, he'd written a derivative recounting of a first-person shooter videogame. Gil talked about the importance of choosing the proper medium for the narrative: the difference between, say, a poem and a story. Or a story and a movie. Or a movie and a TV show. Or a story and a videogame. He was speaking too quickly, but Ned didn't appear to notice. The boy twitched and flinched in his seat, grinning each time he heard the word "videogame," the rest apparently washing over him, nothing but noise.

Susie said nothing throughout the discussion, just stared down at the table. She wore a large black hoodie and kept her hands inside the cuffs, only the tips of her flaking green nails visible. Beside her, Matthew, also all in black—cashmere sweater, black jeans—

was quiet, eyes darting to each person who spoke and fixing steadily until the conversation shifted elsewhere.

At the end, Ned spoke at length about the videogame, getting into an excessively detailed plot summary, and when Gil said that might be more information than they needed, the boy groaned and flopped back in his seat, said, "I just wish you could all see it, you know? It's so awesome. I could probably bring my Xbox and hook it up to that projector."

"Yeah, maybe," Gil said. "If things slow down at the end of the semester." That was never going to happen, but he doubted Ned would remember by the time he left the room.

"All right, next up we have Matthew's story," Gil said. The pain in his back throbbed as he tightened, and he had to blink away spots of light.

Without a word Matthew waved his stack of printouts over his head, as if surrendering, split the pile in two, and handed them around.

"So, should I start?" the boy said as Gil blinked down at the page, trying to focus. He heard a rustle of papers, a clearing of the boy's throat, and then he began to read.

A Favor for a Friend

My mother probably would've thought this part of the Bronx was just like Albania. Mostly because the only people around were swarthy men, smoking between the trucks parked along the street. Also because of the way the sun slammed back off the pale concrete, glinting on the fading loops of graffiti. Chain-link fences topped with unspooling razor wire closed off empty lots, somehow suggesting a post-Communist state, with its squat blocky buildings, its failing infrastructure. Fluttering plastic bags caught in the weeds. The asphalt glittered with green and brown shards. A blue van was parked in the lot with its back window broken out, the wheels flat. There was a faint reek of shit, probably coming from the waste-processing plant down the block. All this was only a few miles from our pristine home. Our double classic eight. Our Russian doormen in their black suits. Our mirrored elevator. Those mirrors, which were somehow never smudged. A few miles away, but a different world, a place my mother would never, willingly, visit.

Thomas had told me to meet him there at noon. Now it was almost twelve thirty, so I was starting to think maybe he'd back out. Not that he even knew, yet, why we were meeting. Only that I'd said I had a job for him, a job that would pay very well. Thomas had been the one to get in touch with me, in fact, which was what set this in motion. A barely coherent email in his broken English letting me know he was in America, visiting his cousin, but if I had work for him, or if I knew people who had work, he was available. He could do lots of jobs.

Back in Tirana, where we'd met, he'd been a driver, or at least that's how I'd known him. He'd been hired by Herbert to give us kids rides into the city when needed. A driver, but also a kind of bodyguard, since we were foreign teenagers who didn't speak a word of Albanian. The Muscle, we called him.

Bulbs of light swelled and burst before Gil's eyes and he pressed two fingers to his sternum to feel the erratic clatter of his heart. This was it. Right here. The truth. The truth that Gil had known, making itself visible at last. And Matthew had turned it in for class. Gil closed his eyes and colors exploded across the back of his eyelids. He put a hand flat on the table, hoped he wouldn't topple, and tried to listen.

Two men, their eyes hooded by crazily thick eyebrows, stared at me from across the lot as they smoked. Better not to wait around as they simmered to a boil, so I walked over and said, "Excuse me, guys, I'm looking for Thomas?"

"What you say?" one of them said, dropping his cigarette and grinding it apart beneath his battered boot. The man's clothes were baggy and vaguely military. Near the shoulder of his jacket was a patch of glue, as if a label, or some mark of rank, had been ripped away, or which he'd pulled off before boarding a container ship in the Adriatic and creeping across the ocean to the waters off America, before somehow slipping away and into the country, hiding out with cousins in Queens.

"Do you know Thomas? He's a friend of mine."

"Thomas?" the man said, shaking his head as if that was the most disgusting thing he'd ever heard. His large nose sprouted long dark hairs and as I watched he rubbed them with the back of his hand.

"Short, glasses," I said, holding my hand at about chin-level. "Thomas."

"Thomas, Thomas," the second man said, in a singsong. This one was chubbier, with a round, puffy red face that was, apparently, always smiling, the better to show off his line of crooked, yellowed teeth.

"I guess you don't know him," I said, and walked back to the spot where I'd been waiting. They kept watching me. The man who'd spoken first was tapping a cigarette on a pack, glaring, and I could hear the faint hum of the other man's voice, still chanting, "Thomas, Thomas, Thomas." Maybe a summoning spell.

And it worked, because up the alley from the water where the Bronx Kill flowed into the East River, came Thomas, waving. He was dressed like the other two men: ill-fitting jeans, flannel shirt over a T-shirt, each article too big, as if he was trying to hide in them. The men watched as we hugged, his cloud of cologne smothering me, and beneath, the sour tang of his body odor. Thomas was small, compact, and though he didn't even reach my shoulder I could feel his strength, the tensile ropiness of his muscles, the hard slabs of his back. I'd always been aware of this strength, coiled and ready. It was, in part, why I'd chosen him.

"My friend," he said, putting his hand on my shoulder. "Come, my friend. We will talk."

He steered me out of the parking lot and down Locust Avenue. Beside us, a retaining wall rose quickly and blocked the view of the river. Beyond the wall swelled green mounds of earth.

"So, you need my help? Matthew, my friend, how can I help you?"

"I have a job for you."

"A job." That's all he said. As if he already knew what it was I wanted. Could it be that Thomas was exactly the kind of man you came to for this sort of thing? I'd seen him do some things in Albania that made me think he'd fit. First, that dog on the road. It'd been limping along the road near the orphanage and Thomas had turned the wheel of the Land Rover, smoothly, no sudden jerk or anything, and there was the thud of the animal's head against the fender, the bump of the wheels going over it. Neither of us said anything about it, just kept on going. And then I'd seen him use his knife, the one he'd carried in Tirana, or probably everywhere. He might've even had it on him there, in the Bronx. I'd seen him hold it to the neck of a man outside a restaurant in a truly squalid part of the city. A smear of blood spread around the edge of the knife as they argued in some Roma dialect. Then Thomas had shoved the man away, looking down in disgust at his blade. So, my point is, it's not like I didn't have some indication Thomas might be right for this kind of job. Plus, you know, like I said, he was poor, with a large family to support. And I was going to offer him the kind of money he couldn't say no to.

I explained what I wanted him to do. I have no memory now of what I said. I remember words coming out of my mouth, probably in a frantic jumble, but the whole time Thomas stood there listening as if he'd known this was what I needed, as if this was what he was *for*.

"You have the money?" He squeezed my shoulder as he said this, as if I might be hiding cash under my shirt.

"I'll get you the money, don't worry," I said, with a flash of disappointment in myself. I was talking as if in a movie. A cliché. "I mean, I can get it. When do you need it?"

"Before," Thomas said. "I need it before." Then he stepped closer and grabbed my arm and breathed his shitty breath all over me. "The money is for my family. You understand this? I would only do this for my family."

"Okay," I said, though you would've thought he'd understand, given the circumstances and everything, that I *didn't* get the whole "taking care of your family" thing. "How about next week?"

"No, not here. This is not a good place. I will text you."

"Fine," I said, though I wasn't sure how I was going to get my hands on the amount I'd offered: a hundred thousand dollars. Twenty thousand I might be able to manage in a week. I guess I'd hoped Thomas would do the job, accept payment after. But I was really hoping that he'd get arrested, maybe deported, or else jailed long-term, and I'd never have to pay up. That'd been my plan, such as it was. Yes, dear reader, I understand it wasn't much of a plan.

"And, um," I said, not sure how to phrase my question. What the hell. "How are you going to do it?"

Thomas squinted at me. Maybe his look was disappointment. Maybe calculation. Something about his eyebrows, massive, bushy, unkempt, obscured the meaning of every expression for me.

"Don't worry," he said. Then he slapped my shoulder and walked away.

I wasn't sure if I was supposed to follow, but I didn't want to be there on the street alone, so I kept a couple hundred feet back. The other men were still there, and they fell silent as I passed. Probably they were considering mugging me. Or maybe just killing me. No running, I told myself, as I pulled out my phone and followed the blue track back toward the relative safety of the subway.

Should I describe my apartment for you? Maybe this will help: I almost wrote "Shall I describe my apartment for you?" That's the kind of place our apartment is. Makes you want to say *shall*. Because the apartment is haughty. We live in a double classic eight on the Upper East Side.

That's all you're going to get from me. No description. It would take too long. Maybe pages.

Goddamn it. Fine.

You enter into the foyer where you're greeted by a huge mirror within a massive coat rack, so you can watch yourself hang your coat beside the one or two others on the multitude of hooks. You see? We're barely in the door. Just trust me: Picture a fancy apartment. Now make it bigger. Bigger again. See the molding along the ceilings, hand wrought and irreplaceable? High ceilings, windows looking out at the ornate buildings across the way and, if you lean close to the glass in the living room, you can see a flush of green that is Central Park. Fancy furniture. You see? I can't stop, and I'm trying to.

I was usually alone in the apartment, other than the cleaning ladies, but I'd trained them not to make eye contact. The key was to never answer them. "Hello, how are you, Mr. Matthew?" they might say. Just stare back. No response. Racist behavior, I guess, since the cleaning ladies were Latina or some variation of Asian. But it wasn't a race thing. Or not entirely. I mean, it was. I'm white. A rich as fuck white guy. They were poor. Here to clean. Not chat. So, piss off.

Maybe, with all this, I'm trying to get you to stop reading. Did you ever think of that? You probably did. You're probably smarter than I'm giving you credit for. Because, honestly, I'm giving you very little credit. Basically none. FYI.

A few of the students snickered at this and Gil looked up from the page. That boy there, just across the room, reading in an even, cool voice, had known Thomas. Had hired him. The story hadn't said what it was for yet, but Gil knew, he felt the tug of the inevitable, that flicker of near-knowing that came while reading a good story, but here it wasn't a product of the narrative. Because this wasn't even a story.

And while we're on the topic of you, reader, I should say: I know what you're thinking. Maybe not actively thinking, though at the back of your mind it's there, lurking, possibly looming: What is this all about? Why so cagey? What are you hiring Thomas to do? Why should we give a shit?

Maybe you think you know. Maybe you think you can see it, far off (though not too far off, I promise): the revelation. And yes, I see no way to keep you forever in the dark. But let's put that aside for now, the what. Be patient. Soon enough, I promise, everything will be clear. But now you've gotten me off-track, with your prurient interest in plot. I was going to put a scene in here with my parents. Give you a sense of them, establish their "character," let you glimpse their flaws, but the truth is, I don't feel like doing any of that David Copperfield kind of crap, so to speak. So let's skip it. Like the apartment, we can just gloss: Imagine your own parents. Now make them richer. Richer again. And again. Imagine the cool distance that comes with all that wealth, how each moment of your life becomes, nakedly, a transaction. There, thinly sketched, I admit, is my life. Perhaps you're unsatisfied? Oh well. On with the plot.

I called Thomas a dozen times before he answered. I'd started to worry he'd changed his mind, so I braced for complaints: He wanted more money, or more money up front. What if he got arrested? How could he be sure I'd send the money to his family? We'd had these conversations before, but now that I'd sent him the time and the date, now that I'd told him, in a voice-mail that he could've saved, the calculus had changed. For the first time, I felt myself to be vulnerable, exposed. Possibly I'd long been exposed, and simply hadn't been aware of it, but now I knew it to be the case. This made me angry. Rage built up each time I called and he failed to answer, so that on the thirteenth-or-whatever call, when he finally answered, I said, "What the fuck, Thomas? Don't you fucking jerk me around, you goddamn piece of shit."

He took it all in stride.

"Matthew, my friend. How nice of you to call."

"Listen, you little shit," I said, blinking wildly out the window, momentarily blinded by rage. "Are you ready? Is everything ready?"

"What about you, my friend? Are you ready? Because there are two of us here, my friend. This isn't just me. You know that, right?"

"Yes, I'm fucking ready. I've got the account info you sent."

"Yes," Thomas said. And I knew it was coming. Exactly as expected. The banal, predictable human greed. "Is that enough, my friend? Do you think? Because I have been thinking. I have been thinking that is not enough. I could go to prison. You know that, don't you?"

"Wow, you think that's a possibility?"

"Yes. I do, my friend. I do think that is a possibility. Fine, fine. I should have asked for more, but my family, I need the money, so, if I am arrested, I want more. You will send the money to my family. To the accounts I gave you. This is for my family, Matthew."

"That's really touching, Thomas. Thanks for plucking my motherfucking heartstrings. And okay, fine. You get picked up, I'll send extra." I had no intention of sending extra. Or sending any, actually, other than the twenty-five thousand I'd already wired from an account I set up through one of my trusts. Someone with the right resources, with real determination, could probably track it back to me, but I also assumed no one would be looking that hard. Not once they got that anonymous tip letting them know where to find that illegal who'd killed two upstanding Americans who'd played golf with the president. The current, orange one. And a couple of others, now that I think of it.

"And you will send me fifty more now."

"Fifty what?"

"Thousand, Matthew. Do not play with me. I know you are not stupid."

"Well, you must think I'm fucking stupid if you think I'm going to send you fifty anything. You want to get caught before you even do it? You gypsy idiot."

On the other end Thomas breathed roughly through his nose, a rattle of snot and anger. After all, he was a grown man. And here I was, a kid.

"You should not talk like that," Thomas said, but before I could launch into another assault, he cut me off and said, "Fine. After. All of it after. To my family. Goodbye."

And he hung up. That was the last time I ever talked to him.

I'd called him from my bedroom, and now I looked across at the apartment of a woman I took to be a ballerina. I'd seen her practicing in a bodysuit many times. How much semen had I expended from those glimpses? Plenty, let me tell you. After all, I was a teenage boy. But perhaps that's too much information? Perhaps you don't care about my masturbatory habits?

What you want to know is: What happened? Enough of these goddamn evasions! Well, dear reader, rest assured, all went as planned, as I'd dreamt it would. On that evening already identified, Thomas drove the stolen truck right into my parents' Ferrari, killing them both. It was impressively done. The moment of the accident, the timing, the precision. I won't call it a work of art, but it was no fucking joke. To T-bone a car intentionally. Action movie shit, right there. Almost unbelievable. But whatever if you don't believe me. It's true. Google it. And despite the Spider's high safety ratings, my parents were killed. Dead. Success. Everything had gone exactly as planned.

Gil's eyes wouldn't focus when he looked up. A messy blur of human shapes around the table. The room was quiet, still, expectant, except for Matthew's voice, calmly reading.

I realize I'm making myself sound cooler, calmer, more "with it" than I was. In fact, I was nervous as fuck. That Thursday, the day of their deaths, I could barely think and my hands seemed not to work—I tried closing them into fists, but they only curled limply into hooks—and I sat in my classes with the feeling that small electric shocks were being administered all over my body, with particular attention paid to my asshole and balls.

I've already told you my parents were not so bad. Not good, but not so bad. My mother, in particular. She wasn't a bad mother. For one thing, she was smart. Much smarter than my father, who was no idiot. Most people would probably assume he was smarter, since he made all the money, but those people would be wrong. My mother was the brains, and she was also mostly kind. Self-absorbed, too focused on her appearance, but not cruel. The one time my father had hit me as a kid— I was nine and we'd been visiting his brother and the family cat had turned up dead and he'd accused me (correctly, though he'd no proof)—she'd stepped between the two of us and said that if he touched me again she'd kill him. My father backed down. He believed her. He was right to do so. She'd protected me. Not all mothers do that, you know. Beyond sadistic mothers, there's the more common mother who pretends not to see that her husband is an abusive/rapist-pedophile. One of my friends suffered through one of those, a father who used to rape him each time they went on vacation. Two hotel rooms, never adjoining, and his father would come into the room with two socks rolled up together. These he'd stuff into my friend's mouth to smother his screams and, well, you can imagine. His mother knew. She did nothing. She pretended not to know. That friend killed himself. Not that his parents thought that's what happened. Overdose. Tragic. So sad, everyone said. A bright young man. Codeine.

Not that I'm doing this for him. Revenge for my generation against our helicopter-but-still-not-truly-nurturing parents. But what justification could I give at this point that would satisfy you? And this is my story. I'll tell it the way I like.

Just imagine me sitting in Central Park, southwest corner, near Columbus Circle, my phone in my pocket with the ringer turned on. I'm waiting for Thomas's call from the burner phone I'd instructed him to buy. Nearby, begging birds flit between the asphalt path and the leaning wire fence meant to keep us all off the grass, their tiny heads darting toward me any time I make the slightest movement. Down the path comes a woman, my mother's age, her body perfect in sleek black running gear, a stripe of reflective material down her leg, shimmering in the light from the decorative lamps that line the path. Beyond the cordoned-off grass a dog lopes beside its owner, some prick who doesn't think the leash laws refer to him. The dog is pretty, a sleek Irish Setter, but that's no excuse. The law doesn't say all but beautiful dogs must be leashed. But this guy doesn't care. Perhaps he lives in one of the buildings behind me, 25 Central Park West, or in the Time Warner Center. Above the law by virtue of his thirty-million-dollar apartment. Of course, he's right.

From my seat on the bench in the puddle of light I can see Seventh Avenue. Just beyond that far dark mass of trees is Sixth Avenue. And down there on Sixth Avenue, just now, my parents are zipping along in their Ferrari. My father is driving too fast. My mother is staring into her phone. They won't see it at all, or not for more than a second or some fraction thereof, the truck, coming for them. I imagine, as I sit shaking on the bench in the cold and the dark, that I can hear the high, piercing shriek of metal as the beautiful car is ripped apart, slicing and crumpling in against my mother, then my father, as Thomas, behind the wheel, fixes his face in concentration, presses his foot on the gas.

Before the call comes, which takes almost two more hours, a calm descends over me. My shaking stops. My hands are steady. I stand, scattering the birds to the top of the fence where they sit in a line and watch me worshipfully. I know just what I'll do next: head to Eric's. Good coke, some eager sluts. But for a few more moments I enjoy my time there in the dark, the shining eyes of birds upon me. And then, the deed done, my life set free, I'll walk out of the park, and back into the soft strange glow of my city.

Gil tried to take a breath but his throat narrowed and with an effort he only managed a wheeze. After a few whispers and an awkward laugh, the students started in without him. *Well, it was pretty disturbing and stuff, but, it was pretty interesting? And the character was interesting? The story was unique?* Alice said there were a lot of colons, which could probably be cut. Tony said he loved the part about the Ferrari. "That's such an awesome car."

One of the students said maybe he didn't need the gypsy slurs, which were, like, racist? And pretty distracting. And it made the character really unlikable. Alice said, "But you're not supposed to *like* him, right? I mean, he's a murderer."

"All right, that's enough of this shit," Gil said. The startled faces of the students swam in and out of focus. "Racist, likable, who fucking cares?" In his rage he could feel the dissonance between the professor he'd tried to be—laid-back, jokey—and how he felt now. Hateful. Violent. The students leaned away from him in their chairs, worried and frowning. "This story, this piece of—" He slapped his hand on the table and one of the students whimpered. "This isn't a short story. Don't you see that? Don't you see what he's doing?"

He gestured at Matthew and couldn't help but catch a glimpse of the boy: smug, smiling, arms crossed over his chest. Beside him, Susie huddled in her sweatshirt, hood up.

"Professor," Alice said, but he ignored her.

"No, Alice, stop. This, this thing, this is a *confession*. Don't you see that?" They couldn't be this stupid. Could they? Maybe they could.

"I mean, I know there are, like, some connections," Alice continued, as if it was her job to rein in the feral professor, "but it's fiction, so, maybe he was using—"

"No, Alice, please, shut up. Listen, just, fuck, listen to me. This is about my sister." Gil glared at Alice, hating her. All of them, actually. Sitting there, listening to this piece of shit, this murder confession, then chatting about its merits, its fucking colons. Fuck her. Fuck all of this. Alice's face went red, and she began to cry. He grabbed the story and shook it so the pages splayed around his face. "All of this is true. Do any of you get that? The driver, the apartment, the accident, my sister, her husband. And he, he fucking, he put it in this—"

He looked at Matthew. The boy's smile simmered beneath a bullshit layer of concern. This was what he'd wanted. To throw it in Gil's face. To provoke exactly this response. *Fine. Here it is, you little shit. Here's your fucking response.*

"Matthew," Gil said, and the name made his voice tremble, "you can't just sit there. Tell them. Tell them what the fuck—" The boy leaned forward, elbows on the table.

"What, Professor? Tell them my parents died in a wreck?" Matthew looked around, bemused, and said, "I mean, it's true. And I used it in this story."

"You know that's not—" Gil started, but the boy cut him off.

"I'm not sure what you want me to say here, Professor. It's a short story. I thought this was a short story class. Guess I missed something."

"It's not a short, not a goddamn— Tell them, tell them what you . . ." Gil wheezed. He sat back, gasping. There were murmurings and a few coughs, the hiss of zippers. From the back he heard Matthew's voice, but couldn't make out the words. A buzzing in his ears swelled into a blare of static. A chair banged against the table. A body moved past him. The door opened with its pneumatic wheeze. He closed his eyes and slumped forward to press the heels of his hands into his face. He had to get control. He had to get Matthew. When he opened his eyes, several students were standing.

"Where are you going?" he said as Tony slung a backpack over his shoulder. Matthew, he could see through the residual haze, was down at the other end of the table, whispering with Susie.

"I don't know, Professor. This is just messed up," Tony said, with a shake of his head, then he walked out.

That set them all free, and they started gathering up their papers and computers, stuffing them into their bags as if the fire alarm was going off.

"Where are you going?" Gil said. "Class isn't over."

Alice, he realized, had already left. A few remained in their seats, and, terribly, Matthew was one of them. The boy reached out to accept a manuscript back from one of his peers, adding it to a stack before him. Gil stared across the room at the boy, trying to focus, trying to make him come clear. "Matthew," he said, trying to keep his voice level. "We need to talk."

"I don't know, Professor," Matthew said, standing up quickly and plucking his jacket off the back of his chair. "I think I'm good."

"No," Gil said, "you can't," but Matthew was coming around the side of the table and fear rose through him. This boy was a murderer. He was exactly the person Gil had always feared, exactly the person he'd suspected, dreaded, and despised. He'd hired Thomas. He'd killed his parents.

"Do you mind," Matthew said, stopping beside Gil's chair. The boy moved toward him, not to strike, but to take the story. Gil jerked the pages off the table onto his lap, crushed them against his stomach. Matthew squinted, as if considering taking this further, but then with a little twisted smile he walked out.

Gil stuffed his books and computer into his bag but kept the story in his hand. Evidence. He could show this to Molly, to the detective. The boy had made a mistake, and now, just maybe, Gil had him.

26

IN HIS OFFICE HE FORCED HIMSELF TO CALM DOWN. THIS WAS NO time for panic. He couldn't let himself collapse, not now, not now that the boy had fucked up, left himself exposed. Once his breathing was under control, he called the 212 number that, he was pretty sure, was the detective from New York. Matthew. Short story. He needed to talk to her. After a single ring he was clicked over to a voicemail box for the New York City Police Department: Leave a message with the case ID and the detective's name. He fumbled through a message, saying it was Gil Duggan, could the detective on Sharon Westfallen's case please call him back, Detective Simpson, that was her name, sorry, anyway, and so, well, he had something he needed to tell her, possibly something that might help.

He sat in his darkened office. Word was probably already spreading around campus. Not what he'd said, or the context, but the mere central fact: Professor Duggan had been abusive in class. He'd screamed obscenities in class. At his nephew. But not only his nephew. He could see Alice in the dean's office now, clutching a wad of tissues as, through hiccups and gasps, she detailed how he'd basically assaulted her. How he'd lost his mind in class. How unsafe she felt. He was so awful! So mean! Yes, the dean might say, sympathetic, as always, to his valued customers. Yes, they would get right on this. She shouldn't worry. They would protect her. Gil grabbed his bag from the floor and hobbled out as quickly as his throbbing back allowed, down the back stairs, out onto the salt-speckled walk.

When he pulled down the drive the house was dark. This was all wrong. Matthew was supposed to be here. Gil had worked out every detail of how the scene would play out, had blocked each movement, each bit of dialogue, so precisely that the empty house was like arriving on opening night to find the doors locked: inside, stretches of red carpet, a shuttered concession stand with a fine layer of dried yellow popcorn along the bottom, chairs stacked in a dark arcade.

Molly and Ingrid would be in Maryland by now, and Chloe was on her way to Sarah Lawrence, so Matthew must've decided he had no cover here and stayed away. Maybe he understood that he'd overplayed his hand, exposed himself. An understandable misstep for a boy of his unbridled arrogance, raised to believe nothing could touch him.

He sent Molly a text asking how the drive had been. He needed to tell her about class, about Matthew's story, to make her understand that all this time Gil had been right. But he'd need to explain it carefully, or he might scare her. Not that she shouldn't be scared. At least she was safely away. Though Matthew knew where they were. Right now he could be anywhere. Beating the shit out of Susie. Or on his way to Maryland to join Molly and Ingrid at the farm with some explanation that would put them off their guard for the night, until he found his way, one by one, into their rooms.

He called Molly but it went to voicemail. The service at her parents' farm was spotty. And as far as she knew, everything was fine.

In Matthew's room the papers had been cleared off his desk, and he'd packed away his duffel bag somewhere. Or taken it with him. The duffel could've been in Matthew's Audi throughout class. Maybe all of this had been planned: Rub it in Gil's face, then disappear.

Except now Gil had the story. He hurried down to his coat, took it from the pocket. He'd scan it, send it to Molly, email it to the detective in New York. It might, he worried, as he dug through the wicker basket of plugs and cords in the corner of the living room, be illegal to send Matthew's story around. Privacy rules, FERPA, all of which he was probably supposed to understand. But surely in this case, with a crime, with a felony, those protections didn't apply. And if they did, so what. This was bigger than his job at Essex, bigger than Matthew's privacy.

He emptied the basket onto the couch and dug through the tangled white and black cords, but the adapter wasn't there. In his bedroom he found the scanner, but that was useless without the right connector. He searched the girls' rooms, then his own bedroom again, then Matthew's, then the cord basket one last time. Nothing. Not a single adapter in the house. Without it he couldn't use the scanner. Cursing and stuffing fistfuls of tangled plastic wires into the basket, he remembered: Chloe had taken it with her to Sarah Lawrence. She was in charge of the research slides, and she had to be able to connect to the projector. She'd asked him. He'd told her of course. Why the hell didn't they have another adapter? Or several more? But buying a backup was one of the many things he'd intended to do for years and had always let slide. And this was the reward for his laziness: He had the story—the proof, or something like proof—and no way to share it.

He made himself a pot of pasta with butter, sat at the counter and watched the driveway while he ate. A text came in from Chloe: They'd arrived at Sarah Lawrence, Lily was her roommate (yay), and her first debate was tomorrow. He wrote to wish her luck—resisting the urge to ask about the adapter—then checked her location in a flurry of anxiety. But of course, there she was, a blue dot in Bronxville. Then he checked Molly's location: not far over the Pennsylvania line in Maryland. All where they should be. All safely away from Matthew. Now he could deal with the boy on his own terms. If he could find the boy. If he ever came home. At nine, while he was scrolling restlessly through the TV, Molly called. The connection was crumbly, and her words faded in and out.

"Hi, honey, how are you?" she said.

"Not good," he said. "Things are a fucking disaster, Molly."

"What happened?"

He tried to explain, hoping she would understand through his muddle of frantic sentences. He tried to stick to the main idea: Matthew had hired someone to kill his parents. He'd written it all out. In a story. He'd turned it in for class. A confession, Molly. And the boy was out there right now, doing who the hell knows what. He told her about calling the detective— She interjected, "Can you send it to me?"

"The story?"

"Yes," she said. "I want to see it."

"I do have it, it's right here. But the scanner—Chloe took the adapter, that white thing, you know, so I can't scan it. But I have it. I could read it to you?"

There was a pause, then Molly said, "No, I don't think—" She stopped and said, softer, "Gil, is he there?"

"No. I'm waiting for him. But, fuck, Molly. I don't know. I don't know if I can just sit here doing nothing."

After a pause she said, "Promise me you'll be calm."

"I will. I'll wait here. I'm in my own house. There's nothing wrong with me sitting in my own house, is there?"

"Stay home, Gil, okay? Just stay there, okay?"

He told her of course he would, and then that he loved her. As soon as he put the phone down, anxiety swelled in his head, swirling out in violent fantasies as he half-watched a zombie movie. Molly emailed and said the important thing was to keep calm and get in touch with the police if he really thought this was serious. But Gil knew better. Molly was being naïve. Now that Matthew had put himself out there, exposed himself in a fit of petty anger, he might try to disappear. If Matthew had orchestrated a murder, he'd surely made contingency plans: money in an offshore account, arrangements with a private jet service to get him out of the country. Gil couldn't just let him go. He'd murdered Sharon. His sister's murderer was out there now, walking around, free.

He woke on the couch in the morning's blue light. As soon as he moved, currents of pain leapt up his back into his shoulders and down through his legs. Gasping, he shuffled to the bathroom for Advil, then lay on his bed, drifting in and out of sleep.

As soon as it was a reasonable hour, Gil called Molly. She said she'd tried calling the boy yesterday, and she'd texted him, but hadn't heard anything back.

"I guess all we can do is wait, Gil," she said. "And you should call the detective."

He did call, finally, while waiting for more coffee to brew, but he ended up in voicemail again. Maybe Detective Simpson was sick, or out on vacation. A slow, shuffling walk in the woods after coffee did nothing to dispel his anxiety, though each slip of his boot in the snow had sent flares up his back, and when he returned he felt sure the boy was in the house, hiding, watching him. He checked the basement, the laundry room, all the bedrooms, and even—feeling ridiculous—the closets, but there was nothing.

There was somewhere he could check: Susie's. But that was dangerous now. He might be recognized by the neighbor, or Susie might call the police. Her professor turned stalker wouldn't leave her alone. He was lurking outside her apartment right now.

He tried to do some work: grading, which he quickly gave up on, then instead he read the Yoko Ogawa stories he was teaching, but even they couldn't fix his loose, panicked mind. Brittle, frail thoughts crashed against each other and shattered. He shouldn't be here alone. Molly was right. But she thought he, Gil, was the biggest risk to himself. Not Matthew, who had wheedled and wooed her and bought her affection with art, with his sophistication and urban sensibilities. Yes, Gil had known for years that Molly missed her city life, but it was obscene to find it in Matthew and then to be blinded by his wealth to the obvious awfulness of the kid. And she was wrong, now, to suggest he just sit around and do nothing. She hadn't been there in the room as the boy had read those sentences aloud. As if they were something to be *enjoyed*. Only Gil knew the truth of the boy. Only Gil could stop him. The day crept into the afternoon, and finally, just as it had begun to snow, Molly wrote.

I heard from Matthew. He's in New York.

He stared at the phone, reread the note. His hands trembled so hard it took several tries to type a reply:

What? When? Call me.

He paced the living room. He needed to go to the city. Now. He should already be in the fucking car. What was he waiting for? Matthew had gone down there to escape. Soon he'd disappear. But if so, why had he told Molly? To try to put them off. As if everything was fine. Spring break, what were they worried about? That story? Come on, man, it was fiction! A joke. Can't you take a joke? And now he was just taking a well-deserved break. Visiting friends. Totally normal. He wasn't on the run. Not at all. Another text came in:

Said he went down to NYC for spring break. Said he told you.
I know it's a lie, but at least we know where he is.

As if that was supposed to make it okay. But apparently Molly was willing to just let Matthew go. Cut him loose. He wrote back:

We can't let him go. We have to get him.

There was a long gap before Molly responded, and when she did he was upstairs, stuffing an extra pair of socks and underwear into his backpack atop his copy of the boy's story.

Get him? Please leave it. Did you call the detective?

He could be in the city in six hours. He'd find Matthew. Keep an eye on him until he got hold of the detective, then let the police handle it, but also be there when it happened, to see it done, the boy, guided into the back of a police car.

After backing up in a three-point turn, he turned right out of the drive without slowing. He'd write Molly when he stopped for gas. But he couldn't let her talk him out of this, not now. The world would be forced to look right into the blank heart of that spoiled rich brat and face the beast they'd all made with their indulgences and neglect and fear of saying the wrong thing. The car rocked over the gravel road. Gil gripped the wheel, sped up, and felt this might be the most important thing he'd ever done.

27

STREAKS OF SNOW WHIPPED THROUGH THE HEADLIGHTS. THE highway was nearly empty in the mountains and he had to watch his speed, especially on the long slopes down through the dark. If he got pulled over it'd all go wrong. He'd end up detained by some dipshit trooper who didn't like his stammering confusion. As it was, he wouldn't get to the city much before eleven, and he'd still have to find parking. Better not to overthink the details. Like what he'd say to Matthew. Assuming the boy was in the apartment. Which he probably wasn't. Unless he was there with Susie. Beating her up.

He checked his phone twice and saw that Molly had called half a dozen times, had left two voicemails and a flurry of texts. *Where are you? Stay home. Please, Gil, don't go after him.* He wrote back a single line: *I'm fine. Don't worry. Back home soon.*

When he passed over the New York state line past Brattleboro he checked his phone and saw that he'd missed a call from a 212 number, at 8:13 P.M. After business hours, if that was a thing for police. Gil pulled off the highway and called the detective, but he ended up in voicemail. He left a message, trying to stay calm. He was headed to the city, Matthew was there, and Gil had a copy of a story the boy had written, and the detective needed to see it. She had to see this, and he was bringing it down with him. He hung up before he could turn incoherent, then got back on the road, pushed his speed higher.

The detective wouldn't call so late if it wasn't important. Maybe Thomas had confessed. And now they wanted to talk to Matthew, which meant it was all the more likely the boy would flee, all the more important that Gil find him.

At a rest stop, after filling up the car and buying a coffee, he called Molly from near the doors where exhausted travelers leaked in and out of the faintly reeking toilets. He shouldn't call. She'd scold him, treat him like a lunatic. From her point of view, it must look crazy. As if he'd come unhinged. But he called anyway. Maybe—he admitted to himself as he tapped the screen and brought it, hot and trembling, to his ear—because he wanted her to talk him out of it. Or, no, to *try* to talk him out of it, and then, instead of giving in, he'd tell all the bits and pieces he'd kept to himself for, well, lots of reasons. But Molly would understand. She had to.

When the phone clicked over after six rings he felt a wash of relief that left him momentarily exhausted. When the beep came for him to leave a message, he disconnected and hurried to the car, put the phone in the cup holder, and pulled back onto the highway before Molly could call back.

He reached the edges of the city after ten, then spent another thirty minutes trolling through the neighborhood, missing spots, trying to back up to them only to find someone else already pulling in, cursing, failing to read the signs right so that he parked in a twenty-four-hour loading zone, finally giving up and heading down to the lots by the East River. Pushing the lock button on his key chain, he checked his phone. No texts, but Molly had called four times.

There was also a text from Chloe. When he opened it, the phone was still on her location. The blue dot resolved, not in Bronxville, but in Manhattan. On the Upper East Side, the low sixties, not far away.

28

MAYBE CHLOE WAS AT DINNER? MAYBE THE TEACHER HAD TAKEN them out? But when he flicked up to see her text it only said the first day was fine, she'd won two of her debates, had lost another because of a stupid judge, and they were going to bed early. Nothing about being in the city. A wave of nausea rose through him with the certainty: Chloe was with Matthew. The boy was here, in the city, not far away, and now Chloe was with him. Hanging out with her murderous cousin, her buddy. And now the boy was running from Gil, was maybe planning to flee more properly, and if he was with Chloe, if they were together now—

He leaned against the car, took a slow shuddering breath. He had to find them. He had to find his daughter before Matthew did something to her. How wrong Molly had been!

When he clicked her location again, the phone took half a minute to locate her, and the dot had moved, was down in the fifties. How had she gotten so far so quickly? Unless she was on the subway. Or in a cab.

Jogging into the wind, he fiddled with the keys to the apart-

ment, not sure if he should knock before going in. Have the doormen call up? Assuming they'd let him in. But wasn't Gil, basically,
as the boy's guardian, the owner of the apartment? The avenues
stretched before him in the cold dark. The streets were littered
with rushing cabs and horns, but those quieted as he approached
Park and Madison, the tall red brick facades, stately, unassuming
palaces. And there, with its green awning, was Sharon's building.

"Can I help you, sir?" the doorman said, opening the glass
door, but also partially blocking access to the lobby so Gil was
outside, beneath the heat lamps.

"I'm Gilbert Duggan. Apartment 14A."

"Duggan?" the man said, crinkling his face, as if the name
meant "Fuck you" in a dialect Gil had no business knowing.

"I'm Sharon Westfallen's brother." He knew it was important to
keep calm. Get past this idiot gorilla without a scene. Find his
daughter.

"Oh, Mr. Duggan. We didn't know you were coming down."

"Well, here I am. Excuse me," Gil said, but when he stepped
forward the man blocked his way—only for an instant, barely long
enough for anyone to have said it happened—and then he stepped
aside with an exaggerated flourish.

Doesn't matter, doesn't matter, Gil told himself as he went past the
desk where another suited hooligan glared at the bum in his hobo
parka.

"You know the way?" the first doorman shouted. Gil punched
14 in the elevator and stared back so the man would know clearly
what he thought of him: He was just a loutish dog hired by the
rich. Soon he'd be too old and weak and they'd toss him aside,
back to his hovel in Queens with its moldy kitchen, its worn shag
carpeting, where he'd hunch over a yellow kitchen table, smoking
cigarettes that would kill him, voting against his interests in some
twisted fealty to the class who'd discarded him like a hunk of trash.
Gil had to suppress the urge to raise a middle finger as the doors
slid shut.

There was no sign of anyone inside the apartment. No coat on the rack, no shoes by the door, no noise.

"Hello?" he said, moving deeper, turning on lights. "Chloe?" he called, stupidly, since he already knew from his phone she wasn't here.

There was no evidence of the boy in the kitchen: not a single dish or glass in the sink. He ran a glass of water from the tap and tried to focus as he sipped, spilling water down his chin, hands trembling. Okay, so, time to go. To find them. At the very least he'd find Chloe, make sure she was okay, send her back to the dorm, or no, maybe not, maybe have her come here, keep her with him. She shouldn't get to just carry on as if nothing had happened, as if she hadn't lied to her father, as if she hadn't, apparently, turned into a bad kid under Matthew's malign influence. That murderer, not content with killing Gil's sister, now had to drag Chloe into it, put her in danger.

He opened his texts again, clicked on Chloe's location, but no map appeared. Below was an option, Share Location. Which meant, what? That she'd turned it off? No, she wouldn't do that. But maybe she'd seen his texts asking if she was in the city. Maybe she'd told Matthew. The boy, evil, but undeniably smart, realized Gil was on to him, got hold of her phone somehow, turned off Share Location.

Gil called Chloe, but the call went straight to voicemail. He texted:

Wondering where you are. Let me know you're OK.

He hesitated. Maybe Matthew was holding her phone right now, waiting to see if his idiot uncle texted. But no, he should send it. She was his daughter. He watched its status shift to Delivered, waited for it to say Read, but it didn't.

Okay, stay calm. He took another trembling sip, set the glass on the counter, hand shaking so badly the glass rattled and he was afraid it might skitter off the edge, shatter, but he managed to pull his hand back without a mess. Nothing had happened yet. As far as Gil knew, Chloe was fine.

He clicked on the lights in the master bedroom—apparently untouched. Next, the guest room, which had clearly been tended to by someone since his last visit, the sheets pulled tight, the pillows precisely arranged. The door to Matthew's room was closed. Gil knocked, and stepped in only after slapping around for the light switch.

On the boy's bed was the weekend bag he'd first seen him with at the airport in Burlington a couple of months ago. The laptop was inside the carry-on, but that was useless, so he went through the papers in the desk. A few tests and a paper from Herbert—all A's, with notes from the teachers such as *Great point!* and *Lovely sentence*—and some receipts clumped at the back of a desk drawer.

Most were ATM slips. Withdrawals of $500, $700, $350. Remaining balance: $34,416.83. The locations were scattered around the city: downtown, the Upper East Side, midtown. The receipts were similarly useless, $3,600 at Burberry for a trench coat, $900 on four pairs of shoes at the Nike store. Why would he need so many? Probably he'd been treating friends, now that he'd been freed from parental constraints. That was somewhere Gil could look: the boy's friends. Except Gil knew nothing about them. Except, no, he did know one name. The friend in the story. The kid whose birthday Matthew had come down for. Eric.

No one Matthew's age used an address book, everything was on the boy's phone, including all the evidence one would need to convict him—but Gil was close, he could feel it. Coming to the city hadn't been an act of lunacy. The hours of suspicion, the spying he'd done, none of it had been a waste. He went back into the living room, then into the kitchen, where, in a drawer beside the fridge, beneath thank-you cards, paper clips, envelopes, pens, and business cards, he found a class list for Herbert, grade 11. Phone numbers and addresses. His finger shook as he ran it down the list, not seeing it the first time, but forcing himself to go over it a second, first names only, and there it was. Eric. Eric Harlan. East Sixty-fourth Street. Gil pulled out his phone and managed to calm himself enough to punch the address into Google Maps. Not far. A sixteen-minute walk. He checked his phone; the text to Chloe was delivered, but not read. Surely, if she was awake, she'd seen it. So why hadn't she read it? Written back? Unless something had happened. Maybe Matthew really had taken her phone, or worse. He pulled on his coat, dug his copy of Matthew's story from his bag, put it in his pocket. Then he ran out of the apartment and slapped at the elevator button again and again until finally it dinged.

The townhouse was red brick, four stories, with a high stoop. In that respect, a bit like the first place he'd lived with Molly. Except that house in Brooklyn had been run-down and neglected since the sixties, peeling paint, crumbling steps, a boarded-over basement window, whereas this one was pristine, a bright coat of black paint on the iron fence, gas lamps whose steady flames cast no shadows. Warm lights were on up in the foyer. Through the first-floor windows he could see a slice of the living room's yellow wall, a triangle of bookcase.

The only option was to use the buzzer. He'd imagined surprising them somehow: Eric's drug-slackened grin fading as he realized it wasn't another debauched teenager, and by the time Gil was in the door Matthew would only just be staggering up from the couch. And then? Bash his head in, screaming Sharon's name?

He pressed the button, waited a few seconds, ready to press again, when a shape moved behind the curtain over the door's glass panes, the side of a girl's face.

"Hello?" A girl's voice crackled out of the speaker.

"Hi, I'm looking for Matthew Westfallen." Gil tried to sound official, as if he was a cop, or at least someone with authority.

"What?" The voice was definitely a teenager's, he could hear that, which meant there was nothing to fear. If adults were there, they'd have answered. And then he'd have had a real problem. It was nearly one in the morning. But so what? They'd be annoyed? Distressed? He didn't know these people. These people meant as little to him as he surely did to them.

"I'm his uncle. Matthew Westfallen's uncle."

"Uncle?" she said, and there was a pause and he heard her saying, "I don't know! Why don't you—" and the gate buzzed.

Atop the stoop he breathed deep, tried to brace himself. Matthew wouldn't like being chased down. Tough shit. Tough shit, tough shit, tough shit, tough shit.

Footsteps. Whispering. Then the door opened a crack.

"Hello?" He could see only a slice of the young woman's face, pretty, blond hair, childlike in her fear.

"Hi, I'm looking for Matthew. Do you know where he is?"

"Matthew?" the girl said, shaking her head and looking over her shoulder, and then she was gone, replaced by a young man. Gil couldn't see much of him other than one brown eye, whose iris was too wide, the white streaked with red.

"What's up, man?" the boy said, a burst of sour beer breath through the crack.

"I'm Matthew's uncle and I need to speak with him. I'm wondering if you know where he is?"

"Matthew's uncle?" the young man—Eric, surely, this had to be him—said, eyes widening. "Seriously?"

"Yes, seriously. I need to find him. He came down to the city and—"

Before he could finish the door slammed shut, then flew open. Eric was much taller than Gil, huge and muscled. His thick neck seemed to be made of rebar over which the skin was pulled taut.

"Welcome to my humble abode, Professor." The boy doubled over as he said this, giggling.

"Sorry, I know it's late, but I was—"

"Fuck no, of course not!" Eric shouted, lunging forward and slapping Gil roughly on the shoulder, knocking him into the foyer.

He could see into the living room: a long leather couch, littered with young people.

"I'm looking for Matthew," Gil said, stepping away to avoid another slap from Eric, who loomed behind him. "He came down to the city this afternoon. Have you seen him?"

"Matthew?" Eric said, fingers rasping through streaks of acne and stubble on his chin. "Have I seen Matthew? Fuck, I really don't know. What about any of you fuckers? You heard the man. Where's Matthew? Any of you bitches hiding him? 'Cause I don't see him. Where's that fucking Matthew at?"

He roared this last bit, tossing his head back, then burst into a fit of laughter that sent him careening into the wall.

The teenagers on the couch watched all this with vacant and glassy stares—two young men and four girls. There was the sharp smell of pot in the room, but he didn't see any other evidence of drugs.

"You haven't seen him?" Gil said, turning to face Eric, who slumped, giggling.

"Nope," Eric said, righting himself, wiping at his eyes. "Not seen him."

"Okay, well, if you do," Gil started, but stopped. What did he want? For them to have Matthew call him? No. But he couldn't ask them to keep quiet about his visit. His stopping by after midnight.

"I could, like, text him," one of the girls on the couch said, holding up her phone. She was the most startlingly beautiful of the four, with a perfect doll's face out of which her eyes shone, pale blue. It seemed wrong anyone could be so pretty, much less someone so young. Her thin legs were tucked under her so her skirt rode up to her waist. Gil looked away and said, "Thanks, but, I'm not—" Too late. She was already tapping away at the screen, silver fingernails clicking on the glass.

Eric surged up next to Gil and clamped a hand on his shoulder, as if to make sure he didn't try to get away.

"Hey, we'll find him for you, Professor," the boy said in his ear. "Don't you worry." He started massaging Gil's shoulder while they watched the girl click away. Was she texting Matthew? Or she'd gotten distracted by some other message, or drifted onto Twitter or whatever.

"I've heard about you, Professor. You know that?" Eric said, sour breath going right up Gil's nose. "Matthew told me about you. *All* about you."

"Okay," Gil said.

"Yep. I mean, we're buddies you know. Me and Matt. He's told me all kinds of fuck-ass crazy stories."

Gil stared at the girl, hiked skirt or no, trying to get her to re-member, to focus, *text Matthew now.* She shifted her legs so he could see right up to the black triangle of her underwear.

"Oh, shit, yeah, he's a crazy motherfucker. But you probably know that. From living with him. *Parenting* him. Or whatever. Crazy bastard. Isn't that right, you dumbshits?" He shouted this last bit at the people on the couch.

"Maniac," one of the boys said, a fat kid with a landslide of acne down his cheeks.

"Yeah!" Eric shouted, giving Gil's shoulder a shake. "That's what we call him. Maniac Matt. Fucker's crazy." He took a deep breath as if to say more, then let out a sigh and said, "That bitch is just the best."

The girl held the phone to her ear.

"He ever tell you about Albania?" Eric said, then went right on without waiting for a response. "You know he went there, right? Like to help out some orphans or some shit. Anyway, so, he went to, like, Albania or whatever, and did he tell you?"

"What?" Gil said, since the boy loomed right next to him, panting with excitement.

"About the rat boys. That's what he called them. Oh, god," he said, his voice rising. "Oh, man. It's so fucked up. I wish Matt was here. When he tells it, Jesus, it's so good. So, like, he was in, like, whatever city that was over there, and there were these rat boys. You know, like street kids or I guess, like, maybe they were gypsies or whatever, just like roaming around, eating garbage and stealing shit, and Matt's like, I wonder if anyone's keeping track of them? I mean, there's no one watching out for them. So, he, like, he starts hanging around, giving them money and shit. To the rat boys. Like, you know, like, trying to act like he's their friend or some shit."

On the couch the girl was talking into her phone, but with Eric roaring into his ear Gil couldn't hear what she said. She frowned at him. Said a few more inaudible words. She opened her legs, slowly, mouth curling into a smile, and Gil shifted his stare to the floor.

"Right, so, he comes up with this plan. I mean, it's why we call him Maniac Matt and he's like—"

The girl lowered the phone and Gil pulled himself free from Eric's grip and stepped into the living room. The other boys tensed, as if he'd crossed a line.

"Did you get him?" Gil said, focused on the girl.

"Yeah," she said, rolling her eyes at the girl beside her. *What's his problem, anyway?*

"Is he here? In the city?"

"Yeah," she said, amazed that somehow this old guy had come up with an even more boring question! Would it never end? She gave her hair a toss to show she didn't need this shit from him.

"Where?"

The girl looked to the others for help—What was up with this creepy dude who was interrupting Eric's story about the rat boys?—but they were immobilized by stupidity.

"Excuse me, where?" Gil said, feeling Eric come up behind him, breathing loud through his nose. Angry. But soon he'd be out of there. Free of these degenerates.

"He's at Drake's. I mean, that's what he said. You know, in Brooklyn."

"Drake's. Where's that?" Gil said. They didn't want to tell him.

But they were kids. Dumb, dangerous, drugged-out kids. But still kids.

"In Brooklyn, right?" the girl said. "Eric?"

Eric frowned. "Yeah, right. Brooklyn. Gowanus. Near the canal."

"Do you have the address? In your phone?"

Eric looked up at him with a sudden, fierce glare, but the boy's resistance had been broken. "I don't know, probably, shit, I mean, hold on."

Gil waited patiently, making sure not to let his parent persona slip for a second. These dopey bastards might turn on him. But he managed it—a slight scowl, as if they were wasting his time, but he understood they were children and so he'd tolerate it—and eventually the girl said, "Yeah, actually, I've got it."

She told him the address.

"Thanks," he said, repeating the address in his head as he stepped around Eric, whose shoulders were tensed, like a leopard about to pounce. "Sorry to bother you."

"Whatever," Eric said, not turning to watch Gil go. "Have fun, Professor. We'll miss you. Good chat."

Gil pulled the door shut behind him but didn't feel he'd escaped until he was clear of the gate, which, thank god, opened easily from within. Drake's. Gowanus. Carroll Street. Matthew was there. And Chloe. He didn't know that for certain, but he felt sure of it: She was there, and she needed him.

The subway was a few blocks. He could take the 6 to the F at Broadway. Sixty-fourth Street was nearly empty now, though over on Lexington, traffic poured through the intersection. It was one in the morning. Chloe was there. In Brooklyn. At Drake's. He was sure of it. During a lull in traffic he ran across the street against the light, then he kept running toward the subway entrance. He'd find Chloe. And Matthew. By the time the detective got to work, Gil would be able to tell them exactly where the boy was hiding.

29

HE GOT OFF THE F TRAIN AT CARROLL STREET AND TURNED DOWN
a quiet block that led toward the Gowanus Canal. Brooklyn, or at
least this part of it, was nothing like he remembered. Not that he'd
ever spent much time down there. In his day this had been the do-
main of mobsters, abandoned warehouses, crack deals, muggings.
Now the wasteland had been converted into luxury condos, with
bits of carefully maintained ambiance. Authenticity, this was what
the new residents wanted, the idea of "Brooklyn," with a bit of
picturesque grit left behind, a neoliberal playground for millionaires.

Even if it was merely decorative, he felt a pulse of the old threat
in the arcing lines of graffiti on a rough concrete wall, in the loops
of razor wire atop a ten-foot fence, beyond which lay a nearly
empty lot: a rusted-out car, a tireless tricycle, three bags of trash
melting against the fence, bottles and cups and papers caught in the
knee-high weeds. No longer burial grounds for mob victims, these
lots were now destined to become another condo development,

like Drake's building, a multilayered cube of brick and glass. Chloe was in there, his girl, with Matthew.

In front of the building, a landscaped path lined with bushes and trees and benches wound above the Gowanus Canal. As if anyone would want to sit and relax a few feet from the turgid green slime, which—some things never change—smelled distinctly of shit and chemical waste. Unnervingly solid bubbles floated on the slow pull of the tide, glimmering in the streetlights.

A scattering of the building's windows were lighted, most free of curtains or blinds. Gil went into the building's grounds and a doorman in the warehouse-sized lobby stepped toward the glass doors to watch him. From the canal side, he could see up into the units. There was a party on the third floor. Young people milled about, laughing theatrically, chatting animatedly as they stared into phones. He tried to find Chloe among them, but mostly they were shapes, their faces flashing occasionally into view, twisted with laughter.

He called Chloe again, but the phone went straight to voicemail. Location was still turned off in text. Then he called his nephew's cell. No answer on the first try, but at least it rang. He tried again. Then a third time. In the window the crowd leaned in flirty clumps, drinking from red cups.

On the fourth call, the boy picked up.

"Hello?" he said, the din of the party surging around his voice.

"Matthew," Gil said. "This is Gil."

"What?" the boy shouted.

"This is Gil. Your uncle." A shape moved toward the glass, and before he could see any particulars he knew it was his nephew.

"Uncle Gil? Are you fucking serious?"

"Yes, I'm fucking serious," Gil said, trying not to shout. The boy above stood with his back to the window, but it was him. A dark shape. A silhouette.

"It's two in the morning. And I'm not in Vermont."

"I know you're not," Gil said. He glanced away from Matthew in the window and saw the doorman standing near the doors, arms crossed over a beefy chest.

In the window above, Matthew turned—yes, it was him—and put a hand on the glass, balancing. Gil imagined the pane breaking, a flaw in the design, a wrongly settled support beam that had caused the finest of hairline cracks, invisible until that pressure, and with it the glass would explode, the boy would hang suspended for a second, then his body would follow the shards out and down. Beneath the window was a black fence with jutting spikes.

"Matthew, where's Chloe? Is she there?"

"Chloe?" Matthew said, laughing. "You want to talk to Chloe? Because, well, I'm pretty sure the feeling's not mutual."

"Where is she?" Gil shouted, his hand tightening around the phone. "Where's Chloe? Is she there? Is she at that party?"

He squinted at the crowd, trying to see her, some proof she was still safe.

"Wow. So, um, you should calm down, Uncle Gil. Get a grip."

"Matthew, where is my daughter?"

"I'm not her babysitter so, actually, I kind of don't give a shit."

"God fucking—" Gil started, then closed his eyes and took a deep breath. "Matthew," he said, his voice trembling, "I'm going to have to call the police." He hadn't wanted to say that, but he couldn't deny the pleasure of watching the boy jerk upright from the glass, shield his eyes to look out. Gil moved behind a tree, through whose bare branches he could see the window, though the boy had already retreated from view.

"What the hell are you talking about?" Matthew said, his voice thinner in the wash of the party's din. Before Gil could answer, the call was disconnected.

The disapproving doorman watched Gil hurry back to the street, where he went up to wait at the corner. He could try going inside. Explain to the doorman that his underage daughter was in that building and he needed to find her. But the man might call up to the party, might tip Matthew off. And the building might have another exit. Surely it did, on the far side. But there was no way he could cover both. And this was the main one. The boy didn't live here, wouldn't know of another way out. Hopefully. As long as he didn't know for sure that Gil was waiting here for him.

Two young men came down the hill smoking cigarettes. One eyed Gil, blew a huff of smoke in his direction, sauntered on. He worried they might be Matthew's friends, coming to meet him, but they went past the building without slowing and crossed the bridge. Gil watched them for several blocks, dipping in and out of the dark patches between streetlights until they turned onto an avenue.

Almost ten minutes went by—Where the hell was he, had Gil lost him already?—before the elevator doors opened at the back of the lobby and Matthew stepped out, zipping up his parka. No sign of Chloe. At the glass doors the boy looked cautiously in both directions. Gil waited, trembling, in the shadows.

As soon as he was outside the boy checked his phone, tapped at it, then jammed it in his pocket and turned toward the bridge. Gil tugged up the collar of his jacket, burrowed his chin into his scarf, and followed. Matthew went quickly out onto the bridge but stopped halfway and put his hands on the railing. He didn't turn, but Gil knew he was waiting for him. The bridge seemed to sway over the canal, as if it wasn't steel and concrete but rope flung across a crumbling ravine. Gil wanted to turn around. To run. But now the boy knew he was there and, inexplicably, Gil felt as if he'd been trapped. As if this was all somehow part of the boy's monstrous design.

"Well, hello there," Matthew said. "What are the odds?"

"Matthew, where's Chloe?" Gil said. "Where's my daughter?"

"Whoa, what the fuck?" Matthew said, putting his hands up. "That's some greeting, Uncle Gil."

"Where is she?" Gil said, stepping closer.

"How would I know? I mean, it's a big city." The boy was grinning and he widened his stance, to make it clear he wasn't afraid of this old man.

"I know what you did. I know everything," Gil said.

"Do you? What do you think I did, exactly? Why don't you tell me what I did?"

"Ingrid," Gil said, stupidly, starting with the least of the crimes, if it counted as one—no, of course it did. Unpunished, but still a crime. "And your parents. I know what you did. I know you paid Thomas. And I know about Susie."

"What?" Matthew said, shaking his head, vaguely amused. "Susie? What the hell does that have to do with anything?"

"The bruises. I know that was you, Matthew. I know what you did. I know you, you fucking shit." He was nearly shouting now and a woman, walking on the far side of the bridge, looked up, startled, then hurried on. Gil grabbed the railing as a wave of nausea came over him. All this time he'd let this murderer live in his house. With his daughters. One of whom he'd already tried to kill, and okay, sure, he hadn't touched them. But he could've. It would've been so easy. There'd been nothing to stop him. He'd let the boy get away with all of it.

Maybe he'd already done something to Chloe, drugged her, gotten her drunk. She might be up there, right now, passed out in some thug's bedroom, so what was he doing here with Matthew?

"Wow. You are truly fucking crazy," Matthew said, tilting his head back to bark a laugh. "I mean, I guess I already knew that. But, fuck me. This is some display. Not pulling any punches, I guess."

"You think it's funny? It's funny that you killed your mother?" Gil choked out the words, stepped closer to Matthew, and that, at least, got the boy's attention. He straightened up. Self-preservation was the one thing he understood.

"What's your proof, you stupid hick? The fucking story I wrote for your class, your *fiction* class? But you'd already decided I'd done it, hadn't you? Before I wrote that. Before your worthless 'proof.'

You were already so sure. And don't think I don't know why, you motherfucker."

"What are you talking about?" Gil said, but Matthew stepped close, their coats rasping together. Gil's body thrummed—fear, hate—and his hands felt numb. If he needed to lift them, would he be able to?

"Not even you're that stupid, Uncle Gil. Money. *My* fucking money. You try to frame me—which, by the way, you can't—then you get the money. Don't think I don't know. I know how to read a will." The boy's breath stank of cigarettes and beer and the sour chemical taint of cocaine.

"This isn't about money," Gil said. "It's about my sister."

The boy seized the front of Gil's jacket with both hands. Matthew was taller, and, it was now terribly clear, stronger. Gil could feel it in the boy's arms, which he tried to pry loose. They were cords of unmoving muscle. "My mother, you fucking bastard," the boy shouted in his face. "My dead mother."

"Don't—fucking—" Gil thrashed in Matthew's grip, tried to shove the boy back, but Matthew didn't let go. Lowering his shoulder, Gil tried to pull free, hurled himself back to get away from the boy. The small of his back hit the railing and his stomach lurched as he felt his balance shift, his shoulder falling out into space above the black oily smear of water. Matthew didn't say anything, but he grunted as they grappled, Gil's shoulder tipping, the balance all wrong, his feet coming loose from the pavement, and then he was falling. His hands were no longer holding Matthew's arms or coat but reaching out into air until one caught against the bridge, a wild flaring pain, and the water was frothing into his face and all around him. His parka filled, a lead weight, dragging him down. Water rushed into his throat before he could clamp his mouth shut. Everything was dark, a thick sludge of black. He thrashed his legs and his foot struck metal, a sharp point stabbing into his shin. He opened his eyes—they seared, burned, but saw only darkness. Down—already his eyes were blurring, failing—was only more darkness, then a white cloud he'd disturbed swirling around his leg, up toward his face, slipping over his chin, his nose, up into his eyes, which he closed. He could feel himself getting dragged by the current. Swinging out his arms, he tried to swim, but his hands hit something metal, debris, a sunken boat, maybe, a coil of fence, but already the current that held him down was carrying him past it. He opened his mouth to scream, but he could barely hear the sound himself and nothing of it, surely, made it to the surface, except perhaps a bubble of air, his last, not noticeable in the froth atop the green-black surface that was already settling back into a fetid sheen of stillness.

30

HE WAS ALONE IN THE CLASSROOM, SURELY BECAUSE HE'D GOT-
ten the time wrong. Eleven thirty-five? What kind of stupid start
time was that? Now all he could do was wait, so he settled back,
checked Messenger, Snapchat, email, and watched the other students arrive, each of them shooting furtive glances at the competition. Along with their glistening anxiety, each was propped straight,
maybe from a booster shot of pride. After all, here they were, in
Introduction to Fiction Writing. You had to apply to get into this
class at Yale. You had to submit a writing sample. Be chosen. One
of the elect.

Presumably he was the only freshman, if indeed he counted as
that, with all the credits he'd transferred. Some of the students
knew one another and talked together in hushed, pompous cliques:
the dorky, overweight Latino boy—obviously gay—telling a story
in a faux whisper to a girl done up in goth gear. Despite the monstrous clothing, makeup, and hair, she was pretty. She sneered at his
stare. *Oh, sweetie. Give it time.*

He'd been informed with great condescension that freshmen

normally took the Intro to Creative Writing course at Yale, for which no application was necessary, so why didn't he do that? He'd explained that he'd already taken such a course, yes, admittedly at Essex College, but he preferred not to repeat material. Plus, wouldn't the professor reject him if the work wasn't good enough? Much hemming and hawing and worry about the rules and regulations. Eventually they'd said okay, fine. Maybe because they'd connected his last name to the donation recently given to the Yale English department in the amount of two hundred twenty-five thousand dollars.

He'd been on campus a week and was still unsure what to think. Certainly it was better than most other options, like Vermont. Vermont had been a shit show, and must've gotten much worse after his uncle disappeared, as the detective who'd spoken with him had put it. They knew Gil had gone to the city. A bag with his things had been found at the apartment. Had Matthew seen him, been in touch with him? Actually, he had—he knew they could check the phone records, better to get it out of the way. His uncle had called him, said he was in the city, that they should meet up. But they'd agreed on the next morning, since Matthew had been with some friends and it was already late. Did Matthew remember exactly what time? No, except that it was late. Wait, he could check his phone. Oh, yeah, so apparently two twenty-one in the morning? And he hadn't heard from him after that? No. It was so weird. It was like his uncle had just disappeared.

There was the next set of questions in which his goddamn uncle had proved himself to be more dangerous than anticipated. Apparently Gil had left messages with the detective about Matthew's story. Had he written such a piece, the detective had asked. He'd said yeah, he'd written about his parents, their deaths and everything, which he thought was pretty natural, considering, but he didn't know what kinds of things his uncle had said about it, so he couldn't say if that description was accurate. The detective asked if he had a copy, and he said no. Really? Not even on his computer? Not in his email? Nowhere? Why not? She was clearly start-ing to think Gil had been right. Or that at least it was worth pursuing. Well, Matthew said, remaining calm, it'd really just been an exercise: Professor Duggan had asked them to take an incident from life and write it from a new perspective. Make the hero the villain, that kind of thing. An experiment. But Matthew had felt bad writing about his parents, writing about them so soon, it felt, well, exploitative, you know? And so when he got his copies back he tossed them . . . The detective hadn't looked convinced. Just to be clear, she'd said, he had no copies anywhere? No, sorry, he should've kept one. But he'd thrown them all away after class and his computer had crashed. Total wipe. He'd had to buy a new one. At least this last part was true—the wipe, though not the crash. Was there a chance any of his classmates had a copy? Maybe, he'd said. Though usually they were passed back to the writer at the end of class, he told her, though he supposed someone might've slipped out with a copy. Alice had nearly gotten away, but he'd found her, sniffling in the hall. And Uncle Gil. But that copy had gone into the canal with him. It must've, since it hadn't been found in the apartment or car or anywhere else. The detective said she would check with the students, see if there was a copy out there somewhere. It just seemed strange, didn't he think, that every sin-gle copy was gone? Well, he'd said, it wasn't exactly Chekhov, so it probably was no great loss to literature. He'd meant it as a joke, but she hadn't laughed, had studied him, assessing his guilt. Apparently the detectives interviewed a few of the students, and who knows, maybe they'd agreed with Professor Duggan that the story was pretty creepy, considering Matthew's own parents were dead, but that wasn't proof of anything. You were allowed to write creepy stories, as far as Matthew was aware.

And after that his lawyers had put their foot down: No more interviews without counsel present; notice would need to be given; there were concerns that the police were violating Mat-thew's rights.

He'd considered going back to Vermont, thinking maybe that would be the best cover, but quickly decided that'd be a mistake. His presence would freak Molly out, provoke her to take more serious action. So he'd stayed in the city, first with Eric, and then, when no one was paying close attention, back in his own place. He'd only been home a few nights when he'd gotten that email from Molly, the only contact he'd had with her since spring break. What did Matthew know? Had he seen Gil? Please, couldn't he tell her anything? Everything would be all right, wouldn't it? She'd known Gil was having a hard time, she probably should've been more aware of that, there must've been something she could do, but what? What could she have done?

He didn't reply, sent the email to his lawyers, thinking it might be useful if there was ever any noise about him getting sent back to Vermont—an unsafe, unwelcoming home. But if he had responded he'd have said, no, sorry, things would almost certainly not be all right, not for Gil. Molly wouldn't be surprised by this. She knew who her husband was, just as he did. He'd heard his mother talking about Gil, about his suicide attempt, a couple of years after their one visit to Montauk, had known since then that his uncle was weak, susceptible. Anyway, one day Molly would get her answer. The cleanup of the Gowanus Canal would move forward and they'd find his body. Or there'd be a storm surge, and what was left of his corpse would float to the surface. Or maybe not. He might've gotten pulled out to sea, out into the confluence. One could hope.

He wasn't sure how his uncle had ended up in the canal. They'd been shoving each other, yes, that's true, but then his uncle had lunged wildly at him and hit the side of the railing and gone over. He remembered the smell when the stagnant water had frothed, a plume of reek, like an unwashed asshole, festering in the summer heat. He remembered his surprise at how quickly his uncle had vanished. As if the canal had swallowed him. Ravenous. Other than a few bubbles, there was no more sign of him. As if he'd passed through that poisonous water to some other place. The answer was simpler: He'd gotten snagged underwater. The canal was full of debris, trash, sludge. Superfund site. Dirtiest waterway in North America.

For a second Matthew had considered jumping in. If only to see where the hell his uncle had gone—maybe it'd be like that scene in the toilet in Pynchon where Slothrop follows the mouth harp—or, you know, to pull him out. But it was the Gowanus Canal. Wouldn't diving in there without a protective suit kill you? Cancer, or worse: a mutation, radioactive sludge. He'd looked around for help but there'd been no one. The girl who'd passed them on the bridge was gone. Up in the bright windows of Drake's apartment the party continued, but no one could see him there on the bridge. No one was pointing and shouting and calling 911. If there'd been police around the corner, it'd already been too late.

Plus, he'd been drunk. And there'd have been questions. What had happened? How? What had he done? And since he couldn't remember how exactly his uncle had gone over, he'd decided it was best to do nothing. More a sin of omission than commission. Once a couple of minutes had passed, what was the point? To involve himself in that? An accident. A death. No, he had enough on his plate.

He'd almost missed the phone, which must've fallen out of Gil's pocket in the tussle. Only when he'd turned to go and glanced back did he see it, the glass screen casting out a chip of light. He'd picked it up, realizing how close he'd come to ruin. His uncle had called him. From there. They'd be able to figure that out, and surely there was CCTV.

And then, as he'd started back toward the building, another close call: The doors opened and Chloe and Lily came out, zipping up their coats. Matthew slipped his uncle's phone into his pocket.

"We have to go," Chloe said when she got closer. "My dad, he's like, he's calling me nonstop and if he finds out, oh my god, he'll totally freak."

Lily stood behind Chloe, grinning in a nakedly lustful way at Matthew, which was pretty much all she'd done since they'd showed up at his apartment, asking if they could hang. Lily was a little horsey, her nose a little squashed, her face a little long, but he could sense total permission in her smile. With her, he probably could've done anything. Except now that was fucked.

"That's cool," he said. "It's getting late."

They were at the edge of the bridge and Chloe leaned on the rail, looked down into the water. For a second, Matthew worried she saw something, a shape, her father, the sleeve of his coat, the pale bulge of his forehead, but when he looked down there was only the black, sluggish surface.

"I can call you an Uber," Matthew said.

"Oh my god, that's going to be so expensive," Lily said.

"Right, but there's no train this late, so," Matthew said.

He waited with them, like a gentleman, until the Uber Black arrived.

"Okay, bye," he'd said, just as Chloe opened her mouth to say something else, maybe some worry about her dad—if Matthew saw him, what if he'd come to the city? Did he know—? but the slamming door cut off any words and the SUV pulled away, and he was, finally, free of the Duggans.

On his own ride back to the apartment he'd had time to plan it all, so he'd taken the phone home and sat up with it for several hours. He knew Gil's passcode, had watched him type it many times. At four in the morning he called Molly, hoping she was asleep. The phone rang four times, though hopefully not on her end, and then slipped over to voicemail. He hung up, turned the phone off, left the building, going out the back way through the staff exit, careful to keep his hood up and head down. On Park Avenue he hailed a cab, asked the driver to take him to the George Washington Bridge.

"Ain't gonna kill yourself, are you?" the cabbie had asked. Matthew ignored him.

In the tangle of underpasses near the bridge he searched for a spot outside the range of any cameras, though it was impossible to be sure. He had the cab pull over beneath an overpass, and as soon as the car curved out of sight he scrambled up a sloping concrete embankment and waited in a dark, fetid moonscape of pigeon shit. As his eyes adjusted he noticed a pile of sodden, disintegrating rags, all fading to the same gray-brown color of the concrete, and there were food wrappers and, probably if he'd picked through the piles, he'd have found more: needles, empty heroin baggies. As a burn deepened in his thighs from squatting in this crease of concrete turned toilet he could almost see Gil there, panting and frenzied, resting in the dark of the overpass, trying to talk himself out of it. Thinking of his girls. Of Molly. What his death would do to them. All that pain, and yet it couldn't push back against the coiled self-loathing that wound itself around his throat, squeezing, crushing, so the only way out was to jump. He had to jump. Matthew could see him stand, nearly losing his balance on the slope, hurrying along the curve to where a patch of grass led steeply up to the bridge above. It was still dark as he went onto the pedestrian walkway, out to where the bridge cleared the Hudson. The dark sluice of water shimmered below. The fence wasn't high. He climbed over easily, stepped to the edge, let go, and the air rushed about him, pushing at his face and also pushing him down, down into the dark rushing wall of water below.

After an hour, he turned on his uncle's phone. Now there was a real risk. It was going on six in the morning. She might answer this time. But this was the plan, so he called his aunt with his uncle's phone, and luck was with him. When the call went to voicemail and there was the beep, he held the speaker up to catch the sound of a passing cab, possibly the faint cry of distant honks. Then he turned the phone off and smashed it, settled it into an oily puddle until he was sure it was thoroughly destroyed.

He'd known they could track the phone and didn't want them looking in Brooklyn. Now they'd focus on uptown and here, by the bridge. Where they'd assume Gil had jumped to his death. Which wasn't entirely off the mark. Presumably all the tracking he'd imagined happened, though he wasn't privy to any of it, and wondered how they accounted for no footage of Gil entering the apartment the night he'd disappeared—Matthew knew for sure there were cameras in front of his building. And he knew for certain there were cameras on the bridge, so how would they account for those missing images, of a bulky man in a parka clambering over the railing? The story would be incomplete, he knew that, but regardless it seemed to have worked, so far. Because here he was, at Yale, and no one had, in any formal way, suggested he'd done anything to his uncle. And he'd taken steps to establish his innocence, so far as he was able, the worst of those being the time he spent attending the trial of Thomas Gashi.

All week he'd sat in the front row, eyes fixed on Thomas, who'd looked at him only once, when the prosecutor had asked if he'd like to take this chance to say something to Matthew Westfallen, sitting in the gallery? Thomas—who'd admitted he'd hit their car with the truck, who claimed he hadn't seen the red light, who'd said it was all an accident, all in his nearly indecipherable accent—looked over. That was a bad moment. Those droopy yellow eyes, like a sick hound dog. Thomas said, "Yes, I would like to say I am sorry. I am very sorry. It was a terrible accident. I am so sorry."

That man, twisted around in the hard wooden chair, might've been the last person to see his parents alive, at least he'd seen his mother's face turning at the onrushing shape in her window, the impossible fact of the truck's grille filling her view. He might've seen her face, her fear, the briefest instant of wild panic when she might have thought of him, her Matthew. He found he was crying and he let it go, the sadness, let it rush like cold water into the tips of his fingers, the end of his nose. There'd been an article about the trial, the verdict—guilty of criminally negligent manslaughter, pleading down from homicide—in the *Times,* and they'd mentioned his tears. That had been in June.

Now he was at Yale, where his parents had expected him to end up. Family tradition bullshit. Though it *was* nice to be free, even if his dorm was apparently full of holier-than-thou, gender-fluid morons.

The fiction professor—he recognized her from the photos on her books he'd read over the summer—came in and sat down behind the desk, welcoming them as she unpacked her bag. She greeted a couple of the students by name and studied the others, including Matthew, as if trying to match them with their writing samples. She handed around syllabi, and then suggested, before getting into all that administrative crap, why didn't they start by introducing themselves? Unfortunately, there was no not-boring way that didn't require them to sacrifice their dignity in some "ice breaker," so how about name, year, major, where they were from, what they'd been reading recently, and what they were working on. Who wanted to start?

When it was Matthew's turn he ran through the requested information—a few of the others perked up when he admitted he was a freshman—mentioned his recent obsession with Nabokov, and said, "Well, in terms of projects, I'm actually working on a novel. Or, you know, I prefer to call it a 'thing' right now, but it's longer, so I guess it might end up being a novel."

"A novel," the professor said. "Ambitious. Can you say what it's about?"

"Well, it's basically about a family in Vermont who have to take in their nephew when his parents die. It's told from the father's point of view as he comes unhinged and becomes convinced his nephew killed his parents."

"Unreliable narrator?" the professor said.

"Well, third person, but limited, so yeah, you could say that."

"If you plan to submit portions of that for workshop," she said, clearly now making the connection with his writing sample, giving him a pleased smile—her own prodigy—"be sure to provide a summary, as much as you can, in order to contextualize the excerpt."

"Sure thing," Matthew said. "Thanks."

Then they were on to the next student, and he felt the hooks of their attention set him free. In fact he'd already finished the novel, had written it over the summer, during and after the trial, helped by his uncle's Moleskine. After what happened in Brooklyn he'd gone back home and searched his uncle's bag, found the journal. Flipping through it that night he'd seen his own name and had known enough to keep it hidden. He'd found it again weeks later, zipped inside an interior pocket of his backpack. Most of the entries were fragments—a few sentences, an image or a simile. And just as he'd guessed, much of it was about him. Monstrous Matthew. Matthew the murderer. Matthew the mastermind. Maybe Gil had thought of it as a diary, though he'd probably called it something dumb like a "writer's notebook." Probably Matthew should've destroyed it, but as he'd read most of the entries he'd felt the stirrings of his novel. He'd hesitated to call it that because he hadn't wanted to sound pompous. But this was Yale, so that wasn't a bad thing. Ambitious, as the professor had said. Yes, ambition was not something he lacked.

31

SIX THINGS AT ONCE. NO DIFFERENT FROM ANY OTHER DAY, SO she should be used to it—*was* used to it, which didn't mean it wasn't bullshit—and then, right at the end of the morning briefing, they tell her, oh yeah, and move Patch. Again. On a Monday. What Patch needed wasn't a new room, but more PT, new tests, a change of meds. He'd opened his eyes last week, only for a minute or so, but still, it'd been the first time. She'd mentioned it to several doctors, but now that there was progress, after all these months, did they care? Nope. Just get him down the hall, out of the way. She'd have to get Jerome to help.

But Patch wasn't close to the top of her list. She'd already checked her charts. She had to get 710 to drink that contrast dye, because the CT scan would soon be backed up to hell. She had to see how her rooms were stocked.

They were, big surprise, stocked like shit. How many times would they have to talk about the fucking linens? And she'd already caught a glimpse of the bathroom in 720. She was going to need a mask just to oversee that mess.

A lull did eventually come—the CT scan came back normal—and though she'd have preferred to stare into her computer, or check in with her mom, she went to find Jerome, knowing he'd be out on the ambulance deck.

"Hey, big guy, I need you," she said as the doors slid open, letting in the heat.

Jerome was way too close to the doors to be smoking. He had that look, like it was only a matter of time before he strangled someone. If he hadn't already. Jerome had given Patch his name, though she'd never figured out what it meant. When she'd asked he'd said, " 'Cause that's his fucking name, obviously."

Now, Jerome ran a hand over his scruffy cheeks and said, "That's nice for you. But I need this cigarette."

He dragged furiously and let it funnel out his nose and said, "What, you want one?"

"I'm fine," she said, stepping out into a square of sun—it must be ninety already. At the far side of the lot two men unloaded a gurney from the back of an ambulance. The body—must be an old person, from the bird thinness of the shape—rocked and jostled, a sheet slipping away to reveal a scrawny, spotted arm, strapped too tight to the mattress. By the time they'd unhooked the wheel from where it had caught on the fender, Jerome flicked his cigarette, sparks scattering over the black asphalt. "Fuck it, let's go," he said, unpeeling his bulk from the wall.

She'd been on duty the night Patch had come in. He'd been picked up near the river in Red Hook: no pants, no jacket, no ID, hypothermic. The assumption was an attempted suicide by drowning. He'd suffered a cardiac event in the ambulance, crashing vitals by the time they wheeled him in. Awful smell, but different from most of the homeless. He'd developed pneumonia, which they'd all assumed he wouldn't survive.

That first night, she'd given him a week. But he'd made it to three weeks. Chances that he'd ever wake were remote, but somehow he hung on. They'd checked with the shelters, but there wasn't a record that matched, not that they had much to go on. Not that anyone cared. But she did her best. Maybe because she had a feeling he wasn't an unknown. Despite the smell, he'd been cleaner than most. His beard had been tidy, no bugs, no lice, no sores or infections, though there'd been a nasty gash on his leg that had required a course of antibiotics. She'd shaved him clean and his skin wasn't rough and cracked the way skin usually got from time spent outside in winter. His hands were orderly, nails straight and tidy. So either he'd been taken care of recently in a shelter and had relapsed, or, well, who knows. She'd talked about it with Dr. Grodin, but he'd nodded in that steady, stupid way of his, then handed her the clipboard and walked off with his tight-assed waddle.

The social worker from the city came that first week, but when she'd suggested they could pull dental records, the man had squirmed, tapped his pen on his notepad, shaken his head, and said, no, he'd keep an eye on the missing person reports. She could barely remember him: baggy brown pants, a mustache, or maybe it was a goatee, lank brown hair. One detail stood out: His shirt had been tucked in wrong, so the front flap was caught on his belt, exposing a bulge of pale belly, slick with dark, wiry hair. She suspected he'd never filed the initial paperwork, because when she'd called to follow up a few weeks later, she was informed he was no longer with the agency and someone else would be taking on his cases. When she'd pressed about this particular case, the woman had gotten huffy and said there was a lot of turnover right now, so be patient. Could she be patient? Could she? Good. She'd never heard from that office again.

Jerome said he had to take a piss and swung off before they reached Patch, so she was alone when she went in, making a mental list of what they could leave attached so as not to need another approval. Definitely the IV could come out, and so she lifted Patch's hand, loosened the tape, and that's when she felt him squeeze. Soft, but steady.

"Hey there. Feeling better?" she said, and looked at him. His eyes were open. But not like last time, not staring vacant. Now they were focused, right on her. His head had rolled on the pillow. Or he'd turned it. There was a wildness in his eyes. Fear.

"Can you hear me, sir?" she said, holding his hand. "Can you hear me?"

He squeezed again and his lips moved, barely managing a putter of air. He tried, a faint moan, his eyes skittering over her face.

She kept hold of his hand and reached down to where the call button dangled beside the bed and pushed it.

He was looking at her, frantic. The bleep of his heart rate quickened.

"Stay calm, sir, you're going to be okay. Everything's going to be fine. We're taking care of you." She felt something she hadn't in a while. Excitement. This man should be dead, or permanently vegetative, but here he was, awake. In large part because of her. She'd taken care of him, not on her own, sure, there were others, but did they care? She'd turned him, washed him, fed him, checked on him, sometimes when he wasn't on her rotation. Because she'd known. She'd known he'd wake. In a way, she'd saved him.

Patch stayed awake for over half an hour, then drifted back to sleep—she worried he'd slip away, one of those blips of consciousness, not uncommon—but three hours later he woke again. He tried to speak but couldn't shape his mouth at all. She asked him questions and he answered by squeezing. Did he remember who he was? Squeeze. Did he know where he lived? Squeeze. Did he know where he was? No squeeze. This wasn't really her place. There'd be specialists who'd want to see him. Someone coming back to lucidity after months and months. Not a miracle. She knew that. Just science. But it *felt* like a miracle. Her own miracle. Saint Helen. Sounded good. She could live with that.

It was three days before he managed any words. She went to his room first thing that morning and asked, "How are you feeling, sir?"

When he squeezed her hand she said, "Sir, can you tell me your name? Can you tell me, so we can help you?"

His lips squirmed and a sound came out, different now. More than a moan.

"Can you try that again?" she said, petting the back of his hand.

The slurring was heavy, but she made him try again, and again, and again. She wrote it down, to see if he could read it, see if she was hearing it right.

She wrote: *Bill.* He shook his head, tried, but now the sound was mash.

"First letter," she told him. "Try that."

The man closed his eyes, focusing. His mouth puckered and he made a sound. *G.* The shape of his lips, the low sound. Had to be. She wrote *G* on the notepad and he nodded, relief washing over his face. Then she had it. *Gill.* She wrote it down. Was that right? Was his name Gill? He squinted at the name, up at her, and nodded. His eyes watering, his heart rate rising.

"Well, hello there, Gill. It's nice to meet you. I hope you're feeling better."

The man closed his eyes, breathing deeply through his nose.

"That's good, Gill," she said. "That's good news. And don't worry. We'll fix you up. We'll make sure you get home."

ACKNOWLEDGMENTS

Thanks to my editor, Andrea Walker, for her incisive editing, guidance, and wholehearted belief. Thanks to the team at Random House, especially Andy Ward, Robin Desser, Emma Caruso, Noa Shapiro, Madison Dettlinger, Windy Dorresteyn, Maria Braeckel, Rachel Rokicki, and Omer Abdi. Thanks to Luke Brown, Drew Jerrison, and everyone at Serpent's Tail. Thanks to Anna Stein, a wonderful agent who guided this novel through many drafts and into all the right hands. Thanks to Sophie Lambert, Claire Nozieres, Enrichetta Frezzato, Julie Flanagan, and Will Watkins.

Thanks to Jessie Chaffee, Brendan Kiely, Cara Blue Adams, Cam Terwilliger, Deborah Treisman, Kenny Cummings, Miranda Beverly-Whittemore, David Lobenstine, Michael Kardos, Katie Pierce, Nicky Beer, Brian Barker, Ashley Van Valkenburgh, Brian Ewing, Bethany Godsoe, and Neil Giacobbi for their friendship and support through the writing of this book. Thanks to my colleagues and students at Seton Hall University.

Thanks to my mother, Peggy Oates, and to my father, Thomas Oates, whom I miss every day. Thanks to my brothers, Tom, John, and Brendan. Thanks to Mary and Tom Wilkinson and to Jenny Wilkinson and Joel English.

Thanks to Sylvie and Baxter, for their patience and playfulness and all the happiness. Most of all, thanks to Amy Day Wilkinson, my first reader, my brilliant, hilarious, patient, endlessly kind friend and partner, without whom I couldn't possibly have written this book. Thank you for our life together.

PHOTO: © AMY DAY WILKINSON

NATHAN OATES's debut collection of short stories, *The Empty House*, won the Spokane Prize. His stories have appeared in *The Missouri Review, Alaska Quarterly Review, Copper Nickel, West Branch, Best American Mystery Stories*, and elsewhere. He has been awarded fellowships from the Writing Seminars at Johns Hopkins University, the University of Missouri, the New York State Summer Writers Institute, and the Sewanee Writers' Conference. He is an associate professor at Seton Hall University, where he teaches creative writing. He lives in Brooklyn, New York, with his family.

nathanoates.net
Twitter: @NathanMOates
Instagram: @nathan.m.oates

ABOUT THE TYPE

This book was set in Bembo, a typeface based on an old-style Roman face that was used for Cardinal Pietro Bembo's tract *De Aetna* in 1495. Bembo was cut by Francesco Griffo (1450–1518) in the early sixteenth century for Italian Renaissance printer and publisher Aldus Manutius (1449–1515). The Lanston Monotype Company of Philadelphia brought the well-proportioned letterforms of Bembo to the United States in the 1930s.